Evidently, Asa had finally decided the time had come to make their lives a living hell.

"Watch out!" Jordan cried.

The two goons knocked Seeley to the mat. They tied her wrists then hefted her to her feet, facing Jordan. The man with the bloody nose mopped his face and then, without warning, hit Seeley in the chin. Her head snapped back as Jordan screamed. Seeley held onto consciousness, though her head swirled and her throbbing chin began to swell.

"You bitch!" the man shrieked, glaring at Seeley. "I think ya broke my nose." He then walked over to Jordan, grasped her chin with bloody fingers, and drooled. "Young—tender—meat—"

The demon restraining Seeley sounded anxious. "Hank, we're not allowed to kill her."

Hank gestured to Seeley. "This lady's fair game, there's a high price on her head. We'll be greatly rewarded."

The other demons nodded with crooked smirks. "We're allowed to stay and play as long as we bag souls for his gain. The more souls, the longer we get to stay."

"Why? Don't you like your fiery perdition?" Seeley said dryly.

Her remark infuriated them and Hank returned to gloat in front of Seeley. Using the distraction, Jordan subtly tried to weasel her way out of the chokehold.

With his left hand, Hank grabbed Seeley's ponytail, tugging her face close to his red eyes. They looked like hot coals as he sneered. "We're not ready to leave, not with all this fun we're having. Souls are jamming the Highway to Hell—we just nudge them in the right direction." A gawky sound rattled in his throat, forcing Seeley to breathe in his foul breath. "Your kind of souls is a pain in the ass."

Hank dug a switchblade out of his pocket. With a decisive snap, he held the silver blade to Seeley's throat.

Haunting visions, unusual strength, and special paranormal talents are the norm for Seeley and her sixteen-year-old daughter Jordan. Their lives become perilous when the leader of The Black Order stalks them, trying to fulfill a prophecy to consecrate Jordan to his lord—Lucifer.

Previously homeschooled and naïve, Jordan is inducted into the social culture of teendom at Elma High, where she encounters Mark, a mysterious new classmate, who is hell bent on keeping her unscathed from the forces of evil. But the battle between Heaven and Hell is escalating—and Earth is their battleground.

KUDOS for *Wickedly They Come*

Wickedly They Come by Cathrina Constantine is the story of 16-year-old Jordan, who is very special. In fact, she is so special Lucifer wants her to be consecrated to him. Jordan says thanks, but no thanks, and dedicates her life to fighting demons, with the help of her mother and a few hunky angels. But the bad guys don't give up easily and Jordan becomes a warrior for good. Now she just has to survive long enough to fight, which is hard to do with both humans and demons trying to kill her. Constantine tells a chilling story, filled with trials, tribulations, and numerous close calls. The plot is strong, well thought out, and unpredictable. I was riveted from the very first word to the very last. I seriously hope there is a sequel in the works. If not, I will be very disappointed. – *Taylor Jones, reviewer*

Wickedly They Come by Cathrina Constantine is touted as YA, and the heroine *is* sixteen. However, the story is very adult—oh there isn't any sex or anything like that in it, but some of the concepts seem a little dark and rather mature for teenagers. But then it has been a while since I have been a teenager myself, or really looked very closely at what they read. Now don't get me wrong, I am not saying that teenagers shouldn't read the book. In fact, they probably should as the concepts in it should make them think and question, and that is always a good thing. What I *am* saying is that even if you don't normally like YA, you will probably like *Wickedly They Come*. Constantine's characters are well developed and show a depth of understanding of human nature that is surprising in a YA author, especially a first time author. The plot is full of twists and turns and really catches your interest right off the bat. If you want a book that is both entertaining and thought-provoking, *Wickedly They Come* fits the bill perfectly. I don't see how you could be disappointed. I, too, am hoping for a sequel. – *Regan Murphy, reviewer*

ACKNOWLEDGEMENTS

I acknowledge my Lord and Savior, and plunge myself in thanksgiving to Him who knows my heart. I am eternally grateful and indebted to my Editor, Lauri Wellington, who said 'Yes,' to this novel, and her patience in offering professional advice pertaining to my countless questions. Also for their expertise, I thank Faith and Karen for editing *Wickedly They Come* which was an overwhelming task. And the art director, Jack for his remarkable help, and everyone associated with Black Opal Books.

Furthermore, I thank Melissa Stevens for creating the awesome book cover which I absolutely love. I am thankful to Rosanne Catalano, the first person to read and critique my novel, and her encouragement when I was ready to throw in the towel.

Blessings upon my daughter, Niki who inspired and aided in scripting the opening and closing poem. Thank you to my sister, Jody, for her unfailing love and enthusiasm and for all my friends for their support which means more to me than you'll ever know. Most importantly, to my family who suffered through endless hours and hours of my morphing into a computer zombie.

WICKEDLY

THEY COME

Cathrina Constantine

A BLACK OPAL BOOKS PUBLICATION

GENRE: YA/PARANORMAL THRILLER

WICKEDLY THEY COME
Copyright © 2013 by Cathrina Constantine
Cover Design by Melissa Stevens
All cover art copyright © 2013
All Rights Reserved
Print ISBN: 978-1-626940-51-2

First Publication: AUGUST 2013

Published by Black Opal Books **http://www.blackopalbooks.com**

DEDICATION

To Jim, my greatest Love
And to my children, whom I cherish with all my heart,
Niki, Robert, Jenna Mae, Noelle and Jordan

To my mom, Frances, you are loved beyond measure

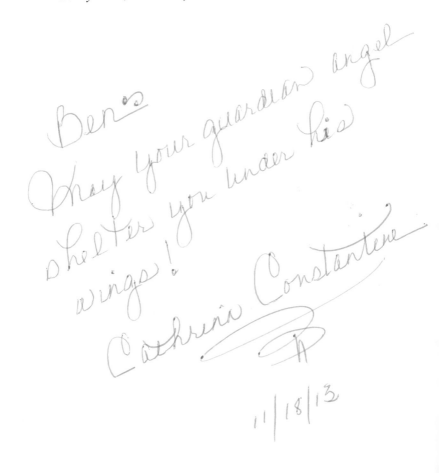

Ben

May your guardian angel
shelter you under his
wings!

Cathrine Constantene

11/18/13

WICKEDLY THEY COME

Eyes like embers burn into my soul
As gnarled fingers stretch to sow seeds of terror
Weaving a realm of pandemonium

Nightmares pour a viscous poison upon sleep's tangled web
And on and on the vision's dance:

I saw the world blind and hollow
Floating in the void of space
Feeding upon the vapors of some
Translucent suspended beast

Disjointed bodies then did appear
Sprinkling death and devouring life
Coaxing earth into silent slumber

Blazing eyes again emerged
Red brightness true to hellish fire
Fixed upon my wandering eye

Flames burst upon the scene
Wild and wily, leaving not one piece to fix upon
Except for those eyes of ember…

CHAPTER 1

Why Do You Glory in Evil, You Scandalous Liar?

Jordan," Seeley said gently. "Jordan, we're here."
The girl stirred. Rubbing sleep from her eyes, Jordan leaned forward. A gothic monstrosity of a mansion was erected on elevated property. Adding to its wretched exterior, a blood moon hung in an ill-omened black sky, painting a grim picture.

Seeley inched the car under a portico, letting it idle. "This wasn't a good idea. I think we should leave."

"We're going in, Mom." Confident beyond her years, Jordan gave her mom a look of pure determination. "We'll be fine, I know it. We have help."

Throughout the day a waffling Seeley had been barraged by Jordan's haranguing on her father's behalf. "We have to go. I'm not scared. Dad needs us. And besides," she said with grit, "Markus and Ezekiel will be with us, right?"

Seeley's ten-year-old daughter had already become a warrior. Seeley decisively counted on Ezekiel and Markus, their ever-present, inexplicable angels. Ezekiel, whom Seeley had nicknamed Zeke, had been with her as long as she could remember. After Jordan's birth, Markus appeared. Two decidedly glorious angels to assist Seeley and Jordan in their unpredictable lives.

A uniformed attendant marched in front of the vehicle and wordlessly opened Seeley's car door. With an outstretched hand, he then indicated a set of gates. The place was built like a fortress. Seeley steered Jordan with a hand on her shoulder. The young girl reached up to hold her other hand as well. Seeley gazed back at the uniformed man, wondering if he knew about the ritual taking place inside. He was busy thumping the tires with his shoe, as if sizing up the car for sale.

The dimly lit grand foyer appeared markedly bare, like it'd been vacant for years. Claw-footed side tables held vases of rotting bouquets, spindly stems long ago denuded, speckling the floor with shriveled petals, turning to dust. Seeley moved her head from side to side. The lofty sandstone walls felt like they were closing in on them and appeared to be weeping— *blood?* Porous stone oozed thick crimson fluid, pooling on the floor. The house's core felt alive. Seeley's pulse accelerated.

A stout, elderly man came sweeping in, wearing a black shroud and holding a candelabrum. Flitting candlelight swayed over filmy colorless eyes and a lipless mouth. His voice was brusque. "Follow me."

Seeley muttered deep in her throat, "Asa Trebane had to be kidding with this horror flick entrance." If she weren't so petrified, she'd chuckle. As she trailed the man who reminded her of Uncle Fester from the *Addams Family*, their steps echoed off the weeping walls as candlelit shadows followed. Bypassing a broad staircase to a concealed door, they descended a flight of steps to a room beneath the main building.

The stout man flicked a switch, stood aside, and waved Seeley and Jordan into a tiny paneled room. A buckling sofa, two plain wooden chairs, and a dusty cobwebbed lamp rested on a small end table. *I guess the cleaning staff wasn't allowed in this room,* she thought, and inspected for any of the crawly bugs she so hated. Lowering into a chair, she extended her arms to her daughter, who burrowed into her inviting, secure lap.

"Something's wrong with Dad," Jordan said softly.

"Why do you say that, Jordan?" Seeley's voice shook. She also felt the presence of death.

Jordan nestled her head into her mother's neck. "I just know."

Seeley froze—listening intently to words being spoken internally. '*Seeley, you are called into battle,*' said Zeke. '*Lucifer's usage of demons to possess unsuspecting humans has caused inexpressible loss of life. Use your talents well.*'

Her eyebrows drew together, seeking clarity. '*I don't understand, Zeke, what are you telling me?*'

'*Remember—you are never alone.*'

Jordan jumped in readiness as the door was flung wide. A completely veiled figure filled the doorway then nodded wordlessly for them to follow. Interlacing their fingers, Jordan and her mother headed toward the cloaked figure. Someone waiting by the door fell in behind them, barring any notions of escape.

"Where's my husband?" Seeley asked urgently. "I want to see my husband. Asa Trebane promised me he'd be here." She nearly bumped into the cloaked figure as it stopped abruptly, swishing around to face her. Taloned fingernails slid back the hood, revealing the malicious woman whose earlier threats had lured them to Satan's coven…

❧❦❧

As usual, Seeley and Jordan had strolled to the neighborhood park. Jordan hopped onto the swing, winding her fingers around the chain. Seeley pushed all the while Jordan urged her to push harder and higher. A few minutes passed when someone sidled up beside Seeley.

"Cute kid."

Seeley looked at the gorgeous stranger then noticed her eyes—liquid black pupils outlined in red that made her appear dodgy. Seeley wondered if she might be an addict—a wealthy addict. The woman was dressed in a plum chiffon Prada blouse and tailored pants. Unique acrylic nails looked like talons, long and curved to fine points, with intricate emblems printed on each nail. Squinting in the blazing sunshine, the pretentious woman looked sinister. She gave the outward appearance of stylish sophistication, except for her feral eyes.

At first Seeley thought she might possibly be a mother of one of the children on the playground. Her thoughts were promptly quashed, however, when the woman remarked, "Seeley, we've been watching you and Jordan."

The woman knew their names. Seeley then assumed the worst—she was a member of The Black Order, an organization with which Jack, her husband, was well acquainted.

An involuntary shiver coursed through her.

Seeley held the chain, bringing the swing to a standstill. Attempting to disguise the tension in both her face and voice, she said, "Jordan, why don't you go and play with some of the other kids for a while?"

"Okay, Mom." The young girl with bouncy auburn hair, so like her mother's, skipped energetically toward the slide, her yellow sandals snapping at her heels.

Seeley kept one eye on Jordan as the woman spoke patronizingly. "Jack's not cooperating. He knows better and yet he continues to deceive the Order."

The woman moved closer to Seeley and sniffed, like she was holding back tears. "Jack and I were bonded at an early age...until—" She never finished her sentence. Her lips formed a definite pout. "Your mystical powers were to blend with those of our Master, Asa Trebane, *and* Jack. But you— you ruined Jack with your holier than thou morality."

The woman's elegant veneer cracked as her face contorted briefly. She purred like a feline ready to pounce. "I wish I could kill you—right now."

Seeley backpedaled, not from the death threat, but from the shadowy ghoul perched on the woman's shoulder. Beady eyes overlooked a pruned, gourd-like snout. Its encrusted hide looked like it'd been salted and cured in the sun. And it had claws like needles.

Undaunted by Hell's emissary, Seeley jerked her chin in the direction of the ghoul. "You have company."

The woman's face twisted into a snarl. "What the hell does that mean?"

"Exactly," Seeley said. "A minion from Hell is on your shoulder."

The woman fanned at her shoulder. The creature was un-moved, just bared a mouthful of thorny shards. Seeley couldn't help but wonder if Jack had once again succumbed into Asa's dark clutches. He'd been missing for over a week. Though, it was not unusual for her husband to be gone for days on his writing assignments. "What do you want?"

Now that the woman had Seeley's full interest, her mouth puckered as if she'd just sucked on a lemon. Her ornate nails brushed at a blond strand of hair that had fallen over her face. Seeley watched as the ghoul squeezed through the woman's parted cherry lips. Foraging in her shoulder bag, the woman coughed like something was lodged in her throat. She handed Seeley a square piece of paper. "Bring Jordan to this address." Her voice was brittle and hoarse. "Be there tonight by two-thirty in the morning. The ritual begins at three."

"I would *never* bring my daughter anywhere near your kind," growled Seeley.

"You and your daughter have Mr. Trebane's assurance that both of you, in fact, all *three* of you will be able to walk away—alive and well."

"I don't trust the devil."

Cherry lips opened and, not one, but two ghouls surfaced and slunk creepily under the woman's clothing. "A sacrificial offering will be made tonight at three. We can slaughter the goat—or your husband. You decide. Jack will suffer the con-sequences if you're not at that address by two-thirty."

"Why does Trebane want to see us? How can I be sure my husband is there, or even alive?" Her mind was a dizzying swirl of misconceptions. "It would be quite natural for you to lie to me."

The woman cackled. Ghoulish forms erupted from her clothing like scary jacks-in-the-boxes. "We know about your...shall we say...spiritualism, and Jack's daughter has been called the warrior. Then there's the prophecy: '*The war-rior will be one with Lucifer, and God will weep...*'

"Mr. Trebane is somewhat...curious. You see, Jack was raised as a son of Satan, and you, a daughter of *your* deity.

Now, to set the record straight, Jordan must be consecrated to *our* lord. Disciples are assembling as we speak."

"No," Seeley gasped. "I won't allow it."

"Mr. Trebane expected your reluctance." The woman withdrew a small wooden box, like one that held tea bags, and offered it to Seeley.

Seeley looked at the item, leery of the contents, and the long sharp nails.

"Take it," the woman said, jiggling the box.

Seeley frowned. The belligerent woman's mouth twisted sideways and shadowy ghouls scuttled back through her lips. Under duress, Seeley opened her hand. The woman slapped the box into her palm, scratching her wrist in the process. Seeley ignored the swelling welts. The box teetered as if it were alive.

Tentatively she raised the lid.

Peering in, she was repulsed, lancing acid burning her throat. Inside was Jack's bloody finger, the wedding ring still attached. The sight triggered Seeley's gag reflex. Snapping the lid shut, she felt her breath come in short spurts as tears jumped to the surface. Covering her mouth in hopes of smothering her cry, she shook with tremors, envisioning Jack's pain as they cut off his finger.

"I almost hope you don't come. I'll take pleasure in snipping off every appendage on his body and rejoice in his howling. And then I will slice the throat of the bastard who turned his back on—on us." Gratified with Seeley's cavalcade of emotions, the woman tossed her head backward and let loose a high-pitched chortle. Pivoting on her heels, she strode away.

ৎৎৎ

Presently the woman's feral eyes were red and swollen. "You bitch, this is all your fault."

Seeley reeled from the woman's verbal abuse, only to bump into the guard behind them. Steadying herself, she wrapped her arm protectively around Jordan.

The woman snuffled. "Oh, you'll see Jack all right." She rearranged the hood and proceeded down the passageway.

They tramped farther below the earth than Seeley thought possible in the upscale neighborhood. It was evident that a wealthy member of the Black Order could make anything possible.

They headed into a commodious murky cave where torches mounted on rocky columns stank of creosote. Rivulets of water tunneling the rock produced pockets of rank, festering puddles, adding to the musty odor. Jordan tried not to breathe, plugging her nose against the nasty fumes.

A forest of black clad people in ankle length robes blocked Jordan's view. She gripped her mother's hand tighter as hooded heads bent to look at her. Where their eyes should be, she saw black holes, only their chins and stiff lips were visible. Someone preaching on a platform drew their attention. A man's silky voice fascinated those assembled.

The Master of The Black Order, Asa, commanded the room and its occupants. Seeley only wanted to find one person—Jack. Her heart clanged into her throat and her short nervous breaths were making her dizzy.

She scanned the area, keeping a wary eye out for the demon-possessed humans she'd foreseen in her mystical visions. The cloaks made distinguishing them impossible. A preposterous thought jumped to mind, if it weren't for the hoods, it would look like her high school graduation class lining up for commencement—only scarier.

Her interest cut back to the podium as Asa spoke of a sacrificial offering and a consecration. "We, your disciples, pledge our souls to you and offer appeasement for the lost soul of Jack Chase—with his own sacrifice." He paused for effect. "And now the time draws near for the consecration of the warrior, a dynamic spirit to be one with you…"

Something dripped on Seeley's shoulder. Then a wet dribble skimmed her cheek and landed on Jordan's arm. There, she could see that the wetness was bright red. Raising her head and sucking in her breath, Seeley gawked at a mammoth pentagram embedded into the rocky dome. The five-pointed star sparkled mysteriously in the flickering light, and a planked balcony bordered the elevated fortification.

As she craned her head and peered directly upward, her bloodcurdling scream split the air. Her knees buckled. "Oh my God! Oh my God! Jack—what have they done?"

Visibly tortured, Jack hung from a cross beam, lifeless and nearly naked. His head angled on his chest, coils of hair veiled his face. Gaping, bloody wounds stripped his pale, bluish skin. Blood filigreed his long juxtaposed legs. Seeley cringed at spikes driven into his feet. His arms were spread lengthwise and led her eyes to the spikes piercing his palms. Blood was draining from his many wounds.

A trembling Seeley rose, not knowing if her legs would support her. She needed to be strong for Jordan and shielded her daughter's eyes from the gruesome sight.

Yet Jordan's eyes were fixed on his tortured body. "Daddy, Dad?" Jordan sobbed. She couldn't believe the bloody man hanging in the air was her father. She remained steady, bearing witness to the nightmarish scene playing out before her.

Suddenly commotion erupted as black robes surrounded Seeley and Jordan. Pushing and shoving, they tried to take Jordan from Seeley's unyielding embrace.

"You lied, Trebane," Seeley howled. "You lied!"

Asa raised a hand, quieting the tumult a bit. "We belong to the Great Deceiver. The three of you will be welcome to leave after the consecration of your daughter." The pretense in his voice was plainly audible. His lips curled in a malevolent smile. "Though, I fear Jack is feeling somewhat…out of sorts, shall we say. My condolences, Mrs. Chase."

Her arms and legs felt like jelly. She was losing it. Somehow she managed to unearth an inner calm and braced her shoulders. Within seconds, Seeley felt an enigmatic power building within her. Outwardly, she sizzled. "You are the devil's spawn!"

"Why, thank you, my dear." Asa's tone was more than despicable. "Bring the child forward!"

Seeley scooped Jordan into her arms.

A burdened wheeze came from above. "No—Seeley." All heads shot heavenward. Jack was alive and speaking, "Do not let them—do it. Seeley, stop this—now."

Tears bathed Seeley's face as she gazed at the man she so desperately loved. How could this happen? What could she do?

"Why, Jack, you're still with us, I see." Asa's oily voice wavered. "Have you explained to Seeley why you're in such a predicament? My prodigal son has deserted me." Black masses parted like the red sea as Asa paced unhurriedly toward Seeley and Jordan, his baleful eyes judging Jack.

"Jack, Jack, Jack. You became a holy thorn in my side—let's see…" His head veered to Jordan, his gray eyes turning black. "About ten years ago—Yes, I believe that's right."

Jack's painful gasping was heart-wrenchingly evident as he struggled to breathe.

Asa's accusing eyes pierced Seeley. "You—" He pointed a finger at her head. "You caused my Jack to rebel against us. Together, we could've been great Sovereign Rulers. I planned for him to take the reins of a worldly kingdom." Asa snorted. "Jack's betrayal cost us billions and now he pays the ultimate price. If he wants to fight for Christ, Jack will die like Christ."

Seeley heard Zeke's slight undertone. *'Now, Seeley—now.'*

Asa held out his arms. "Give me the child." Callously, he ripped Jordan from her arms.

"Ezekiel! Markus!" Seeley bellowed.

An iridescent flash stunned the cluster of hooded men and women. They slumped to the ground. Dozens remained standing—demons.

Asa ferried a flailing girl, sprinting to a rectangular slab situated beneath an inverted crucifix. He had one purpose—to consecrate Jordan to Lucifer.

Zeke appeared, not as a glorious angel, but as a human, fearless and powerful. He spun toward a demon man who broke from his confining robe. The red-skinned demon, covered with flaky ulcerations, pounced. Zeke's fists smashed into its flesh, caving in the demon's chest cavity. He finished him off with an uppercut to the chin. A splintered jawbone drooped awkwardly to the side.

A red-eyed devil taunted Markus, slobbering from a gaping orifice while wielding a stiletto. Dodging swiftly and accurately, he gashed Markus's arm. Instead of retreating, Markus ducked inside the slashing hand. Getting a grip under the man's armpit, Markus tore the demon's arm from its torso with a stomach-churning crunch of bones.

Boiling over with pulsating energy, Seeley leapt on the back of a medium-sized woman, getting a headlock on the snarly fiend. Profound strength rippled in every muscle as she easily broke the woman's neck. The demon spirit fled like smoke from a fire as the human frame sank to the ground.

Spotting Markus fending off three demons, with another one about to attack, Ezekiel transformed to his ethereal state. Out of thin air he materialized a serrated blade that glimmered like an icicle. With perfect timing, he threw the icy blade to Markus, who caught it gracefully, as if it were light as a feather. Infused with Markus's power, the blade had the strength of a broadsword. In a synchronized move, he split one demon's head like a melon, swiveled, and decapitated another.

In such an unholy place, Ezekiel felt the drain on his angelic potency. Knowing he couldn't remain in spirit much longer, he morphed back to human form, but not before pulverizing a wily critter with fangs. It looked more like a wolf than anything human. Adversely, an unseen blow struck, dropping Ezekiel to the ground. An enormous creature hunkered over him, aiming a pistol straight at the fallen warrior's skull.

Accurately flying through the air, Markus toppled the creature just as the pistol fired. Markus jolted. He merely laughed at the bloody hole in his shoulder, turned back to the hulking demon with the pistol, and adroitly juggled the blade in his hands. With one precise stroke, he severed the demon's gullet. A volcano of blood erupted from the wailing carcass. Gunky gray fluid littered Markus's sneakers.

As Seeley pursued Asa, an arm encircled her neck. Choking, she jabbed her elbow into her mugger's diaphragm. He buckled, freeing her neck. Seeley spun and kicked, putting her heel in the evil one's eye.

"Seeley—" Zeke hollered. "Help Jack. You can release him. Concentrate on the nails."

Disorientated, Seeley yelled, "Jordan—I must get to Jordan."

"Markus will protect Jordan. You help Jack."

Seeley threw an agonized glance at the altar where Asa was wrestling with Jordan on the concrete slab. She then observed a lightly muscled teenager striding purposefully toward them. Feeling Seeley's concern, the angel looked back briefly. His face was resolute and his eyes were flashing blue fire. Seeley decided to leave her daughter in her guardian angel's care.

Jack knew he couldn't hold on much longer. Now he hoped only for time before he died, time to explain important details to Seeley.

Seeley stood beneath him, his blood showering down on her, and concentrated on the nails lodged in his hands. Blocking the curses and grunts, the crunching and snapping of bones, she let her mind dwell on her husband.

Her mind blended with Jack's. His labored breathing and suffering moans wounded her heart. Eyes shut, and with a split-second plea, she imagined the nails inching from the wood, one-by-one. She experienced a sensation of drawing brainpower. Seeley heard the tiniest clink, succeeded by several more. Her eyes opened. The spikes, dripping with blood, lay scattered on the floor. Her head jerked up, Jack dangled limply, held up only by the rope tying his chest to the beams. She thought for sure he was dead.

At the altar, Jordan calculatedly chomped on Asa's lower arm. Her jaws were like a steel trap. Her grip loosened when he slammed her back onto the concrete, holding her shoulders with both hands. He swore under his breath at the dotted teeth marks. While Asa was distracted, Jordan sank her teeth into his other arm. A metallic taste filled her mouth.

He yowled, "You little brat," and backhanded her across the face. "You'll get yours."

Jordan's head swam and disgusting blood clogged her throat. She watched as the man slipped a dagger from his cloak.

Rushing the unholy mantra, Asa began the consecration. "*Erth Baalrog, Lucifer—endula—se—nobili—bellator…*"

Although the words meant nothing to Jordan, Jack would have known their meaning: *All mighty Lucifer accept and honor this consecration—a warrior to battle for your world.*

Asa held the dagger aloft. Suspended in time, as if in a void—Jordan wasn't a bit afraid. Almost subdued, she would give her life peacefully if it meant saving her mom and dad.

She turned her head and glimpsed her mom reaching her arms up to her father. She looked up at the balcony and was shocked to be able to meet her father's magnetic eyes. Jordan's throat stung with inhibiting tears as she gawked at his mutilated body. Miraculously, she heard each drop of his blood splash on the floor. She noticed his lips were moving. She wished with all her heart to hear what he was saying. Her wish was granted. His voice was in her ears. "Fight, fight back. You are the warrior."

In slow motion, the dagger plunged, Asa's face warped in an expression of victory.

All hell broke loose as Jordan regained her senses. She heard nerve-racking screeches, metal clanging, and heavy feet running. Asa was impelled ruthlessly off of her, thwacking into the cement wall. Everything came to a halt.

Jordan couldn't take her eyes off of Markus's hand—hovering just above her heart.

The bloody dagger, thrust through his palm, quivered there, its tip grazing her shirt and staining the white fibers a brilliant red. Gripping the hilt and clenching his jaw, Markus gradually withdrew the dagger from his hand.

There wasn't time for pity as creatures bombarded Markus.

Jordan, teetering on the altar, hopped over to seize the neck of Markus's current attacker. Just then sinewy arms gripped her waist. Ezekiel actually smiled as he set her on the floor and directed her toward Seeley.

Cloaked worshippers had run amok during the confrontation and were nowhere to be seen. Asa, along with his legions, had vanished. Adrenaline subsiding, drained of color, Markus wobbled, grimaced at his battle wounds, and glared at Ezekiel who looked perfectly fit except for a few scrapes.

Taking three strides, Ezekiel hooked his arm under the hollow of Markus's shoulder for support and smirked playfully. "You're young and strong, Markus. But you block when you need to disarm."

"Good thing you've got my back, bro."

Their human bodies were beaten and bruised. The angels joined Seeley and Jordan where they waited sorrowfully for Jack Chase. An unfamiliar, lustrous angel leaned over the balcony, untying the ropes from Jack's chest. He effortlessly carried Jack along the railing and descended the stairs to his waiting wife and daughter.

Seeley's legs crumpled as she broke into despairing sobs. The angel, respectfully and with honor, laid Jack's body in her arms. She lovingly swept the blood soaked hair from his once handsome face. Recoiling at the yawning cuts and bloated contusions, she bowed over him and tenderly brushed his lips with hers.

Jack stirred, his eyes slit open. He managed a faint smile.

The embodied angels knelt, humbly bowing their heads. The angel who carried Jack spoke. "I'm Rafe. For years now, Jack has fought valiantly, banishing satanic cults."

Stunned, Seeley said, "I thought Jack was helping them."

"No. He didn't confide in you because he feared for your life and the life of your daughter. Apparently, he was right."

Jack moaned.

"We need to get him to the hospital," cried Seeley "Before it's too late."

"I need—to explain—" Jack's voice was thinning.

Jordan gazed at her father. Nuzzled safely between her mom and Markus, her memories of the ghastly incident lost their sharp edges. Her voice was a mere squeak. "Da–addy." She hugged her father's wounded hand to her chest, his blood transferring to her shirt and mingling with the blood of her angel.

Jack choked through his words. "The manuscript—in a box, under the bed. Read it, you'll need to know. My car—" His chest heaved, searching for oxygen. "It's parked on Clover. Journal, in glove compartment—use it. Go home—to your parents. There's strength, protection with family."

Seeley looked pleadingly at Zeke.

Ezekiel and Markus stood, stepping back. They took on their angelic forms, saturating the room with serenity.

"Seeley," Jack's voice was failing. "Consecration—more fittingly called desecration of a warrior is—the death of the body. Lucifer binds—the spirit, shapes it—into a vengeful demon like him." Jack's eye fell to Jordan. "I'll be with you always."

Seeley wept. "Jack, I love—love you—"

"I regret—the damage I did and hope, I've helped, some way—these past years. Seeley, it was all—all for you—I love—" One last breath rattled in his chest, as his weary, swollen eyes locked on Seeley's. His mouth was engraved in a permanent smile.

Seeley couldn't breathe. Her throat a tangled lump, she gulped for air, suffocating. Scalding tears streamed uncontrollably, washing Jack's face. Trembling fingers stroked his jawline. His lifeless head swayed to the side.

Seeley raised her teary eyes and witnessed the manifestation of her past confidant and priest, Father Edmund Posluszny, standing before them. The priest held his arms out toward Jack. Implausibly, Jack stretched and rose. Father Edmund embraced him. "Well done, good and faithful servant—well done."

Awed, they looked at his lifeless body, then at Jack's diaphanous spirit. Radiant as the angels, Jack's gilt-flecked emerald eyes emitted pure love as he gazed at Seeley and Jordan. He then dissolved into a wisp of gentle breeze. Seeley looked desolately at Ezekiel.

He said simply, "Go home to your parents."

CHAPTER 2

Mortals Are Mere Breath.
Fear No Harm, for I Walk with You.

Traumatized, Seeley and Jordan took refuge in the quaint village of Elma. Henry and Emily, Seeley's parents, wanting to shelter them, insisted that Seeley sleep in her old bedroom and converted a cozy attic space into a room for Jordan.

Months after Jack's death, Seeley gathered her courage and opened the box containing his manuscript. Scrupulously and guardedly she flipped page after page, reading about Jack's macabre upbringing and how Asa, through a blood rite, made Jack his 'son' and eventually a polished sorcerer. Jack conveyed truly terrifying tales of psychic phenomenon and the ubiquitous rise of supernatural demons.

Seeley felt empowered to warn the public and began to submit query letters to literary agents and publishing houses throughout the country, only to receive rejections. Jack's investigation, his extensive work, and his self-sacrifice were slipping down the proverbial drain.

Discouraged about the book, Seeley had found the dog-eared journal from Jack's battered jalopy to be a valuable resource. He had recorded page upon page of names, places, addresses, and phone numbers, along with specific transactions and dealings within the Order's organization.

Studying the journal, they learned, among other things, how demons possess a human body. Horrified, Seeley and Jordan read Jack's explanation: *Once the body was possessed, the person's soul withered and died over time. The demon inhabited the human shell until the innards started to deteriorate and the demon had to find a new host.*

☙❦☙

Years passed, devoid of devious demons or Asa crossing their paths. Yet, Seeley always had the sensation they were being watched. She continued to look over her shoulder and persisted in homeschooling Jordan for her protection.

At sixteen and strikingly beautiful, Jordan knelt in the antiquated chapel within St. Mary's of the Holy Angel's Church. Anyone meandering into the church would have looked twice. She stared upward at a life-sized statue stationed on a shelf, her emerald eyes unblinking, lost in the discipline of prayer. Her satin, brunette hair, highlighted with hints of reddish-gold, danced over her shoulders. She rested her delicate chin on her laced fingers. Her lips moved ever so faintly as she sought advice on a recent vision.

Next to Jordan appeared familiar, sparkling dots, like miniature firecrackers. The dots coalesced into her guardian angel, Markus. His flashing blue eyes looked at Jordan, then he gazed aloft to the womanly statue, as if anticipating something or someone. Jordan followed his gaze back to cold granite.

Immediately, she was distracted again when dazzling light radiated from the statue. Now clothed with the sun, the statue seemingly breathed life. The ineffable woman's translucent mantle and ebony hair billowed in an arcane breeze. Her loving eyes smiled at Jordan.

Entranced, Jordan stared at the apparition. "*Salve*, Regina."

"Daughter of my heart," a heavenly voice lilted. "There is a terrible battle waged above all levels of spirits. Those who are good against the wicked—angels against demons. The battle grows fiercer, calling all beings into combat. Remember that you are never alone. Your faith will be tested through unimaginable tribulations—be strong." Her pink lips curved, although the woman's eyes filled with crystalline tears that tripped over her lids—tears of heartache, and love.

Swiftly, life left the woman, turning her back into cold granite. Jordan turned her head and looked at the glorious angel beside her. His fathomless eyes were distressed, yet, unwavering. Markus faded into pure mist.

Heavenly apparitions, prophetic visions, and foreseeing future events had not only plagued Seeley, but the gift was inherited by Jordan. Along with developing oddities such as their telekinesis and remarkable strength, mother and daughter had discovered an adept priest, Father James, to help sort through their peculiar reality.

While picnicking at Chestnut Ridge, Seeley and Jordan were both distractedly practicing their telekinesis. They sat under a shelter, giggling like best friends, as swings on the nearby swing set rocked back and forth—their power at work.

"Awesome," The swing swished upward and wound around the pipe.

"Show off." Seeley teased.

Jordan covered her ears. "Do you hear that really annoying dog barking?"

"I don't hear any dog."

"I can hear pretty good." Jordan clipped a strand of hair behind her ear. "Like—do you hear water?"

"Water?" Seeley strained to hear this water she spoke of, without results, the extent of Jordan's talent constantly amazed her. "Take me to this water."

Seeley trailed Jordan past oak trees and pines and over a craggy crest, roughly a quarter of a mile into the wooded park. They stopped at a babbling brook. Jordan gestured. "There—water."

Seeley chuckled. "I hear it now."

꽃꽃꽃

Employed with *The Courier Express*, the city's newspaper, Seeley found working and homeschooling her maturing daughter quite frazzling. It didn't help that her opinionated parents frequently added their two cents.

"Seeley," Henry groused. "Send Jordan to school. Lighten up on the kid."

"Dad, I like homeschooling her," she said. "What's wrong with sheltering my daughter from the outside world for a while?"

Secretly, Seeley reflected on the prophecy hanging over Jordan's head. She'd been biting her nails for years waiting for Asa to make his move.

"For a while? Jordan's sixteen. It's high time she made a few friends and experienced life."

"I have a friend," Jordan said. They paid no attention to her. She shrugged indifferently, grabbed a cookie, and sat down.

Em agreed with her husband but eased the stress by adding, "You and Jordan have been through so much." She paused. "You know, Seeley, Dad and I don't live with blinders on. We've always known of your...your gifts, and I know you keep things from us. However, Jack would want you to live your life."

In a way, her mom was right, but like she said, Seeley would never tell them everything.

"What I need is to find a place for the two of us." Seeley looked from Em to Henry. "I've mooched long enough, don't you think, Dad?" Seeley really wasn't serious. She'd felt secure in knowing Jordan was safe with her parents.

Henry harrumphed but Em interjected, "Absolutely not. After losing you for all those years, I'm thoroughly enjoying a full house." She was still miffed that, after Seeley had married Jack, they'd left Elma.

But what Em didn't know was that the young couple had fled from Elma *and* Asa's influence.

Seeley grinned at her pigheaded parents, shaking her head. "I've saved some money from my job at the paper. Maybe I can find a place nearby."

Henry and Em did not like that idea one bit. Seeley cut off their protests before they got started. "Omigosh, look at the time." She glanced at the clock. "Jordan and I are late for class."

The lines around Em's mouth deepened. "Seeley, what's going on? Why are you and Jordan taking these martial arts classes and…what's that other stuff?"

"We're learning to defend ourselves. It's a crazy world out there."

"Yeah, Em." Jordan piped up. She whipped her leg through the air, demonstrating a kick. "It's really a riot. Someday, *if I ever have a boyfriend*, he'd better watch out."

Unappealing as it seemed, Jordan was growing-up. Seeley knew her parents were unbelievably correct. She needed to untie the apron strings. She snagged her purse and hustled Jordan to the car.

Driving forty-five minutes to the city to take classes at the accredited Jacob Adams Academy was well worth the effort. Their private lessons built confidence and precision. For five years Seeley had been preparing Jordan for the unimaginable. Her plaguing visions of soulless humans were becoming a nightly event. Seeley merged into traffic and soon became agitated with the congested highway. "Cripes—" Seeley veered into the far lane. "We're going to be late." The red needle on the speedometer spiked.

"Chill, Mom," said a positive Jordan. "It's no big deal if we're late."

The stress lines relaxed into a smug grin as Seeley darted a peek at her daughter. They now stood shoulder to shoulder and she even wore her reddish-brown hair well past her shoulders, just like Seeley. Jordan's delicate heart-shaped face, glowing with good health, masked a core of fortitude. It was Jordan's eyes that reminded Seeley of Jack—the same compelling, gold-flecked green, fanned by plump black eyelashes. She'd also inherited his easy-going personality and, admittedly, his stubborn resolve.

Seeley considered her father's comments about Jordan enrolling in high school. "You have friends, don't you?" she inquired casually. "Like Cayden and—what's that other girl's name?—Oh yeah, Kristin."

Jordan knew what her mom was getting at. "Yeah, Mom, I have a friend." Then she decided to go for it. "I've been thinking about it a lot lately. Maybe I should register at the high school this year."

Squirming, Jordan waited for the rebuttal. Instead, her mom merely nodded. She felt somewhat guilty about not confiding in her about the troubling dream. Though if her mom had known of what was lurking in the school's corridors, she'd never let her enroll. And it was time for Jordan to step into battle mode, as the woman clothed with the sun had foretold.

Parking was at a premium near the academy. Seeley had to drive around for twenty minutes before finding a space. In the baking heat of late summer, they both were wearing shorts and tees and broke a sweat walking.

"I'm almost looking forward to winter," Jordan said, running fingers through her hair and tying it up in a ponytail. The two ladies received admiring glances. They looked like sisters with their swishing ponytails.

When they arrived at Jacob Adams, the doors were locked. Seeley knocked on the window, wondering if Jacob had forgotten about their session. An average-looking man in his thirties unlocked the doors and let them in.

"Sorry about that," he said with a slight accent. "Jacob's running late. I'm his brother-in-law, Hank, and he asked me to start the lesson."

Hank lowered his face and motioned them in with his arm. Seeley noted his workout clothes and dirty bare feet, though she didn't get a good look at his eyes. With a brief sigh of relief, she chuckled privately at the notion of a demon wearing a kimono. Jordan and Seeley went into their usual workout room, where two other men dressed in jean shorts and shirts leaned against the wall, as if they were waiting for a lesson. They straightened up when they saw the ladies.

Seeley's inner demon-detection antenna started to click away. Evidently, Asa had finally decided the time had come to make their lives a living hell. Heedless of Seeley's vibes, Jordan had stripped off her flip-flops to stretch and then jumped and twirled, executing perfect martial art skills.

Keeping one eye on the men and one on Jordan, Seeley actually thought it looked like Jordan was warming up for the melee to begin. She hastily browsed for the nearest exit, wanting to save her daughter. When the men stalked the border of the mats, Seeley's scalp prickled.

Responding instantly, Jordan and Seeley dodged their clumsy, yet furious, attack. Jordan got hold of one man's slashing arm, jarred her hip into his side, and flipped him to the mat. Before he had a chance to recover, she landed a solid kick to his ribs. While she was in the process of turning back around, a second man tagged her from the rear, binding her wrists in an excruciating hold.

The man who'd opened the door joined the attack. Seeley smashed the heel of her palm into his nose. A spurt of blood stained his face. Then she rammed her foot into his abdomen. The man doubled over and Seeley swiveled toward Jordan, who had cried out in pain. The third man had one arm around Jordan's neck while the other held her wrists behind her back. Seeley saw the telltale red-ring around his pupil.

"Watch out!" Jordan cried.

The two goons knocked Seeley to the mat. They tied her wrists then hefted her to her feet, facing Jordan. The man with the bloody nose mopped his face and then, without warning, hit Seeley in the chin. Her head snapped back as Jordan screamed. Seeley held onto consciousness, though her head swirled and her throbbing chin began to swell.

"You bitch!" the man shrieked, glaring at Seeley. "I think ya broke my nose." He then walked over to Jordan, grasped her chin with bloody fingers, and drooled. "Young—tender—meat—"

The demon restraining Seeley sounded anxious. "Hank, we're not allowed to kill her."

A meager inch from Jordan's face, Hank clearly had red-ringed eyes. His repellent breath fanned Jordan as his fleshy tongue darted out, slathering her face from chin to temple. "Tastes as good as she looks, guys."

"Disgusting," she gagged and tried angling her head to her shoulder to wipe the rank saliva on her T-shirt.

Hank then gestured at Seeley. "This lady's fair game, there's a high price on her head. We'll be greatly rewarded."

Seeley pulled herself together enough to mock him. "Lucifer's let you out of Hell?"

Her question caught them off guard. "Humans crack the barrier on a daily basis," the fiend with the chokehold on Jordan said in a dubious manner. They're begging for us to come play, and besides, our lord gives us free will."

The other demons nodded with crooked smirks. "We're allowed to stay and play as long as we bag souls for his gain. The more souls, the longer we get to stay."

"Why? Don't you like your fiery perdition?" Seeley said dryly.

Her remark infuriated them and Hank returned to gloat in front of Seeley. Using the distraction, Jordan subtly tried to weasel her way out of the chokehold.

With his left hand, Hank grabbed Seeley's ponytail, tugging her face close to his red eyes. They looked like hot coals as he sneered. "We're not ready to leave, not with all this fun we're having. Souls are jamming the Highway to Hell—we just nudge them in the right direction." A gawky sound rattled in his throat, forcing Seeley to breathe in his foul breath. "Your kind of souls is a pain in the ass."

Hank dug a switchblade out of his pocket. With a decisive snap, he held the silver blade to Seeley's throat.

Jordan needed to act, quickly. Silencing her mind of demon interference, she linked all her concentration on the hand weights. The twenty-pound dumbbells jiggled in place. Then one detached from the stack and launched across the room, crushing one demon's skull with a nauseating thud. He collapsed and a gloomy configuration fled the lifeless frame.

A jumbo Markus boldly manifested, clutching a showy bejeweled sword and extending feathery effulgent wings, confusing Hell's legions. With Markus posed like a warrior, the blitz was swift as Seeley and Jordan disposed of the horrid beasts.

Panting, Jordan asked Markus, "What took you so long?"

Markus shrank to human size, transmitting the sword into the heavens. It disappeared. "You handled it well."

"Handled it well?" Jordan blasted. "We could've been killed."

"We're not supposed to interfere unless it's crucial."

"Crucial? It's always crucial," Jordan fumed.

Ezekiel then became visible, looking at the exasperated Jordan. He shifted his gaze to Seeley. "You live in apocalyptic times. We clash and purge against Lucifer's legions, but mediums around the globe continue to expedite their freedom. Some occupy human bodies while others prowl in their own distorted forms. Don't be deceived, Lucifer does not allow free will—he binds and takes."

"We cannot kill humans—only in extreme, unavoidable conditions," Markus added. "And then, we mourn each loss."

"Demons are fair game though, right?" Jordan actually looked excited.

Markus and Zeke exchanged faint smirks.

"Demons are not living creatures," Markus answered. "They don't have souls. They sow wrath on earth and drag souls to Hell. So—yes, they're fair game."

"Jack wrote about possession and how a person's soul dies after the demon takes over the body," Seeley said. "Could that person still be saved?"

Zeke nodded. "You know the answer, Seeley."

"Exorcism," Jordan exclaimed.

"Yes, a holy priest. Specific men and women have the power to vanquish demon spirits. Unfortunately, a person's soul doesn't necessarily choose to spend eternity in heaven, and Lucifer collects those souls with great pride."

Jordan's mouth twisted. She was revolted at the thought of choosing Hell.

CHAPTER 3

You Know My Folly, and Again You Have Rescued Me.

The congregation had dispersed after mass and only a few people remained. Jordan sat quietly, thinking about the next chapter in her life. Seeley had begrudgingly consented to Jordan starting at her old alma mater, Elma High. Although, Jordan was secretive about her vision of demons hunting in the school, she felt it was time to take control of her life. And her mom would hold her back. As a precautionary measure, and for his expert advice, Jordan had recounted the vision to Father James. He felt it was very significant, though he just didn't know why—yet.

Not sweating the demons, Jordan worried more about starting high school in her junior year; her stomach curdling at the prospect. Jordan's inner psyche turned to Markus just before he appeared. Indiscernible to humans, he brought heaven's glow with him. He easily read the concern on Jordan's face, but she had less luck studying Markus's unchanging features.

"Always carry holy water."

"Where am I supposed to put that?"

"Your purse?"

"I don't like to carry a purse."

"Then in a pocket or something. It's for your own protection. And you should wear a blessed holy medal."

"Why?"

"Are you going to argue about everything?"

Jordan pouted. "I just want to know why."

A little girl with pigtails, sitting at the end of the pew, looked at her strangely.

Markus's eyes softened. "It's like a shield. Sacramentals ward off evil."

Jordan's shoulders sagged. Trying not to draw the little girl's attention again, she took a breath and said delicately, "I thought you were my shield?"

"Yes—one of them." He looked at her calmly. "I know you're nervous about school. Maybe even a little scared?"

"I'm not scared," Jordan shot back. "It's just...all those kids...staring at me."

"Stare back." His expression was almost comical.

She held onto a snicker.

಄಄಄

Elma High School was built in 1956. The low-rise building supported three stories, with adjoining athletic fields, and was secluded on the outskirts of town. With less than eighty-five students in the junior class, obscurity was unattainable for Jordan, and since the start of the school year, it had felt like everyone was prodding, pointing, and goggling at the new girl. Jordan had lived in the village for six years and chiefly home-schooling was an obstacle with her peers. The kids thought of her as some kind of geek, a weirdo who lived in the woods. Henry and Em's Cape Cod home, far from any central thoroughfare was within walking distance, and for the past month, Jordan had been one of the few students who didn't ride a bus or drive to school.

She hated the noisy corridors and felt like every single teacher and student must be in the hallway, bellowing and jabbering. Carrying an armload of books, she bumped a knot of whispering girls on her way into algebra class. They glared at her as if they thought she'd been eavesdropping. Just to irritate them all the more, she hiccoughed a chuckle to make them think she knew what they were saying.

The room was practically empty. Jordan headed for the corner, her usual desk in the last row by the windows. Despite the various free desks, a mousy girl with buckteeth took the seat next to Jordan. Returning her toothy smile, Jordan understood the social benefits of braces.

Without moving her head, Jordan noticed an overconfident girl striding toward her corner desk. Her sleek mane, tinted like black enamel, cascaded well below her shoulder blades. She had three silver hoops the size of bangles in her ears and mystifying almond eyes. She stood in front of the mousy girl and said, "Move." The girl shot from the seat as if electrocuted.

"So you're Jordan." The dark-haired girl slammed her book on the desk. "I'm Ronan. What's your next class?"

"English, with Mrs. Kinvara."

"She's pathetic."

Jordan smirked.

Mr. Basinski cleared his throat nosily as a precursor to drawing everyone's attention to him. Glasses perched on his bulbous nose, his eyes swept the room. He held Jordan's gaze a beat longer than the others. She returned his gaze, curious, until he turned to the board.

"Jordan…" Ronan sounded cagey.

With the teacher scrawling numerals on the blackboard, Jordan glanced at Ronan, who asked, "Are you up for some after school activity?"

Jordan thought quickly, examining the girl's liquid black pupil—no red-ring. "Sure."

"Come to the students' parking lot and wait by the steps. We'll pick you up," Ronan whispered hurriedly as Mr. Basinski looked at the girls.

Math was Jordan's worst subject. She was relieved when the bell rang and she could shuffle out of the room with the rest of the horde.

"See you later," Ronan called.

Jordan nodded.

Jordan was thankful for her only friend, Cayden, who'd accepted her and all her weirdness. But she was also grateful for this odd invitation to hang with someone new. Either her classmates had deemed her acceptable, or she'd better be wary.

English with Mrs. Kinvara was boring. She droned on and on about the perfect five paragraph essay. Jordan groaned inwardly when Mrs. Kinvara produced last week's assignment, asking each student to read their essay aloud. And Jordan had thought math was bad.

Distracted and curious, Jordan thought about Ronan's invite. Ronan didn't appear to be the library type, so the afternoon would prove to be interesting. When the bell trilled, Jordan snatched her flannel jacket from her locker and speedily located the back doors to the parking lot.

The whole school seemed to tumble from the building as Jordan leaned on the brick wall, trying to look casual. Students walked by, their voices raised an octave above normal, each attempting to talk over the din, girls with their heads together, more than likely spreading the latest gossipy news, and everyone racing to their cars. Some cast strange glances Jordan's way, and she wondered if Ronan had stood her up.

Eventually a car horn blared and a voice hailed, "Hey, Jordan!"

A classic, dusty blue Chevelle Malibu pulled up to the curb. "Hop in." Ronan ordered,

Pleasantly surprised, Jordan got in. She was relieved to see Cayden in the back seat with a big, burly blond guy who smiled at her. "Hi, Cayden."

"Hey, Jordan." Cayden waved curtly. "Squish back here with us."

Ronan turned around from the front seat and introduced the big guy as Rolly and the standoffish girl sitting next to Ronan was Paisley. The cute driver was named Thrill.

Jordan cocked her head. "Thrill?"

"Thrill." Paisley leered at Jordan. "Like a thrill ride."

Thrill glanced at Paisley. "Wouldn't you like to know?"

Paisley stuck out her tongue in his direction, but he just smiled, obviously not offended.

Looking over his shoulder, Thrill explained, "I was a lovable, adventurous tyke."

"Yeah, your mom said you were *real* lovable," Paisley countered. "Especially the time you climbed out the second floor window to sleep on the roof 'cause you said it was too hot in the house."

"Oh, yeah, I forgot about that." Thrill's mouth gathered to one side as he grinned. "Once I jumped out of my parents' upstairs window into the pool at my sister's birthday party. I thought my mom was going to hemorrhage."

Paisley scoffed. "You wanted the girls to think you were really cool or something."

Thrill chuckled. "I thought I was cool *and* brave." He blasted Paisley with a salacious eyebrow tweak. "And so did Brinkley Warton."

"Brinkley—ugh, that slut."

"Seriously, though Jordan," Thrill reasoned, ignoring Paisley's commentary. "I pulled pranks on my brothers and sister. My parents said I was like a thrill ride—they never knew what I'd do next. So my brother started calling me Thrill instead of Bill and the name stuck. I should go back to William, though. I've totally calmed down."

Jordan thought it sounded like Thrill and Paisley shared some history.

Reversing back to the steering wheel and putting the car in gear, Thrill said, "Let's punch it!" He hit the gas. "Suckers!" he yelped out the open window, cutting off a shiny red Mustang and bypassing the school's exit by driving over the lawn to the main road. Their tires fishtailed on the asphalt, leaving scores of rubber marks.

Not amused, Jordan dug her hands into the vinyl cushion for support. *Yeah, he's certainly calmed.* The rest of the kids laughed. Thrill drove through bustling Main Street and past the village library. Jordan had been right—they weren't the bookish type.

Rolly, whose nickname fit, had everyone in stitches as he reenacted his attempt at eating the cafeteria's spongy macaroni and cheese. His sausage-like fingers scraped the roof of his mouth, as he pretended to remove gummy noodles and then clutched his throat as if he were gagging to death while swallowing. Jordan frowned, finally laughing out loud when Rolly demonstrated how to hack up a gooey cheesy glop and then burped with gusto.

Everyone said, "Eeyew."

After Rolly's theatrics, Jordan listened to the group discuss the upcoming Winter Ball.

Wholly in command, Ronan remarked, "We're going together as a group. We'll have a better time. What'd you think?"

Cayden and Paisley nodded, but Thrill spoke up. "I was going to see if the new girl wanted to go with me."

Startled, Jordan knew he was talking about her. An eye-catching Thrill threw a mischievous grin over his shoulder, causing a rapid rise of heat to her cheeks.

Ronan saved her. "No way, Thrill. This sweet thing's with us. Right, Jordan?"

"Ah–h–h…I wasn't planning on going to the dance," Jordan replied with uncharacteristic timidity.

"C'mon, Jordan." Cayden peered around Rolly. "You'll have fun and get to meet everyone. You've lived here for so long and no one actually knows who you are."

"Who are you anyway?" Twisting to scrutinize Jordan's face, Paisley broke her icy silence. "Rumor has it you go to church—*a lot*. Are you one of those geeky holy rollers?"

Irked, Jordan recalled her mom's warning about her own deprecating school years. Well, she wasn't her humble mother.

Jordan held her anger in check while Ronan's snicker dampened their tempers. "Chill, Paisley. Let's all be friends." Then Ronan laid her head on the back of the seat, clearly relaxed. "Now, what were we talking about? Oh yeah, the dance. I think it's December tenth."

"Ronan, are you going to ask that new guy to the dance if we go as a group?" Cayden asked,

Ronan turned and looked at Jordan. "Have you seen the new guy?"

"I don't know, everyone looks new to me."

"You warned us to back off," Cayden declared, in her nasally voice. "The new guy was yours. We thought you'd be asking him to the dance."

"You're such an idiot sometimes, Cayden," Ronan jeered.

"O–o–o–o, you were dissed." Thrill gloated. "No wonder you want us all to go to the dance as a group."

Ronan slapped Thrill on the shoulder.

"Ow—" he said, rubbing the spot, "—just kidding, Ronan."

"I never asked him." But Ronan's sideways glance at Paisley told a different tale.

After twenty minutes, Thrill banked left and clouds of dirt swallowed the car. He was content in careening over the bumpy road, bouncing the kids like pinballs. They thumped in and out of potholes until Rolly bashed his head on the roof. "Hey man, slow down. You're killing me back here."

They'd plainly taken a road less traveled. While her head bounced like a bobble-headed doll, Jordan checked out the scenery. The car trundled under an impressive tunnel of arching tree branches. "We're here," Thrill announced.

Leafy limbs painted in an array of russet, yellow, and red leaves wagged in the tepid breezes. A sighing wind rustled branches and a rainbow of colors floated to the ground as they straggled from the car. Jordan was startled by a dissonant squawk. The desolate area was coming to life and thrummed eerily. Raucous caws and the thrashing of wings made everyone look up as a flock of crows sailed by in shrieking squadrons. Minutes passed and a peaceful quiet returned briefly, then nervous giggles gushed from the girls.

The group trooped toward a crude pathway between immense oaks. Jordan inhaled the loamy scent of the crackling dead leaves. She was lagging behind Cayden and lengthened her stride to keep pace. Stifling a niggling uneasiness, Jordan realized she was being led into a forest with people she hardly knew.

They scampered to the surface of a large boulder and sat in a circle. Jordan started to squeeze between Cayden and Paisley, but detecting Paisley's sneer, she changed her mind. Thrill saw her hesitate and offered his arm, wedging Jordan between him and Rolly.

"What's today's poison, Rolly?" Ronan inquired expectantly, rubbing her palms together.

Rolly extracted a flat, clear bottle from his side pocket and set it on the boulder with a clink. "It's all I could snag from my parents supplies. Not much—might give us a buzz."

Jordan rolled her eyes. Adjusting to hanging out with this new group might get tricky.

Paisley saw Jordan's eye roll. "Ever get a snoot full, Jordan—or are you too high and mighty?"

"Hey, hey," Thrill said brusquely, albeit in an amiable voice. "Let's be nice, okay?" He put a protective arm over Jordan's shoulder, pulling her close.

Paisley sulked.

Rolly uncapped the bottle and gulped heartily, passing it to Cayden, who took a healthy swallow. The bottle made its way to Thrill, who downed the contents, leaving a few drops at the bottom. He grinned slightly and passed it to Jordan who thanked him with her own smile. Wiping the mouth of the bottle with her sleeve—like germs mattered—Jordan consumed the remaining drops. Snatching the empty container from Jordan's hands, Ronan whipped it at the nearest tree, shattering glass.

"To the log." Paisley pointed her arm, eager to lead the way.

Though she had generous curves, Paisley could not compete with the stunning Ronan in looks. Paisley's shoulder-length hair, dyed platinum, had ashy roots. She had a shiny gem for a nose stud and an obvious tattoo on the back of her neck—a circled snake biting its tail, centered in the middle of a five-pointed star.

Paisley managed to flaunt it by constantly flipping her hair. Her muddy brown eyes, however, kept up with Ronan for sheer intimidation. She shot Jordan a look and hopped to the ground, her jelly belly jiggling.

Clambering over fallen trees and zigzagging through masses of brambly bushes that snagged and scraped at her jeans, Jordan trailed obediently. Scurrying squirrels and a herd of deer leapt away gracefully in response to their intrusion.

Sunbeams shafted through the verdant canopy, casting shaded lacy patterns on their faces. Paisley slowed as they approached a clearing, where a broad, sturdy log created a natural bridge over a ravine. Padding gingerly to the ravine's precipice, Jordan peered down. Broken tree trunks studded a treacherous decline. She thought the sheer drop resembled an archaic torture device. Soil shifted under her sneakers as rocks and pebbles tripped over the shelf. She watched their flight and at last they pinged off jagged boulders.

"It's time," Ronan said in a singsong voice.

Cayden slipped a brown cotton scarf from her jacket and twirled it in the air.

"Wait." Thrill's tone was cautious. "I'll show Jordan what to do."

Jordan scanned their faces. "What's going on?"

"It's initiation time," responded Paisley. "We've all done it."

"Done what?"

"Crossed the log—blindfolded," Rolly answered. "It's easy. Don't freak," he added, noting Jordan's rounding eyes. "Watch Thrill, he's the expert. Even did it backward once."

Ronan wound the scarf over Thrill's eyes. Raising his hands like a blind man, he groped the air. "Okay, let's go."

Cayden and Paisley obliged, guiding him to the natural bridge. They raised his left foot, placing it on top of the log's crusty bark. Like a tightrope walker, Thrill balanced his weight. Making it look easy, he scuffed his feet to the opposite side without incident. When Thrill reached the log's decaying edge, he jumped to flat ground, removed the blindfold, and spun, lifting his arms. "Ta-dah!"

They all clapped—except for Jordan, who felt a bit queasy.

Thrill shuffled back to her side and challenged, "You're up, Jordan."

Before she knew what was happening, the blindfold was tied tightly over her eyes, rendering her helpless. Any mulish effort to hold her ground would be useless. Her foot was squarely placed on the broad log. For a fraction of a second, she nearly tore away the cloth. However, she was here on a mission. She felt it was vitally important that she be accepted into their clique. If she could kill demons, Jordan reminded herself, then crossing the log should be a piece of cake. Needless to say, her mom would probably blow a gasket when she found out.

"You're all set to go, Jordan." Thrill said evenly. "It's easy—just go slow and straight."

Her fear vanished with Thrill's encouragement and a cold resolve set Jordan in motion. Edging her foot forward, feeling the rough bark through her sneakers, inch by inch she slid across. Behind her, she heard crunching twigs, and a commotion of voices. She hesitated and wobbled a bit. *Concentrate*, she thought. *Concentrate*!

"Stop her," a vaguely familiar voice commanded.

"She's fine," Ronan yelled. "Doing great, Jor!"

Hushed voices and a few gasps hung in the air as her foot slipped, but she recovered quickly. It was all about survival at this point. Her breathing labored, Jordan carefully felt for her next step.

"You're almost there, Jordan," Thrill assured her. "One more step."

Her nerves jangled. When she heard a faint crack of splintering wood, Jordan flung off the blindfold and leapt to level ground. With a rush of relief, she copied Thrill, twirling and cheering, "Ta-dah!"

Jordan winced—strangers were gawking at her—but everyone else applauded her accomplishment. Tearing her eyes from the stares, Jordan stepped up on the sturdy log and held out her arms for balance. A puff of wind whipped her hair over her face. She stopped in the middle of the log to peel away the blinding strands and made the mistake of looking down. The height was enough to paralyze her. Jordan swayed.

"Jordan! Jordan!" The cacophony of voices broke the spell, but she'd lost her balance and began to fall.

Miraculously, a strong arm circled her waist, hoisting her up and over the last couple of steps. The arm released Jordan and dropped her unceremoniously to the ground. On the verge of tears and humiliation, Jordan faced Ronan.

Ronan gave her a high five. "Knew you'd do it. Easy, right?"

Jordan shrugged warily as Ronan's eyes strayed over her head.

"Jordan, this is the new guy who started school last week." Ronan gestured with her hand. "I'm sorry. I don't remember your name?"

"Mark." His hard, low voice made Jordan's stomach clutch.

Revolving into his hard chest, Jordan stepped back to look into his face. She met his fierce eyes and, in startled delirium, she whispered, "Markus?"

Ronan eyed them suspiciously. "Do you two know each other?"

Mortified by Markus's angry glare and Ronan's question, Jordan performed a fast about-face and hemmed, "Um-mm...kind of...a little."

Her human angel apparent for all to see, she couldn't think of a quick comeback.

"Our families go way back," Markus drawled lazily. We've helped each other out a few times."

Ronan sighed, relieved. "Oh, you're related—like cousins?"

"Not exactly," he told the puzzled group.

Unsatisfied with their explanation, Ronan was decidedly miffed.

Thrill congratulated Jordan, spinning her around, then addressed the new guy. "Thrill McKenna, and this here is Rolly."

Markus extended his wiry hand. "Hey, man, Mark Evans." They shook hands, Rolly's chubby fingers engulfing Markus's hand.

Jordan tried not to stare at her angel, who acted like a typical guy, as if he was—*one of us!*

A pretty blonde, well formed under her beige sweater, said to Jordan, "I'm Beth Schaffer, and this is Kristen and Jeff. I guess you know Mark." Pausing for a second, Beth strode to Mark, putting her arm around him possessively. She looked at Ronan with knowing eyes. "I enlightened Mark about the initiation—the one we'd agreed to stop after the accident."

She looked sweetly up at Mark. "Our friend Gwen Kinski fell—she nearly died. Nobody talks about it much, though." Her eyes looped back to Ronan. "For some reason, Mark insisted on coming out here. It stands to reason you'd be here with the new girl, Ronan." A flicker of resentment flashed between them.

"Mind your own business, Beth," Ronan retorted as she stormed past Beth, bumping her shoulder.

"We agreed to stop this nonsense before someone gets killed," Beth repeated stubbornly,

"I'm not your friend anymore—remember?"

Jordan, aware of Markus's close proximity, felt his warm breath tickle her ear, launching a shiver up her spine. "That was a stupid—no, idiotic—thing to do."

"I needed to be accepted."

"They'd accept you either way, without you nearly killing yourself."

"Shush, Ronan's watching us."

Scowling conspicuously, Ronan had watched their exchange, torn between curiosity and outrage. Then Jordan remembered the chatter in the car. Ronan expected more than just friendship with Markus, or now should she call him, Mark?

"Let's get out of here." Ronan's tone was terse. "It's a little too crowded."

Departing from Markus with her new acquaintances, Jordan felt eyes boring into her back. Laughter and mingled voices leapt from tree to tree as they hiked out of the forest.

The drive back to the village was quiet, each lost in their own thoughts. Jordan stared out the window, her thoughts on Markus until she noticed the pewter sky. "Omigosh. What time is it? I never called Henry, he'll be mad."

Checking her cell phone, Paisley said, "It's after 6:30."

"Thrill, could you drop me at home?"

Thrill gave her his dimpled smile. "Sure, Jordan."

"Why do you use your grandparents' first names?" asked Paisley, her eyes scouring Jordan's face as if she were an odd-ball.

Jordan shrugged. "I've always called them Em and Henry."

Thrill's car rumbled into the driveway, and Jordan saw her grandfather sitting on the porch, his bushy brows gathered over irate eyes.

"See you tomorrow." Jordan shut the car door and trudged to the porch.

Pushing himself to a standing position, Henry gimped through the screen door with Jordan on his tail. "You missed dinner."

Once tall and virile, now his back was stooped and Henry walked with a dawdling gait. Jordan knew he was mad. Under his sparse grey hair, his weathered face looked grim as he eased into the recliner.

Jordan looked around. "Where's Mom?"

"She had to work late tonight, and it's a good thing. She called twice asking about you. We had to lie—said you called and would be home shortly." Henry snapped his newspaper to attention.

Sitting placidly in her comfy chair, Em cleared her throat. "That's all right, Henry. Calm down." She smiled kindly, the smile not quite reaching her eyes. "Jordan, there's a plate in the fridge. Just warm it in the microwave. Your mom should be home any minute."

Jordan apologized, glimpsing at Henry, whose bushy brows looked like fuzzy caterpillars peeking over the top of the newspaper. He accepted her apology with a curt nod.

Jordan walked into the kitchen just as her mom bustled in. She heard a murmured debate in the living room, then high heels clacked in her direction. Jordan expected a reprimand. Instead, her mom simply stated, "We're getting you a cell phone."

CHAPTER 4

Angels Walk Among Us, Yet So Too the Demons.

Jordan was finishing homework when Seeley marched into the bedroom. Since Jordan's inappropriate arrival, she'd been expecting a sermon on the undue stress she caused her grandparents. Except her mom inquired cheerfully about her day, interested in what had brought her home late.

Explaining why she'd missed dinner, Jordan described her first chance to hang out with classmates. "This girl invited me. Her name's Ronan, and I met a funny guy named Rolly— you'd like him, Mom. Another girl, Paisley—" Jordan's head waggled, with a minor crinkle to her nose. "She's okay—the jury's still out on her—and Cayden Rotella was with us, so at least I knew someone. I didn't feel too much like the new kid." Her voice then changed to optimistic. "And the guy driving, he's kind of...cute."

"O–o–o, Jordan, I've never heard you say anyone was cute."

"Well, I think he is. His name is William, but everyone calls him Thrill." She saw the flinch in her mom's eyes. "I know what the nickname implies. Thrill said he used to be pretty wild when he was younger."

"You're trying to tell me he's not wild now, even though he's still young?"

"Mom–m–m," Jordan whined. Then she remembered the tire tracks he'd left on the schools lawn and realized that discretion had to be enforced when conversing with her mom. She was treading into new territory. "I just met the guy. He seemed nice and he actually said he was going to ask me to the Winter Ball, but I think he was kidding."

"What makes you say he was kidding?" Seeley noted how Jordan's eyes lit up when she said the boy's name. She studied her daughter, an innate beauty and utterly naïve of the fact, which made her even lovelier. Seeley knew it wouldn't take long for the guys at the high school to start snooping around.

"Ronan came up with the idea of us all going to the dance together, and then Thrill said he was thinking of asking the new girl, meaning me." She cocked her head, looking cutesy, then turned theatrical. "I wanted to crawl under the seat. I was *soo* embarrassed. Ronan didn't go for it, though."

"Looks like this Ronan kind of rules the roost."

"Looks that way."

"So where'd you go with these…friends?"

"We drove down past town, farther south to a neat place where the trees were at their peak. It was really pretty. We hiked around for a while, and mainly talked. It was nice." Jordan sat on the bed in a lotus position, winding and unwinding a strand of hair on her finger like a yo-yo and hoping her mom couldn't read her mind as she reflected over the afternoons events.

"That's it? Just went for a joyride with a bunch of strangers, walked in the woods, and came home?" Seeley eyed Jordan skeptically. "What'd you find yourself—a bunch of nature lovers?" She felt certain that, like all kid's her age, Jordan was withholding information and, as a mother, Seeley was ignorant of the goings-on in the life of a teenager.

Concurrently, Jordan thought her mom wouldn't understand typical teens, because she'd never been one. She'd totally freak if she knew about the liquor, and any mention of her tightrope act on the log would send her mom into a fit. Even now, Jordan wrestled with keeping her vision a secret. She still felt certain her mom would pull her out of school, saying she wasn't ready to handle it. She preferred not to lie but, in her mind, this wasn't lying, just not revealing the whole truth. "They're a little different, I guess."

Seeley was sure her daughter was concealing a secret. "Is there something you're not telling me, Jordan?"

"Nah, I had a good time today, but I'm tired." She'd purposely left out Markus's appearance. If she even hinted that he created a human identity, her mom would more than guess she was hiding something—she'd know. Jordan hoped Ezekiel would keep his mouth buttoned, at least until she could figure out what these new friends were into.

Seeley pecked Jordan's forehead. "It's late. We'll talk more tomorrow." She shook her head, clearing the cobwebs. Without a doubt, her daughter was turning into a typical teenager and keeping Seeley on a need-to-know basis.

☙☙☙

Jordan punched the droning alarm and moaned. Midautumn mornings were black as night. Clanging around in the grayish dawn, she poked through her closet for a shirt and jeans. The house had a damp chill at this hour. She dressed hurriedly and then tiptoed down the stairs while her grandparents slept.

Already at the kitchen table sipping coffee, Seeley studied Jordan's drowsy eyes. "You need to get more rest." She held out a plate stacked with crusty bread. "Here grab a piece of toast before you go."

"Thanks. See you tonight."

Munching on toast, a heavy-eyed Jordan slipped through the back door into a dreary silvery morning. The brisk cold was like a spray of ice water, enough to rouse the senses. She scuffled along the driveway. A mantling frost touched the region, and Jordan scraped her sneakers over the slippery pavement. She liked the crunchy noise and kicked up crinkled leaves just to trample on them.

Looking back, she grinned at her random outline and was startled to see Markus striding purposefully behind her. She was bemused at his human appearance, and now he looked like a common teen in his zippered gray hoodie, black jeans, and brand new sneakers. Nobody would suspect anything different.

The first streak of morning sunlight set fire to his golden hair. *Now that's different*, Jordan thought. Markus noticed Jordan's gaze and ran a tousling hand through his hair, extinguishing the sparks.

"Where've you been?" She sounded annoyed. "I was calling for you half the night."

Markus's mild glare did not go unnoticed. "Being human has its difficulties. I feel like your comic book character, Clark Kent. It's not a good idea to disappear when people are in the same room. There is a need for secrecy, don't you think?"

"We need to talk, Markus," Jordan said as he whisked by. "I don't understand what's happening. Why are you human?"

"I'm here to fortify you for your mission," Markus informed her in a precise, formal tone. "You cannot overcome evil spirits on your own."

Jordan had to double-time it to keep up with his long stride and, at the same time, she pondered his words. Elma High came into view, teeming with activity. Some guys, and a few girls, tossed a football on the frosty lawn. Cars sped past, maneuvering into the crowded parking lot. Jordan wanted answers yet, glimpsing Markus's stern brow, she knew her questions would have to wait. He held the glass door to the school's vestibule open for her.

"Have a good day, Jordan," he called over his shoulder, sauntering along the corridor.

"Thanks, you, too," she muttered, trudging in the opposite direction to her locker. Musing on the uncanny emergence of her guardian angel, she was bowled over by Paisley and Cayden, who'd hustled on either side of her.

"Was that the new guy Mark you were just walking with, Jordan?" asked an enthusiastic Cayden. Her skinny jeans and knit shirt only made her look extra lanky as she looked down at Jordan.

"Yes, we met on the sidewalk."

Paisley wasn't as enthusiastic. "Ronan wants us in the gym after school" she ordered, rather than asked. "Ronan said you'd be interested. Be there, okay?"

Treading to her locker, Jordan decided these new friends were interestingly strange. The log stunt was unwise, dangerous, or what Markus said—stupid. Nonetheless, the fear had been exhilarating, like taking down demons. And Jordan needed to gain their trust. In order to conquer her nightmares, she needed to be accepted into their group.

The day had dragged. After school, Jordan looked around the crowded gymnasium and caught sight of the girls on the top bleacher. They waved her up. Mounting the bleachers two at a time, careful not to bungle her footing, Jordan reached them without incident and sat next to Ronan.

She appeared intent on the action below. A team of guys played basketball and a bunch of girls, some in cheerleading uniforms, practiced their routines. Not sure why they were there, Jordan inquired, "Hey, what's up? Are we trying out for cheerleading?"

Ronan flicked sleek hair over her shoulder and thrust her chin toward the girls on the floor. "Look there."

"What, or who, am I supposed to be looking for, Ronan? There's lots of people down there."

With a baton-like finger, Cayden pointed to a girl Jordan recognized from the woods. "Right there—Beth Schaffer."

Beth looked regal in the fitted cheerleader outfit. Her curvy body executed a twirling round-off and landed perfectly. Jordan suddenly felt inadequate. Without thinking, she let her hair fall over her petite face and absently pulled at the hem of her worn green and yellow T-shirt.

"She makes me sick." Ronan crunched her nose as if she'd smelled something rotten. "Did you see the way she put her arms around Mark, like they're already hooking up?"

Ronan's conclusion, though totally wrong, disturbed Jordan. Just thinking of Markus hooking up with anyone made Jordan's stomach feel like it was full of nettling butterflies. What if they actually knew that Mark was an angel—a real live angel?

Ronan leaned forward with her elbows on her thighs and lowered her voice. "Girls, concentrate your energy on Beth." She glanced at Jordan. "Listen and learn, Jordan. The power within you is great…concentrate." Ronan, Paisley, and Cayden centered their narrowed eyes on Beth. They appeared to be in some kind of a trance.

Ronan's lips stirred ever so faintly as she stared, utterly absorbed. Jordan jumped when Ronan hissed, "Not me, Jordan. Focus on Beth…"

A sharp cry of pain drew Jordan's attention to the gym floor, where Beth had landed wrong after a routine pyramid. Slumped on the hard wooden floor, she rocked, gripping her ankle. Cheerleaders rushed to her aid, helping her to the bleachers.

Paisley and Cayden's faces mirrored Ronan's smirk. She signaled the girls with approval. A tall guy with unruly hair loped over from the basketball court. Markus stopped beside Beth and checked her ankle. Even from where they sat, Jordan saw Beth wince in pain. Markus raised Beth's leg to the bleacher and her teammates packed it with ice to stop the swelling.

Apparently, Jordan's instincts were correct, but the girls weren't demons. During her mom's tutorage, they'd read her father's manuscript inside and out. And most recently, his journal had advanced her otherworldly studies. Her new friend, Ronan, more than likely had some type of psychic power.

Beth shooed Markus away. He jogged slowly back to the court, peering over his shoulder at Beth. A pang of envy touched Jordan when she realized that Beth, with her blonde ponytail, was very nice-looking, even when grimacing in pain.

"I knew he'd be here somewhere," drawled Ronan peevishly. "Beth has her claws deep into him."

With a wry smile, Jordan watched Markus bag the ball into the net with a high jump shot. As wacky as it seemed, Jordan couldn't help noticing Markus's well-developed build. She shook her head over the improbability of an angel playing basketball.

Ronan arranged her arms over the girls' shoulders in a conspiratorial huddle. In a measured undertone, she said, "We're g–o–o–o–d." She looked fixedly at each girl. "The four of us together are going to try that again, but this time we'll concentrate on Mark. We have the power on our side." Definitive almond eyes came to rest on Jordan. "I feel the force, don't you?"

Jordan sensed a foreboding spark in that glance.

Four pairs of eyes were riveted on Jordan's angel.

Mark halted, swerved, and looked with his own lancing gaze. Ronan's concentration was broken. She grinned and gave him a little finger wave. Paisley and Cayden followed her example. Ronan rose and the girls filed out of the gym.

"What was that all about?" Jordan questioned.

"You'll see." Paisley performed a sneaky, excited wiggle. "Are you intrigued?"

"Kind of, I guess," Jordan replied, wondering what she was in for.

The rim of Ronan's mouth curled into a secretive smile. "Spend the night at my house on Saturday. My father's out of town, again, and the girls are keeping me company. We'll play…some games."

Paisley and Cayden snickered.

"I guarantee a hair-raising good time," Ronan added.

Again, the girls covered their mouths, holding back the laughter.

Alerted rather than deceived by the contrived joke, Jordan said, "I'm sure it'll be all right." They had accepted her.

⋯⋯⋯

Jordan heard someone puttering in the kitchen and, assuming it was her grandmother, she yelled, "Em, I'm home."

Unexpectedly, her mom answered. "Did you have a good day, Jordan?" Seeley angled a shoulder on the doorframe, wiping her hands on a dishtowel. She smiled tenderly at her daughter.

"What are you doing home from work so early, Mom?"

"Come in here and sit down. I'd like to speak with you."

Her mom was a tad edgy, judging by the sound of her voice. Jordan dumped her book-bag on the nearest chair and hung her jacket on the rack. She wondered if Ezekiel had snitched about her tightrope act, or—her vision. She watched her mom pour a glass of orange juice. She didn't appear too terribly upset, so Jordan relaxed, somewhat.

"Here," Seeley said, handing Jordan the glass. "Sit down for a minute."

Jordan took a sip of juice and sat down, observing a strained look on her mom's face as she lowered to a chair.

Striving to engage her daughter by keeping things light, Seeley said, "Jordan, I'm going on a business trip. I guess that's what you'd call it." She hooked a rebellious strand of hair behind her ear and clasped her hands together on her lap.

"I don't know what you mean," she said. "Like a writing assignment for the paper?"

"Not exactly…" Seeley's voice trailed off. Then, clearing her throat, she explained, "Remember how hard I tried to get your father's book published?" She waited for Jordan's nod. "Well, years ago, you know, I spent lots of money to self-publish the book. That's one reason why we've lived with your grandparents. The other reason was for your safety." She put her hand up to stop Jordan's protest. "Let me finish."

"Father James has been instrumental in helping to distribute the book throughout district parishes and the state. Widespread interest in the book has taken an unexpected turn. There are people just like us out there, hunting and encountering these…demons."

Relieved beyond belief to hear the news, Jordan sighed deeply. She had wondered if she and her mom were the only two candidates fighting the vile breed. Now, there were numbers.

"Father James will stay behind to supervise you," Seeley continued. "At any time of the day or night, you can contact him. Don't forget the holy water and do wear your medal. You understand?" She shot Jordan a blazing look. "I'm convening with several groups to discuss…tactics." Unclasping her fists and kneading her eyebrows, Seeley sighed. "I don't know what I'm doing."

"Tactics?" Jordan repeated cynically. "Mom, say it honestly. Methods of slaughtering demons and sending them back to Hell where they belong."

Seeley's lips turned up at the corners in a tight smile. Mother and daughter nodded in unison.

Banging through the door with arms loaded with grocery bags, Henry and Em interrupted their banter. Seeley and Jordan rose to lend a hand.

That night, the four of them dined on chicken potpie, chatting happily. When Seeley discussed her departure in the morning, a tense undercurrent enveloped the table.

"Everyone has my cell number," she reminded them, wanting to keep the topic light. "I don't know how long I'll be gone, but I'll keep you informed. Mr. Donavan at the paper said I'd have a job waiting for me, so don't worry about that."

After drying the dishes, Jordan sulked to her bedroom and crashed on the bed, slinging her arm over her eyes. She hated being left behind. She worried that her mother might get hurt—or worse. Jordan felt grateful for her grandparent's protection, but she was looking forward to a time when she could accompany her mom on her travels. A wink of movement alerted Jordan as her mother sat on the side of the bed, drawing Jordan into her arms.

"I'm an optimist," Seeley breathed into her ear. "I believe love conquers hate, faith overcomes despair, and that life is stronger than death. We'll be together in spirit—I love you, Jordan."

"Love ya, Mom. Be careful."

Jordan listened to her mom in the next room opening and closing drawers as she packed. She suddenly remembered Saturday's sleepover at Ronan's, but decided not to bother her mom with the details. Snatching her new cell phone, she called a friend instead. Cayden answered after the third ring.

Without beating around the bush, Jordan said, "Cayden, we've known each other for a while now. You never mentioned your friends, Paisley and Ronan, and I'm a bit curious about what they're into. What kind of games are we playing Saturday?"

"I think it's great that your mom's letting you go to school now," Cayden commented, evading Jordan's question. "People won't think you're such a geek—Oh, sorry. I didn't mean that the way it sounded."

"Apology accepted—I guess," Jordan said, clearly waiting.

"Ronan and Beth Schaffer were best friends for years and the most popular girls in school. I was lucky enough to hang with the group last year—but—something happened—and...um...it had to do with boyfriends and jealousy and crap—and Beth's group parted ways—from Ronan—and—and—Maybe we should talk about this some other time? Saturday will be a riot. Don't worry. I gotta go." Stumbling for words, Cayden hung up.

Jordan had a hunch she wasn't telling the whole story.

Showering and shoving on a pair of sweats, Jordan could still hear her mother bustling about the room. She pounced on the mattress and rolled under the warm quilt. After a perplexing meditation, she whispered, "Markus, Markus..." then waited soundlessly. As he materialized next to the bed, Jordan propped up on her elbows. "Finally. We need to talk."

"I've found a place to live," Markus related quietly. Transforming into the young man Jordan saw at school, he straddled the bedside chair.

Jordan sat cross-legged on the mattress, confused. "I don't get it. Angels are supposed to be anonymous. Why are you creating an identity?"

"My Father's not pleased with Lucifer and his legions, especially when it comes to children and young adults seeking answers."

Stunned, she stared at him. "You've spoken with God?"

An inner glow softened Markus's chiseled features. "Occasionally I have the awesome pleasure."

"Cool." Jordan couldn't fully fathom that reality. "Then can you explain why He can't just squash Lucifer?"

Markus inhaled, expanding his chest, then blew out a gusty puff. Pure, violet-blue eyes fastened on Jordan. "Lucifer had been a reverent angel at one time in history. But vanity and pride, his greatest sins, veined a deadly pattern through him. He wanted equality with our Father. Lucifer became disobedient and felt beneath the duty of babysitting humans. His nature was despoiled and he could no longer abide in the kingdom. His odium grew toward humanity.

"And so Lucifer acquired followers, other angelic beings who followed him freely, and were cast to a place that you call Hell."

Markus closed his eyes for a short hiatus while raking fingers through his hair, displacing it every which way. "To answer your question a little—people are blinded by greed, lust, and so on. You get the picture. To squash Lucifer and all that he stands for, we would have to wipe out a grave majority of souls."

"Very…very interesting." Jordan twirled a strand of hair then trapped it behind her ear. "You still avoided part of my question. Anonymity is the usual angel rule, right? Why are you human?"

His eyes evolved from a violet-blue to a reflective amethyst, and his tone sharpened like a blade's edge. "You'd be dead today if I hadn't been there to tote you off that log."

Her eyebrows popped up, then drew together. "I thought I handled it well."

"No, you didn't." Jordan felt the cold reserve in his voice, as he said, "Exemplify yourself with these teenagers."

She stifled a laugh, due to the severity on his face. "Markus, these kids aren't turned on with thy old 'Holy, Holy, Holy' bit!"

"You need to prove, by example—"

Jordan examined the angel's human face, a bit agitated. What did he expect of her? Should she walk around the school like a righteous nun? *No way. That's not me.* He just needed to understand and listen to her.

"I registered in school because of that awful dream," she retorted. "And you know that! I thought I might be able to thwart those creepy spirits, or whatever. Now I think Ronan will talk to me—she's definitely behind some of the bizarreness."

She paused, peeking at Markus's unreceptive expression. "But there's more, right? Without you, in person, in human form, I'd be dead. Correct?"

Markus dipped his chin to his chest and stared into Jordan's eyes. "We're not playing by the rules."

"Well, neither is the devil, so who the hell cares?"

"You need to be careful," he stated prophetically. "Evil snares are all around you."

Jordan winced at his choice of words. "Then tell me. What should I expect from Ronan? She's dabbling with some kind of power."

"Ronan's lashing out in hatred because of her maimed mind. It's not my place to expose or criticize her. She needs help before it's too late." Hastily, he shoved off from the chair. "I need to go before I'm missed."

"Wait, Markus, where are you staying?"

Markus grinned. "Deacon Schaffer was kind enough to take in a youthful stranger who's considering the priesthood."

Surprised, Jordan drawled, "Deacon Schaffer, as in Beth Schaffer's Dad?"

"Yes."

"Oh, no," she groaned. "Ronan won't like that at all."

Markus tilted his head, clueless. "Why not?"

"Angels—You don't understand teenage girls, do you?"

Markus hitched up his broad shoulders and was gone in a flash.

CHAPTER 5

Your Power Does Not Come from Above

With her grandparents' permission to spend the night at Ronan's, Jordan packed a small duffle bag with accessories and her flannel pajamas. Then, on second thought, she ripped the pajamas from the bag, stuffed in a pair of sweats, and looked longingly at the cozy flannels with prints of playful puppies.

Her conscience gave a twitch when Henry said, "What about church on Sunday?"

"I go so much—one week won't matter. The kids already think I'm some kind of freaky Holy Roller."

"Jordan," protested Em. "I remember what your mother went through growing up, but she shouldered the burden without such comments."

"But, Em, I didn't say anything wrong. It's true."

"Jordan, your grandmother and I worry about you and your mom," Henry said in a disgruntled voice. "We're not completely ignorant of what's going on. Your mom holds back from telling us all the details. She thinks she's sparing us, and perhaps, it's a good thing." Henry looked at his concerned wife of fifty years. "All we can do is stand by and support the two of you. Now, what's so important at this girl's house?"

Jordan felt miserable at that moment. She dearly loved her grandparents, even if they could be meddlesome and suffocating at times. In the nicest voice possible, she said, "Henry, it's part of growing up. You know—friends, parties, sleepovers. Didn't mom have friend sleepovers?"

Her grandparents shared a discreet glance "No, not really," Em said ruefully. "Your mom was somewhat reclusive. We thought she'd become a nun. Her spiritual advisor, Father Posluszny, said Seeley needed to live her life."

"Good for him." Jordan pictured her mom as a hard-assed mother superior, jamming her Naturalizers into a demon. "But I'm not my mother. Henry, didn't you say you wanted me to go to school so I could have friends?"

Henry wilted, his face seeming to age another year. "You're right, Jordan."

"We're glad you have friends." Em was obviously tiring. "Aren't we, Henry?"

Henry ambled to his bedroom, grumbling incoherently.

〆〇〆〇

As per Ronan's instructions, Thrill was picking Jordan up. And now, more than a little nervous, Jordan paced back and forth until she nearly wore a hole in the carpet. Em and Henry watched her every move. When two beeps sounded from the driveway, Jordan shrugged on her jacket and bade her grandparents good-bye. Stepping outside, she peered at the odd bluish-gray sky and predicted snow. She belted the jacket firmly, barring the cold.

As she got into the car, Thrill's welcoming smile warmed her cheeks. Jordan adjusted the seat belt and aimed at being carefree, at least on the outside. "Hi, Thrill, is Rolly coming tonight?"

"He's meeting us there." Thrill sped down the driveway and headed for Ronan's.

Jordan peeked over her shoulder at the window, hoping her grandparents hadn't seen his speedy reverse, or she'd be hearing about it tomorrow. Self-conscious and tongue-tied, Jordan was alone in a car with a boy, for the first time. And that boy was Thrill McKenna, the celebrated Redskins quarterback and the catch of the school, as she now knew. She'd been keeping tabs on the gossip in the lunchroom and rest-rooms for signs of the unusual—girls liked to talk.

Attempting not to appear obvious, Jordan straightened her head and kept her eyes to the windshield, all the while inspecting the quarterback with her excellent peripheral vision. Thrill kept his burnt sienna haircut short. Dark stubble highlighted the square chin that went with his straight pleasing nose. He wore a maroon, fleecy pullover and light denim jeans, but he discarded the traditional sneakers for a pair of cowboy boots. Striving to maintain her poise, as if she drove in cars with guys on a regular basis, Jordan was bothered that he was perfectly at ease. Like Thrill picked up girls every day of the week.

As if reading her thoughts, Thrill's eyes flit to her. His lips twitched. Thankful for the dimness in the car, Jordan felt her face flaming, first from embarrassment, and then because she was mad at her body's betrayal. He cleared his throat. "I should warn you. Ronan and the girls like to play games that I'm not too crazy about. I don't get off on that creepy stuff. Rolly and I probably won't stay long."

His words were not what she'd expected. Though, Jordan was happy that Thrill and Rolly were not part of the cult as she'd suspected. Unfortunately, Jordan's life was full of creepy stuff that he didn't like. Her thoughts then turned to the games mentioned. He definitely did not mean charades, or whatnot.

"What kind of games?"

"You'll see, soon enough."

In a village like Elma, most people lived within minutes of town and, Ronan's house was only a few miles from Jordan's. Parking the Chevelle along the curb, Thrill nodded toward the house. "This is it, and there's Rolly's car. He must be here already."

The rustic Dutch colonial reminded Jordan of the classic movie *Amityville Horror*, which was not what she needed to think about right now! They trekked to the doorway as the threatening clouds split open, pelting them with icy pebbles. Thrill clutched Jordan's arm, carting her swiftly into the house. They chuckled while brushing ice bits from their heads and shoulders.

"Here, let me take your coat." He draped Jordan's wet jacket over a chair sitting in the entry. Like an adoring fan, Jordan watched as he pulled the fleece over his head. His T-shirt rode up, revealing firm skin above his belt, and flexing broad muscles. With a blitz of flush stealing up her throat, her eyes rebounded to anywhere besides his body.

Barking laughter echoed through the hallway and Thrill ushered Jordan forward. A pestering chill struck Jordan, alleviating her recent flush, and a mysterious quiver chased along her spine. Scattered throughout the kitchen were differing heights of numerous candles. Their flickering flames sent exaggerated silhouettes all over the room. The thought of her warm jacket crossed her mind as Jordan chafed her cold hands. However, the lacquered Ouija board centered on the table distracted her.

"All right, our new member has arrived," Ronan announced. She hooked her arm over Jordan's shoulders and led her to a chair. "Jordan, have you ever played with a Ouija board?"

"No...never had the opportunity." She kept her tone level and controlled.

"Then you go first," Paisley suggested,

"No. No, why doesn't someone else go? I don't know what to do."

"We can all play, but I'd like to see your abilities, Jordan," Ronan confessed.

Sneaky, Ronan, Jordan thought. She decided to play dumb. "I don't understand—my abilities?" She figured the only way to see how deep Ronan's involvement in the mystical realm went was to play along.

"It's easy," said Ronan. "Just hold on to this." She stroked a heart-shaped piece of wood, imprinted with strange symbols, as if it were a precious item. "It's called a planchette or an oracle, because it can tell the past, present, or the future." She then added curtly, "Sit down, Jordan."

Jordan sat opposite of Ronan while Paisley and Cayden each settled in a side chair. Thrill and Rolly hovered around the table, observing.

"Place your fingers lightly on the oracle. Now we speak to the spirits. Go ahead ask a question—anything."

"The s–spirits," Jordan stuttered. "This is a joke, right?" Uneasy, she remembered her father's book and the consequences of playing spirit games. Communicating with the dead might create an opening for possession.

"Come on, Jordan," said Paisley, annoyed. "Lighten up, it's only a game."

Jordan's reluctance aggravated Ronan, whose eyes narrowed. Jordan acquiesced and lightly positioned her fingertips on the planchette.

They waited.

The air suddenly felt electric, stifling, and silent. The only distinguishable sound was their breathing. Ronan shut her eyes and drew in an extended breath, then parted her lips and exhaled. In a melodramatic voice, she asked, "Are the spirits with us tonight?"

Astounded, Jordan watched the oracle creep to the letter Y, then E, and then S. Ronan must be better attuned supernaturally than Jordan realized.

"You're moving this thing, right?" Jordan inquired suspiciously.

A low snicker went round the table. Ronan glared and hushed everyone. Again she pinched her eyelids tightly, concentrating. "Do you like our new friend?"

The oracle spelled V-E-R-Y.

A tingling sensation in her fingertips gave Jordan goose bumps. She considered releasing the oracle but, wary of Ronan's scorn, she unwillingly held on.

"Can you help us?"

Again the oracle spelled Y-E-S.

"What's your name?"

The oracle dragged to the J, A, then C, and lastly K.

"Jack!" Paisley exclaimed. "Wasn't that your father's name, Jordan?" Heated excitement showed on her plump face, as she stole a glimpse at Ronan.

Jordan bolted, tripping over the chair with a resounding, "*No!*"

Thrill detained Jordan in a two-armed embrace. She buried her head into his chest. She was ashamed of her outburst, but her mind was whirling. *Is my father trying to tell me something? If anyone could make contact, he could.* Yet somehow, she doubted the spirit's veracity.

"You're all right, Jordan." Thrill hugged her ardently, in a more-than-comforting way.

"Sorry, Jordan," Ronan said. "We should've warned you. Cayden told us your father died. Sometimes they break through and speak to us."

Paisley backed her up. "People pay good money for psychics and mediums to contact their loved ones. They want closure or something. Really, Jordan, it's okay to be scared, but we do this all the time and nothing terrible has happened. It's awesome to speak to the dead."

Disentangling from Thrill's arms, Jordan reminded herself of why she was there. She needed to know how involved the girls were in paranormal activities. And apparently, the main instigator was Ronan *Will I be able to deter Ronan from conjuring unwanted spirits?* Jordan wondered.

"Hey, I know," Cayden supplied. "Let's ask something silly…like, will Ronan dance with that new guy, Mark, at the Winter Ball?"

"That's good," Ronan said, appeased. Her almond shaped eyes skipped to Jordan. "You ask, Jordan."

Jordan wanted to tell the girls about the reprehensible damage they risked in testing paranormal spirits, but they'd probably laugh, ridicule her, and boot her butt out the door. *Be patient*, she thought. *The time will come when they'll listen to me.* Jordan lowered to the chair, placing her fingertips on the oracle again. As instructed, she repeated mildly, "Will Ronan dance with Mark at the Winter Ball?"

She felt the dawdling movement, first to N, then O.

Hurriedly, Ronan chimed in with, "Will Mark dance with Jordan?"

Y–E–S.

Jordan glanced at Ronan. She registered distrust mixed with envy before Ronan masked her expression, gracing Jordan with upturned lips.

"I'm not even going to the dance," argued Jordan, prying her eyes from Ronan to look at Cayden.

"I thought that was all settled. You're going with us," Cayden stated matter-of-fact.

"No, it was never settled. I—I'd rather not go."

Strong hands came to rest on Jordan's shoulders, and Thrill's handsome face touched her cheek. "Come with us, please?" His polished tone was cajoling.

With everyone staring at her, the mortifying heat spread to her cheeks. Jordan managed to say, lamely, "Maybe, all right—prob'ly." Thrill squeezed her shoulders, shooting a fine sensation up her neck.

"Great," Cayden chimed and changed the topic by asking, "What does everyone think of the new guy?"

"Man, he's to die for." Paisley gushed. Her eyes shot to Thrill as if she were trying to make him jealous.

"Mark's body is divine to the max," Ronan added. "But it's his eyes…

"Yeah, his eyes," Cayden concurred. "Like you lose yourself in them…almost…like…"

"Like he can read your soul," Ronan finished.

Both Paisley and Cayden nodded. "Yeah, that's it."

Rolly and Thrill groaned, rolling their eyes.

Then Thrill drawled, "We're out of here."

"Where you going, guys?" Cayden asked. "The night hasn't even begun."

"These games suck," snapped Thrill, indicating the Ouija board. "And listening to you all getting hot and bothered over some guy was not what I had in mind. I've got better things to do."

"So, you two guys going to The Watering Hole to meet up with Jen and Hilary?" Paisley demanded, jumping down his throat.

Rolly's expression brightened. "That sounds like a good idea, thanks, Paisley. Definitely better than this." Rolly smacked Thrill good-humoredly on the back. "Now why didn't we think of that sooner? A little drink, a little dance—a night of…whatever…"

Amidst strangled chuckling, the boys donned their jackets and left through the front door.

"Good riddance," barked Paisley, her tone extremely snide. "Thrill's so conceited. He's probably mad 'cause the girls have someone new to check out." She shot Jordan a blistering look.

"Jealous, Paisley?" Cayden goaded her.

"Not in the least. I hate him…sometimes."

"Now back to Mark," Ronan said, taking command. "He's plain gorgeous, like, out of this world."

Jordan couldn't contain herself. She burst out laughing, startling the fawning girls. "Oh, sorry—Mark's okay—kind of nice-looking—Yeah, you're right," Jordan admitted, wondering what Markus would say about a bunch of teenagers ogling him.

"Did I mention that he's in my earth science class?" said Ronan. "I've spoken to him a few times. Something's different about the guy, though, I can't figure him out." She turned back to Jordan. "I heard you were walking to school with him," she said, her voice unduly argumentative. "What's that all about?"

Caught off guard, Jordan didn't know how to respond except to be honest. "I was surprised to see him. He walked up from behind me and just started to chat."

"What did he say?" Ronan persevered.

"Er–um–mm…nothing important. I can't really remember."

"Rumor has it that Mark's living with Beth Schaffer's family," Paisley confided.

"Oh snap!" blurted Ronan. "Now I really despise her. She'll be rubbing him in my face all year. Are they together…like…you know?"

"Nah, Deacon Schaffer wouldn't let that happen, you know, under his roof. He's old-fashioned."

Jordan didn't know if she could handle any more ludicrous talk about her angel. "What does everyone wear to the Winter Ball?"

The dialogue flipped to whether evening gowns should be long, short, slinky, or strapless and on to pedicures, manicures, and hairstyles. Then there was a heated catfight between Paisley and Cayden, both intent on wearing a French twist. Next, the speculating trio gossiped about who was taking who to the dance and eventually they lost Jordan's interest altogether.

Jordan surveyed Ronan's crusty kitchen, noticing a thin layer of scum on the cherry wood cabinets. So unlike her grandparents' kitchen, which was scrupulously scrubbed and polished, from laminate flooring to whitewashed ceilings. Whereas, Ronan's countertop was a jumble of crumb-covered plates and filthy smudged glassware. Blooming from dual sinks was an avalanche of pots and pans. She guessed that, with her father gone, Ronan didn't feel the pressure to tidy up the place. Even Jordan's sneakers were suctioned to the floor.

Ronan distributed soda cans and tore open bags of chips and pretzels. When she'd offered drinking glasses, Jordan declined, saying she preferred to drink from the can. They were munching on salty chips when Ronan enthusiastically leapt from the chair. "It's time—the witching hour."

Cayden, Paisley, and Jordan tagged behind Ronan and into the living room. Like the kitchen, the room was in shambles with couch cushions awry, dirty plates, and half-filled glasses dotting the coffee table. Under a layer of newspapers and magazines, indistinguishable crud had been smashed into the carpet. Nodding to Paisley, Ronan said, "Help me." They moved the oval coffee table to the side. "Everyone take a seat."

Cayden and Jordan bundled the scattered mess into a hasty pile and sat down. Ronan and Paisley went to the kitchen and reappeared, carrying lit candles. Under her arm, Ronan held what looked like rolled parchment or cloth. Paisley arranged candles on the floor and then switched off the lights.

Jordan figured they were in for more tantalizing spooks. A qualm tore through her as Ronan unrolled the cotton cloth in the middle of their circle. She recoiled at the intricate penta-

gram, knowing the design had promoted worship and summoning of the devil. Jordan should've been prepared, but she
never guessed Ronan's psychic abilities went so far beyond
teenage games. Impulsively, she reached for her holy medal.
Glancing at her chest, she realized it was missing. She reached
for her pocket, only to remember that the holy water was in her
jacket at the front door.

Jordan's confidence slowly ebbed. "I'm really not into
devil stuff."

"Don't be such a dweeby-geek, Jordan," Ronan scoffed.
"A séance is a cool rush. We usually end up scaring ourselves." Then pantomiming a stage magician, she raised her
hands, crisscrossing them in front of her face. In a low mono-
tone voice, she said, "It gets us in the mood, like watching a
scary movie."

Paisley and Cayden giggled at her interpretation.

Jordan's bravado returned, especially after Ronan's
dweeby-geek comment. She sent out an internal call for
Markus. "Then let's do this thingy."

"Everyone hold hands. Whatever happens...*if* anything
happens—" Ronan said, her black pupils skirting their circle.
"—stay connected. Now close your eyes. Keep them closed
and concentrate on the atmosphere around us.

Paisley and Cayden practically crushed Jordan's hands
and shut their eyes. Jordan obliged and lightly shut her lids,
peeking every now and then.

Minutes passed.

Nothing

Breathing

Jordan liberated a suppressed giggle, releasing stress.
Paisley squashed her hand like a nutcracker, putting an end to
her chuckles.

"Feel their presence," Ronan breathed. "The spirits are
nearby. Make yourselves known. Come, come and join us."

Ronan began to mumble some gibberish under her breath.
Jordan thought it might be Latin, but wasn't sure. In her own
head, Jordan repeated, *Don't come, Dad, Don't come, Dad,
Don't come...*

A convincing clairvoyant, Ronan's hypnotizing voice sealed them into a mystifying state. A wispy cool draft skimmed Jordan's forehead, and she heard heavy footsteps approaching. Her eyes flew open.

Candlelight made their faces appear ghastly, like the walking dead. A stiff wind whisked around their circle, flickering the candle flames as flimsy images appeared. Jordan glanced around at the girls, whose petrified eyes observed the increasing nightmare. Muffled murmuring mingled with their strained breathing as the hair on Jordan's neck stood on end.

Please, Dad, Jordan implored. *Don't be an evil spirit.*

"We know you're here. Can you communicate with us?" Ronan said eagerly.

Jordan froze. The voices became more discernible. Her short-lived bravado was dissolving and she couldn't take her eyes off the blurry gray forms.

"As you can see, we have added someone to our circle," Ronan crooned. "Our new friend is Jordan Chase. We believe her father, Jack, is with you. Don't be afraid to speak to us."

Jordan's stomach somersaulted. Evidently, Ronan's task was to contact her father.

There was a temporary silence.

Then—BANG! BANG! The girls jumped in place, their shrieks cut off. Jordan swung her head to the side. A cold hand touched her shoulder, a cry wedged in her throat.

The floating gray matter gradually congealed into a hazy figure of a man. His stature commanded the room. A looming menace, he surveyed the girls before him.

He glided effortlessly like smoke in the wind, coming precariously near Ronan. Jordan thought her eyes were playing tricks but, implausible as it seemed, the shadow melded with Ronan. The bond was immediate. Her eyes protruded abnormally, their reddish membranes pierced Jordan. A tinge of fright, then calculated fury disfigured Ronan's face.

A moment of silence.

A sluggish, throaty voice sighed. "Rooonannn..."

Ronan moaned. Her body convulsed then became stiff. Rolling eyes tipped back into their sockets and her head lolled from side to side. She expelled a deep, gurgling breath. Then with an unnatural twist, Ronan's head jerked up. A diabolical tale of suffering escaped those red-rimmed eyes. Ronan, or whoever it was, drew near.

Ronan's mouth, disfigured by the spirit, opened to speak. A tang of fetid breath entered Jordan's nostrils. Paralyzed, she was helpless to flee the toxic demon.

A foul, guttural voice resonated in the room. *"Jack Chase betrayed us! Seeley—she—she snatched him away. Jordan is* Mine! *We want—Retribution!"*

"No–o–o–o!" Jordan's spine-tingling scream rattled the windows. Breaking the trance, she crawled on hands and knees away from the riled demon.

A gust snuffed the candles, leaving the room in total darkness. Jordan heard gasps and pleas in the gloom. Her fingers fumbled until she felt the wall. And then, absurdly, she heard Paisley's low giggling and Cayden's nasal, high-pitched squawk. Someone scurried to the lamp. Light returned.

Ronan lay prostrate on the floor. Paisley and Cayden crouched on either side of her. Each seemed to be waiting—for what, Jordan didn't know. Then Ronan's shoulders began to heave. She broke into hoarse, almost hysterical laughter. Jordan recognized relief in Cayden and Paisley's faces. They erupted in a fit of giggles, rolling on the carpet in some kind of euphoria.

Gathering her wits, Jordan held the wall for support. She rose guardedly, expecting to see Ronan's red eyes and the contained demon. Cautiously approaching the girls, Jordan inspected Ronan's laughing eyes, which seemed perfectly fine.

Paisley snorted gracelessly. "Wasn't that awesome?" She lay sprawled on the floor, looking up at Jordan.

Cayden and Paisley stood then extended Ronan a helping hand. It was then—Jordan perceived a diluted shadow escape Ronan's face.

Paisley tilted her head and looked at Jordan. "Somebody don't like your daddy," she said in a southern vernacular.

"Maybe Jack was warning Jordan earlier," Cayden suggested, sounding uncertain.

Jordan fell silent, her brain revolving a thousand miles a minute. She heard the tiniest hint of a whisper in her mind, '*Warn them.*'

The words stiffened the weak space between her shoulders. With courage, she said, "These…games…they're not what you think. One day, maybe even the next time you play, something bad—something really bad—could happen to any one of you. These *things* aren't your *friends*." Jordan's voice sounded unconvincing, even to her. She looked at each girl in turn and they all cocked their heads as if she was speaking a foreign language.

Indignant, Ronan glared, her eyes throwing daggers. "You act like an expert on psychic phenomenon. But you know what I've learned, Jordan? These spirits help me more than any person."

More than frustrated, Jordan elaborated. "These spirits are hellish beings oozing from the abyss and materializing into despicable fiends." Seeing Ronan's ear-to-ear grin, she added, "Ronan, I'm serious."

"Wow," Ronan said caustically. "I guess you've read your father's book from cover to cover. Do you really believe what he wrote? I found it quite instructive, although probably not in the way he expected. I'm quite the psychic myself, if you hadn't noticed."

Jordan felt like she'd been punched in the gut. Inhaling jaggedly, she glimpsed at Cayden, who hid her beet-red face. Years ago, Jordan confided in her one friend about her mother's efforts to publish her father's book.

"You know what, Jordan?" Ronan said. "I think we can help each other. You know more than you're letting on, and there's some big reason why your father's trying to make contact. Surely, you must be curious?"

Jordan knew it would be a mistake to reveal family secrets. "Ronan, I think you're wrong."

With arms akimbo, Paisley and Cayden hung on every word. "Ronan's never wrong," Paisley interjected spitefully. "She has special powers, so you better be careful what you say—"

Ronan held up her hand, stopping Paisley. The right side of her mouth curved. "Jordan, we're all friends here. I'm trying to help you, and I think you can help me." She set her hand on Jordan's shoulder and leaned in with self-assurance. "I can contact a powerful spirit, Davian. He can uncover the answers. He's temperamental, but gifted."

Weighing Ronan's budding power demonstrated over the past few hours, Jordan wasn't shocked to learn that she was on a first name basis with the spirit. Why did she feel they'd crossed an extremely dangerous line?

Looking away from Ronan's spellbinding eyes, Jordan sighed. "You're creeping me out, Ronan." She shrugged free of the girl's confining hand. "I'll think about your offer."

Hugging herself, Jordan felt like freezing blood coursed through her veins. She brushed the gooseflesh on her arms, needing to get away from the haunted house.

The girls moved the coffee table into place and switched on the television. Unrolling sleeping bags, they prepared for what was left of the night. Jordan snagged her jacket and dug in the pocket for the vial of holy water. It was gone! She looked over her shoulder at the girls.

She'd been outfoxed, but by whom?

CHAPTER 6

Softer Than Butter Is Their Speech.

Seeley swept into the Warner Theater and settled on a cushioned seat near the stage. Ezekiel, unpredictably in human form, claimed the seat beside her. Unlike those gathered, he wore frayed jeans and a black T-shirt that accented his muscular frame. His ebony hair was pulled back into a low ponytail, his steely eyes pinned on Seeley. "Are you here to stir up a boiling kettle?" he asked point blank.

"Something like that." Her roving eyes inspected him from head to toe. "I see you've dressed inconspicuously."

"You're here to make a statement." Ezekiel was rarely facetious. "And I'm here to be noticed by *the Master.*" The border of his lip curled as if the word tasted repugnant.

The highlight of the symposium on financial success was tonight's guest speaker—billionaire, Asa Trebane.

Seeley, motionless during the dull facts and figures, clapped stiffly as Asa, clothed to impress in a licorice black Brioni suit, a white Eton button-down with diamond cuff links, and Italian loafers, strode in like a peacock. He reeked of superiority.

Asa's silver-tongue twined an invisible noose around the audience. People snickered time and again at his airy, depraved jokes on the economy and the ignorant poor bastard without a brain to help himself.

In a deliberate clerical tone, Asa addressed the issues at hand. "Financial success can be achieved by all!" More applause. "Look around you." He gestured exaggeratedly toward the financial experts seated on the stage. "We are here to help you reach your richly deserved goals."

Seeley wasn't shocked to see the woman with the feral eyes nodding her head sagely during Asa's dissertation. "They call her Veronka," said Zeke quietly, noting Seeley's obvious scowl. "She serves the higher echelons around the world with Trebane as her so-called boss. Even teenagers have formed cults to worship the devil."

Seeley frowned. "Is she human?"

"Feel her essence, Seeley. Look at her closely. Human or demon—what gives them away?

Seeley remembered the reddish eyes. "Demon." She should've known.

"We are here to advise and instruct," Asa clarified. "To offer a decisive formula to begin your road to success. How to achieve financial stability? Hard work and shrewdness! You there—" He pointed directly at a man sitting in the front row. "I notice a medal around your neck, a holy cross? Do you pray to help you financially? Does He help? A resounding no! Clean those notions from your mind! Win financial security, stability, and material possessions by the sweat of your brow. *Money* is our goal! *Money* is our power! *Money* rules the world!"

Beguiled souls gave him a standing ovation, cheering.

"If anyone here wishes to become a millionaire or even a billionaire, follow my advice—you must eat or be eaten. However, anyone who can't stomach my methods—or who wishes to remain inferior—feel free to leave."

A hushed silence reigned as necks craned right and left. Seeley rose, a lone woman, with silky auburn hair, wearing a fitted pastel blouse and a charcoal-gray pencil skirt that clung to her curvaceous figure. Heads turned in time with masked whispers, wondering what the woman was going to ask. Holding Asa's critical gaze, she intentionally turned her back on him.

Stifled mutterings mixed through the theater. Shoulders defiantly straight, the audacious woman strode straight up the aisle. The click-clack of her heels sounded like a discreet alarm. She left through the dual doors into the vestibule. They slammed behind her like a slap in the face.

Seeley waited briefly. Zeke was the first to barge through the doors and, with a curt nod to her, prudently disappeared. Her mouth spread into a smile as a steady exodus followed her example. *Not all souls are duped into believing Asa,* she thought. Once outside, she hailed a taxi and asked to be driven to the nearest church.

Her knees still knocking, Seeley lit a candle, thankful for certain accomplished deeds. Replaying her exit, Seeley could almost hear Asa gasp when she stood. A smug grin touched her face and, after a fleeting glance around the church, she slid into an empty pew.

She closed her eyes. Dragging in a profound breath, Seeley cleansed her mind for the Spirit to lead her into contemplative prayer.

She heard the creak of a kneeler and hot breath in her ear. Intuitively, she knew who it was, but did not give Asa the satisfaction of acknowledgment. She remained immobile, despite her drumming heart.

Then she realized that she couldn't have moved even if she tried—Asa's refined sorcery was imprisoning—so she opted to remain unruffled. Seeley warily remained, positive that the church was a safe haven.

Asa had had years to cultivate an unquenchable desire and hatred for Seeley, since Jack's duplicity, which had eventually grown all out of proportion. "I'm biding my time because I enjoy our cat-and-mouse games." It was said in a sardonic undercurrent that whisked pass thin lips. "But once you become...*unappealing*, so to say, I will find a way to break your protective shield and you will be annihilated." He paused. "Think, Seeley. Think back to the day your daughter was conceived." His voice weaved threads of distant memories. "You know the answer, and you know Jordan will be ours. The sacrificial consecration will take place, within the year..."

cɔcɔ

Astounding even herself, within a week's time, Seeley had fallen for the handsome, charming Jack Chase. She later learned that a touch of Jack's distinctive magic had pushed her along. She would follow him anywhere—even into the devil's den. Timidly, Seeley agreed to visit his place of worship.

Mutinous thickets claimed the building, inconspicuously buried in the deteriorating industrial park. Weathered gray planks, sucked dry of their color, shuttered gothic casements. When Jack parted the heavy oaked doors and shepherded her into the dim vestibule, Seeley instinctively wanted to bolt. A whiff of rotting timber and something else, something Seeley couldn't quite place until later—the smell of blood—greeted them.

Little did Seeley expect that her existence would come unraveled on that fateful night.

In an ocean of black-robed people, she gripped tightly to Jack's arm as he tugged her forward. Seeley then spied the bleating, horned ram and the strange altar with the inverted crucifix. Her soul cried in agony. Disillusioned with Jack and the heinous members who'd pledged their allegiance to the Devil, she wanted to escape.

The rhythmic chanting overcame her. Its spell robbed Seeley of her ability to function. She was emotionally and physically bound. Terrified and unable to object, she watched in horror.

Asa swayed one arm upward like a traffic cop, magically steering a lethal axe. It floated precariously in the air and came to a standstill, dangerously teetering over the ram's head.

Indefinable utterance escalated. Seeley felt her lungs were going to implode. She couldn't breathe.

Suddenly, the chanting stopped.

Asa's expression was purely demonic. His arm slashed through the air. And the axe hewed the ram's neck in one ugly stroke. The body crumpled to the ground and Asa hoisted the head by the horns, blood gushing for all to see. Seeley nearly fainted as men rushed with buckets to catch the draining fluid.

Jack steadied a swaying Seeley. When robed figures offered her the sacrificial goblet, she refused. Shaking her head, she pressed her lips tightly together.

"You must!" Jack breathed in her ear. "You're obligated by the rite to consume."

With tears coursing down her cheeks, she stammered, "No, Jack, don't—don't make me."

Jack snatched the goblet, filling his mouth. Then grasping Seeley's face with both hands, he feverishly kissed her, prying open her lips and forcing the warm, tinny blood into her mouth. She tried pushing him away as the metallic gore clogged her throat. Hooded creatures gazed favorably, jeering their approval.

There must've been a mind-altering drug in the liquid, because she'd felt obscenely inebriated. Loving Jack in a capacity she'd never felt possible, she had given him all she had to offer—body and soul.

In the wee twilight hours of the morning, she woke in Jack's bed, thunderstruck and mortified by her passionate memories of the night before. Stabbing tears stung as she evoked the aftermath of Jack's assault—she wouldn't call it a kiss. Seeley dressed quickly and quietly, but Jack stirred. He leapt from the bed, imprisoning her in his arms. Shriveling from humiliation, she couldn't look at him. Yet Jack sent shivers through her body as his tongue traced her neck and found her lips, savoring each moment.

Placing his hands on either side of her face, he gazed into her eyes and took a ragged breath. "Thank you, Seeley. I've never felt this way before."

And Seeley was pregnant.

ഈരാഈ

Seeley burst free of the spell—reuniting with the present. How long had she been under Asa's influence? Unfurling her fists, she peered down. Her fingernails cut bloody half-moons into her palms. Standing shakily, she checked the church. She saw unoccupied pews, and no Asa. Sagging into the wooden pew, pressing fingertips to her brow, Seeley knew she would never forget that day—or night.

Her nose and eyes were flowing like a faucet. She scrambled in her purse for a tissue. Seeley mourned for the short time they had together. Reflecting on Jack's unshakable love brought another rush of salty tears. He'd fought so hard for them.

Taking a rocky breath, she swabbed at wet eyes. The tissue came away smudged with black mascara, and Seeley rubbed at the raccoon-like rings bordering her eyes. She then pushed trembling fingers through her hair.

She couldn't let go of Asa's warning. He believed the blood ceremony uniting Jack and Seeley had been ordained by Satan. And the warrior born to them, Jordan, rightly belonged to Lucifer. Burying her rickety hands in her lap, she worried over Asa's prediction. The image of a crucified body haunted her, only this time, it was Jordan.

At the breaking point, she tried pulling herself together. Checking her watch, Seeley found she was late for the meeting. Looking somewhat respectable, she left the church, only to run into Veronka. For some reason, Seeley wasn't surprised—Asa had many methods of persecution.

Determinedly ignoring the woman, Seeley hurried to her destination.

Veronka strode doggedly at her shoulder, glaring at her with red-ringed eyes. "You're presumptuous of having the upper hand," she said, her voice threatening. "Asa's holding back, for some reason. He hates you for killing his son, but he speaks…fondly of you."

Faltering abruptly, Seeley felt her stomach cramp. Her response was tenable and terse. "Asa killed Jack."

"No, it was you, Seeley." Veronka let her words absorb before saying, "You killed Jack. If you would have joined us, he'd still be alive."

She knew Veronka was screwing with her mind. "I'd die first." Her teeth clenched.

"Someday, somehow, I will get my revenge on you and your precious daughter," Veronka said in a withering tone, needing the last word. Then she dashed across the intersection without a backward glance.

Seeley gripped her cell phone and punched in Jordan's number. She waited until it went to voice-mail. "Call me, Jordan. Just wanted to hear your voice and make sure you're all right. Call me."

She dialed her parents' home, but no one answered. Seeley reminded herself to call after the meeting.

e/se/s

It was after eleven when the taxi dropped Seeley at her motel. She keyed in Jordan's cell number and waited. It went straight to voice mail again. Annoyed, she called her parents. Henry picked up on the first ring.

"Hey, Dad, how are you?"

"Fine," he yawned into the phone. "Where are you?"

"Erie, Pennsylvania. Sorry to call so late, but I can't get through to Jordan. Is she home?"

"She's staying at her new friend's house. Hang on."

Seeley heard Henry ask her mother what the girl's name was and then some shuffling. Emily spoke into the phone. "Hi, honey. Are you all right? We miss you so much."

"Thanks, Mom, but it's only been a few days. Where's Jordan?"

"She's sleeping over at a friend's house. The girl's name is Ronan Beckman. Jordan seemed excited, so we said it was all right."

"She's not picking up her phone, and that's what worries me."

"The girls are probably listening to that loud music or something. You know how teenagers are nowadays," Emily reasoned, though not precisely sure what kids were into these days.

"Father James set up a few meetings," Seeley said. "I'll be in Virginia and Kansas, and then I hope to be home in about a week. Call me anytime."

"Talk to you soon, Seeley."

Seeley anxiously called Jordan again and was relieved to hear her daughter's voice.

"Hi, Mom."

"I was worried when you didn't answer. Emily said you're at Ronan Beckman's?"

"Yes, I'm here," she answered. "Cayden and Paisley are here, too. We're just talking about the Winter Ball next month. How's everything going? Are you okay?" Jordan spoke too fast and guiltily. *Mom would die if she knew about the Ouija board*, Jordan thought. Especially since her mom was attempting to abolish the accursed ones, while she was cracking open the chasm.

"I don't want to brag," Seeley said. "But I went to Asa Trebane's financial conference and caused a little anarchy without speaking a word—sometimes action alone is enough to knock some sense into people."

"Cool. Did you have the first meeting that Father James set up?"

"Yes. For some unknown reason, a neighborhood demon felt his presence was required. Thankfully, the man in charge spotted him."

"What happened?"

"Let's just say there's one less creature to deal with." Seeley unzipped the suitcase, flung open the lid, and rummaged for pajamas. "We'll talk more when I get home in about a week. Have fun with your friends. Oh—do you have holy water?"

"Mom," Jordan griped. "I'm fine. Everything's good."

"Love you, see you soon."

Seeley peeled off her skirt and blouse and slipped into the bathroom. Luxuriating in the balmy spray for half an hour, she at last felt her mental strain wash away. Winding the white fluffy towel around her flushed, stress-free body, she breezed in a blast of steam.

"Hello, Seeley." The slimy voice came from a shadowed corner of the room.

Frightened, Seeley whirled and gasped. Asa sat on the cushioned chair like a king, his pointy chin lifted as he ogled her.

Clinging to the towel, Seeley stepped back. "Get the hell out!"

Asa frisked her with his eyes, his mouth curved with an optimistic quirk. "I've come in peace. A truce, so we can talk."

"Your pompous arrogance precedes you, Trebane. Why would I wish to speak to the devil?"

"Please, call me Asa."

Asa's smirk crinkled his eyes into a most sinister expression. "I could give you anything and everything the world has to offer." He lifted his palm briefly to stop Seeley's outburst. "I may reconsider the consecration of your daughter. I'll call off the hounds, so to speak. But Jack left us high and dry. The marker must be paid—by Jordan or by you."

Seeley studied him coldly. Asa's proposition intrigued her for a few unspeakable moments. Then she shook her head, incensed. "Do you truly think I'd be gullible enough to believe a pathological liar?

His lean frame pushed upward, confident. "We would execute a blood oath, sealing the bargain, you for your daughter."

Seeley actually paused to consider his obscene proposal.

"You'd better act quickly. The oath would put a stop to Veronka's revenge."

Now interested, Seeley struggled to keep her emotions from showing as Asa reeled her in like a floundering fish. "How would that stop her?"

"Veronka would have to comply with the oath. She would rather comply and maintain her worldly deployment than rush to perpetual misery." He rubbed his hands together, sure of the deal.

"What would you want of me?" breathed Seeley. Her heart was throbbing, and not in a good way.

Bit by bit, Asa closed the distance. He caressed Seeley's bare shoulders. His breath fanned her neck. "I think you know what I want."

The man's repulsive touch shattered Seeley.

CHAPTER 7

The Chill has Iced My Bones.

Jordan. Sh-h-h, it's okay, honey. I'm here, Grandma's here."

Em's hands kept sliding off Jordan's arms, which were slick with perspiration. Astonishingly quick and sturdy for her age, Emily finally harnessed Jordan's flailing arms. She hugged her granddaughter, sticky sweat and all, smoothed her matted hair from her forehead, and calmed her screeching.

"I'm okay, Em," Jordan panted. "Really."

Her nightly shrieks had reached her grandparents' bedroom, bringing them racing to her bedside. Jordan's mother, scarcely gone a week, and the nightmares increased after the sleepover. In the dim room, Jordan saw concern on her grandmother's elderly face. Emily made no move to leave and instead, she nestled beneath the quilt. Actually glad for Emily's company, Jordan rolled over, and her grandmother massaged her back with a maternal touch.

Soon Jordan heard Emily's light snore, the sound allaying her fretfulness. Afraid of dozing and returning to her nightmare, she kept her eyes open, gazing into the darkness. Jordan watched the sky melt from navy to muted grays. Finally she eased off the mattress and dressed for school, leaving Emily still whiffing.

December lived up to its reputation. Jordan slouched out the back door and a glacial gale nearly tore it from its hinges. When she looked up from navigating the icy patches on the driveway, Markus stood there with arms crossed, leaning on the mailbox post.

He smiled disarmingly. Jordan suddenly remembered the girls' gushy commentary and, as she strolled near, she took inventory. Yes, Markus was tall with a nice body, windblown golden hair, longer than the norm and, most of all, fathomless eyes, like the autumn sky right after sunset, glossy bluish-purple. She returned his contagious smile. "Where've you been?"

"I'm around, always around. Do you mind if I walk with you?" Markus seized Jordan's backpack and flung it over his shoulder before she had a chance to answer.

"That'd be great." Her voice sounded quirky. Jordan glimpsed down and frowned at her scruffy sneakers, definitely not a fashion statement. "How's it going living at Beth Schaffer's? Does she know you're here with me? It must be kind of *weird*."

"Beth and I are friends, and I leave early before she wakes. They think I'm an exchange student from South Africa considering the priesthood, as I told you before. Samuel Schaffer's a good man, and we can converse about faith on all levels." Markus caught Jordan's crazy eye roll. "The Schaffer's opened their home without questions, and Deacon Schaffer insisted on leasing a car for my use."

"Oh, you have a driver's license?"

Markus grinned. "Everything's been arranged."

Jordan inspected his attire—a trendy navy pea coat and straight denim jeans that accented his long legs. "Must be nice," she scoffed, trying not to think about her worn jeans and sneakers. "I wish Henry would offer me his car. I haven't driven in a while."

Markus and Jordan walked, each lost in thought, hearing only the crisp of sneakers grinding frozen leaves. Friends drove by beeping, then stopped, and asked if they wanted a ride. Markus looked at Jordan and then said they'd rather walk.

Markus hesitated. "Perhaps you're over your head with Ronan."

Jordan stopped in mid-stride. "What'd you mean?"

"Ronan Beckman's in league with a controlling demon named Davian, as you already know." He perceived Jordan's chagrined expression. "She knows your father had some form of mystical powers, and I suspect she's conjuring spirits to answer questions that eventually could hurt you and your mother."

"I've been training. I want to help. Please, Markus."

His face was impassive. "I'll support you, Jordan, but be on guard. Ronan's known in the spirit world. Indeed, she has gone beyond just playing games."

"If you're an angel..." She had to tilt her head back to look up into his face. "Why don't you know everything that's happening? Like, what the heck are Ronan's capabilities? And...and how's my mom? And...is she safe?"

Markus grunted. "I'm not God. And becoming human limits my...potential."

The whole angel turned human, living an ordinary teenage life seemed totally, *totally* bizarre. Slowing down, Jordan asked, "Markus, are you human or an angel?"

"Technically, both, for now."

"What does that mean exactly?"

"I'm an angelic spirit graced with humanity, which isn't uncommon." He peered into her eyes. "Believe it or not, angels walk among humans on a daily basis. I've just set up residence, which is unusual, but it's been done before."

"Really?" Jordan persisted. "Then is there a difference in your abilities?"

Markus shot her a lopsided grin. "I'm powerful in either form, although a bit quicker and more transportable in spirit."

"I mean...like...what if a truck hit you right now? Could you die?"

Markus wavered. A keening draft whipped his golden locks into his eyes. He removed the strands with his lean fingers while Jordan waited impatiently for his answer. At last, he said, "Possibly, yes."

Disturbed by Markus's acceptance of his existence, Jordan dipped her head sadly, the conversation disbanded in an awkward silence. Shriveled leaves scampered past their feet, as the brick formation of Elma High loomed on the horizon. Then it looked like the heavens parted, liberating white flecks of snow dust, flittering breezily.

Stashing Markus's existence in the back of her mind, Jordan switched gears. "The first snowfall of the season," she said gleefully. She stretched out her palms and the flakes melted on contact.

Amused by her exuberance, Markus breathed softly, "Jordan."

Happily bringing her eyes back to Markus, she saw his creased brow and tried to wipe the smile from her face. "You know better than to play with the Ouija board and invoke spirits," he counseled. "I shouldn't have to tell you how precarious these games can be. And Ronan appears to have quite a dependence on the supernatural."

"I want to stop Ronan before my dream becomes a reality, before it's too late. I needed to see exactly how far she'd ventured into the dark."

He gripped her shoulders, his features taut. "I know you're capable, though a little headstrong." His eyes dimmed. "I'm not going to stop you, only guide and protect you, as well as I can."

At first, Jordan felt like she'd been dissected. Then when she gave a brisk nod of her head, he released her shoulders. Buoyed with his unexpected support and feeling confident, she practically jogged to the school's entrance, with her angel keeping pace easily. Surveying Markus, who didn't break a sweat, Jordan chuckled at her own exertion as he handed her the weighty backpack.

"Thanks. Talk to you later, Mark."

Jordan sprinted to her locker, where Ronan waited, wearing her leggings and shirtdress with a wide belt. Jordan felt drab and common in her jeans and long-sleeved, striped T-shirt. Never one to make a fashion statement, she liked to blend. Maybe next year, when she got acclimated, she'd go out on a limb and wear something risqué, like a skirt—if she owned one by then.

Dark almond-shaped eyes slit at Jordan's approach. "What's going on between you and Mark?" Ronan demanded, her voice cold.

"Mark?" said Jordan, muddled. "There's nothing going on between us. Why?"

"You were walking with him—again, this morning." In a show of aggravation Ronan flipped her silky hair over her shoulder with the back of her hand. "I saw the way he was holding you." She stamped her foot like a spoiled brat and, not waiting for a reply, said, "Thrill drove me to school this morning. We would've stopped to pick you up, but you both looked—intense."

"It was just a...a coincidence, we bumped into each other." Jordan knew her voice sounded insecure.

The history textbook slipped from her hand, slamming to the floor. She stooped to pick it up, feeling somewhat strained. When she stood up, Ronan, with hands on hips, surveyed her from her hair down to her scruffy sneakers.

"What's wrong, Ronan?"

"What do you *have* that sucks Mark in? Definitely not your fashion sense."

"Me? He's not interested in me." Jordan emphasized each word. "I know you've already called dibs on the guy. Don't worry. I won't stand in your way."

Ronan's face relaxed. "What do you think goes on at Beth Schaffer's house?" She noticed Jordan's wide-eyed confusion. "You know what I mean? *They live together.* She hangs all over him, it really makes me puke."

"Mark says they're friends, nothing more." Jordan wanted to boost Ronan's confidence before she sent Davian after poor Beth.

Ronan astonished Jordan by saying, "Mark asked me to go to Taste after school today." Satisfied with Jordan's shocked expression, Ronan pivoted away to her first period class.

In a way, Jordan was upset that Markus never mentioned his coffee date with Ronan. Why would he keep it a secret?

The lunchroom pulsed with energy with the Winter Ball just around the corner. Animated chatter filled the space and building to an outrageous racket. Threading among tables and chairs, Jordan nearly lost her pickle when someone backed their chair into her hip.

She couldn't help overhearing students ragging about every little thing. One girl complained, "…committee voted on silver and white. Weren't those last year's colors?" A group of guys were discussing music. "…better not play crappy music or the dance will suck!" Jordan strode past another table. "…dress Paige is wearing? It's the hideous…"

Wow! Tough crowd, Jordan thought.

Jordan felt dwarfed seated next to Cayden, who swiftly leaned and pilfered the pickle from Jordan's tray, taking a hearty chomp. Pickle juice dripped along her chin, and she helped herself to Jordan's napkin as well

Her voice was somewhat garbled with pickle chunks. "Just about everyone saw you and Mark walking to school this morning."

"Um-hm," Jordan admitted. Her dry turkey sandwich was sticking to her teeth. "Why is everyone so bothered? We were just walking." With her finger she dislodged a hunk of bread behind her front teeth.

"Let me give you some advice." Cayden glanced over her shoulder conspicuously. "Ronan wants Mark. I mean, she likes him." Then, cupping her hand around Jordan's ear, she confided, "Like I tried explaining over the phone, last year's Winter Ball ended badly. Beth and the popular kids blamed Ronan for what happened and they've ostracized her ever since." Cayden stiffened. Her eyes circled like a deer's in headlights when Ronan entered the cafeteria.

Puzzled by Cayden's sudden panic, Jordan watched a dynamic Ronan make her way to the table. "What's up, Cayden?" Ronan's tone was sharp. "What were you whispering to Jordan about?"

"I was telling Jordan the Winter Ball isn't as exciting as everyone makes it out to be," Cayden lied.

Ronan's head bobbed in consideration. "Unfortunately," she remarked lightly. "Cayden's right. All the hype and it's just a lame dance in the school gym." Her voice lowered. "Do you think the Ouija board is right and Mark is going to ask you to dance?"

"I wish I wasn't even going. And Mark will probably dance with anyone who asks," said Jordan. "Do you even know if he's going?"

"Oh, he's going." Ronan's pupils dilated. "I believe he's going with Beth's group. So—do you plan on asking Mark to dance? Is that what you're saying?"

"Not a chance," related Jordan. "Why would I ask him to dance?"

Startling Jordan, Ronan reached forward, picked at a loose lock of Jordan's hair, and hooked it behind her ear. Then in an odd gesture, she skimmed her finger the length of Jordan's jawline, producing a shudder from her scalp down the length of her backbone. "Will he ask you?" Ronan whispered.

"I dunno." Jordan said.

Ronan's upper lip rolled derisively. Without another word she sauntered to the lunch counter.

Jordan scrubbed away Ronan's touch and looked at Cayden "We've known each other for a while and I know we're not best friends or anything like that," she said, her tone rather peeved. "But why didn't you warn me about Saturday night? And why's Ronan so crazed about Mark?"

She instantly regretted speaking harshly to Cayden.

Blotchy-faced, Cayden sipped on a juice packet. "Ronan asked me all kinds of questions about you for weeks and I remembered you'd mentioned something about your mom trying to get your dad's book published," she said miserably. "I thought your dad was a writer. Then she'd planned the log initiation to see if you'd be receptive to crazy stuff." Her eyes turned catty, peering at Jordan. "By the way, you passed with flying colors." Cayden paused to shred a napkin, thinking. "Somehow Ronan got a copy of your father's book. I couldn't give her the information she wanted about your dad, because all you ever told me was that he died." Her eyes darted to Ronan. She was slanted against the sidewall, talking with a boy but keeping a close watch on Jordan and Cayden.

Cayden appeared so forlorn Jordan almost felt sorry for her. "So what were you talking about before Ronan walked in—something that happened last year?"

Cayden started to cough, a fit that shook her slim body. Sipping more juice, she nervously glanced at Ronan. In the midst of coughing, Cayden muddled through to say, "Maybe you should ask Thrill, or someone else." Standing, with her hand covering her mouth, she stumbled out the doors.

Between classes, for the rest of the afternoon, Jordan hiked the crowded halls, searching for Thrill. She'd only managed to walk into an open locker. Massaging her bruised shoulder, she peeked around and found a solitary girl smirking at her indignity. With the end of the last period class, Jordan's plan was to beat Thrill to his car.

The flittering snowflakes amassed into a heavy snowfall. Jordan's sneakers sank into the wet slushy snow as she trudged through the parking lot. Generally, Thrill usually drove Ronan home, but she was going for coffee with Mark after school, so Jordan assumed Thrill would be alone.

Unexpectedly, two arms engulfed Jordan from behind, lifting, and twirling her in a circle. "Hey, Jordan!" Thrill exclaimed. "Want a ride home?"

Jordan giggled, loving Thrill's enthusiasm. "Sure. I was looking for you—and you found me."

Tracking Thrill to his car, Jordan attempted to step in his snow-flattened footprints. Obviously her sneakers weren't holding up well in the snow.

"You were looking for me?" he said over his shoulder. He unlocked the door holding it for Jordan.

Frowning at the globbed snow on her sneaks, Jordan felt guilty tramping it into his car. She knocked them on the cars ledge, but it was too late, water had already soaked into her socks.

"My car's used to the snow, don't worry about it." He smiled. Jordan was glad for the cold weather as her blush mingled with her rosy face. "So what's up?" he asked.

Jordan enjoyed his flushed cheeks as well, and the way he ran his fingers through his hair. For a nanosecond, she forgot what she wanted to ask him. He revved the engine and switched on the defrosters, giving Jordan time to gather her wits.

"I was wondering if you could help me." Jordan paused as he put the car in gear. "Er…Cayden said something happened last year at the dance. I'd like to be informed before I get myself in trouble."

Thrill seemed agitated and swerved onto Main Street. "Why? Does this have something to do with Mark?" Jordan must've looked a bit stunned, because his next words were, "Ronan told me she's nuts about the guy. She doesn't like the idea of him living with Beth, and then you've been seen with him lately. In fact, we saw you two walking again this morning. Are you crazy for this Mark guy like every girl in school?"

Jordan didn't know if she should be affronted. "Mark's…nice," she said meekly. "We're friends, that's all."

Thrill nodded, but clearly wasn't convinced.

"But, Thrill, I'd really like to know what happened last year. It has nothing to do with Mark."

Thrill gnawed on his inner cheek. Jordan could tell her question really bothered him because his fingers were tense and turning white around the knuckles as he gripped the steering wheel. All of a sudden, he veered the car to the side of the road and switched off the ignition. Taking a cleansing breath, he said, "What do you know?"

"Not much. Cayden had started to explain how the Winter Ball ended badly, but as soon as Ronan walked into the lunchroom, she got all weird and jittery. That's about it."

A snort rumbled Thrill's throat as he rolled his eyes. "It's a long story, Jordan. I don't have all the facts. We might never know what really went down."

"Please enlighten me a bit, Thrill." Intent on hearing the story, Jordan had no idea what her intense green-gold eyes and fluttering lashes were doing to Thrill.

Thrill's full mouth curved engagingly. "Are those beautiful eyes flirting with me?"

Confounded at first, and then mad at her traitorous blushing cheeks, she joked, "Not really, but if it'll help...then yes."

With a spurt of a chuckle, Thrill conceded. "It *always* helps, Jordan."

She loved the way he said her name, sugary—no, more than sugary, like an unripe strawberry dipped in sugar—a little tart and sweet. She couldn't think straight. She was positively out of her league when it came to this boy. She did her utmost to rid the silly grin from her mouth.

"I have to give you some background first," Thrill said, beginning his tale. "Ronan was part of the popular pack all through school. She can be very...intimidating." He shared a perceptive grin with Jordan, both of them on the same page. "And through the years I've seen how she can sway people to her way of thinking." Thrill hesitated, running his fingers over the steering wheel. He seemed to be refreshing his mind.

"Anyway, she fell hard for a guy—his name was Robert. They became quite an item, or so it seemed. I felt sorry for the guy. He couldn't look or even talk to another girl." Thrill laughed humorlessly. "It was like she cut off his balls or something. My friend Megan—a very hot chick by the way." He smiled. "She was rumored to like Ronan's guy. Needless to say, Ronan found out, probably from Paisley. Then at the Winter Ball, Meg asked Robert to dance—not once, but twice. Meg hated Ronan and the way she ruled the group. She especially disliked the way Ronan treated Robert. But that nitwit Robert blew it. He enjoyed dancing with Meg way too much. If you don't know by now, let me tell you, Ronan's insanely jealous. She has a nasty streak when it comes to anything she wants."

Thrill grabbed a water bottle, lying on the seat, and drank generously. "Wanna sip?" He extended the bottle.

"No, thanks." Jordan was getting antsy, wishing he'd get to the point.

"So, it'd be advisable not to make her jealous." He looked intentionally into her eyes, though he didn't mention Mark.

She nodded, knowing what he meant.

Thrill's brows drew together, then he started again. "It was the last dance of the night. It happened so fast—Ronan stood up, got a fistful of Meg's hair, and yanked her head back. Megan swore. Then Ronan whispered something in Meg's ear and shoved her head, hard. Then she dragged Robert onto the dance floor, like a puppet. I went over to ask Megan to dance. Just as I got there, her eyes popped out of their sockets, like she was scared to death. Her entire body started shaking, and her hands held the table, kind of like...for support. And then..."

Pressing on his eyelids with his fingers, distracted by the past, Thrill stared at the car's windshield as if watching a movie.

"It's hard to explain..." His voice sounded far away. "But Megan looked like she was playing tug-of-war with the table. Her mouth opened wide as if she wanted to scream, but she couldn't get out any noise. Then she started making this gross gurgling and some kind of foamy saliva dripped from the corner of her lips."

Thrill glanced at Jordan. "I thought she was having a convulsion or some kind of seizure." His haunted gaze wandered back to the window. "Her head flung forward—no. She *hurled* her head forward and smashed her face on the table! Man. I can still hear the thud—blood gushed from her nose—her mouth—it was everywhere. It was disgusting." Thrill rotated toward Jordan. "Can you believe it?"

Dazed, Jordan reflected on her mental picture of the peculiar event. Undoubtedly, Ronan Beckman had delved deeper into the black arts than she'd imagined. Although futile, she asked, "Was it a seizure?"

He shook his head negatively. "It wasn't a seizure. Right afterward, Megan was hysterical, hollering that Ronan did it. She was blubbering, holding her face. I grabbed the tablecloth to help soak up the blood. She was inconsolable, saying that Ronan smashed her face. I looked for Ronan on the dance floor, only to find her right in front of the table with Robert, watching the whole time. Ronan was livid at Megan's accusations. Still, there was something about the way she looked—smiling, like she was *happy* seeing Meg a bloody mess." He scraped two hands over his grooved forehead. "Arrgh—I don't know. The whole thing was frickin' wacked."

"Do you think Ronan had anything to with it?"

Thrill didn't act surprised by her question. "Meg and Ronan hated each other, but I keep asking myself one thing. Would Megan deliberately break her own nose and blame it on Ronan to get Robert? I doubt it."

"Do you know what Ronan said in Megan's ear?"

"Now that's bizarre. A couple days later Megan told me. She was scared to tell anyone, because the whole school thought she was a lunatic for blaming pretty Ronan." Thrill shook his head. His mouth curved sideways, like remembering was unpleasant. "Megan was crying on my shoulder—and it wasn't cute. Two black and blue eyes, bandages, and packing in her nose. Ronan had whispered, 'My friend, Davian, wants to meet you.'"

Davian? Who'd have thought Ronan really had the power to command wicked spirits. "What happened after that?"

Thrill tried to laugh, but it sounded flat. "Robert—he panicked. He broke up with Ronan the day after the dance, and Ronan made his life a living hell. Called his mom and dad, crying about how much she loved Robert and how badly he hurt her. This lasted weeks. Finally Robert's family moved. Ronan has a way of making life miserable if she's out to get you." His amber eyes sought Jordan's face.

"I don't know how Meg found out about Ronan's *games*, but man, she started a smear campaign. She began to call her a witch behind her back, telling the whole school stuff that *I* didn't even believe." Thrill grinned. "I liked Meg's fabrication of seeing Ronan flying on a broomstick at midnight. Now that was a hoot. Ronan didn't think it was funny. She was enraged. One day Megan tripped down the bleachers, and she blamed the witch again. Some of the guys started to take Megan seriously, and gradually kids distanced themselves from Ronan. And Megan's family moved shortly after the New Year, which was probably a good thing, considering Ronan was out to destroy her.

"Beth was one of the first to shut Ronan out, but soon everyone did. This past year I've seen a big change in Ronan, and it's not for the better. I've known her since the second grade—she was cute and nice, then her mom died. It devastated her, and her dad kind of abandoned Ronan, always on business trips and whatnot. She got bitter—hard. I figured playing with the Ouija board was Ronan's way of trying to contact her mom. It always freaked me out, especially when I've seen some strange stuff—well, maybe Ronan is a witch. And sometimes, I almost believe Megan, and if that Davian *thing* attacked her…" Thrill raised the water bottle and glugged the remaining contents.

Absorbing Thrill's explanation, Jordan felt pity for Ronan, but then she thought about the poor girl with the broken nose. "Were you close with Megan?"

Thrill gave Jordan a direct look. "Kind of…we were going out."

The frigid air had crept into the car. Jordan shivered from her frosty feet—and from Thrill's enlightenment.

CHAPTER 8

Beware of the Wicked Curse.

I thought you'd be home by now," Jordan whined into the cell. "It's been over a week."

"Father James set up meetings with specific groups, more than I imagined, and all intent on sharing knowledge in these strange times," Seeley explained patiently. "Jack's book has caused quite a stir. This was interesting—I talked with a holy mystic who'd foreseen demons emerging to harvest souls for the devil. She visualized darkness over the earth then what looked like gleaming flares shooting through the darkness, dispelling it." Seeley sighed. "There's hope, Jordan."

"You sound tired, Mom. Is everything okay?"

"Fine." Seeley's voice shook faintly. "A run-in with Trebane sort of spooked me, and a few tailing demons, but other than that, I'm good. But it's you who should be careful. Watch your back."

"Are you really not going to tell me about Mr. Trebane? What did he want?"

Like an invasion of microscopic spiders, Seeley's skin crawled remembering Asa's touch. "You know Asa's threatening tactics." She was talking too fast. "Riling me up about your father's deception and how the marker must be paid. Just be on the lookout for anything out of the ordinary. I don't trust that demon Veronka." Seeley needed to change topics. She'd discuss Veronka's stated revenge when she was face to face with

Jordan. She didn't want to scare the crap out of her, though Seeley knew better—Jordan didn't scare easily. "Let's talk about something else, like—how's school?"

Jordan cringed. Her mom would flip when she found out about Ronan's Ouija board—and Davian. Jordan figured that uptight exchange could wait.

"School's boring as ever." With absolute reservation, Jordan decided she'd better mention Markus's human appearance before her mom heard, or eventually saw him standing on their front porch. Her tone blithe, trying to make it sound like angels attended high school every day, she said, "The funniest thing has happened." Her casual timbre wasn't quite cutting it, but she persisted. "Markus isn't just an angel anymore. He's formed a human identity and, believe it or not, he's living with Beth Schaffer's family."

Seeley's scalp bristled. Inadvertently, Jordan had alerted her to impending danger. Seeley fought to remain calm. "You're not telling me everything, are you, Jordan?"

Her mother's authoritative voice was prickling. "Mom, everything's fine. Markus said it was easier for him to get a grip on the situation if he accompanied me to school, kind of like a bodyguard." Jordan's explanation sounded full of holes, even to her.

Her mother didn't respond.

"Mom, are you there?"

Seeley took a deep breath. "I wish I could be in two places at once. I'll cancel my last meeting. I'm leaving Quenemo in the morning. I'll be home sooner than expected."

☙❧❧

Jordan had summarized their conversation to Em and Henry, who were looking forward to Seeley's homecoming. As Em put ham sandwiches on the table, her eyes twinkled. "I noticed the nice-looking young man who drove you home from school yesterday. I hope you don't mind—I peeked out the window when I heard a car pull in the driveway."

With a satisfied smile, Jordan said, "That was Thri— William McKenna. He's a nice guy." She decided to use his real name since she wasn't in the mood to explain.

Henry harrumphed. "Don't go getting involved with any guys, Jordan. You have college to look forward to."

"Henry—" Em retorted. "Jordan's sixteen years old and there are some fine young men in Elma."

Under his shaggy brow, Henry's irascible eyes looked at Jordan, then he slowly produced a genuine smile. "You're pretty, like your mother. I'm just saying...be careful."

Jordan nodded to Henry, acknowledging that 'be careful' referred to certain interactions with the opposite sex that could have serious consequences. For Henry, Seeley's teen pregnancy created resentment for his son-in-law, resentment that was never forgotten. Jordan chugged a glass of milk and finished her sandwich just as the doorbell rang.

She jumped up from the table, and when she swung open the door, she was shocked to see Markus framing the archway. "When was the last time you had a sparring partner?" he asked.

"Guess it's been a while...why?"

"I thought we'd go over to the school's gym and workout."

"The gym's probably crowded with activities."

"Nope, they're cleaning for the Winter Ball," he told her. "But Mr. Harrington, the gym teacher, said the crew would likely be done after one o'clock."

"Well then it's probably locked up. How would we get in?"

With an impish grin brightening his usually serious features, Markus dangled a set of keys in front of her face. "Mr. Harrington supplied me with the keys. He said I looked trustworthy."

Jordan chuckled. "Okay then. Let me grab my coat." She turned to dash into the kitchen and almost collided with her grandparents.

"Who's this young man?" Em inquired, her face aglow as she stared at the flawless Markus.

Jordan introduced him as Mark, an exchange student living with Deacon Samuel Schaffer's family.

"Known the Schaffers for years, a wonderful family," Henry complimented.

"Yes, they are," Mark agreed.

"Sam mentioned something about an exchange student last week after church." Henry extended his arm and pumped Mark's hand. "Nice to meet you. Where are you taking my granddaughter?"

"Thought we'd go to the school's gymnasium and workout with some of their weight machines, if that's okay?"

Em tittered like a young girl. "Of course, that'd be fine."

Jordan plowed between her grandparents, buttoning her coat. "See you in a while," she said and then was startled to see a metallic green SUV parked in the driveway.

Markus released the passenger side door and Jordan settled into the warm interior. Adjusting the seat belt, she saw Em and Henry flanking the doorway. Henry's face was dubious and Em's a joyful ear-to-ear grin. Jordan waved as Markus pulled out of the driveway.

"Nice car, Markus."

"It was all Deacon Schaffer's idea."

Changing the subject, she asked, "How'd your coffee clutch with Ronan go the other day?"

Markus tensed a little. "I think it's imperative we keep a close eye on Ronan. Somehow, someway she needs to be coaxed away from indulging in her magical charms. I've deduced that her mind is crippled from years of abuse and neglect. She's yearning for love and, with that, for the power to control situations."

"You got all that from a cup of coffee?" she said, in full cynical mode.

Unique midnight blues cast Jordan a mordant glance. "When did you last see Father James?"

Turning her head to the side window, Jordan shrugged. "It's been a while." She knew she needed to talk to her spiritual advisor, yet the chore was more than bothersome at times.

Sunshine glittered over the windswept afternoon, but provided little warmth. A current of air rocked the vehicle. Markus drove to the rear of the school and the two of them skated on icy pavement to the gym's entrance. Once inside, Jordan tossed her coat on the bleachers. Shucking her wet sneakers, she frowned at a toe poking out of a fraying hole in her sock. She rolled them off and made a mental note to buy new ones. She smoothed her long-sleeved, orange T-shirt. At least it was in decent condition. Luckily, she'd been wearing her fairly new black sweats.

Markus assembled padded mats and slipped off his sneakers as well. Jordan couldn't help feeling peeved about his pristine white socks. Then she really looked at him. Wearing navy-blue sweatpants and a matching tank, he looked like a model for a workout magazine.

For no specific reason, she said, "I wish I could make a sword appear out of thin air like you and Ezekiel."

Markus straightened with legs parted and hands balancing on his hips. "Try it."

"What'd you mean—*Try it?* Try what?"

"You need to stretch your mind, beyond this earthly sphere. Ask, seek, and knock, and it will be given, if it is our Father's will."

"It doesn't seem right to pray for a weapon."

"Remember—we're not playing by the rules."

"How do I do it?" Her thoughts ignited at the prospect of attaining a magical weapon. "Just think about a sword or something?"

"No—more than just *think.*" While pushing hair off his forehead, Markus took a step forward, his expression indistinct. "It'll take practice, patience, and delving into your subconscious. You need to grasp the realm outside of this dimension."

Puckering her face in pursuit of a prized sword, Jordan's hand shot in the air, her fingers itching for the presence of something cold and sharp. Digging past mental chains on a quest to unlocking her subconscious, Jordan lowered her eyelids, blinding herself to interfering sights.

Meditating to an astral degree, her brain seemed to bulge from the effort.

Jordan then felt her body, or was it her psyche, shift—somewhere.

Instead of something cold, the air circulating her fingers was hot. Opening her eyes, she saw a mirage of a short blade distorted in layers of undulating air. Jordan's fingers tried circling the hilt, but they passed through the image. Losing concentration, she felt the air surrounding her hand cool considerably.

"That was an excellent first attempt." Markus clapped his hands twice in laudatory praise. "Although, you looked like you were having an aneurysm."

"You said I had to delve dee—" She never finished her sentence, perceiving Markus's laughing eyes and pearly white teeth. "Now you're being *too* human, making fun of me."

"Sorry." He collected himself. "Do you need to warm-up before we begin?"

"*If* you don't mind. I'm not a lofty seraph." She didn't mean to sound crass, but it came out that way.

Stretching and bending her arms over her head, Jordan then lunged to slacken her thigh muscles. When ready, she rotated rigidly to Markus who signaled with a finger command to begin.

"Hit me," he ordered. "Hard as you can."

Jordan thought for a moment then kicked her leg swiftly at Markus's defenseless thigh.

He grasped her leg, easily flinging her to the mat. "You can do better than that."

In a split-second decision, Jordan scissored his ankles then rolled. She nearly toppled Markus to the floor. Yet he recovered, slinging his muscular arm across her neck. With his other hand, he gripped her arms behind her back, always her weak point. He released her, flinging her forward again. Their sparring became a mental and physical game. Ambition scarred Jordan's pleasure. She was determined to beat Markus, though she didn't know how.

For such a tall boy, Markus feinted swiftly and accurately. She tried to outmaneuver him, with some success, but she assumed he was just being kind by letting her get her licks in. Jordan felt like she'd just come out of a sauna. Her skin was dewy, and beads of sweat dripped from the tip of her nose and chin. Then tricking Markus, Jordan pretended to have a stunned look on her face and pointed to something behind him. And when he wasn't prepared, she clobbered him in the abdomen. He barely flinched then laughed as she shook out her hand. It felt like she'd hit cement. She promptly twirled and aimed her heel at his groin, which he blocked, sending her crashing to the mat.

She landed with her arms and legs spread eagle like Leonardo DaVinci's famous sketch, *Vitruvian Man.* "Okay, okay, have you had enough?" she said, breathing heavily.

"We haven't even begun."

Soon after Markus's prophetic words, growling sounds reached their ears. A bevy of demonic men and women darted sinuously around them. As the first attacker charged, Jordan's core seemed to have a mind of its own. She did a front round-off over the man, leaving him muddled. Before he could turn, Jordan twisted his scrawny neck like a corkscrew. "Wow, I didn't know I could do that!"

Simmering in the wings was a she-devil—her putrefying guts smelled like death. Skin hung revoltingly from her bones, and burr-holed sores were swarming with squiggly maggots. The creature's deformation didn't deter her ability to jaunt toward Jordan, arms outspread.

Jordan fanned her nose. "Pee-yew. You're way past the expiration date."

The thought of touching the fetid she-devil made Jordan gag, but she executed a flying kick with both feet and thwacked the creature in the chest, hollowing it in to her vertebrae. Ichor and maggots splattered everywhere. Jordan squirmed over the crud on her bare feet, grimacing.

Markus's voice rang out. "Jordan, get out of here!"

While Jordan dealt with the woman, the entourage had wrangled with Markus. He threw his arm above his head, instantly acquiring a heavenly weapon, the singing sword proficiently culling the soulless herd. Monstrous demons lured Markus farther away from Jordan. That was obviously part of their plan, for Veronka and Asa burst through the doors. Asa whipped up a combustible hex. Hellfire surrounded Markus, cutting him off from Jordan.

Diverted temporarily by the inferno then, wheeling around, Jordan came face to face with Veronka. Her fist crashed into Jordan's jaw, sending her backward. Jordan hit the ground.

When she came to, Veronka had her in a back-crushing hold. Hot breath brushed Jordan's neck as the demon's chin rested on her shoulder. Jordan's mouth ached. Parting her lips, she slowly moved her jawbone from side to side. The brackish tang of blood covered her tongue.

"Welcome back," Asa said mildly.

Jordan's eyes darted to the dancing flames imprisoning Markus. They burned nothing, but the angel could not pass them.

"Just a little Hellfire to detain our friend while we speak," Asa said.

Veronka's secure hold gave Jordan little room to breathe.

"You killed my father," Jordan wheezed. "I have nothing to say to you. I wish you were dead!"

"Jordan, Jordan, you'd like to save your mother, wouldn't you?"

"Just like you spared my father?" She gave him a poisonous look. "I'd never trust you, Trebane, never—you son-of-a-bitch!"

"What a rank mouth, my dear." Asa's lips bent to one side. "You and Seeley need a lesson in respect. I will succeed—at the opportune time. My power will break through your heavenly fortification"

Markus hollered from inside the wall of flames. "Jordan, you can block the fire! Release me!"

Veronka gouged her knuckles into Jordan's spine. Jordan trapped the cry of pain in her throat. She didn't want to give them the satisfaction.

Veronka began to retch, repugnant gurgling noise. Her jaw obtrusively distended, allowing a gross python to slither from her oral cavity. The python slunk over Jordan's shoulder, along her chest, and entangled her body, constricting it. Jordan panted for air. Her head swam as she struggled to focus on blocking the fire. She felt faint, utterly ineffectual.

"The omen must be fulfilled." Asa stated. He sucked air between his barred teeth, his nostrils flaring. "I promised Lucifer your consecration by year's end, the date has been settled. I've been waiting for your abilities to develop. With those powers, you will be an asset to our lord, don't you think?"

His tongue darted across his lips, out of character with the dastardly villain in his double-breasted, brushed, cashmere Canali suit. He did not disturb a hair on his styled head as his manicured hands boxed Jordan's face. His gloating eyes were inches from hers. So close that Jordan felt herself being tugged into those dilating pupils. His cultivated voice drew her in. "You will be ours or your mother will die a slow torturous death. You'll hear her screams burrowing into your brain," he breathed. "Her screams of affliction, and then you will beg me to take you in her place."

Again, Markus yelled, "Jordan, don't listen to him!"

Asa's black orbs hypnotized Jordan. In vain, she tried to lower her lids, but she could only stare as he cursed. "*Screams* of agony, *screams* of torturous pain, groaning screams that will fill you to the brim…"

Jordan heard her mom's raw scream searing into her brain like a branding iron. Dimly, somewhere in the background, she heard Markus. "Jordan, close your eyes! Concentrate on someone else!"

She sank into oblivion.

ာ၁ၔၐ

Jordan wrenched upright, ready for a brawl, nearly knocking Markus in the forehead. Realizing that he held her in his arms, she looked around the room. It was cleared of fire, demons, Asa, and his sidekick, Veronka.

"What happened?"

"They left."

"That's good, right? Why the long face?"

"He's cursed you somehow."

Jordan rose and stretched. Every joint and muscle cried out in pain. She cupped her swollen chin where Veronka had socked her. "I feel...kind of all right," she said. "What happened to the fire? Why couldn't you walk through it?"

"Hellfire detains both angels and demons. Since I was in my human form, I attempted to pass, though it scorched my fingers to ash."

Jordan glimpsed his charcoal-colored hands.

"I heal quick." He shook his head, looking glum. "You need to speak to Father James. I'll drive you to the rectory, now."

Jordan's objections smothered in her throat as Markus tossed her sneakers and coat onto her lap.

"Get dressed."

By the sound of his voice, there'd be no arguing with him.

She had scarcely stuffed her arms into her coat sleeves when he grabbed her hand and jogged to the car. His urgency baffled Jordan, who felt perfectly fine.

The car skidded on the frozen street as they headed for Holy Angels Church. By the time they reached the church, the world looked fuzzy and lopsided like some kind of psychedelic maze. Jordan's head was aching. She massaged her temples, fighting her annoyance as the usually complacent Markus fidgeted. He rang the rectory's doorbell and then impatiently slapped his opened palm on the panel, nearly jarring the lock.

Father James, wearing a traditional priestly cassock, released the bolt. He was younger than most parish pastors, though faint silvery strands laced through his head of jet-black hair. Even at his age, the priest was already showing signs of strife. As soon as he saw Jordan's bloodshot eyes, he sighed, gravely concerned.

Without saying a word, Markus swept speedily past him with Jordan in tow and deposited her on the rectory's couch.

Aware of Jordan's guardian, Father James stared as Markus recounted the battle and Asa's curse.

"I know you're an exorcist. Only you can help her," Markus said in haste. "I feel a vital call and must leave immediately." His figure faded from their sight.

Father James and Jordan looked at each other, stupefied by his brisk departure. "Now explain in detail—every little word or action you can remember," Father James ordered.

As she endeavored to recollect the past hour, Jordan's head was igniting. Incessant screams jangled her brain. Futilely, she planted her hands over her ears to stop the noise, but the screeching shredded her from the inside. Her eyes felt like hot, molten lava.

Father James uncapped holy oil of chrism for anointing her eyelids, ears, throat, and forehead. Thumbing pages in a book he utilized for an exorcism and, clutching a crucifix, the priest situated the cross directly over the bridge of her nose.

His compelling words plaited an intrusive, binding cord. The priest admonished curses, hexes, and enchantments. He concluded with, "We rebuke Satan and all his evil works, snares, and approaches. By the power of Jesus's precious blood, we soak and cleanse the body of Jordan Chase inside and out…"

Her body felt like a bedraggled dishrag as she gazed upon the priest who rebuked Asa's curse, over and over, for more than an hour. His eyes looked sunken and dull, and his shoulders hunched like an old man sapped of energy. Jordan's head still ached, although not as badly.

Gently smoothing the dog-eared pages in his book, Father James said, almost feebly, "I'm vaguely worried about Asa's spell rebounding. It's hard to vanquish. And you, Jordan, are blessed with a substantial armor of protection."

She recalled the séance, which undoubtedly added fuel to the fire. "Father, I involved myself in a séance to wheedle my way into the confidence of some girls," she confessed. "I think one of them might be the catalyst that brings about my…dream. Ronan Beckman can command spirits, and I need to find a way to stop her. But that night…I felt like I crossed over to something very dark." Under blinking eyelashes she monitored the pale priest. He didn't seem pleased. She added, "My mother doesn't know, and she's on her way home. What should I do?"

Slightly unsteady, he lowered himself onto the nearest chair and stroked his eyebrows. "How many people are involved with these…games?"

"Three girls right now and I participated, but only once." She dislodged a damp string of hair from her forehead. "Two boys know about it, but I don't think they've contributed to their conjuring, at least not when I was there. And rumors are flying around the school about Ronan being a witch. Most kids think it's a hoax." It hurt her head to even talk.

"Jordan, in that school, you are called to transcend adolescence and harvest souls for God. *Not the other way around.*" Inflating his lungs to their fullest capacity, Father James went on. "It's highly unusual for both you and your mother to receive such extraordinary mysticism, but I recognize that we live in a dysfunctional world. We must believe with all our hearts that God's in control."

Then lowering his chin and closing his eyes, with his hands steepled in prayer, Father James didn't move, yet he seemed to have shifted into another dimension. Stillness. When he became alert, his gaze centered on Jordan.

The priest leaned forward, his elbows on his knees. Lacing his fingers, he rested his chin on his thumbs and peered pointedly at his charge. "You're on a different level than most teenagers. You are morally solid. You can easily avoid the evil snares of worldly possession. I know that your subterfuge is a way to avoid distressing your mom. Nevertheless, you hurt her by not confiding." Father James's chest expanded. "Séances can damage you. Your soul is not likely to be possessed, yet your spirit is more easily attained. You, in and of yourself, would be a great advantage to the spirit world. You need to be on guard."

Contrite, Jordan let her head fall back. "May I go into the church for a while?"

"Yes, come through the rectory and I'll let you in the side doors."

He touched Jordan's shoulder and cautioned, "I'd been forewarned of Mr. Trebane's—shall we say—talent. It is well known. My exorcism may not have countered all of his incantation. Come back to see me as soon as possible." He directed his young parishioner to the church and then limped away.

To Jordan, the faintly lit church felt like home. Tiers of votive candles flickered placidly beneath life-sized statues depicting the church's Holy Saints. Her eyes browsed to the perpetual candle next to the Tabernacle, its oscillating flame like a joyful hello.

Kneeling respectfully, hands knit in prayer, Jordan implored the Lord's forgiveness for her mistakes. She had her eyes closed, engrossed in prayer, when a resplendent shine pierced her eyelids. Straining to see through the blaze, Jordan was immersed in an arcane luminosity.

"Lucifer does everything possible to separate your heart from My heart," a heavenly voice said softly. "You can dispel the strongest demons, for they are nothing in My name. Trust in the mercy of My cross and it shall become a flame of divine love to assist you in conquering the demons of the evil one."

The sanctuary dimmed.

Drifting to earth after the inspiring interlude, Jordan observed her splendid angel kneeling reverently. He rose upward, his essence hardening into Mark.

"I'll take you home."

Exhilarated, Jordan could only nod. The sublime apparition had resulted in wobbly legs. Jordan took Markus's offered arm and shambled to his waiting vehicle.

CHAPTER 9

You Are Never Alone.

Jordan, you're not being entirely truthful with me," Seeley had fumed into the cell phone. "I need to know all that goes on in your life. You're not in this alone!"

The debate with her mom ended on a sour note. Zeke had informed Seeley of the attack at the school gym. Markus had asked several principalities, including Ezekiel, to be on the lookout for demons in Elma. Markus, however, forgot to mention that Jordan preferred for Seeley to be left out of the loop.

Annoyed with Markus, Jordan was having a hard time getting to sleep. Except Markus was not truly at fault—*she* was. Hiding secrets from her mom, as Father James said, would only hurt them both. Plumping the pillow, Jordan propped her hands behind her head and stared at the ceiling. The whistling wind clattered the windowpanes, drawing her eyes to the crystallized flakes outside. It looked like a roiling snow globe.

It was around this time of year, six years ago, that Jordan remembered transporting their meager belongings to Elma. Their lives had been in ruins after her father's death and, without faltering, her grandparents had opened their home and their arms to Seeley and Jordan. Grumpy Henry and sweet Emily offered them sanctuary.

Despite the whistling wind, Jordan finally sank into a fitful slumber, transported yet again to the spacious, hazy room where black-clad bodies pressed in on her. Hooded cloaks revealed glowering eyes and pinched lips...

Drip, Drip, Drip Something splashed on Jordan's hair. She brushed the wetness away and gaped at her hands, bathed in her father's blood. Trapped in the recurring nightmare, she didn't want to look up. Though, the dream was in control, and her neck craned backward toward the suffering sacrifice. She knew what her eyes were searching for—her father's bruised, bloody body.

Unbelievably, Jordan had plunged into a new horror.

Not her father—but her mom's half-lidded eyes begged Jordan for release. Seeley's mangled body, clothed in blood, cried out in agony. Jordan's mouth opened wide to scream at the horrendous spectacle, but she gagged instead—and gagged again, until she vomited a repulsive slimy snake.

Choking, clutching her throat, Jordan vaulted from the bed. Her screams died in the depths of her chest as her head swung back and forth, inspecting the dusky room. She sucked in cool air as her battering heart slowed.

The shadows retreated as the light entered. A tall figure drew forward.

"Omigosh, Markus, you scared me!" Jordan cried.

"Another nightmare?" His lean fingers touched the side of her cheek, sweeping away the damp hair that screened her face.

"Yes." Her voice broke. "But it was—Mom—Mom was hanging on the cross. The way she looked at me—almost like—like I failed her."

Markus hid his troubled expression. "Go back to sleep. I'll stay with you."

Jordan's body drooped without further coaxing. Markus tucked her in bed. After a few seconds passed, Jordan heard a faint whisper. Rolling over, she slurred, "What did you say, Markus?"

"I didn't say anything. Just calm down and get some rest."

Jordan fell asleep, or so she thought. When a white light woke her, she squinted into its glare. And rejoiced when her father appeared, his face as handsome as she remembered. He had a toothy smile as he scooped her into his arms.

"Dad—Dad!" Jordan cuddled into his neck, not wanting him to disappear.

"I needed to see you, to hold you," her father said softly in her ear.

Tears sprang to her eyes as Jordan melted in his arms. "I miss you."

A nurturing light encased them. Her father rocked her from side to side.

"Jordan, are you all right? Jordan?"

She pried open her eyes, hot with tears, and looked at her angel. "What happened to my father?"

"Jack?"

"Yes, he was here, just now, holding me." She glanced around, half expecting to see him beside them.

Markus's skeptical look gave Jordan her answer.

"Another dream," he whispered.

Jordan pouted and burrowed under the covers. "No, not this time. He was real. I felt him."

❧❧❧

Em shook her head at Jordan when she yawned broadly for the umpteenth time during church. Boredom had set in, and Jordan began to people watch, a jumbled assortment of textured woolen coats, jackets, shapes and sizes. Unexpectedly it was to a pair of unwavering sapphire eyes that she was drawn. Markus sported his friendly, lopsided grin. Beth sat next to him, along with the rest of the Schaffer family. Catching their brief encounter, Beth inched closer to Mark's elbow. Jordan quickly looked back at the altar.

After church, the congregation filtered through the glass doors. Em and Henry exchanged greetings as Jordan bounced from leg to leg in the cold. A raw current whisked through the fibers of her coat as she warmed her frosty cheeks with fleecy mitten hands. And wished for once her grandparents weren't so talkative.

"Hi, Jordan."

Hearing his voice, Jordan turned. Markus's features shone in the morning rays. Standing beside him was Beth, looking glamorous in a full-length, faux fur coat. Her arm was linked through his elbow.

Jordan uncomfortably pulled on the sleeves of her shabby, woolen coat.

The Deacon, Mrs. Schaffer, and their two kids surrounded Jordan's grandparents. "We're going to breakfast at Lucky's Diner. Would you care to join us?" Deacon Sam asked Henry.

No—say no, Jordan thought. The last thing she wanted was to be stuck at a table making small talk with Beth. Nonetheless Henry replied, "That sounds like a good idea. We'll meet you there."

Jordan's head bobbed absently. Dredging up a crooked grin, she thought about the whole preposterous state of affairs: Her guardian angel, now human, impersonating an exchange student living at Beth's, and to top it off—a witchy Ronan playing tug-of-war, with Jordan caught in the middle.

Breakfast proved to be tolerable. Jordan needn't have worried. Beth and her sisters were fairly nice, updating Jordan on Elma's fresh gossip. And Deacon Schaffer and her grandparents had pulled Markus into their conversation. It was hardly two hours later when Henry made the right hand turn onto Hickory Road that Jordan spied her mom's car at the curb. She bounded from Henry's vehicle before he parked. "Mom! Mom," she shrieked.

Seeley raced from the kitchen as Jordan flung herself into her waiting arms. "Miss me?"

Jordan chuckled. "A little."

Henry and Em ambled through the door, their faces wreathed with smiles.

Em hugged her daughter's cheek. "Seeley, so glad you're home and safe."

Henry's grouchy face glowed. He took a turn hugging his daughter. "Can you tell we don't like it when you leave?"

"Love you, too, Dad."

The kettle whistled. They hustled around the table where Seeley poured the boiling water and added tea. The four of them squandered Sunday afternoon, talking in turns. Seeley described the meetings, leaving out a few major elements. And with her parents adhered to every detail, she spoke mainly of the scenery and the cities she visited. "All in all, the trip was worthwhile."

Em and Henry conversed about breakfast with the Schaffers, rehashing the good-looking, intelligent exchange student and how he took Jordan to the gym to workout.

Seeley nodded absently, attempting not to judge Jordan before she heard the whole story. "I'm going up to unpack," she said, and left the table.

Jordan couldn't help but notice her mom's eye command and followed.

Upstairs, Seeley snapped, "So what's going on, Jordan? I had another vision a few days ago. I was in Elma—I recognized the school—and there was an invasion of soulless creatures."

Jordan sat on her mom's bed, wringing her hands. The story poured out of her, from beginning to end. She started with her first vision of demons terrorizing the school's hallways, then described Ronan's demon, the séances, and the strong call she felt to stop Ronan. Jordan also related her talk with Father James, ending with the transcendent apparition.

Her face stern, Seeley marched from one side of the room to the other with her arms crossed over her middle, listening to her daughter's tale. She stopped every once in a while to gawk and then shake her head.

Jordan's confession weighed heavily on Seeley's heart. Upset that her daughter withheld information, she questioned her own decision to keep Asa's indecent proposal from Jordan.

She'd give her life to save her daughter. Now, on the verge of agreeing to Asa's offer to save Jordan, her conscience revolted. Not naïve any longer, Seeley knew better than to trust that Asa would leave Jordan alone—even if Seeley *did* agree to his *arrangement*. She knew the devil dealt in money and souls—Jordan would not be spared.

Seeley summarized her negotiations with Asa, watching a look of shock bloom on Jordan's pretty face.

"How could you?" Jordan gaped at her mom. "After all the grief you gave me, you were ready to...to..." Jordan couldn't even say the words. "You said we're in this together—never alone."

CHAPTER 10

Pandemonium.

After another night of disturbing images, Jordan crawled from the comfort of her bed and hunted in the gloom for something to wear. Glancing quickly at the clock, she wondered if she had time to talk to Father James about her dreams before school. She groaned. It was already past six-thirty.

By lunchtime, Jordan felt like she could curl-up in a corner and sleep for hours. Hunched over the table, poking at a mound of mashed potatoes, she attempted a subtle yawn, although it morphed into a fully-fledged gape. Paisley came up beside her, setting a tray heaped with food on the table. "Look at this swill. They call this healthy?" Scuffing the chair on the laminate flooring, she sat.

Jordan snickered when Paisley dug into the beef crumble with gusto.

Blotting her chin with a paper napkin, Paisley nudged Jordan with her shoulder. "So you went out with Mark on Saturday? And then with Beth and Mark for breakfast on Sunday?"

Slurping up the last of her chocolate milk, Jordan sputtered, "A–are you f–following me?"

"Ronan wondered what Mark did on his weekends. Apparently he spends them with you and Beth."

"Ronan and Mark aren't a couple," Jordan protested. "Why's she being so possessive?"

"They've been on a few…dates. Ronan thinks it's going somewhere. She doesn't want you and Beth messing things up."

Jordan rolled her eyes. These girls were clueless, and Markus wasn't helping the matter. "Mark and I are friends."

Paisley's eyes tapered to slits. "You'd better lay off. Ronan won't be too happy when I tell her about Mark's weekend with two other girls."

"You haven't told Ronan yet?"

"Nope, I thought I'd talk to you first to see what's going on. But I did mention Beth Schaffer to Ronan—she hates Beth." Paisley started in on dessert, biting into a peanut butter cookie and spraying crumbs as she talked. "Ronan wants you to come to her house. Something you'd be very, very interested in."

"I can only imagine what Ronan feels I'd be interested in." She prepared herself for another session with the Ouija board, though she leaned closer to Paisley. "They're risky games. Where demons take over, Paisley, it's kind of hazardous for your health, if you get my drift?"

Paisley's head reared back in understanding. She stabbed Jordan with a malicious look, undaunted. "Be at Ronan's tonight, by nine o'clock, or I'll tell her all about your date with Mark." She stood and then slanted over Jordan, her lips touching Jordan's hair. "Your father has contacted Ronan. Jack wants to speak to his daughter." Paisley poked Jordan's shoulder and snickering headed toward a display of doughnuts.

Paisley's claim blew Jordan away. Dwelling on the recent dream of her father—was it just a dream or did he really have something to say? Jordan didn't care about Ronan's jealousy over her so-called date with Markus, though she'd wondered if Paisley had followed them into the gym. How much had she actually seen? No matter what, Jordan knew she'd have to make another visit to the spirit realm.

છ૭છ૭

Seeley loathed the idea of her daughter partaking with the conjuring crew. Nevertheless, the time had come to untie the apron strings. She understood—the warrior was needed to avert danger. She plied Jordan with holy water, following the explicit instructions in Jack's journal. Added to Father James's recent ministrations, she assumed her daughter would be protected from whatever the girls had up their sleeves. Seeley stipulated that Jordan should be home by midnight, or she'd come looking, and lobbed the car keys.

An onslaught of chunky snowflakes clumped on the windshield wipers, which beat in time to her favorite song as Jordan negotiated carefully down the streets, arriving at Ronan's at the designated time. The girls were waiting restlessly, but before she took off her coat, Jordan checked to make sure she had the tiny vial of holy water in her jeans pocket.

"Lighten up, Jordan," Ronan said, sensing Jordan's anxiety. "This will be a riot." Her lips twitched. "Come into the kitchen. We have the board set up."

Ronan ushered them down the hall, her stoic expression unnerving. "Everyone take a seat." Her biting eyes centered on Jordan. "We can learn more today. My sources tell me your father was highly involved with the cult, and I suspect he was disloyal."

Jordan's clipped intake of breath was noticeable by all.

Ronan's theory wasn't finished. "I believe your father offered his firstborn child to Satan in exchange for a high rank in the organization. But Jack Chase betrayed the cult and now you are the sacrificial consolation prize, if you know what I mean. What I couldn't quite grasp was something about an omen." She raised her face to the ceiling with her index finger tapping her lips and then looked back at Jordan.

Ronan waited as if Jordan would say anything at this point. Then, precise and to the point, she breathed, "The warrior will be one with...with..." She smirked sideways. "Lucifer..."

Stunned, Jordan figured Ronan's condemned spirits helped her in more ways than one. She ignored Cayden and

Paisley's big eyes—they looked at Jordan as if she were the devil's advocate.

"What's a warrior?" Cayden said, breaking the suspense.

"Oh, shut it, Cayden," Paisley snipped.

"That's what we'd all like to know," said Ronan, looking at Paisley. "Sometimes there are compromises, ways to pacify the spirits. Your father might be able to help." Ronan lit the candles stationed on each corner of the Ouija board while chanting an unintelligible verse and switching off the kitchen lights.

She moved confidently. Obviously, she had done this before.

"Okay, hold hands," Ronan coached. "Close your eyes and concentrate. They are here, just waiting for us. Come, come, we are waiting. *Atelum—ergo—pastillom devaloag.*"

There was a brief silence, then Ronan invoked the spirit of Davian. Her voice dredged the bottom of her diaphragm.

She was hooked.

Her head rocked from shoulder to shoulder like a metronome, and her almond eyes rolled from side to side. The words of her spell transcended time, mantling them in some sort of stupor. Her face twisted, disrupting her impeccable features.

Jordan tensed, struggling to manage her unbidden tremors. Her heart pumped frantically against her ribcage. She inhaled and exhaled shakily. Fluid puddled in her palms as she held tightly to Paisley and Cayden's hands.

"Jack Chase, your daughter is here for you," Ronan said, her tone oddly wistful.

The candles flamed higher, a freeze blanketing the room. Clouds of cool vapor formed before their gasping mouths as inky silhouettes drew their eyes toward the walls and ceiling. Then an obscure form hovered precariously close. An unsightly sneer ruffled Ronan's mouth, satisfied with the arrival of her spirit *friends.*

Jordan's body shivered from head to toe.

"I feel the spirits among us. Speak. Speak." Ronan's voice came from somewhere deep inside. Her head lolled backward as the throaty words rose to a higher pitch.

Like a magnetic current, the bristling hair on Jordan's arms came to life, pulling them to attention. Her gut impulse—that inner voice—issued a distinct warning.

A condensed humidity grew and the girls gagged as a putrid odor sealed the room. Candles plumed upward like geysers, staining the ceiling. Churning smoke merged into unsettling, ghostly shapes that billowed capriciously about the room.

Cayden's crushing grip cut off circulation to Jordan's fingers. Jordan glanced at her. Her forehead rested on the table, her eyes crunched shut.

"Jack? Jack?" Ronan asked with relish. "Do you have something to say to Jordan?"

"Dad…" Jordan's lips moved almost soundlessly.

"He's here, Jordan," confirmed Ronan, her voice beguiling.

Scarcely controlling her body, Jordan watched in disbelief as the planchette began to move—without being touched. Ronan's insistent, domineering voice rang out, "Jack, can you help Jordan?"

The planchette came to rest on the B then slid to E-W-A-R-E. Then it paused.

"Beware," Ronan repeated.

Sluggishly, the planchette began to move again, first to M, then A, then R. Suddenly, a turbulent gust of warm air swept it off the board. Airborne for a fraction of a second, it slammed violently against the wall, where it smashed to pieces.

Cayden's head bolted up. "What was *tha–a–t–t?*"

Jordan hurriedly fished in her pocket for the vial. It fumbled from her fingers and rolled to the floor.

The gust ramped to a squall, roiling smoky figures with gaping maws: bloated, panic-stricken, half-faced entities. Horrible shrieking cries of anguish pierced their eardrums as they streamed by, in what appeared to be pain. They exploded from the room. Jordan clamped her eyes shut, ducking her head toward the table. Murky figures splattered her face. Unable to avoid inhaling the airy sludge, she choked.

The figures vanished. Relieved, Jordan wiped the inside of her lips and tongue on her shirt. Paisley and Cayden frowned, grumbling to themselves as they swiped at ashy particles. They rubbed burning eyes, blinking back tears. The upheaval even rendered Ronan speechless.

Incredulous, they stared at what was left of the planchette. Even more extreme, the candle flames seemed unaffected by all the wind. They burned just as they had when Ronan lit them.

"That won't stop me. I have another oracle in my room," Ronan hissed, more to herself than to the girls.

"Ronan," Paisley said, spitting and mopping her face on her sleeve, "was that Jordan's father telling her to beware?"

Collecting her thoughts, Ronan answered, "Yes. I believe." She swiveled to Jordan. "You'd better beware, Jordan. Who could M-A-R possibly be? Maybe Mark?" Her opinion was clear.

Jordan wished she could speak with her father—though not like this. Ronan's rip-off disappointed her. She had played Jordan, bringing up her father to make sure she would go along. And Jordan certainly didn't need to *beware of Mark.*

What was the real message behind the séance that Ronan and Davian had staged? Jordan recalled Thrill's words regarding Ronan's insane jealousy. More than likely, Ronan had picked this childish prank as a way of getting back at Jordan for spending time with *her* Mark.

Needless to say, Jordan had no doubt that Ronan was an established clairvoyant and this made her a threat to everyone. And now, she faced the impossible task of discouraging Ronan from releasing more spirits. All the same, Jordan played the game and asked Ronan doubtfully, "Why would my father say to beware of Mark?"

Cayden and Paisley had snuffed the candles and toggled on the kitchen lights. A little warmth had returned to help dispel Jordan's goose bumps.

Ronan held her shoulders in a shrug. "There must be a reason, but only your father knows. I'll try to get more information. The powers get stronger every day, and I've become

like a receptacle. I feel them and hear what they're saying...most of the time. It's like they drop the veil. They open
the door for me to get in. I love it."

Jordan promptly thought, *And for them to get out.*

"What do we really know about Mark?" Paisley asked.

"Nothing." Ronan's brow furrowed. "But I'll find out—
soon. Mark and I are more than just friends." Her lids half-
shaded her lying eyes. "We talk about the Ouija and séances.
He says they're practices of the devil and we should stop dabbling with the unknown, but he seems definitely interested."
She snorted. "I'd like to tell him I more than just dabble." She
didn't elaborate.

Easing the heels of her feet onto the chair, Jordan
wrapped her arms around her knees, listening to Ronan's bab-
ble. Her dialogue confirming, wicked spirits seeped through
the chasm created by people like Ronan.

"The spirits are getting clearer, more distinct," Ronan
said. "I have gifts you can't even imagine. Mark doesn't get
it—the magic, the power." Her cryptic stare was creepy. "I get
such a rush when we break through the barrier and talk to
them. Jordan, you should have been here last week. They were
literally in our heads."

Jordan glanced at Cayden and Paisley. From their
blanched faces, they weren't too keen about spirits being "literally in their heads." In fact, Cayden, her eyes weirdly haunted, looked entranced. Jordan clapped her hands, aiming to get
her attention.

"Cayden, Cayden?"

Cayden belched. "What happened? I feel sick." She doubled over and puked on the floor.

Jordan scrambled to Cayden's side, dragging her to the
bathroom. She applied a wet towel to the back of her friend's
neck and forehead. Jordan heard Paisley griping about slop-
ping up puke while Ronan chuckled, either at Paisley's displeasure or Cayden's.

"I'm better, Jordan, thanks," Cayden said tonelessly.

Poor Cayden was physically and mentally beat. Jordan
grasped her elbow and helped her into the kitchen. The maca-

bre house reeked. Jordan fought an urge to run, lugging Cayden with her.

Propping Cayden against the wall, Jordan muttered, "I'd better drive Cayden home."

"You can't leave yet, Jordan. We need to substantiate what Dav—what your dad was trying to tell us." Ronan's face gave her away. She knew she'd blundered.

"I *know* I need to beware," Jordan said succinctly and uncaring. "Now I'd better get Cayden and myself home before the roads get worse or my mom will come out searching for me."

Paisley had rallied and interceded. "Cayden, you'll be okay for a few minutes while we talk, won't you?"

She hiccoughed "No, no, not really."

Jordan draped Cayden's arm over her shoulder, getting her to the front door where she scrabbled with their coats. Ronan and Paisley watched, leering.

Ronan held her hand aloft. "Here, I think you dropped this."

She sauntered over and dropped the vial of holy water in Jordan's upturned palm. Unperturbed with Ronan's attitude, Jordan pocketed the vial.

Her eyes not disclosing her thoughts, Ronan peered at Jordan. "I'll find a solution for the sacrificial offering."

Ronan's remark left Jordan speculating. Either Ronan wanted to help her or kill her. With her mind whirling, Jordan clutched Cayden's waist and hauled her to the car.

ℰᦔℰᦔ

That night Jordan rolled from one side of the bed to the other as nonstop deviltry stalked her through the hours of darkness. Even in her dreams, her pulse skyrocketed with monstrous scenes of sadistic torture.

The next day Jordan moped through the school in a daze. She felt feverish, cold, and damp. Her nightmare persisted even though she was fully awake.

The hallways became a hellish transport to pandemonium. Knotting fingers in her hair, Jordan cradled her head, striving to protect herself from incessant urges. She was losing control.

Over and over, she called for Markus's help, trying to keep her psyche to a minor growl. Classmates gawked strangely at her stumbling. Surely word was already spreading that Jordan was on some kind of drug. An hour before lunch, delirium set in. Jordan marched out of the school, coatless, in subzero temperatures. Without a second thought, she tramped home.

By the time she'd barged through the front door, her face was a bluish-white. Every patch of Jordan's body felt hot, then cold, as she shivered. When Henry saw her condition, he hobbled over and helped her up the staircase. He tucked her into bed while Em scuttled for hot tea and warm blankets.

Jordan slept till dinnertime. She opened her eyes, unprepared for a muted, familiar room, then plodded downstairs.

Seeley took in her daughter's disheveled, colorless appearance. "Jordan, I just checked and you were sound asleep. You should stay in bed. I'll bring something up."

Jordan's head was swimming, as if she were drowning in a nightmare. Her mind registered the woman's concern. A surge of hostility rose like a volcano. It took all her control not to shake. "I'm fine, and I'm not hungry," she groused. Pivoting fast, she took the stairs two at a time. She ran into the bedroom, slamming and bolting the door.

"What'd you think?" Seeley asked, baffled. "Is she getting sick? Jordan's never acted like this before."

Henry grumped. And Em's lips pressed together. "Could be boy trouble. This past weekend we saw her go out with two different boys."

Seeley frowned. "Two? What two boys?"

"Jordan said one of the boy's was William McKenna—he drove her home from school, and remember Deacon Schaffer's exchange student, Mark, picked her up last Saturday."

Seeley nodded, though not convinced. After dinner she tapped on Jordan's door. When there wasn't a response she jiggled the handle. "Jordan, it's Mom. Can you open up?" She heard the bed squeak and the lock click.

With the curtains drawn, the light in the bedroom was bleak. Jordan had gone back to the bed and lay curled in a ball.

"Jordan," Seeley whispered. "What's wrong?"

Shaking her head, Jordan muttered, "I don't know. Maybe I'm getting sick? I–I feel...different." More than different, Jordan thought she was going crazy. One minute she recognized her mom, and the next...

Seeley switched on the bedside lamp and squatted in front of her daughter. She pulled Jordan's hands away from her face and scrutinized weary, puffy eyelids. "This has nothing to do with a boy, does it?"

"No. I didn't sleep a wink last night. So many bad dreams, I need—I need—sleep."

"What kind of bad dreams?"

"Bad—Really bad, now leave me alone." Jordan glared at the woman, and for a nanosecond, wondered why she couldn't remember her.

"Here I've been meaning to give this to you." A chain of rosary beads threaded from Seeley's pocket. Unfolding Jordan's hand, Seeley poured the rosary onto her palm then curled Jordan's fingers over the beads. "I know they're worn. Prayer shackles Satan. Use it often." Jordan flinched, the beads felt extremely hot, like they were burning her hand. "Perhaps Markus could help."

Jordan's face grew livid. "Now that he's *human*, I'm nothing. Not as important as Ronan or even Beth. He couldn't care less about me. Mark thinks he's so...so high and mighty. He makes me sick."

Astounded at her outburst, Seeley said soothingly, "Okay, honey, okay." Spreading the quilt up to Jordan's shoulders, she felt her warm forehead. "You might have a smidge of a fever. I'll check in on you later. Get some rest."

With the woman out of the room, Jordan's fingers unfolded, rosary beads tinkling to the floor. She gaped at the red swelling blisters on her palms.

An hour later, quietly slipping into Jordan's room, Seeley halted. A young man hunkered above her daughter. Seeley registered Jordan's flushed face and the sound of her ragged breathing.

Markus looked at Seeley, troubled. "She appears ill."

Seeley uncapped a jar she held and, dabbing her fingers in the holy oil, anointed Jordan's sweltering forehead. Jordan recoiled and cried out, burying her head under the pillow.

"I thought Father James helped her on Saturday," Seeley said. "And I assumed that would protect her from the séance."

"Trebane's a powerful enemy. Father James definitely alleviated his curse, yet the séance could have countered his protection. Father told Jordan to see him again, but I doubt if she made the time."

Her eyes implored Markus for guidance. "What do we need to do?"

"You need to leave the room."

"No. I want to be here—to help."

Markus transformed, bathing the room with angelic brilliance. His sparkling eyes looked at Seeley. "If I expel a legion from Jordan, it might transfer, tunnel within you, and remain hidden."

Seeley knew Markus was right. In her travels and busy days, her prayer life had taken a backseat.

Jordan's brain was in a turmoil of horrid visions. She saw souls gnashing their teeth in a fiery pit, clawing at the walls, beckoning pitilessly. She faced suppurating corpses and disjointed orifices, verbally cursing, while blank eye sockets eerily sought her. Then Jordan saw her once handsome father, searching. His body was deteriorating, rinds of blackened flesh peeled from his torso. His arms and fingers were groping robotically. Mesmerizing emerald eyes fastened on her, then they altered to a blazing red. She tried to run, but her legs felt like they were sealed in concrete. Her father's face progressively faded, only to be replaced by an angelic man. Markus.

Beware of Mark?

Beware of Mark!

In her dream, Jordan was able to back away in terror as Markus transformed into a fiendish devil.

From a faraway place, Jordan heard his voice, strong and patient. Sitting feebly up in bed, she found Markus looming above. His intense gaze frightened her.

He examined Jordan's bleary eyes and ashen face, evaluating the signs of possession.

"Leave me alone," she growled.

The abrasive croak was not Jordan's voice. Afraid to glimpse his face, afraid to see him deforming, she felt her bones seemingly liquefy in aversion to Markus's presence.

Someone in Jordan's head screamed, '*He's a demon! He's trying to hurt me!*' She leapt from the bed, skittering around—out of control. "Markus, are you the answer to Jack and Seeley's prayers?" She did not recognize the harsh voice as her own.

Markus used his angelic presence to herd her, keeping her in the room. "Something like that."

"She must be sacrificed. Jack initiated the blood rite—and the prophecy cannot be evaded." The voice was vile. "Your deity will weep…"

"Is the prophecy inspired by my Father?" Markus argued, his tone steady. "All the virtuous may seek divine intercession."

"We will find a way," the demon insisted. "Ronan has become capable—"

Markus cut him off sharply. "She has a gullible nature and a fragile mind."

The creature within Jordan glowered. "You're here to protect more than one soul? How clever!"

With a rapid jerk, the demon filched a pair of scissors from the dresser. "You don't want this supple young thing disfigured, do ya?" The shears bit into Jordan's cheek, raising a pink ridge. "Stay back or this perty girl loses an eyeball," the creature warned.

Markus maneuvered in front of the demon. Both circled the room, their eyes locked, waiting for the next move. "What's your name, beast?" the angel demanded in a low tone.

The creature chortled. "Wouldn't you like ta know?"

Scissor tips dipped to her throat, penetrating her pliable skin. The cut deepened and split a vivid scarlet stripe. Blood ribboned Jordan's neck like a lacy collar.

Grimacing, Markus released his breath. "*Davian*?"

"Ho, ho—close, but no cigar. Davian's my brother, I'm called Legion. I no longer have a name except what my master calls me." With a flick of Legion's wrist, the sharp point pressed into Jordan's stomach. The demon sidestepped closer to the window.

"You know you can't win this, Legion." Markus said, stepping forward.

"You don't want her damaged!" Legion's tone was shifty. "Or worse—dead!"

She heard the command in her mind. '*Jump out the window. That's the way to escape him.*'

Vanquished somewhere inside a torrid dimension, the tiny spark that had been Jordan fought desperately. Unable to find a passageway back to her body, she lost the struggle and dove toward the glass.

Phenomenally agile, Markus caught the beast, wrenching the scissors from her unyielding fingers. The creature howled when Markus's iron grip clamped her waist. Jordan lashed out, pummeling his rock hard chest. His hands held her roughly, shaking her, then pinning her against the wall.

"I warned you, Jordan. What have you done?" His once friendly eyes were condemning.

The demon burrowed within Jordan, cognitive of the potent angel and wary of his brutality. "I don't know what you're talking about. Let me go." Her body squirmed, grappling to break from his embrace.

"The demon spirit is in you, Jordan," Markus spat, revolted by the beast within. "Fight back—stave him off."

Legion yowled.

"The spirit is having fun possessing your untarnished soul. Legion can destroy you."

"Markus, I should beware of *you*." Her voice rose hysterically. "You're the demon! You're the evil one!" Again she thrashed, trying to break his grasp.

Markus's eyes softened. Releasing her arms, he crushed Jordan to his chest and caressed her hair.

Untamed tears wet Jordan's cheeks. Markus spoke. His tone was mellow, albeit with grand authority. His divine words bound the besmirched Legion.

The imploding rampage came from within—Jordan's head felt like a balloon pumped with water, nearing its breaking point. Instinctively, she endeavored to find some form of stability.

Markus gripped her firmly. His ceaseless prayer felt like he was sucking the life from her soul. Hatred ruptured her brain and her body seized jerkily as Legion departed, leaving her defenseless form withered in revenge.

Markus gathered Jordan in his arms and gently laid her on the bed. Her burning eyes opened briefly. His distraught, angelic face swam out of focus.

CHAPTER 11

Untoward Talons.

Shirking the curtains, a crack of light crossed the windowsill. The beam speared Jordan's eyelids. Her battered body, soaked in icky sweat, sprawled over the mattress. She chucked the quilt to the floor, hoping cool air would revitalize her. Then she felt just plain cold, so she dragged herself off the bed. Staggering upright, she noted the brightness of the room and, glimpsing the clock, she grumbled—two hours late for school.

Padding into the kitchen half an hour later, her hair still wet after a hasty shower, Jordan found her grandparents and mother eating breakfast. "Why didn't you wake me?"

Seeley examined Jordan's face. "I thought you could use the day off to rest."

"That was some party you had in your bedroom last night," Henry butted in. "All that noise and banging around."

Seeley saw Jordan's muddled expression and realized she had no memory of the night. She turned to her dad. "Jordan was sick most of the night. I kept running to check on her. Come on, Jordan. Let me take you back up to bed."

Jordan started to piece together random memories as she tailed her mom up the staircase and into her mom's room. Jordan flopped on her mother's bed. "Was it as bad as I think it was?"

Jordan knew something had gone terribly wrong. And was saddened when her mom turned. Her face revealed anguished fatigue, fine lines, and shadowy bloodshot eyes.

"Yes, it was bad." Seeley pinched the bridge of her nose. "I don't know what I would've done if we didn't have Markus and Zeke."

"Was Zeke there too?"

"He was standing by...for support." She turned toward the closet. "I have to go to work today. I need you to rest and then borrow Henry's car and go see Father James again."

"That was the creepiest feeling ever." Jordan's mind filled up with unpleasant thoughts. "It felt like...like I was there, but...screaming behind some kind of blockade. I feel so used."

Seeley placed a tender kiss on Jordan's head and hurriedly climbed into black linen slacks, a white button-down blouse, and a tweed jacket.

Already an hour late for work, Seeley hoped Mr. Donavan wouldn't be too angry. Thankfully the snowplows had cleared the highway to the city. Traffic thinned as Seeley veered off the ramp to Swan Street. Out of the corner of her eye, she saw a dreadfully familiar face. Decked out in a designer zebra coat and corresponding leather boots, that provocative stride and those hand movements belonged to none other than Veronka. To her right walked a girl with silky black hair, possibly Jordan's age.

Seeley felt an imperative need to warn the girl of her dire mistake in hanging with a demon. Did the young girl even know? Obsessed to the brink of madness, she slammed on the brakes, parked, and bolted out of the car. People bundled in winter apparel crammed the sidewalk, blocking Seeley's erratic advance. She prodded and snaked her way among the throngs and spied the striped fur entering a coffee shop.

Seeley paused for a moment before she went in. A plan was needed. She peeked through the storefront window and glimpsed the girl's profile.

Veronka suddenly swerved her head—meeting Seeley's gaze. Smug red lips sneered, and Veronka leaned toward the girls head, whispering in her ear. The girl's mouth parted in laughter. Veronka then wound her arm around the girl's back, almost maternally, and turned her away from Seeley.

The motherly gesture was more than Seeley could stomach. She headed in to confront Veronka, whose talons embedded the naive teenager. As she marched in, her heels skidded on a patch of ice, hurling her backward. A pair of arms rescued her from utter humiliation.

"My, my, so nice of you to drop in, Seeley," said a superficial voice.

Seeley came face-to-face with Asa. She flicked her eyes toward the coffee shop window. Apparently, today's schedule included a congregation of fiends. Retreating from his inscrutable gaze, Seeley felt the mystifying electricity the man transmitted.

"Are you recruiting, Asa?"

"Whatever do you mean, Seeley?" He relished her name on his lips.

Seeley angled her head, indicating the coffee shop. "Your demon slave is holding a teenager hostage."

"The *girl* came to us through, shall we say, channels." He made a throaty noise, pleased with his own witticism. "She needs our expertise in handling certain…devices and skills."

Seeley brushed her coat sleeves, shaking off the sensation of Asa's contact. Feeling ill equipped to rescue the girl from their clutches, Seeley sighed. "Does she even know what or who she's dealing with?"

"It was her choice to meet with us on numerous occasions."

"I want to talk to her."

Asa clasped her wrist in a surprisingly strong hold. "Enough. Enough of your savior exploits," he ordered harshly. "You can't stop people from seeking spiritualism."

Seeley wrestled her wrist out of Asa's grasp. "So that's what you call it?"

"I give up." He lifted his hands as if he was surrendering. "Go and talk with the girl. But be warned, you won't like what you hear."

Seeley moved toward the store's entrance. Behind her, Asa's voice sounded like it was wound so tight, it was ready to snap. "I'm no longer a patient man, Seeley. I'll need your decision soon—very soon. We'll meet again."

Seeley shrugged off the man's threat and stepped into the tantalizing aroma of coffee. Scanning the patrons from table to table, Seeley counted a majority of red-ringed eyes scowling at her. She walked briskly to the restrooms then back to the front. Veronka and the girl had vanished. Shouldering the doors, she stepped outside and looked in every direction. She saw no sign of the women, or Asa.

Repressing her abhorrence for the creatures, Seeley shoved her hands into her coat pockets. Her fingers twiddled with a plastic container of holy water. Mustering her courage, she uncapped the container and held it beneath her coat sleeve. With her arm across her chest, Seeley headed discreetly back into the coffee shop.

She meandered around the room, feigning interest in sketches exhibited on the walls. Lowering her arm, Seeley dribbled holy water over the shop floors, already pooling with tracked in snow.

Scrambling out the door, she leaned her back against a brick wall. Her heart pumped with energy. She concentrated, focusing her psyche on the restaurant's wet tile. She couldn't see it happening, but felt the intensity, inside of her. The water rippled faintly and then began to bubble and sputter, as if it were boiling. The shop rang with fiendish shrieks as a shower of holy water rained—from the floor up.

Striding to the car, a confident smirk on her face, Seeley complimented herself on a task well done.

ოჯო

Seeley was editing a controversial article on euthanasia, when her boss, Declan Donavan, signaled her into his office. Smothering an irritating yawn, she grabbed pen and paper. As she settled into a less than comfortable wooden chair, she analyzed the pragmatic man shuffling paperwork. As standard procedure, he had discarded his suit coat early in the morning. An indigo, linen, button-down shirt stretched across his shoulders and was tucked crisply into tawny pants at a trim waistline. She admired Mr. Donavan's distinguished salt-and-pepper hair and rugged features. Looking up from a hodge-podge of paperwork, his intense eyes captured Seeley's scrutiny.

With a cocky grin, he handed Seeley the *Business First* newspaper, featuring a photo of Asa Trebane and his associates at the Financial Seminar in Pennsylvania.

"This affluent man lives in our area." Mr. Donavan tapped the picture with his hand. "He's secretive, wealthy, and a hometown boy. Seeley, I want you to interview Mr. Trebane for a feature article for the business section."

Her mouth dropped open. She'd never refused her boss an assignment, but this was too much. "Declan, this isn't for me. Ask Charlie or Max. They're the financial experts."

Declan leaned easily on the edge of his desk. "Yes, but they'd never dig down to the nitty-gritty of the man as you would, Seeley. They'd get the facts and figures, but I want more than that."

"How can I get more information from Mr. Trebane than Charlie?"

Declan's gaze surfed over Seeley. "Have you looked in a mirror lately?" His tone was husky, lower than normal. "Who wouldn't tell you their whole life story? And don't start harping on sexual harassment. I think you're capable of going deeper and getting the scoop."

Her cheeks flushed at Declan's candid compliment. Tucking a stray piece of hair behind her ear, she asked, "Can I think about it, Dec?"

His gaze was disquieting. "Don't think too long," he snapped. But the corner of his mouth bent up, softening his eyes.

Back at her desk, Seeley noted the time and called Jordan to check on her.

"Feeling great, Mom, no adverse reactions. By the way, I talked with Father James. Everything's cool."

"Good, I'll be home shortly," confirmed Seeley, keeping her voice level.

"I know you're probably wiped, but could we go to the mall tonight? The Winter Ball's coming up and I don't have anything to wear."

Seeley couldn't help smiling—anything to get her mind off the assignment. "That'd be fine, but only for about an hour or so. I definitely need to get a good night's rest."

ᆼᅩᆺᅩ

The mall, overcrowded with holiday shoppers, was bedecked for the season in bright red, gold, and silver balls, plus myriads of sparkly trees and holly swags. Christmas carols rang loud and clear, enticing shoppers with the spirit of giving.

Seeley and Jordan rifled through formal and informal, strapless and beaded, racks and racks of pricy dresses. Sorting the array of offerings, they gathered armloads and found a fitting room. Seeley helped her daughter with zippers, buttons, and opinions.

A red sequined gown exposed more than Seeley wanted to see of her sixteen-year-old. Jordan sashayed to the threefold mirror. Seeley bit her tongue, hoping Jordan would reconsider. Jordan struck an assortment of modeling poses and both women snickered. Their laughter bounced gaily off the walls.

"So what do you think?" Jordan paraded elegantly past her mother. The exquisite gown molded every slender curve.

Seeley hemmed, her expression peaked. "You look …nice."

Jordan rolled her eyes. "Really, Mom? I wouldn't be caught dead in this dress. I just thought it'd be fun to try on."

"Phew." Seeley swiped her forehead. "For a minute I was worried."

They giggled. An hour later, they'd purchased a tea-length emerald dress, now slung over Jordan's arm.

"How 'bout stopping for coffee or hot chocolate?" Jordan asked her mom.

"Sounds good. Shopping always makes me thirsty."

They made their way to a trendy café and unwound in a booth, indulging in hot mocha with gobs of whipped cream. After a bit, Seeley recounted the events at the coffee shop, though she left out Asa's warning.

Her eyes blazed with fervor as she spoke, sharing her worry about the young girl with Veronka. Though, she could not restrain her modest self-satisfaction as she told Jordan how she had expelled Lucifer's legions.

It was after ten when they'd breezed into the little white house.

"Wow, Em, the house is so festive," Jordan cried out.

With her head in the downstairs closet, Em called back, "We thought we'd surprise you girls."

"You did," said Seeley, concerned. "But you should've waited for us to help. You and Dad must be exhausted."

Em shuffled to the living room and parked herself on the overstuffed blue lounger. "Your dad's already snoring in bed, and I'm ready to follow him. But I waited up to see the dress Jordan picked out for the dance."

Seeley could only imagine her mom's comments if they'd come home with the sequined red. Pegging their snowy coats on the rack, Jordan then slipped off the plastic bag containing the emerald dress and held it up for her grandmother.

"Lovely," Em said, beaming. "You'll look stunning, Jordan. Now I'm off to bed."

"I'm right behind you, Mom," said Seeley.

Jordan ambled through the home, checking out the Christmas decorations fondly and carefully displayed.

Whimsical snowmen and Santa Claus collectibles sat on poinsettia doilies and garlands of fake holly and ivy looped the stairwell.

A ceramic Christmas tree sparkled with multicolored lights and a three-tiered German carousel with wooden figurines rested on the end table.

It depicted the manger scene on the middle tier with shepherd and sheep below and angels tooting horns on the upper deck. Jordan set the top wooden slats in motion, delighted as the figures twirled. She smiled.

CHAPTER 12

Celebrate, the Worst Is Yet to Come.

The internal strain Jordan had experienced all day melted under hot cascading water. Fairly uptight about her first high school dance, she scrubbed fastidiously, striving to keep her mind a blank, but it wasn't working. She'd heard the words often enough, "geek" and, recently, "the weird girl who lives in the woods." She told herself that it didn't matter what they thought of her. She went to the school to do a job—like saving them from the beasties.

Not usually one for primping, she took an inordinate amount of time drying and brushing her hair. Satisfied with its shine, she applied a light layer of mascara. Sliding into the green dress and slipping her foot into her new high heels, Jordan felt extremely clumsy. She tottered across the room, then back again, trying to walk in a somewhat dignified manner.

Her mother stood in the doorway, beaming with pride. She held a small velvet box, which she offered to Jordan. "I have something for you. These are from your father. He'd want you to have them."

Confused, Jordan lifted the lid to discover exquisite, glittering emerald studs. She looked up at her mother. "Mom, I can't take your precious earrings."

Seeley's encouraging smile warmed Jordan. "I loved your father's eyes, and yours are exactly like his. When he gave them to me he said, 'So you'll always remember me.'"

છબલ

Rolly, Thrill, Cayden, Paisley, and Ronan gathered at Jordan's house, the closest to the school. Her friends assembled in formal attire, looking out of place in her rinky-dink living room.

Full-bodied Paisley had stuffed herself into a rosy-mauve gown that flattered her bodacious curves. Her platinum hair, caught up in a French twist, showed off the tat Jordan had learned was called an ouroboros. A fragile chain connected her nose ring to her right earring, a knotted series of links that hung to her shoulders.

Cayden's maroon dress made her appear even thinner. Well over six-feet tall in pumps, she had her wispy locks drawn back in a rhinestone clip with matching earrings. However, no one compared to Ronan, sensational in a silk magenta halter dress. A dipping cowl collar revealed an expanse of olive skin. The silken fabric hugged her passionately. Her glossy hair layered in ringlets tickled her bare back. Dark almond-shaped eyes were emphasized in kohl outliner. The effect was bewitching. Thin strands of diamonds pierced her earlobes, and circling Ronan's neck were woven threads supporting a lone pendant, a horned diamond that drew every eye as it rested, sandwiched between her fleshy mounds.

Thrill spiffed-up exceptionally well, accenting his athletic build with a charcoal gray suit, a white button-down shirt, and a multicolored striped tie. His affable amber eyes glinted adorably under artfully tousled sienna hair. Jordan decided no girl would be able to resist the eligible quarterback.

Rolly, large and in charge, the constant jester with his barking laughter, had borrowed his father's exceedingly big brown suit coat, which made him look even larger. Wearing the suit coat over a pair of jeans, he said, "I'm not out to impress."

Seeley grinned proudly, admiring her daughter. Jordan lacked a pretentious nature, and her beauty came naturally. Her mane of burnished-auburn hair carpeted sumptuously over her shoulders. Jordan was adorned in satiny emerald with a light mesh overlay embellished with swirls of gold and silver glitter. Held up by spaghetti straps, the princess neckline had tiny pearls dotting the bodice and shaped Jordan's curves tenderly, down to a sash which accented her tiny waistline, then flowed slightly below her knees. The dress's hue heightened Jordan's vivid emerald eyes and defined cheekbones.

Henry, sprawled in his brown recliner, scrutinized the gregarious guests' comedic nonsense. Jordan glimpsed his toothy grin as he chuckled noiselessly over their antics. After all the introductions, Seeley wrestled the rambunctious, reluctant teenagers, trying to get them to hold still for pictures.

She took one last candid snapshot of the group laughing. Checking the camera's screen to see if it came out, her whole body tensed. Ronan's laughing profile transported Seeley back to the coffee shop. It was Ronan—the girl with Veronka!

It made perfect sense. Being in league with Veronka would explain the girl's supernatural skills. Snatching a small purse from the hall closet, Seeley stashed a vial of holy water in it—just in case.

"Here's your purse, Jordan."

"Mom, I don't have a purse," Jordan said, baffled.

Seeley opened the clutch so Jordan could see the vial. "You do now."

Jordan took the purse begrudgingly. "Thanks, Mom."

A motherly grin curled Seeley's lips, and she watched as Thrill helped Jordan into her coat. They all piled out the door, but not before Seeley hugged Jordan and whispered, "Have fun, and be careful."

They walked out underneath an infinite velveteen sky, and the background for a superb waxing moon and winking stars. The walkway was a sheet of ice as they carefully shuffled to Thrill's car.

Cayden performed a graceless slip and fell into Paisley's arms. "You're so clumsy, Cayden," Paisley said snippily as she righted the tall girl, chortling at Cayden's expense. Cold breath wreathed their heads.

The car was bursting with high expectations as Thrill zoomed down the driveway. Halfway down the avenue, he

said, "Perfect out of the way street for a few strategic doughnuts."

Everyone in the car yelped, or laughed, as the Chevelle
whipped around, full circle, on the slick asphalt. Jordan
couldn't decide if the ride was fun and hoped they were out of
range of her mom's eyesight.

Cars and limousines unloading passengers jammed the
school's drive. Most kids parked in the lot and walked, mindful of the slush as plump snowflakes fell lackadaisically. Rolly
and Thrill stationed themselves on either side of Jordan.

Thrill angled near Jordan's ear and said, "I didn't want to
say anything in front of your mother, but you are hot tonight,
girl!"

On hearing Thrill, Rolly bobbed his head in agreement,
grinning from ear to ear. Thrill steadied Jordan's elbow as they
crossed a snowdrift.

The decorating committee had performed a miracle, transforming the gymnasium into a winter garden. Twinkling miniature white lights and shiny silver stars hung from the ceiling.
Variable sizes of artificial pine trees sprayed with fake snow
glittered along the perimeter of the gym. Silver melamine covered the tables, topped with glass jars which were filled with
pillar candles.

Jordan wasn't surprised when, one by one, girls clung to
Thrill's arm, asking him to dance even before the music started. His mouth curved charmingly, confidently handling the
parade of starry-eyed teens. Needless to say, every girl eyed
Jordan up and down as if she was some kind of freak of nature.
Then when Thrill put his hand on her shoulder to guide her
through the tables, Jordan spied the same scowl on Paisley's
face.

One couple had claimed a prime table next to the dance
floor, but not for long. Ronan stalked around them, and they
bolted without confrontation. Jordan shrugged apologetically
at the duo as Ronan announced tactlessly, "I found a great table, guys. Take a seat."

Perceptibly rubbernecking, Jordan was amazed at the
metamorphoses. Sophistication graced the rural village of

Elma. Guys looked polished and acted courteously in their suits, while the girls in elaborate gowns made a vibrant bouquet of rich fabrics.

Ronan and Paisley drew Jordan's gaze to the door, where Beth Schaffer, along with Markus and friends, had just entered. With his height and good looks, Markus stood out in the crowd. His wheat-colored hair was uncharacteristically groomed, emphasizing his prominent cheekbones and strong chin. Something Beth said to him produced a perfect smile. Beth, of course, looked spectacular in a strapless, champagne, crimped wrap. Jordan couldn't help observing as girls and guys alike turned their heads to stare at the newcomers.

Markus waved to Jordan and, leading his friends to the table, asked kindly, "Mind if we join you?"

"Of course you can," Ronan said amiably. "Here sit next to me, Mark." She shooed Cayden off the chair for Mark to sit. Jordan made an effort not to smirk at Ronan's obvious mania—and not to blush when Thrill stroked her arm.

Finally, the music boomed to a round of applause. Not one to dither, Thrill immediately asked Jordan to dance, and a look of envy shaded Paisley's face. The Winter Ball rocked with a pumping, rhythmic beat as students converged, circulating around the gymnasium. Thrill wasn't only an excellent football player, his dance movements flowed with the beat, not jerky or overly awkward like so many of the guys on the floor.

Jordan barely caught her breath before Rolly yanked her onto the floor. "I love this song. Come on, Jor."

He danced outrageously and enjoyed making a spectacle with every move. Jordan laughed as he twirled her like a ballerina and, for a finale, wound his bulky arms around her waist and spun her in the air. Unwinding at this point, thanks to Rolly, Jordan decided to have a good time and not care how many people criticized their demonstration.

Thoughts of séances and demons flitted from Jordan's mind. She watched in amusement as Thrill dodged a pack of female admirers who were tailing him as if he were a king and they were ladies in waiting.

Paisley had asked Thrill to dance, and Jordan noticed the strain between them. Not wanting to be nosy, though she really was, Jordan asked Ronan, "Does Paisley like Thrill?"

Ronan's head wobbled from side to side, as if the answer was yes and no. "They've been friends forever. She just about lived at his house when we were younger. They were close, but this tarantula, Megan, got her fangs into him. Thrill thinks of Paisley as one of the guys. Paisley knows how he feels, and she needs to get over it."

Jordan nodded and kept her mouth shut about Megan, Thrill had explained that already.

Everyone appeared to be having a good time, though Jordan monitored the tension rising between Beth and Ronan. Each flanked Markus, attempting to grab his undivided attention.

Taking the initiative, Beth rose. "Mark, let's dance." Her tone was temperate, though crisp.

And Thrill joined the activity, in effect, hoisting Jordan to her feet and carrying her into the middle of the dancers.

"I think you can put me down, Thrill."

He chuckled and set her lightly on her toes.

Buried in Thrill's embrace, Jordan craned her neck to see Ronan's expression tied up in a knot. "Thrill, ask Ronan to dance. I think she feels uncomfortable with everyone more than likely remembering last year's...you know."

"Sure." He flashed Jordan a charismatic smile. "We wouldn't want Ronan to get mad at anyone." He administered a lasting squeeze to her waist.

Thrill headed toward Ronan and Jordan scanned the room, meeting the penetrating sapphire eyes of her human angel, so worldly that it almost scared her. She grinned.

The first hour passed speedily, though Ronan was unmistakably provoked. She wedged herself between Paisley and Jordan. "What the hell's going on with Mark? He hasn't asked Jordan to dance yet."

"Why would he ask me?" Jordan answered, stumped.

"The Ouija board—remember?" clarified Ronan. "Mark has to ask you to dance."

"That's a bunch of crap, Ronan," Jordan said tersely. "Let's forget about that and enjoy the dance." She saw a shadow shift in Ronan's eyes.

"We shall see, Jordan," Ronan said, her tone grim. "We shall see." She glided to the refreshment table and returned, carrying bottles of soda. She offered one to Jordan.

Jordan accepted gratefully, and they both watched Mark and Beth dancing nearby. Even though the tune had a fast tempo, Beth snuggled enticingly against him.

"She makes me sick," Ronan hissed. "Let's create a little havoc. What do you say, Jordan?"

Hoping to have a night free of spiritual warfare, Jordan sighed and asked cautiously, "What are you planning, Ronan?" She was anxious about Beth's welfare—the poor thing hadn't a clue what was in store for her. Before Jordan even finished her thought, a hollow shriek resonated down the school's hallway, mixing with the music. Everyone laughed. The product of a prank—or so they all thought.

Then after another scream and some girl running into the gym looking like she'd seen a ghost, more people started laughing. Then a voice in the pack shouted, "Hey, this isn't Halloween!" generating more chuckles.

However, Jordan kept her eye on the girl. She was speaking to a friend and pointed down the one of the corridors. The girl was obviously crying as she wiped under her eyes and walked to her table, visibly shaken.

When Jordan swiveled in her chair and saw Ronan studying Mark and Beth, she decided to take matters into her own hands. She foraged in her purse for the vial, soaked her hand with water, and then calmly walked over to Markus and Beth. Pretending to intrude, Jordan placed her hand on Beth's shoulders, coating her with traces of holy water. Then she said, "Beth, would you mind if I cut in and dance with Mark?"

Beth's lips parted, ready to object, but she relinquished her place, giving Mark a yearning look. "Sure, he's all yours—for the moment."

The upbeat tune ended, and a melodic slow song began. Jordan raised her hand to Markus's broad shoulders and felt his warm hold on her back. In silence, she moved stiffly, her legs pacing from side to side. Somehow, it was odd, circling the floor with her angel.

Markus broke the silence. "You danced easily enough with Thrill. Why so inflexible with me?"

Looking up, Jordan caught Markus's sarcastic grin, and she began to relax in his electrifyingly safe hold. For some reason, his fiery gaze flamed her cheeks in the twinkling lights. Ambivalent to the lapse of time, they glided together, two connected spirits magically skimming the dance floor.

The song faded and the moment passed. "Ronan's not happy," Jordan said, almost dreamily. "She's plotting something. Why don't you ask her to dance, maybe that'll cool her down?"

"If you think that'll help," Markus replied. Their fingers laced, and he guided her to the table.

"For a guy who's taken Ronan out a few times," Jordan said softly. "It would seem logical to ask her to dance—and stop being so cozy with Beth."

"Jealous, Jordan?" drawled Markus, a half-smile lighting his face.

"Absolutely not," she retorted. "Did you happen to notice the guy sitting next to me—sweet, built, the high school's star quarterback?"

"Be watchful of Thrill," Markus responded in a hushed voice. Then the angel wondered why he felt so dispirited. What was that feeling in his chest?

He had dragged her chair back, and Jordan shot him an inquiring look. It was too late to ask him what he meant by his remark.

People played musical chairs during a twenty-minute break for pizza and wings. Devouring cheesy pizza and greasy wings wasn't quite the gourmet meal Jordan had imagined.

Ronan swished past Jordan, saying bitterly, "I need some air—it stinks in here.

Paisley and Cayden huddled round Jordan.

"What's up? One minute Ronan was happy and the next..." Paisley's eyes narrowed and glared at Jordan. "You pissed her off."

"What do you mean?" said an exasperated Jordan, knowing full well that no one could hear her with all the noise.

"Ronan's probably furious because Mark hasn't asked her to dance." Cayden explained. "Then you go and ask him—and I distinctly remember she told you *not* to ask, remember? Duh—the Ouija board—and then the way the two of you danced..."

"You guys are idiots to think the Ouija can actually predict the future," said Jordan. "How many times do I have to tell you that Mark and I are just friends?"

Cayden and Paisley swapped looks.

"It was like...magic," Cayden said, becoming emotional. "The two of you seemed so...so...connected."

Jordan snickered, wondering what they'd say if she told them they'd been connected since her birth.

When Ronan returned her face was venomous. She sat broodingly and closed her eyes. She remained unusually quiet. Jordan peeked at her then shuddered with the changing environment. Heavy dread encompassed them like a pall.

Jordan stiffened as a chilling breeze brushed her face. She looked at Markus; his expression was grave and his lips moving silently. His eyes flicked over to meet hers.

An appalling gurgle brought him swiftly to his feet, overturning the chair. Beth's face was turning brick red as her eyes bulged, and her hands pawed at her throat.

Everyone was riveted as Markus clutched Beth's ribcage and performed the Heimlich Maneuver. The ominous sensation dissipated, and a miniscule piece of pizza flew out of Beth's mouth. She drew a life-saving breath as her beautiful face evolved from red to her natural tan.

"Wow man—that was brilliant!" Thrill clapped Markus on the back. "You've got to teach me that."

Not amused Markus slowly pivoted his head in Ronan's direction, his eyes scathing as she shrugged apathetically.

Bending over Beth, Markus asked, "Are you all right? Would you like to go home?"

"No, no," she croaked and smiled brokenly. "I'm fine, and the dance is only half over. That's what I get for always eating too fast."

Beth's friends Kristen and Jeff snickered lightly as relief rounded the table.

The disc jockey revved up the gym with a fast beat, impelling everyone to the floor. Markus tendered his hand to Ronan. A pleased look of triumph crossed her face. Bumping Jordan's chair as she passed, she wound her arm possessively though Markus's. Then, instead of leading Ronan to the dance floor, Markus escorted her out of the gym altogether.

Hardly able to contain herself, Jordan wondered what Markus was discussing with Ronan. In her opinion, Ronan had cast that spell to hurt Beth and to threaten Markus. Jordan then feared the worst. What if Ronan knew Mark was an angel?

Thrill's warm breath floated in Jordan's ear. "How about we dance?"

Jordan's thoughts evaporated with the touch of his hand. A delicious tingle swelled her insides when Thrill brushed his fingertips along her back. Settling her cheek on his chest, she sighed as they circled at a snail's pace. Jordan was beginning to loosen up when Ronan's giggling interrupted them.

Jordan looked over, grimacing. Ronan was grinding her hips provocatively against Markus. Her arms entwined his neck, pulling him toward her lips. He swerved his head, avoiding contact. Ronan seized the opportunity to nuzzle his throat and nibble his earlobe. Jordan felt an unexpected pang, but then she saw a grinning Markus admonish Ronan. Jordan hoped he was setting her straight. She was glad when the song ended.

As they headed back to the table, Thrill said, "I know how much Ronan likes Mark, and she said they'd gone out a few times, but he'd basically ignored her half the night while dancing with Beth. I have to admit, I was worried about a repeat of last year's fiasco. And then when Beth started choking…" Thrill searched Jordan's face. "Just a coincidence, right?"

Jordan arched her brows ambiguously.

A girl stood by the table, waiting to snatch Thrill from her hands. His cheeks dimpled as the girl dragged him in the opposite direction. Jordan's eyes canvassed the gym. She was itching to speak with Markus. She spied him at the refreshment table, chatting with some people Jordan only knew in passing. Markus seemed more at ease at being human than she felt herself. She was on the opposite end, not a social butterfly.

She butted into their conversation and said to Markus, "Can we talk?"

Markus slid his hand onto Jordan's shoulder and steered her into the sparkling pines, where twinklers pricked their clothes and faces. When they were alone, she leaned close and whispered in his ear, "I think Ronan knows you're an angel."

Markus stared down at her, marveling at her clear beauty, even when red, yellow, and blue lights colored her complexion. Unconcerned, he said, "How'd you come to that conclusion?"

It seemed entirely ordinary for Markus to sweep Jordan's hair back off her shoulders, freeing her heart-shaped face from its veil. "I wish people could see your inner strength and beauty."

Jordan pushed at his hand, a little insulted. "So you think I'm homely?"

"That's not what I said."

Whipping her fingers through her lengthy hair, Jordan drew the locks forward again. "Well, when people compliment someone's inner beauty, it's because they can't honestly say that they're…you know…pretty."

Markus shook his head. "Humans judge too much based on what they see on the outside. They dismiss the inner-self."

"So I'm homely, but I look good on the inside." She hugged her arms around her waist, feeling like the geek everyone had originally called her.

Markus brushed the masking hair back again and blasted Jordan with a fantastic smile. "You're acceptable…for a human."

"So, what? There's not one bad-looking angel in the universe? You're all glowing, perfect, and dazzling?"

His puckish grin reached to his eyes, now the shade of amethyst. "You've taken me totally off topic." She huffed, slightly peeved at his impishness. "Like I said, I think Ronan knows you're an angel. It seemed like Ronan, in her skillful way, was letting you know how *mad* she was—at you. She wanted to embarrass Beth, and knew you'd be there to help. It seems obvious, don't you think? Especially after I'd just slathered holy water on Beth—how come that didn't ward off the spell?"

"It helped, look at Beth now." He actually approved of her tenacity. "If you hadn't splashed her with holy water, she'd be lying in a hospital bed on a respirator."

"But you were here."

"I weakened Ronan's spell."

"What's going on?" She looked into his taciturn expression. "What'd you say to Ronan?"

Markus rubbed his head, returning his hair to its untidy state. "For the past few weeks, I've endeavored to persuade Ronan to put an end to her magical charms. She's a competent witch, self-righteous, egotistical, and full of pride—untoward personality traits that cause disaster—and all the while Lucifer applauds her aptitude."

"What can we do? If she knows you're an angel, then what?" Jordan clenched his arm, her voice like simmering water. "Is she plotting to use you to her advantage?"

Tapering his eyes and rolling his lips into his mouth, he didn't look fully convinced. "I don't think she knows I'm an angel, at least not yet. And I don't think Ronan's thoroughly lost. There's still a spark of goodness, possibly because she sees it in me. She says she wants to attain my light."

"Well, that's a good thing, right?"

Markus hesitated. "She's interested in more than just my light."

Tilting her head, Jordan stared at him, mystified, until it dawned on her. "You're an angel, don't go there, Markus!"

Totally chagrined, she added, "No matter how tempted you are."

She'd never thought of him in *that way*. Jordan remembered the countless times she'd woken up screaming after her father died. Markus had always been there for her. He'd crawl into bed with her and she'd curl up in his arms. He'd douse his light—although now, she wondered if he'd turned human. He would hold her, pressed against her back most of the night, or until she rested peacefully.

Then a few years ago Markus stopped sharing her bed when she woke from those terrible dreams. When she'd confronted him about his absence when she needed him most, his face had been hard to read. He'd said, "I'm always here for you, but you're getting older now."

Jordan had thought he meant it was time for her to grow up and handle matters on her own, but maybe not.

He grinned. "Don't worry about me."

Tap-tap-tap-tap. Repeated clicking interrupted them. Ronan stood there with her hands on her hips, compulsively tapping the floor with her foot. Jordan thought of the old adage, *If looks could kill*.

"What's going on over here?" reproached Ronan. "Jordan, you said Mark was just a *friend*."

Jordan's mind froze. Before she could summon a reply, Markus cut her off. Swinging an arm over Ronan's shoulders, he led her away, saying, "Jordan needed advice about Thrill."

Jordan saw Ronan's ringlets wiggle as she nodded.

Walking back to the table, Jordan was surprised to find a boy from her art class waiting to ask her to dance. "I've wanted to ask you all night," he said. "But you've been hanging with that jock."

The guy was nice enough, but his ungainly moves made it a rough dance. As soon as the song ended, another guy took his place. This one was less klutzy, though his eyes seemed stuck to her boobs, until Thrill came to her rescue. She was enjoyably secluded in his embrace the remainder of the evening and detected more than one envious glare.

A headache had gradually been building behind her eyes. Now it pounded like a jackhammer in her temples. She massaged her forehead, and luckily, the Winter Ball came to an end with a flash of harsh fluorescent lights. And then there was a mad scramble for the coat racks, all the while, the teacher chaperones yelled over the hubbub. Paisley had organized plans to head to the Elma Grill with most of the student body, though Jordan just wanted to end the night.

"Would you guys mind dropping me at home," she said tiredly. "I have an awful headache."

"Are you sure?" Thrill asked in a sympathetic tone.

"If you don't mind."

Plainly disappointed, he nodded.

It was bedlam outside. Kids swarmed everywhere, firing snowballs that descended like mini-bombs on unsuspecting victims. The snow had stopped, but slush leaked over and into their shoes as they tread carefully to the Chevelle.

The fresh air helped Jordan's aching head somewhat. She chuckled merrily at the high-spirited mob then crouched on wobbling high heels to make her own snowball.

Jordan took aim and whacked Thrill between the shoulder blades. He whooped heartily and scooped up snow to return her volley.

She promptly learned that heels make terrible snowshoes as she gleefully dodged his expert aim. She swiveled and then felt the hard blow as if she'd plowed into a brick wall. When her head cleared, she discovered she'd run right into Markus's powerful chest.

He held her steady. "Whoa, are you okay?"

"Oh, I'm sorry," Jordan blundered, as another snowball came thundering their way slamming into Markus's face.

Releasing Jordan, Markus shoveled up a handful of wet snow. Chortling, he threw and watched until it hit its target. Jordan couldn't recall the last time she'd heard him laugh so hard.

"Stop it!" Ronan complained, standing in front of Markus's car. "I'm freezing. Let's go, Mark!"

Not anticipating his next action, Jordan gasped as Markus lifted her and carried her in his arms over the slushy puddles. He set her down next to Thrill's Chevelle, and said to Thrill, "Drive safe."

"Yeah, man, you, too."

CHAPTER 13

Wicked Spirits Create Chaos.

As daintily as possible, Jordan climbed the stairs. A band of light was spilling from her mom's bedroom door. Jordan poked her head around the doorframe. Seeley was reading in bed.

"I saw your light on," Jordan said softly.

Seeley patted the side of the mattress. "I waited up. You're home awfully early for your first dance."

Jordan dove beneath the covers and then thumped a pillow under her head. "I have a headache," she mewled while pressing the palms of her hands into her eye sockets.

Seeley didn't want to pry, but she was ready to burst. "Did you have a good time? Did you dance with any boys?"

"Mom, you're making it worse." Jordan yawned as her mom combed her fingertips through her hair, alleviating the ache. "That feels good—and yes, I had a very good time. Yes, I danced with boys."

"If you're feeling that bad, we can talk in the morning."

With her eyes closed, Jordan sighed. "Something's wrong. I can tell by your voice."

Seeley hesitated. "Your friend Ronan was the girl with Veronka in the city a couple of days ago. I only saw her back and profile, but it was definitely her."

Jordan sat up and angled herself against the headboard. "Tonight, Markus said Ronan performs witchcraft—he meant it literally. He says Ronan doesn't know he's an angel, at least not yet."

Seeley seemed unconvinced. "If Ronan's in league with the Order, surely they'll supply her with whatever damaging information they can, and it worries me, because Veronka's out for revenge. And now I'm more convinced than ever of Ronan's powers. She must've unlocked the gateway that liberated Legion. It really would've thrown her when you arrived in school acting perfectly normal. Maybe that was Veronka's plan all along. She might be pulling Ronan's strings."

"Just because Ronan can invoke spirits, doesn't mean they tell her everything, or even tell her the truth," Jordan reasoned. "We've read what dad wrote, and even Markus says wicked spirits create chaos. They're known for being tricksters."

"You might be right," Seeley mused.

Burying her head in her hands, Jordan tried, unsuccessfully, to make sense of the situation. She then moved her head from side to side. The headache was still prevalent. "I think Markus is wrong," she mumbled in utter frustration. "Ronan *must* know about his involvement."

"Markus wouldn't lie. Perhaps he's protecting you? That's his job, isn't it?"

"I'm afraid for him. I have an awful feeling, deep inside of me."

"Markus is a powerful angel. Why would you be afraid for him? I think he can take care of himself."

"One day I asked Markus if he could get hurt or even die while he was human, and he said, 'Probably, yes.' What if—" Jordan's temple throbbed brutally.

"Zeke never told me that. I assumed they were invincible. But then, Zeke never created an actual human identity," Seeley mumbled. "Jordan, don't think about *what ifs*. You'll drive yourself crazy."

"Mom, my head is spinning. I need to sleep. We'll talk more in the morning, okay?"

"Sure, honey, get some sleep." Seeley watched Jordan slog from the room. Switching off the bedside lamp, she tried not to think about their crazy life.

Jordan conked out as soon as her head hit the pillow. She woke a few hours later with a glow pricking her eyelids. Markus, in angelic form, stood by her bed. When her eyes opened, he knelt, propping his elbows on the mattress with his chin on his hand.

Jordan squinted, shielding her eyes with her arm. "What're you doing here?" she said sleepily.

"You're kind of like my assignment. I watch over you, a lot," he whispered. "Any nightmares?"

"I slept like a log, not a peep—until now. You could've doused your light before peering into my eyeballs." A full-blown yawn warped her face.

Markus tipped his head and rose. He'd started to recede when Jordan blurted, "I think Ronan knows, or at least is suspicious about you. My mom's seen Ronan with Veronka."

"I just dropped Ronan at home. She wanted me to spend the night."

Jordan climbed to her elbows, irked by Ronan's gall. "Geez, Markus! You didn't, did you? I know she's gorgeous and all—but ge–e–ez…"

He recoiled at Jordan's presumption. "Of course not."

Glancing at the time, she said, "It's 4:15 so you had a late night. Did everyone go to the diner?"

"Yes." Putting a fist to his mouth, Markus cleared his throat, apparently to warrant Jordan's undivided attention. "I'm leaving after the holidays for a while." He seemed guarded, as if he knew she wouldn't understand. "But you'll have protection."

She stared at him in disbelief. "What'd you mean—leaving for a while?"

"Unprecedented occurrences have unfolded. It's necessary for the Powers to convene."

"Unprecedented occurrences, like what?"

Markus gritted his teeth, nullifying his anger. "I can't say—not now."

"Oh?"

Though superficially composed, Markus flexed his fists. "Get some sleep," he said, his voice soothing, then he retreated until she could no longer see him.

Too sleepy to absorb any more, her head sank to the pillow, and she drifted thankfully into a dreamless state.

eße

Em, Henry, Jordan, and Seeley lounged around the decorated Christmas tree, admiring their handiwork. With the holidays just around the corner, the family had spent the last couple of days on last minute details.

"One more week and then no school for almost two weeks," Jordan cried happily, leaning back on the couch with her hands behind her head. Contented, she wore sweat pants and a robe. She refused to dress, citing that it was nearly vacation, time to vegetate.

"I wish I could say the same," Seeley said wistfully. "A week off with nothing to do but put my feet up and rest would be just what the doctor ordered." Then she looked at her daughter. "And Jordan, exams come before vacation, so get studying."

"Thanks for putting a damper on my frame of mind, Mom."

"You kids have it easy nowadays," Henry added with a grin. "Not like when Em and I were young. I'd rise at the break of dawn because the house was freezing, and all during Christmas vacation I'd spend my days shoveling coal in the chute. And then shoveling off the driveway and sidewalks, and all that was *before* my father left for work. When I was thirteen, I helped support the family with a job at the Five and Dime. I walked to work in all kinds of weather. My parents didn't have an extra car to cart my butt all over the place."

"Yeah, Dad." Seeley's tone was full of cynicism. "And you'd walk ten miles in a blinding snowstorm, uphill—going *and* coming, right?" She turned to Jordan. "We've heard this story before."

Everyone giggled.

The house phone rang, and Em grabbed the cordless on the end table. "Seeley, it's for you." She covered the mouthpiece and whispered, "It's a man."

All ears perked up, listening to Seeley's dialogue. After a minute or so, she banged the receiver, muttering under her breath.

"Seeley, is anything wrong?" Em asked.

"That was Asa Trebane."

"Isn't Trebane that despicable man Jack lived with when he was young?" Henry asked, his voice full of distaste. "The one who was responsible for his death?"

"Yes—but remember, it was never substantiated." Seeley collapsed on the couch next to Jordan. "The police said the house where Jack was killed had been vacant for years. And, go figure, Asa had a solid alibi. The detective thought I was psychotic as soon as I mentioned The Black Order and human sacrifice. I had to keep my mouth shut. They were ready to lock me away."

"Seeley, with your affiliation in the media, isn't there some way to expose this man?" Henry looked like he had a unibrow when he scowled. "I can't even call him a man. He's more like a devil."

"Asa's one of the affluent untouchables." Seeley explained, compressing her hands between her knees. "He's right when he boasts that money rules. Asa has legitimate corporations around the world and illicit organizations overseen by his colleagues. He's a puppet master and a powerful evil mystic."

"Why is this dreadful man bothering you, Seeley?" Em cheeks flushed, and her eyes darted around the room as if Lucifer might appear at any given moment. The topic of the devil visibly distressed her.

Seeley caught Jordan's cautious expression. She didn't have the courage to tell her parents about Asa's sordid offer. Instead, she remarked, "The paper wants me to interview Asa for a feature article." She wasn't totally fabricating. Declan had been on her case for weeks to finish the assignment.

"Nasty business," grumped Henry. "What the paper won't do for an exclusive."

Just then the doorbell pealed. Jordan ran and opened the door to a frozen Father James. His teeth chattered. "Jordan, may I speak with your mom?"

"Sure. Come in, Father."

Snow caked his shoes. He stamped on the porch before stepping inside.

Henry ambled over to the priest and pumped his gloved hand. "So nice to see you, Father James."

"You, too, Henry and Emily." Seeing Seeley, he asked, "May I speak to you, Seeley?"

"While you're here, Father, could you possibly find the time to bless the house again?" Henry added hastily. "It's been years."

Father James nodded. "Yes, Henry, that's a good idea."

Jordan hung up the priest's coat. Father James, wringing his cold hands, followed Seeley into the kitchen. He seemed to have no energy and his shoulders sloped as if he bore a heavy burden. Seeley pulled out a chair. Falling into the seat, the priest sighed heavily.

"You're not well, Father?" Seeley said, concerned.

With a flick of his wrist, Father James dismissed Seeley's comment. His eyes trailed Seeley uneasily as she switched on the burner to heat a kettle. "Did you hear what happened in Kansas, in Osage County?"

"No, I haven't heard from them since I left weeks ago." By the tone of his voice, she knew it was bad news. She crossed her arms over her chest and waited.

"It's been hushed-up. They've had unusual decapitations." The priest's face crumpled. "Bishop Stevenson wired me yesterday. Tragic, tragic."

"Decapitations?"

"Yes." He paused. "People are hacking off their own heads."

Seeley winced, and then sat opposite Father James. "Is that even possible?"

"Gory. They found—"

Seeley plastered her hands over her ears. "I don't want to know the details!" She rose briskly, fetching two mugs and tea bags, then poured the boiling water.

"People are misguided," Father James said. "Led astray by meritocracy and the pursuit of wealth. They fall, body and soul, into the darkness of self-love." He sighed deeply and placed his hand over the rim of the steaming water. "The atrocities are widespread. Be vigilant, always on guard, Seeley. I've ordered another one hundred copies of Jack's book to be printed." Lifting his hunched shoulders, he sat up straighter. "Religious bookstores are selling out and are asking for more. I see this as a good sign. We need people to be informed. They must not put on blinders nor be indolent of the awful truth."

"Father, I'll give you the money for the printing," Seeley offered. "Are there more groups you'd like me to meet?"

Swallowing the hot, calming tea Father James answered gratefully, "If it wouldn't be too much of a bother, I'm celebrating healing masses at area churches and I'd like you to speak on the dangers of satanic manipulation, how people are misguided by the slight, clever pull of the devil."

Seeley shrank at the idea of giving a speech from the ambo. "Father, I…what if…what if I screw up?" Her voice trembled. "I'm not a public speaker."

He cupped his chilled hands around the warm mug. "You're a respected reporter and journalist," he replied firmly. "Your psychic experiences need not be revealed, yet. But don't you feel it's time to use your knowledge to warn people of what's hunting for their souls."

As much as she hated speaking in public, Seeley consented, with a queasy stomach. Then she mentioned her pending interview with Asa.

"You must remember, he has no power over you whatsoever. Your convictions are healthy and strong. Use justice and discretion," he said. "But show the public who he is. Of course, I need not advise you to print anything that can't be corroborated. He might be a damned man, but I still pray for him."

Seeley nodded even as she grimaced.

Tipping his mug and finishing the tea, Father James stood. "Well, let's get this house blessed again. Do you have any holy water handy, or should I bless some?"

Seeley swung open the end cupboard, every shelf filled with plastic containers of holy water. "Take your pick, Father."

CHAPTER 14

They Strike Out at Friends.

Jordan trudged out the back door, late for school as usual. A blustery current of air tackled her, whisking her hair into a messy nest. Rotating her face into the wind, she attempted to gather the rebellious strands into a ponytail. Bitter cold nipped her nose. She shouted into the wind, "My soul for a warm car..." Her words were drowned in the breeze, her voice barely reaching her ears. She had to admit—the snow-encrusted trees and drifts that looked like peaks of whip cream gave the yard an awesome grandeur. She rounded the corner of the house and was surprised to see Markus perched on the hood of a car.

"Hey, Mark, am I getting a ride to school?" she joked, happy to see him.

He jumped to the snow-dusted ground, holding wide the side door, waving his arm flamboyantly. "Your carriage awaits, my dear lady." His voice changed to a skeptical tone. "And what's with calling me Mark?"

"Everyone calls you Mark. I thought maybe I should, too."

Markus gave her a crooked grin. "If you wish—you can call me Mark."

Warming up in the car, and aiming to right her wronged hair, Jordan studied him. "Last time we talked, I thought you'd be away for a while."

His head tilted. "I was, but then I needed to return."

She noticed his stubbly chin and shaggy hair. "What's going on? What's happening?"

He hitched his shoulders and shook his head. "I don't have a clue. I'm not privy to God's omniscience. But it's important that I stick around." He stroked his bristly chin. "I just shaved a day ago, and now I have to do it again. Facial hair is very annoying."

"Don't angels shave?" Jordan said unsure, checking out Markus's scruff.

"How many angels have you seen with beards?"

"Make sure you do shave. You look more like a guy in his twenties than a seventeen-year-old."

His mouth rumpled with his nod. "Some of the guys look at me weird. They probably think I flunked a few grades."

As they parked in the school's lot, Jordan inquired, "Have you made any headway with Ronan?"

Markus turned, elongating his arm on the back of Jordan's seat. "I've been thinking about that and, after all my attempts, I've done nothing except hit a nerve. And then she seems to think we're, like—how do you say it?—an item." A weary noise gurgled in his throat. "I'd thought the three of us could get together and have an adult discussion on the risks of witchcraft. Perhaps she'll listen to you."

"I doubt it, but it's worth a try," Jordan conceded.

"I'll arrange it with Ronan. Meet me at the car after school. We'll go to Taste."

Jordan nibbled her lower lip. "Do we have to be ethical about the whole thing? Couldn't we just scare her into submission?"

Whump, whump, whump, whump, on the side window startled both of them. Turning, they faced a seething Ronan. She flung the door open. "What the hell's going on?"

Taken aback, Jordan scooted out of the car and dragged her backpack from the floor. Boyfriends, girlfriends, and dating were not her expertise. Maybe Markus could set Ronan straight. She headed into school, already late. Charging around a corner, she bumped head-on into Thrill. Books and paper scattered all over the hall as Thrill supported an unstable Jordan.

"Slow down there, Jordan. What's the rush?"

She swept her hair out of her eyes. "I've been late almost every day, and I'd wanted to make sure I made homeroom on time."

Sitting on his heels, he helped her retrieve her things. "The guys are going to Hidden Lake Friday after school to hang. Do you want to come?"

Jordan sat up, looking Thrill in the eyes. "Sure, sounds like fun."

He smiled broadly. "It's usually a blast—tons of snow, so dress warm. I'll pick you up at your house right after school."

She grinned dreamily as she watched Thrill saunter down the hallway. Then aware that she was in public, she shook her head and giggled, realizing she sounded like her grandmother.

☙◦❧

Hopping up and down to keep warm, Jordan shivered next to Markus's car. She couldn't help but cheer up when he emerged from the school. She knew she would soon be seated in warmth. But then she noted Ronan wasn't with him. "Where's Ronan? I thought she'd be with you."

"She said she'd meet us there."

Jordan heard the asperity in his tone but didn't comment.

Elated students departed at the end of another school day and, unperturbed, Markus eased through the traffic on the way to Taste. Cruising Main Street looking for a parking spot, Jordan surveyed the street lamps wreathed in twinkle lights, illuminating the cobblestone roads. Charming shops displayed Christmas decorations. The Pie Hole's window depicted elves, balancing pies on their heads, serving a merry Mr. and Mrs. Kringle. The Five and Dime, with its red and white awning, featured an impressively life-like nativity scene in one picture window and, opposite, statues of old-fashioned carolers with children ice-skating. A unique sweater store, The Lamb's

Wool, displayed two wooly sheep sprouting reindeer antlers and wearing a silver-belled harness to pull Santa's sleigh.

Despite the crowds, Markus and Jordan arrived at Taste Coffee House ten minutes after school. Jordan appreciated the mouth-watering scent of fresh coffee. "Um-m-m, that's such a great smell," she said to no one in particular.

At the glass counter, she lingered over a variety of delectable baked goods. There were three shelves of fudge brownies, coffee cakes, and oversized macaroon, peanut butter, and chocolate chip cookies. The menu, a mammoth blackboard, listed various wraps, sandwiches, soups, and breakfast foods.

Markus paid for two coffees and opted for a sunny window seat, offering them the illusion of a summer day—if they didn't look out the window. They draped their coats over the back of their chairs. Markus's V-neck sweater molded to his chest and, as always, his jeans looked brand new and they fit to perfection. Jordan happily showed off her new white knit sweater and twilled corduroys. She enjoyed keeping up with Markus—at least as far as clothes went—for a change. And she wondered again how he got his endless wardrobe.

Smoothing the sweater's cuff, she saw a brown smudge, and remembered eating pudding at lunch. "Oh, darn, I'm such a klutz." She scraped at the dried pudding and then gave up on the stain. At least it looked good most of the day. She raised her coffee to her lips and watched the pedestrians scampering in and out of the inclement weather.

Finally, she broke the silence. "I'm stunned Ronan didn't come with us. She has quite a jealousy problem, you know, and catching the two of us this morning probably blew her mind. Especially if she thinks the two of you are, like…um…a couple."

"I've made myself perfectly clear," he said firmly. "We're friends. I don't understand how Ronan could mistake my meaning."

"Girls construe things differently than boys. You took her out a few times. I know you're trying to put a stop to her shenanigans, but…she's definitely interested in more."

"All right, all right, I get the picture. Teenagers, bah." Markus squirmed, burned his lip on the hot coffee, and made a sour face.

With an off-center grin for his clumsiness, Jordan thought—right at that moment—Markus acted completely human. She wasn't sure if she liked the idea.

"Why the strange look?" His eyes, like the violet sky at dusk, stared straight into Jordan's.

"Oh, nothing..." Usually he could read her so well. "Doesn't Ronan have a guardian angel?" she asked softly so no one would hear and think she was nuts. "I know most people can't see their angels like I see you, but I thought everyone had an angel."

Markus chewed on his top lip. "She did, but angelic beings, pure in spirit, cannot dwell in evil for very long, and Ronan's been practicing the dark arts for years. I'm able to endure evil spirits longer in human form." He shut his eyes tightly. "Although—Ronan insisted I meet with her father and, after an hour in her house, my body felt like it was on fire."

"Markus, when a girl wants you to meet their parents, it's because they want their parent's approval," she said a tad riled. "You haven't the slightest notion of how dating works."

"I'm trying to help Ronan and protect you at the same time. I don't like the society you humans are burdened with. Dating, you know...whatever." He flicked his hand, defeated.

Jordan pressed her fist to her lips, holding back her bubbling laughter, then she clutched Markus's hand and squeezed. "This is a great experience for you. Now you'll understand how it feels to walk in our shoes."

A chill ran through Taste when a cluster of kids filed through the door. Ronan, Paisley, Cayden, Rolly, and Thrill headed to their table, chafing cold hands. Like an eclipse of the sun, Ronan's eyes darkened as they focused on Jordan's hand.

Conscious of her fingers covering Markus's, Jordan released his hand and buried hers in her lap "Oh, golly."

Thrill clapped Markus on the back. "Hey, man, what's up?"

"Just waiting for you guys to show," Markus responded, his tone casual.

Jordan couldn't think of a worse time to speak with Ronan. She flinched when Ronan said awkwardly, "What'd you guys want to talk to me about?"

Ronan looked at Markus, then at Jordan, her expression almost childlike.

Jordan nearly fell off her chair when Markus, in a low, friendly voice, said, "Ronan, we're your friends." He glanced at each person's face, then back at Ronan. "We don't want you to get hurt. We'd all like to help you."

Ronan was dumbfounded. "I don't understand."

All eyes were on Markus. "The Ouija board, the séances—not to mention the incantations—you're infiltrating the spirit world," he said. "You're skating on thin ice, my friend."

Jordan could hardly believe it but Cayden, Rolly, Thrill, and even Paisley, who was generally Ronan's number one cheerleader, nodded in agreement. Jordan suddenly realized that Markus had anticipated this the whole time. He was more insightful about human nature than Jordan gave him credit for.

Regrettably, caring friends looking out for Ronan's well-being didn't fly with her. "We were just fine before you showed up, Mark," she snarled.

"No, not really, Ronan," Thrill retorted.

She rounded on him like a viper ready to strike then turned on Cayden and Paisley, her voice biting, "You agree with them?"

"Ronan, it was fun for a while," Cayden, said in her nasal whine. "But last week freaked me out. I like being in control of my own body."

"You've always been pathetic, Cayden," Ronan spat. "And what about you, Paisley?"

Paisley's face, a brilliant shade of pink, fell. Her shoulders lifted in a slight shrug. "I dunno."

Ronan looked at Jordan then Thrill. "Since we're being truthful—Thrill, I know you have the hots for Jordan. Do you see what's going on between Mark and her? They're hooking up behind our backs, just like Meg and Robert last year!"

Jordan shot up. "Not that nonsense again, Ronan."

Ronan appeared crushed, and then, a slow Cheshire-cat-like sneer developed on her face. She turned to Markus and purred, "Markus, be an angel and drive me home, okay?"

Stupefied, Jordan looked at Markus. If the exposé registered, his face stayed expressionless. He shrugged on his coat and said to Thrill, "Would you mind giving Jordan a ride home?"

"Of course." Thrill grinned at his good fortune. He then asked Markus, "You're going Friday, right?"

Ronan answered for all of them. "We're *all* hanging at Hidden Lake on Friday."

It was then that Jordan saw a trace of worry in Markus's eyes.

ɕↃɕↃ

Jordan knelt in the closet, busily discarding dilapidated jeans and shirts. Nightfall overtook the room and, as she stood to switch on the light, Markus materialized, bringing his glow.

Shoving through piled debris, Jordan sighed. "She knows—Ronan knows."

"It was only a matter of time."

"You knew she'd find out?"

"Ronan's woven into the deadly fibers of Asa's cult. He's helping her refine her talents."

"When did Ronan learn you were an angel?" she cried. "And why are you keeping secrets from me?"

His angelic form paced from one end of her bedroom to the other, with his chin buried on his chest, thinking.

"Did Ronan drop any hints while you drove her home?

"Not a word. She acted contrite, telling me that she wants to end her association with the spirits—to make me happy," he said. "I estimate that Ronan's witchcraft compares to the most adept of sorcerers." He leaned on Jordan's bureau, crossing his arms on his chest. "I feel this frantic pull. Something's…terribly wrong…"

She sensed his charged energy. "What's wrong? Do you need to leave, again?"

Anguished, he spun and supported his body with his hands pancaked on her dresser. "No, I can't leave—not yet," he said decisively. "The darkness draws near..."

A shiver danced up her spinal column. Jordan slumped onto the bed, pulled her legs to her chest, and stared at the wall. Her thoughts were a jumbled mess. Advancing shadows darkened her bedroom. She moved her head to look at Markus—but he was gone. Someone downstairs was calling her name. She hiked down for dinner.

CHAPTER 15

I Have Sunk into the Mire of the Deep.

The confrontation at Taste exasperated Jordan. Unspoken words were making her head ache. What could she possibly say to Ronan? *Do you know Mark is an angel?* or *Are you a conniving bitch, conspiring with the Order that killed my father?* Jordan held her tongue in check and waited for Ronan's next move.

It was the last day of school before the holiday break and, as originally planned, Thrill's Chevelle, crammed with the usual gang, picked her up on Friday for hanging at Hidden Lake. A pleased Ronan sat in the front seat, looking prim and pretty in pink.

Straggling out of the heated car and into the bracing outdoors, Jordan admired the patina of iridescence on the fallen snowflakes. She shoved on gloves and wrapped her scarf securely around her neck. Gradually their eyes adapted to the brilliance. Impressed, Jordan gazed in wonder at frost-encased tree limbs glistening with frozen droplets of thawing ice captured in time, giving them a surreal clarity. In the distance, she saw a coppice of bare trees interspersed with immense hemlock and black spruce, sheathed in mounds of snow.

"This place is awesome," she exclaimed. "I can't believe I didn't know it was here."

"It's a great hangout, away from townies and prying eyes. We come here a lot." Thrill gestured to numerous idling vehicles. "We're lucky today. The snowplow must've come through. Once last year it was a real mess. We came to party, but the plows hadn't been here in a while. We used our cars like plows and barreled our way in." He chuckled. "About eight cars got stuck in the snow. It was a good time."

Jordan flipped up her hood, warding off the chill, as they forged a path to a rusty steel bridge. Car doors began to open and people garbed in layers of winter garments descended upon the once-deserted area, yammering noisily.

"Hey, Ronan, Beth and her friends are here," Paisley announced snidely.

Thrill glared at her. "What the fuck, Paisley? Can't we just have a good time without your constant commentary?" He saw the hurt in her eyes and softened. "Sorry, Pais. No trouble, okay?"

"A little harsh, William," Ronan reproved, though her eyes danced in merriment at Thrill's lash. She shouldered the pouty-faced Paisley off to the side while everyone continued onto the bridge. "You went to his house last night, didn't you?"

"What's the big deal?" Paisley lowered her eyes. "So, I like to grovel."

"Stop it, Paisley, he's not interested."

"He was, before Meg, real interested. You—you could make him interested again."

Ronan glared at her best friend and confidante with disdain. "I took care of Meg. The rest was up to you. Thrill has moved on, and I suggest you do the same. Besides, I'm not into love potions."

"Yeah, except for when it suits you," Paisley said, nearly whimpering.

"What the hell's that supposed to mean?"

Paisley hunched her shoulders and joined the group on the bridge, leaving Ronan to bring up the rear.

Out of breath by the time they reached the bridge, Jordan teetered precariously over the hand railing. "This bridge is cool." Blood rushed to her head, making her dizzy as she observed the opaque surface below.

"Hey, little one." Thrill snatched her away from the rail. "It's not a good day to jump." His winsome smile brought more color to her rosy cheeks.

Sunshine flared in Thrill's amber gaze, filling Jordan with all kinds of odd sensations. She stooped, clumped snow into a tiny ball, and popped it between her lips, cooling herself off. Boisterous revelry drew their attention to the clearing. A football went smoking through the air. All eyes tracked its spiraling flight until it landed in two feet of snow. The guys attempted to run in knee-high drifts. Jordan giggled. It was like watching football in slow motion. Beth's friends, Kristen and Jeff, lumbered to the landing site and excavated with gloved hands in pursuit of the prized pigskin. Shouts of victory heralded from Kristen's team when she held the ball aloft like a trophy.

Jordan headed for the clearing with the girls slogging behind. "That looks fun."

Rolly barged to the front like a locomotive, hands and feet flying in the air. His burly body channeled a passage through the cumbersome snow. "I call dibs on Thrill," he hollered. "He's on my team."

Trailing in Rolly's wake, Jordan recognized the boy now lobbing the football. He sat in front of her in math class. She lost sight of the ball's ascent in the glaring sun. Markus and Beth, gloves sheltering their eyes, searched skyward. Beth pointed and Markus lunged for the ball, snagging it easily. Beth tackled him around his waist, falling backward into a powdery drift. She had landed on top of him and they both burst into laughter.

Ronan yanked Jordan's wrist, spinning her around. "Have you walked on water lately?"

That sounded a trifle absurd. "Walk on water?" Jordan said warily.

"Follow me." Ronan towed her along, Paisley and Cayden following dutifully. Ronan paused at the embankment, where stacks of snow were piled high, presumably by the occasional snowplows.

"Come on." Ronan began to scale the bank.

"Is this safe?"

"It's probably iced over by now. We used to skate here all the time," said Cayden.

"My dad brings his row boat and fishes here in the summer," Paisley interjected.

A smidge uncertain, Jordan relented and clambered up the embankment. Losing her balance, she tripped and tumbled sideways. The girls hooted at their clumsy climbing.

"Looky, looky who's watching." said Paisley.

Markus and Thrill, inclined against the bridge rail, both with hands crammed in their coat pockets. Jordan's breath caught in her throat. She could not possibly be seeing a giant halo enclosing Markus—and big enough to include Thrill? Slightly paranoid she wondered what Ronan would think?

Cayden spoke first, clearly in awe. "Wow, look at the way the sun is shining on Thrill and Mark."

"Yeah, like a couple of angels," Ronan said with a curl to her mouth as she waved to the boys. They tipped their heads in response.

Jordan comprehended her hint and couldn't shake the coldness scraping her bones.

It was so unlike Jordan to be uncoordinated. She blamed it on Thrill watching as she toppled recklessly to the frozen shoreline. Giggling, the girls each grabbed an elbow and lugged Jordan to her feet. Carefully testing the ice, they slowly eased onto the lake.

"It's frozen solid," Paisley claimed.

"This is great!" Ronan hollered. She skittered across the ice, slipping and sliding to the opposite shore.

Demonstrating an inability to run on ice, Jordan skidded and fell, landing soundly on her butt. She chuckled at her unusual lack of agility, got to her feet, and brushed the wet flakes from her backside. She felt justified in blaming her newfangled boots with raised tread.

They twirled together, releasing each other to glide over the polished surface. Enjoying the harmless activity, Jordan laughed easily with these girls who just wanted to have fun. Their clowning attracted the football enthusiasts to the frozen lake and, with a flurry of action, everyone exhibited their abilities to scrabble and slide on the ice.

"It's getting crowded. Let's go further up the lake," Ronan suggested.

Interlocking elbows, the girls scuffled away from the others. They rounded a bend and the sound of gaiety faded.

"I think we should go back," Cayden said cautiously.

"Don't be a baby, Cayden," Ronan said.

Paisley agreed with Cayden, but spoke carefully. "She's right, Ronan, we're too far out."

"Okay, but one more slide," Ronan dared, signaling them onward.

Ronan made her way over the slippery surface with Paisley and Cayden swooshing toward her. But Jordan remained motionless, feet planted firmly in place. She heard the girl's delighted squeals, then they whirled to peer back at her.

Jordan saw the intensity of Ronan's contemptuous look and noticed her mouth moving.

To Paisley and Cayden, the strange scene unraveled. It appeared as if Jordan was wrestling with herself. What they couldn't see was the invisible entity threading around her body.

She couldn't shake free from the entity's pressurized embrace. Terrified, she heard the thunderous crack beneath her feet. Perilously vulnerable, she had little or no time to react. Her body ripped through the ice.

Flailing her arms, Jordan desperately tried to paddle. The ominous pressure heaved her downward. Her eyeballs felt frozen, but she could see the horrific entity tangling her body, dragging her to a watery grave. She struggled to free herself, but her coat and boots weighed her down like an anchor. Viscerally paddling, she was losing the battle. The freezing water was paralyzing. Her lungs were ready to burst. She needed to breathe. Jordan knew she wasn't going to make it. She was drowning.

Her mouth automatically opened for life-giving oxygen. The deluge of frigid water trampled her throat, burning her insides.

A premonition had alerted Markus, who streaked around the bend in time to witness Jordan in the menacing clutches of a murky form. Implausibly, the ice cracked and the creature dragged Jordan beneath the surface. Markus ran as fast as—humanly—possible. Afraid he was too late, he yanked off his coat and plunged into the gaping hole, instantly transfiguring.

He was fearsome in his angelic form, and the entity vanished. Jordan floated lifelessly like a rag doll, her long hair splayed like swaying seaweed. Markus, now faster than a bullet, shot her to the surface.

A crowd waited anxiously, keeping back from the crumbling fissure. Venturing closer on his belly, Thrill gripped Jordan under the arms, fishing her from the water. Markus easily hoisted himself up onto the cracked ledge.

Torturous convulsions tore at Jordan's chest. A constant bashing caused her unbearable pain. A mouth covered hers, breathing. The burning sensation returned tenfold as Jordan choked and coughed, spewing icy water from her distended lungs. She flopped back limply as many hands labored to remove her coat and boots. Swaddled in something warm, on the brink of consciousness, she opened her eyes to stare at dozens of fretful faces above her.

A pair of muscular arms scooped her off the ice and supported her firmly against a muscular chest. Jordan knew it was Markus and felt his breath on her face. He mumbled indistinctly. Markus effortlessly handled the embankment with Thrill jogging ahead to the car.

Feebly attempting to extricate herself from Markus's embrace, as she shook with cold, Jordan croaked, "I–I'm o–k–kay. L–let me d–down."

His features drawn, Markus ignored her pleas. Thrill opened his car door and Markus got in, holding Jordan in his extremely hot grasp. He chaffed her bluish, pimpled skin.

"I s–said, I–I'm o–o–kay," Jordan complained with chattering teeth. In actuality, she was beginning to sweat.

From the driver's seat, Thrill glanced worriedly at Jordan's glassy eyes and pasty flesh, which was turning pinkish under Mark's hands. "Where to?" he asked.

"We should take her to the hospital," Markus said, his fingers kneading Jordan roughly. Jordan wrenched herself up, ready to object, then he added, "Let's take her home."

Revived after suffering Markus's abrasive ministrations and, with the thirty miles drive, Jordan edged off his lap, though he kept his arm sheltering her shoulders. The ordeal had zapped her energy. Sleepy, she closed her eyes and leaned her head on Markus's chest.

Jordan didn't wake until they reached her house. Then she noticed the guys' drenched clothes. Toasty warm in Markus's pea coat, she felt a twinge of guilt as she observed the coiled tendrils that hung like dank rope, framing his face.

She started to remove his coat, but he stopped her hand. "Keep it for now. Do you want me to carry you?"

"That's a definite no," she said.

Thrill held up Jordan's sodden coat and new boots. "You might want these."

"All right, both of you can carry me."

Markus and Thrill crisscrossed their arms, making a throne. Jordan circled an arm around each neck and sat like a queen on their proffered arms.

"Now this is what I call servitude," she said. Easily they carted her to the front door, setting her down ceremoniously on the inside landing. They both bowed. Jordan giggled, shyly eyeing Thrill. "Thank you."

"I'll call later," Markus said, his voice distinctly dour.

Jordan understood his message.

Not to be put off, Thrill grinned. "I'll call tonight, too."

Fastening the door behind them, Jordan jumped when her grandfather barked, "Why the heck are you all wet?"

Not wishing to worry her grandparents, Jordan explained in half-truths. "Really had a great time in the wet snow." She tore up the stairs before they had a chance to drill her with more questions.

Peeling away her frozen clothes, Jordan crawled into the bathtub, filling it to the brim with hot water, and stayed there until she wrinkled like a raisin. Her skin restored to a rosy flush, she dressed in lamb's wool sweats and an overly large

sweater. She knew the worst was yet to come—having to tell
her mom.

☙☯☙

Jordan recounted the incident, sending her mom into a
frenzy. Dog-tired, Jordan just wanted to go to sleep, but Seeley
kept vigil, edgily waiting for Markus to appear. Jordan was
spread eagle on the mattress, Seeley rigidly sitting in the chair
with her knees crossed, bouncing her ankles at a rapid speed.

"What's keeping him?" Seeley checked the time. "It's after midnight, for crying out loud. Doesn't he realize you need
to get some sleep?"

"Oh, Mom," Jordan said, stifling a gaping yawn. "He'll
come."

Within the blink of an eye, Markus towered in the small
bedroom, his expression solemn.

Seeley jumped down his throat. "Markus, how could this
happen?"

"Now I know why I needed to stay for a while longer."
Markus pressed his brow with the heel of his palm. "Two people could've died today, thanks to Davian.

Jordan threw her feet over the edge of the bed and sat up,
a tad muddled. "Two people?"

"You and Thrill." Markus peered between his hands. "If I
hadn't been there, Thrill would've gone into the lake to save
you. You both would've drowned."

Jordan shrank back, her breath caught in her throat. "How
do you know that? I thought you didn't have God's omniscience?"

"I receive acknowledgement, beyond the course of human
time, when my presence alters life situations."

"And that...thing was Ronan's...Davian?"

"Yes, a rogue spirit, not easy to banish."

"So Ronan truly tried to drown me?" She just couldn't believe it. One minute they were all having such fun, and the
next...

"Why, Markus?" Seeley asked. "Why can't something simply be done with this...this girl?"

"You know it's not that easy, Seeley," he said, deflated. "Should I affront my Father's law and kill her?" His eyes wavered then regained their resoluteness. "Ronan's loveless and abusive childhood has twisted her mind. She's found solace in the supernatural, unleashing vile spirits that she calls friends. And, as we all know, Ronan's skill has caught the interest of the Order. They've infected her with harmful power."

"Killing her would be the best solution," Seeley said in an irrational moment. Then she realized her insolence, and the rash statement gave way to her bottled-up emotions. She broke into a strained sob.

Jordan swung an arm over her mom's heaving shoulders. "That *was* a bit harsh, Mom, but don't beat yourself up too much. 'Cause deep down, I think we all somewhat agree."

"Oh, Jordan."

When the flood subsided, Markus reported, "I'll be assembling with Ezekiel and others for a brief reconnaissance. As I've told Jordan before, anomalies have come to our attention. We will regroup and take action. I've been away far too long, and lately I've been feeling more human than angelic."

"I can't believe you'd leave us now with this girl prowling around." Seeley wiped at her wet face. "Who knows what she'll pull next?"

"Ronan doesn't scare me in the least," Jordan lied. "It's those flimsy spirits who are so hard to get a hold of, that's what's so bothersome."

Markus knew Jordan was putting on a show of bravery for her mom, yet when he looked into her eyes he saw the ambiguity. It was almost enough to disregard his summons. He drew a tense breath. "I must leave, now."

"Why can't you tell us more about these anomalies?" Jordan asked.

"I will tell you—when I'm able."

His body evaporated before their eyes, leaving them somewhat somber and depressed.

CHAPTER 16

Even in My Joy, Darkness Trails Me.

After the holidays and the celebration of Jordan's seventeenth birthday, Seeley felt brave enough to arrange an interview with Asa. She declined his invitation to meet at his mansion on Delaware Avenue, one of his many properties. Alternatively, they agreed to meet at Spot Coffee on Chippewa Street, during the hectic lunch hour.

Classic and fashionable in a Paneiss herringbone coat, each bronze button embossed with an iconic symbol, Asa portrayed a worldly man for all seasons. He systematically answered her financial questions. It wasn't until she touched upon his parents and childhood that he became ill tempered.

"My parents provided me with a childhood of torture," he spat. "They swore they'd beat the devil out of me." He smirked. "I don't think they succeeded."

When she asked if he'd ever been engaged or married, Asa scoffed. "Ah, the American institution of wedded bliss. I fell madly for lovely Leela. I was hardly twenty, but, when push came to shove, my satisfaction with her dwindled swiftly. The poor thing died of a heart attack at the ripe age of twenty-four." Boredom slipped into his tone. "Then Olivia tempted me into matrimony when I was thirty. She was quite entertaining and thoroughly pleasurable—for a while. Olivia and I shared the same interests. But alas, a fluke accident—her car careened off a cliff in Mexico. So sad."

Asa examined Seeley from under hooded lids as he ran his tongue suggestively over his thin lips. "Gratification comes in countless forms, my dear."

Sick to her stomach, Seeley changed the topic. "To whom do you attribute your success?" She knew that answer. It was as plain as the hawk-like nose on his face.

"Let's just say that I dragged myself from the gutter, successfully achieving—" He made air quotes with his fingers, his voice dripping pure arrogance. "—the American dream."

Seeley jumped on his statement. "You've achieved the American dream? What—in your own opinion—*is* the American dream?'" she asked as she scribbled notes.

His eyes roved over her shiny, golden-brown hair and caramel wool coat, which parted to reveal slender legs encased in knee-high brown suede boots. Asa grinned haughtily when Seeley swung her legs under the round table, away from his scrutiny.

"Money, money, and more money," he said dryly. "Wealth provides everything."

Seeley was repelled by his unbridled avarice. "Is that what you want me to write, Asa? I will gladly put that in quotes." She cocked her head. "And what about your extracurricular activities? The public always likes to know about a businessman's religious associations."

"I don't give a damn what you write," he jeered. "Do you honestly think I care what people think of me? If I give to the poor, feed the hungry, shelter the homeless, help the sick, it's only as a tax shelter. What else?"

His answer was the straw that broke the camel's back. The interview was a sham, and she started packing up her clipboard and notes.

"Wait." Asa yanked her wrist. "We're not finished—not by a long shot."

"Let go," she hissed, her face rigid.

His intimidating eyes grazed over Seeley. "Are you foolishly overlooking my generous bargain?"

Seeley settled into her chair, glaring back at him.

Asa removed his fingers one by one from her wrist. "As I've said, my patience has run out. Decide—now." He spoke passionately, his face full of lust.

Afraid for her daughter's life, Seeley had procrastinated for months. She knew the time had come to lay her cards on the table. Writhing under his look, she steadied her voice. "You can go to Hell."

Asa's unforgiving gray eyes blackened. "You've just made the biggest mistake of your life, Seeley."

Veronka stepped into view, her expression screaming for revenge.

Undetected by Veronka and Asa, a man lingered in the rear of the coffee shop, biding his time. The man advanced. Broad-shouldered with his long, black hair tied back, he came up behind Veronka. "Excuse me." His voice sounded like galvanized steel. Without waiting, he nudged past Veronka's shoulder, hooked Seeley's elbow, and led her from the coffee shop.

Once outside, Seeley glanced back. Veronka and Asa appeared to be engrossed in a heated tête-à-tête. She sighed with relief. "Thanks, Zeke."

☙❧☙

Jordan had time to spare as she put witch-watching, meaning Ronan, on the back burner. She helped her grandparents with their nonstop housework, and motored to the grocery store with Em's scrawled list of produce. Essentially, Jordan liked being a normal girl, except when she'd seen a pile of laundered clothes hanging out on her bed. Closing the door, she smirked and levitated each article. The items found their way into a bureau drawer without lifting a finger. Every night she'd lie in bed and mentally lambast Ronan, sometimes imagining a good thrashing, but then reality set in and so did the alarm clock.

Jordan filled Markus's palpable absence by steeping herself in her schoolwork. Like her mom and dad, Jordan had a gift for writing. She had researched Abraham Lincoln's assassination, using her findings to write a short story. Her English teacher, Mrs. Kinvara, raved about the yarn, but that didn't stop her from assigning a revision, so Jordan could work on punctuation, grammar, and the correct southern vernacular.

Jordan decided to stay clear of Ronan's crew, not answering or returning phone messages, and even skipping lunches. Despite feeling that she was being rather foolish, Jordan scoured the halls for the attractive quarterback. Thrill had called once—the night of her near death experience. He made her laugh, describing what she ate for lunch that day, because it was spewed over the ice.

Math class with Mr. Basinski proved a test of sheer willpower with Ronan's gauging almond eyes glaring at her. Jordan claimed the desk nearest to the door and retreated swiftly at the sound of the bell, before anyone had a chance to corner her.

By Thursday, Jordan's stomach demanded food. She headed for an open spot next to Cayden.

"Hey, where you been?" Cayden asked. "I've wanted to talk to you."

"Been bombed with extra work." Jordan knew her voice sounded dodgy. "I used my lunch periods to finish my art project. So what's up?"

"I can't hang with Ronan anymore." With shaky fingers, Cayden combed back her thin hair. She looked pitiful, with hints of half-moon patches centered under each eye and hollowed cheeks. She'd lost weight, more than her body could afford. "I haven't slept well in weeks. Ronan's séances are freakin' me out." Then she said hastily, "Why haven't you returned my calls?"

Jordan opened her mouth to explain, but Cayden continued. "I bumped into Mark yesterday, and he sat down with me after school. We talked for quite a while. There's something different about him, something that's…that's peaceful, like he could solve all your problems." She steadied her fingers by linking them together. "No wonder Ronan likes him. He helped me feel so much better, almost brave enough to spit in her eye…I think…"

"You talked to Mark? Yesterday?"

"Yeah, he was so nice," she told Jordan. "And last night was the best sleep I've had in a while."

Jordan stared, perturbed. Markus was off being more angelic than human, convening with the Powers. When did he return, or did he ever really leave?

Cayden closed her eyes and leaned back. "O–o–o–oh, you're not jealous, are you? I know the two of you have a special relationship, and that's driving Ronan nuts, but then, I thought...you and Thrill?"

Jordan ignored Cayden's long-winded sentence and asked, "Is Mark in school today?"

Cayden decided Jordan *was* nuts. "I just saw him."

Scratching the back of her neck, Jordan sighed. "I'm sorry I interrupted. What were you saying, Cayden?"

Looking at Jordan strangely, Cayden scarfed the last bite of cookie and brushed off the crumbs with the back of her hand. "At first, being included in Ronan's clique was cool. All the guys used to hound her, and I thought I might be lucky enough to get one of her castaways. But now I get scared just looking at her, or when she looks at me in that...weird way. And what really worries me—" Cayden tilted closer to Jordan. "—are those spooky *things*, and Ronan's spells, I'm afraid if I ignore Ronan, she'll curse me. Something bad's going to happen, like...like what happened to you at the lake." She saw Jordan's eyes widen. "I'm not ignorant, Jordan. I know Ronan was behind it, and that's why you're staying clear."

Jordan nodded sympathetically and slipped the holy water out of her pocket. She slid it into Cayden's hand. "Holy water—use it well, every morning and night, or whenever you feel funny. You know what I mean. And if you're a religious person, I'd start practicing your faith."

Tipping the vial, Cayden sprinkled a few drops into her palm then smeared her hands on top of her head. Jordan smiled on the inside, watching as Cayden wet down her hair.

"I'm devout—starting today." A trace of a grin spread over Cayden's lips, not quite reaching her eyes.

ↄﻬↄ

January's snowfall exceeded expectations, even without the customary blizzard. Plows heaped masses of downy flakes the length of every roadway, creating mountains.

Today, Jordan was horizontal on the couch, content to watch television and enjoy the scrumptious scent of roast turkey. Henry snored in the recliner, while Em tinkered in the kitchen. The days were blissfully uninterrupted by scavengers from Hell, dicey mishaps with Ronan, or run-ins with the Order. Even Asa and Veronka seemed to be keeping a low profile.

Jordan shoved the math text and spiral notebook to the side and flipped channels. Her mom swept in the front door with a trailing frigid breeze. She yanked off her snowy boots, smiled at Jordan, and dashed up the stairs.

Within moments, Seeley trekked down to the kitchen, wrapped in a bathrobe. "Mom, it smells amazing, but I have to miss dinner tonight. I'm sorry—don't be mad."

Em's eyes narrowed. "What's so important that you have to miss my turkey dinner?"

Seeley's mouth tightened, obviously trying not to grin, but her eyes twinkled as she replied, "I have a date." She twirled on the balls of her feet like an excited little girl.

"A date!"

On hearing her mother's announcement, Jordan raced to the kitchen. "You have a date? With whom?" The prospect of her mother having a date seemed weird. Shouldn't Jordan be going on dates while her mom stayed at home doing laundry or something?

Seeley danced up the stairs with Jordan hot on her heels. "I know, I know. I haven't been on a date in so long. But Declan is so dynamic, I couldn't say no."

"But, Mom, do you even know anything about this guy?"

"Jordan, I've worked for Declan for years now. He's a good guy. He always gives me the time off when I need it, without questions."

Jordan nudged her mother's shoulder. "That doesn't answer my question."

Meticulously applying mascara, Seeley paused and fixed her lively blue eyes on her daughter. "What if I interview him tonight, and give you all the details tomorrow?"

"Am I going to meet this guy?"

"He's picking me up in an hour, so let me get ready, okay?" Seeley started rifling through her closet, discarding dresses and pants suits in heaps.

Jordan leapt onto the bed and watched her mom go berserk standing in front of the mirror, holding up hanger after hanger of clothing, analyzing every flaw.

Seeley turned to Jordan with a ruby dress that looked ancient. "What'd you think?"

Jordan's nose scrunched. "Nah, too awful. It might've worked ten years ago."

Moaning, Seeley tossed the dress on a pile and displayed another outfit, a navy blue suit. She posed, facing the mirror. Her eyes went to Jordan, whose face scrunched again as she shook her head. Flinging down the pants suit, Seeley threw her arms in the air. "I have nothing—absolutely nothing—to wear."

Bounding off the bed, Jordan flipped through the mishmash of outdated garments and, pushing hangers aside, pulled out a little black dress hidden between two gaudy sweaters. "This is perfect, Mom, classic black, sophisticated, and fashionable."

Seeley looked at her daughter, realizing she'd grown into a woman overnight. "Thanks, Jordan. How could I manage without you?"

Jordan pointed to the navy blue pants suit. "You would've worn that ugly contraption."

"That's one of my favorites."

"I know, and I think it's time for the Salvation Army."

Seeley looked at her tawdry clothing, defeated. "Okay, now vamoose so I can get ready."

Within an hour, Jordan sprinted for the front door. A relatively broad-shouldered man in his forties, not overly attractive, yet ruggedly nice-looking, waited on the stoop.

"May I come in or are you going to gape all night?"

A flushed erupted from her neck and spread up to her cheekbones. Jordan guessed he made a demanding boss and wondered what her mom saw in him. She stepped aside to let him enter. He swept his hand through his hair, sending snowflakes everywhere.

Declan Donavan assuaged Jordan's embarrassment with a pleasant, teasing smile. "You must be the beautiful Jordan I hear so much about." He extended a hand the size of a dinner plate. Losing her hand in his grip, she shook it.

"Declan." Seeley breezed down the staircase. "Come in, come in."

By this time Em and Henry had hobbled to the narrow entry to examine Seeley's boss and unexpected date. Seeley made introductions, then Mr. Donavan turned to her. "We have reservations at eight in the city."

Seeley snagged her coat, but Declan took it from her hand and spread it out for her.

Em tittered and whispered in Jordan's ear, "What a gentleman."

Seeley gave Jordan a bear hug and breathed, "Don't worry, he's a good guy."

Jordan, Henry, and Em, temporarily speechless, gawked from the front door as the couple drove away. Jordan's only consolation was the turkey dinner getting cold on the kitchen table.

ⱸⱾⱸⱾ

After unearthing his wife's extra-marital affairs and a messy divorce three years ago, Declan had sought refuge in his work. He rode his employees hard, thanks to an infinite drive to unveil the truth and bring newsworthy articles to the public. Known as the standoffish, hard-nosed editor-in-chief, he'd shown Seeley his soft side by gruffly allowing her to come and go as she pleased, as long as her articles and commentaries were of the highest quality. And with Declan's coaching, Seeley's stories were always top-notch.

For the past six months, Declan had given Seeley a yellow rose each week, along with an invitation to dinner. For six months, she had kindly declined. Seeley knew dating her boss could easily backfire, and then she'd find herself pounding the pavement. Notwithstanding, her topsy-turvy lifestyle had left little room for fun. Though lately, the calling had subsided somewhat, and she'd contemplated her own heart's desire. With her thirty-sixth birthday knocking on the door, Seeley yearned for male companionship. Invigorated, feeling reborn, Seeley finally agreed to an evening with the incalculable Declan Donavan.

The Chophouse Restaurant, situated in an elite section of the city, posted signs for valet service. As Declan rounded the drive, a young man in a red suit coat and black pants opened Seeley's door and, taking her hand, assisted her from the vehicle.

Declan smiled at the attendant. "Take care of her, son."

"Of course, Mr. Donavan."

Evidently Declan was well known. Seeley couldn't help but wonder how many women he'd dated over the years. He swept the coat from her shoulders and handed it to the coat check girl, who seemed enamored, issuing Declan a sweet smile. Seeley approved of the restaurant's subdued atmosphere and ocher-suffused lighting—very romantic. The bar was an artwork of burnished mahogany where intricately carved grapevines adorned the rail. In the corner, a woman dressed in a flowing evening gown plucked soft melodies on a stringed harp.

With a flourish, Declan pulled out a leather captain's stool which Seeley gracefully occupied. "What will you have?"

Seeley thought a moment. "Pinot Noir."

Declan hovered protectively beside her chair, checking out the room, as if he were casing the joint. Seeley chuckled at the silly way her mind worked and sipped the heady vintage.

Glimpsing over the rim, she looked into a pair of alert steely eyes. Then Ezekiel lowered his lashes, and Declan's touch on her shoulder drew Seeley's attention back to him.

They made small talk, discussing her next article until the hostess arrived to seat them, escorting the couple up a magnificent mahogany staircase to the second floor.

In a private alcove, a flaming candle danced cheekily as Declan held the cushioned Queen Anne chair for Seeley. After a fleeting glance at the other diners, she fidgeted with her dowdy hair then sighed as she noticed a snag on her dress.

As if reading her thoughts, Declan complimented her. "You're lovelier than everyone combined."

Seeley hated feeling insecure, though his compliment boosted her confidence. She raised the fluted glass to her lips while gazing into his steady powder-blue eyes.

"Seeley, we've worked together for years, but I hardly know anything about your personal life. Would I be insensitive if I asked about your husband?"

Virtually six years had passed since Jack's tragic death, and Seeley still loved and missed him. Even with time, the harrowing scene was still raw. "Jack died when Jordan was ten."

"I'm so sorry. Cancer?"

Not wanting to reveal the particulars of Jack's death, Seeley sidestepped the question. "No, murder, and not my best subject."

With a startled nod, Declan drained his bourbon. They passed the evening chatting about co-workers and miscellaneous events, like the recent downsizing economy. A few funny stories from Declan's childhood had Seeley in stitches, and she shared a few tales of her own childhood. Gazing at Declan in the candlelight, she admired his unpretentiousness and riveting tales. She scolded him blithely for not writing a novel to share his humorous and mostly ironic views with the public.

His hardy face lit up, but he laughed. "I'm too damn busy. Maybe someday, when I'm old and gray—which isn't that far off."

Soon the couple savored a fabulous meal of seared strip steak, five-layer au gratin potatoes, and root vegetables. Seeley waved away dessert. She couldn't eat another bite.

Then, in her peripheral vision, Seeley spied a recognizable sway. Turning her head, she observed the backside of Veronka and, a few feet ahead of her, Asa. She couldn't believe the coincidence.

Declan had also detected the couple. "Isn't that Asa Trebane?"

"Yes, unfortunately."

Momentarily serious, Declan said, "Your interview raised eyebrows. I've been expecting retaliation, a lawsuit, or worse from Trebane's organization. I went with my gut and printed it, though."

Seeley saw Declan shift in his seat and rise, then she heard Asa's distinct voice. "Mr. Declan Donavan, am I correct?"

Declan pumped Asa's offered hand then gestured to Seeley. "Yes, and this is—"

"Ah, yes, Seeley Chase, so pleased to see you again."

Seeley nodded, but refused to meet the man's eyes.

"Mr. Donavan, I hope Seeley's article about my life and loves has boosted *The Courier*'s circulation?" Asa said, somewhat churlishly.

"I'll have to check, Mr. Trebane. Thank you again for the interview." Declan was unnerved by Asa's forceful presence. "Perhaps you'd consider a consultant position to reform our business section. It's been floundering lately."

Seeley jerked backward, shocked by Declan's absurd offer, but Asa's prideful answer relieved her. "I'd be quite an asset to the newspaper. Alas, the time spent would lose me money. But thank you for the offer. We shall meet again."

Asa's parting stroke of Seeley's shoulder did not go unnoticed.

Seeley felt a surge of hatred rush to the surface and barely restrained herself until Asa prowled pompously over to his table to join Veronka. Then Seeley shot from her chair and insisted Declan take her home.

Once safe in Declan's car, Seeley felt like a discourteous child. He must have thought her request an unjustified overreaction. She apologized. "Sorry, Declan, that man makes my blood boil, and not in a good way."

"Yes, I could tell."

The car idled and Declan cranked up the heat, deicing the windows. Without warning, he leaned forward, cupping Seeley's delicate chin in his hand and tenderly tasted her supple lips. His hand slid behind her neck and he buried his fingers in her hair, drawing her toward him. With Seeley's full cooperation, the kiss intensified.

Declan released her, wanting more. "Will you come to my place—for a drink?" In the confines of the car, his eyes were dark.

Seeley hesitated, fighting the desire to lose herself in him. "I–I don't think so, Declan."

"I'll never force the issue. Your call, Seeley." His voice was thick with longing.

"You and the dinner were both wonderful. Thank you, Declan, but I'd like to go home."

"Perchance you'll give me the honor again, sometime soon. I'd hate to wait another six months for dinner."

Seeley's face lit up with her smile.

CHAPTER 17

Though I Walk in the Dark,
Angels with Gilded Wings Follow Me.

Carting a cardboard box packed with the final Christmas decorations down from the living room, Jordan set it on the floor, brushed her grimy hands on her jeans, and glanced at her mom. "Thrill McKenna asked me to go sledding. That's all right, isn't it?"

"Oooh, Jordan, you have a date?"

"Mom—" Jordan said with a scolding tone and an eye roll. "Tomorrow night, okay?"

"I can't remember the last time I took you sledding. It's been a while, huh?"

"Yeah, I'll probably freeze my butt off."

Jordan followed her mom up the basement steps to kitchen, where they joined Em and Henry at the table.

"Well, that's done," Seeley said, smacking her dusty hands.

"Thanks, girls." Henry blew over the rim of his mug and sipped.

Seeley couldn't resist. "Jordan has a date tomorrow night."

Heads turned to look at Jordan. She groaned. "Mom, give me a break."

"Well, it's your first official date, isn't it?"

"Who with, Jordan?" Em piped up.

"Thrill McKenna. You met him before the Winter Ball, remember?"

Em's eyes sparkled. "Oh, yes, that good-looking young man. I thought his name was William?" Her bamboozled expression doubled the wrinkles between her eyebrows and forehead.

"Yes, his name is William," Jordan said. "But everyone calls him Thrill, just a nickname."

Henry looked disquieted. "I hope that name isn't an indication of his character?"

"His parents started calling him Thrill when he was a baby," Jordan explained, swiftly putting an end to their way of thinking. "It's got nothing to do with his character now."

They accepted her explanation with tentative nods. Then changing the subject, much to Jordan's relief, Emily looked at Seeley. "So will you be seeing Mr. Donavan again?"

"I think we're going to the theater on Saturday." Seeing Jordan's surprise, she added lightheartedly, "You're not the only one who has a date."

ℰↄℰↄ

The temperature held steady at a balmy thirty degrees with a wind chill factor of twenty as Thrill veered into Chestnut Ridge's full-to-capacity parking lot. Jordan's abundant layers—including thermals, sweater, hoodie, scarf, gloves, and coat—prohibited any possible gracefulness as she attempted to help Thrill unloaded the inflated tubes.

He chucked a tube to the ground. "I hope you're warm enough, Jordan."

"I can barely move." She twined the rope in her hand and began to drag the tube. Her nose and mouth produced exaggerated puffs of mist as they shambled toward the thoroughfare. Towering lights, like those used on football fields, saturated the area with brightness, making the sky above appear pitch black. The park swarmed with adults and children. Lively shrieks echoed all over the ridge. Jordan was astounded by the exuberance of the young children, diving on tubes and flying over the edge to uncertain mayhem.

"Hey, look who's here." Thrill waved to Beth and friends.

Beth signaled for them to come over.

Jordan couldn't believe her eyes. *Her* guardian angel was hanging out—like one of the gang. Apparently, Markus had resurfaced without making himself visible to her. She was piqued over his inferred exodus, yet here he was sledding with Beth—not to mention rambling through the school without so much as speaking to her. She issued him a brusque nod. She was ticked-off, no—more than ticked-off—mad.

So she snubbed her angel and stayed close to Thrill. It only took a minute before Jordan felt Markus's hot breath in her ear. "Jordan, can you give me a minute to explain?"

Without even acknowledging his appeal, she tromped out to peek over the ridges cusp. Her stomach squeezed like an accordion as she watched people rocket through the air, rolling and bumping on the snowy ground. She didn't quite remember that steep incline. Imitating Henry, Jordan harrumphed and shuffled away from the commotion.

Thrill stood on what Jordan thought of as the Ledge of Certain Doom, holding the inflated tube. "Come on, it's our turn," he shouted. Before she had a chance to protest, he captured her gloved hand and gathered his arms around her waist, drawing her with him onto the tube.

"No, Thrill, I don't think I'm ready." Her feeble attempts to disengage herself went unheeded as Thrill securely locked his legs around her.

"Let's go," he called.

Jeff and Kristin heaved and sent them over the ledge. The brisk cold burned Jordan's eyeballs before scrunching them tightly. She was scared out of her mind as they sped toward the tumult below. The tube picked up more speed. Her scream reverberated along the ridge and Thrill added his mimicking squeals. Striking a bump, they went airborne for brief seconds before landing soundly on the tube and sliding briskly to the bottom of the hill. Coasting about twenty feet, they hit another bump, which flung them tumbling on their backs.

"Are you okay?" Thrill asked, worried. He thought she was crying.

Trounced with snow and laughing rowdily, Jordan exclaimed, "That was great!"

Hand in hand, they traipsed up the hill. On their next jaunt Thrill and Jordan followed Beth and Markus's example. Thrill lay on his stomach with Jordan on his back. Her arms choked him to death as she held on for dear life and her screams nearly burst his eardrum as well. She face-planted at the bottom, and a surge of riotous whooping came from Thrill at her obvious displeasure. Recovering some dignity, she chuckled while wiping her snow caked face.

Unstoppable, Jordan turned into a sledding guru. She clasped a tube across her chest and, head first, recklessly flung herself over the edge without a second thought, swooshing over the snowy pathway. At the bottom of the hill, instead of slowing, she kept gliding, almost picking up speed. Her jouncing tube sliced near a tree and slid into the woods.

That was a close call, Jordan thought. The air in the murky evergreens suddenly felt extremely bitter. The wind wailed through the trees, bending the branches, creating a deafening din. Jordan became aware of a sickening presence.

Without a sound or warning, Jordan was suddenly hanging in midair. She barely had time to register what was happening when she was thrown backward, just missing an ice-covered rock. Though her vision adapted to the shadowed grove, she still couldn't see a person, only an obscure presence. Bending her mind, she snared a nearby rock, which flew forward, passing straight through the muddy shape.

"Jordan." Markus appeared, flinging a tube behind him. Mottled moonlight filtered through pine boughs, falling on Markus, who appeared to glide toward her. He turned his head toward the spot where, only a minute earlier, Jordan had spied the eerie form.

"Markus, over there," Jordan cried, pointing. "Something's here."

Taken off-guard, Markus was yanked five feet in the air and smashed against a huge tree trunk. Huddled in the drift, he recovered, transforming into an angel—an angel in overdrive. He raised his hand.

Jordan's eyes bulged when she saw lightning sizzle from his fingers like a javelin and strike the imperceptible being. "Awesome."

A mysterious stranglehold clamped down on her throat. She couldn't breathe. As she clawed at her neck, she was winched upward. She kicked her legs behind her only to come in contact with—nothing. She gurgled, trying to get Markus's attention as her consciousness faded. She could only think, *This thing's going to snap my neck.*

Markus whirled toward Jordan. Without hesitation, he threw himself at the inky creature. Its grip loosened. Jordan fell into a drift.

Gulping for air, massaging the column of her throat, she watched in horror as Markus and the obscure creature crashed from tree to tree. A blaze of light and dark, they fought their way out of sight.

Waiting, every nerve alert, Jordan heard crunchy footsteps. She looked for an angelic glow, yet none was seen. Finally, not her dazzling angel—but a human, Mark stooped and lugged her from the powdery drift. She breathed a thankful sigh.

"Why don't you use that lightning thingy more often?" she asked. "It'd save a lot of time."

"It zaps my strength too quickly." His fair hair was a mesh of soaked whorls, and he sounded out of breath. "I don't like this!" he said, clearly irked. "Why are they seeking you so frantically? It's almost like...like there was a price on your head."

"I must have a bull's-eye from hell on my back," Jordan interjected. "Markus, you've been back for a while. How come you haven't come to see me?"

Clomping footsteps foiled any explanation. Her answer would have to wait as they prepared for another beastie.

"Jordan? Mark?" Thrill yelled. He stumbled through the trees to find Mark shielding Jordan. "Am I interrupting?"

"No, Thrill." And unflappable, Markus patted at Jordan's snow-covered jacket and jeans. "Jordan hit a tree. She seems a little dazed."

"Oh." He looked at Jordan, relieved. His tone softer, but was still skeptical. "Are you all right?"

"Yeah, fine." Her voice shook as she swatted away Markus's helpful hands.

"Thrill, why don't you help Jordan? I'll carry the tubes."

Thrill's arm circled her waist. "We were wondering what was taking you two so long."

Hightailing into the Ridge's casino for hot cocoa, they found everyone jostling around a stoned fireplace, a roaring blaze crackled. Shrugging off gloves, scarves, and coats, they bathed in the warm heat.

"Ahh, this feels good." Beth slipped off her mittens and raised her hands to the warmth, while Kristen and Jeff heated their backsides, smiling. "Wow, Jordan, you could've been really hurt if you'd hit a tree."

Jordan's gaze skated past Markus. She knelt on her heels, facing the fire. "Missed the tree by inches."

Thrill looked dubious. "I've never seen anyone sled that far into the woods. Seemed pretty unusual." Heads bobbed, agreeing with Thrill. The conversation faded, each person caught in the trance of undulating flames.

Jordan broke the spell, saying dryly, "I think I'm done for the night, but don't let me stop you, Thrill."

"Nah, I'm freezing. Let's get out of here." He swigged the rest of his cocoa and helped Jordan to her feet. "See you guys later."

"Bye, everyone." Jordan snagged Markus's glinting eyes. "See you later."

Unusually quiet on the ride home, Thrill finally looked at Jordan. "It was strange…"

As casually as she could, Jordan said, "What was strange?"

Thrill shrugged. "I saw you sledding too close to the trees and was ready to come after you when Mark just about ripped the tube from my hands and flew down the hill."

"Oh?"

"And when neither of you walked out, I thought you must be hurt. I had to wait until Kristin walked up with her tube to follow. I thought I saw a flash of light, though…"

Jordan trembled to think of Thrill being trapped in that skirmish. "I was a bit shaky and Mark made me sit awhile."

A muscle jumped in Thrill's jaw and Jordan wondered if he suspected her lie.

They both felt damp and cold by the time they reached her house. Thrill walked Jordan to the front door and, without warning, gently held her face, kissing her warmly on the lips. "I'll call, okay?" he breathed gently.

Jordan nodded with an inane grin, watching Thrill walk to the car.

Practically floating up the stairs, she went quietly into the bathroom. She passed the mirror and groaned, seeing her blotchy face, wet snarly hair, and red, obviously runny nose. She groaned again.

"Jordan, how was your night?" Seeley called softly.

Jordan slipped into her mom's bedroom, noting that she had Jack's journal in her lap. Jordan grinned, completely forgetting the eerie spirits. "It was great. Thrill's nice."

Seeley noticed her rosy cheeks and dreamy eyes and smothered a little giggle. "Do you want to talk about it?"

"Sledding was a riot. I forgot how much fun it can be." Then it hit her—the confrontation in the woods. Her brow furrowed. She didn't want to think about it, not now.

"What's wrong? Did something happen?"

"No, no." Jordan paused then spoke in a rush. "Thrill kissed me, but I wasn't ready. I think I flubbed it."

"Did he ask to see you again?"

"He said he'd call."

"You did fine," Seeley said, smiling.

Dead tired, and thankful to be alive, Jordan crawled beneath her cozy quilt. With an indelible smile, she wondered what Thrill thought of their first official date. She ran her fingers over her chapped lips, remembering the soft pressure of his mouth.

Jordan's mind flopped to her weird life. How could she have a boyfriend? Thrill could get hurt, physically and mentally. Her mom must have the same worries about Mr. Donavan. Now Jordan understood why she hadn't dated for so long after her father's death.

An hour went by as she waited for Markus. With her eyes drooping, she decided to snooze until Markus showed up.

It wasn't her angel singing in her ears, but her alarm clock that woke her in the morning.

CHAPTER 18

The Crossroads Have Become an Abomination.

Despairing, Father James knelt in the first pew, propping his head in his hands. The church was dark except for the perpetual candle beside the tabernacle. He was plagued with uncertainty and doubt about the possessive demons on the rise, constituting loss of life and impurity. He wept for the end of innocence.

Raising a teary face, he spoke to his predecessor, Edmund Posluszny, pleading. "Edmund, ungodliness ravages the world. Even our own little village is suffering. We need help." He paused to take a tattered breath. "Are we losing the battle?"

A hiss drew the priest's head upward to the lofty crucifix. The sole candle fluttered, casting sporadic shadows on Christ's Corpus. A massive serpent rose from the top beam of the cross. Its split tongue hissed repeatedly. Deliberately, the serpent coiled sinuously around the corpus, enveloping it. A faint splinter sounded as the beast applied pressure, crushing the granite.

Father James stared at the apparition, transfixed. A crackle of wood roused him from his state of shock. He blinked to rid himself of the offensive scene. The cross teetered. He gasped—it would topple at any moment.

"Saint Michael the Archangel, defend us in battle," he murmured in a harried voice. "Be our safeguard against the wickedness and snares of the devil. By the power of God, cast into Hell Satan and the evil spirits who prowl the world seeking the ruin of souls."

Another sound made him raise his eyelids. The statue of Christ flushed with color—breathed to life. Seraphim and cherubim filled the sanctuary with splendor. Then Father James saw Father Posluszny prostrate before the altar. A heavenly choir of angels sang sonorous praise. In the midst of the serpent's coils, Jesus raised His pierced palms, beams of light issuing forth from the wounds. Father James sheltered his eyes, rapt with the experience.

The serpent, engorged with evil, shuddered, unable to abide in divine sanctity. Its treacherous grip slackened and it dropped to the ground. A beatific woman clothed with the sun, appeared. Raising her foot, she crushed the beast's head with her heel. Resplendence enraptured the sanctuary of St. Mary of the Holy Angels.

Father James blinked in the radiance. His eyes reopened to the one lit candle and silence. The sanctuary, and the crucifix, remained unchanged.

In the solitude, hushed footfalls breezed up the aisle. It was after three in the morning. The church doors were locked. With a racing pulse, the priest vaulted from the pew and spun to face two men. He recognized them immediately.

"Father James, we must talk," said Ezekiel, with Markus by his side.

cseco

Cruising the school corridors, searching for one memorable face, Jordan ran into Ronan who, uncharacteristically, said nothing. Jordan stepped back, inspecting the once beautiful girl and was shocked by her lanky unkempt hair and weary bloodshot eyes. She looked like she'd been crying nonstop, and she'd lost weight. Her clothes seemed to hang on her.

Jordan felt compelled to ask, "Ronan, are you all right?"

"No. Do I look all right?" she said. "My friends have abandoned me. I'm all alone. My dad's gone, again, on another business trip." Ronan swiped at her runny nose with the back of her hand.

Pathetic, thought Jordan. She felt somewhat sorry for the girl. "Do you want to go out for a cup of coffee after school and talk?"

"Look at me, Jordan." Ronan held her arms out like preparing to be frisked for inspection. "Do I look like I want to be out in public? I don't even want to be here. In fact, I think I'll take the rest of the week off." She started to walk away.

"Wait, Ronan—" Jordan didn't know what to say. "You should call Paisley and Cayden to keep you company tonight?"

Ronan's face twisted into a broken grin. "You'd love to come too, right?" Then she blended into the corridor full of students.

Jordan lagged behind Ronan. And noted the girl's head veering sideways and mouthing words, like she was talking to someone—someone not visible. A nippy shiver rocked Jordan.

After dinner, she called for Markus, then again after her shower, and then again. Like a caged animal, she stalked around her room and hallway. Markus had picked a great time to ignore her. Jordan couldn't stop wondering why he'd talked to Cayden and then to Paisley, and completely hidden himself from her.

When Markus had said that he'd be gone for a while, Jordan took for granted that he'd meant from school, the country—the earth. And he hadn't been gone at all! Her temper hitting the boiling point, Jordan slammed off the light and walked into the hallway. Something caught her eye in the dark bedroom, a spark.

She trounced back into the room, aware that staying calm wasn't working for her. She pointed accusingly. "Where've you been? I thought you were going away, and then I find out you've been here the whole time. What's going on?"

Jordan gasped slightly when another angelic Markus appeared. There was two of Markus, side by side. "You were never alone," the one on the right said. "And I couldn't very well miss school, could I? My disappearance would've caused quite a stir with the Schaffer Family." Markus's hand flipped to the duplicate angel. "Meet Rafe."

"You have another angel impersonating you. Why didn't you just tell me about Rafe?"

"Because I know how you think," he said, not expounding further.

The duplicate angel dipped his head and vanished, leaving Markus and Jordan alone.

"Then that wasn't you sledding with us," she said. "It was the other Markus?"

"Oh, that was me," he stated emphatically. "Rafe notified me of your date to go sledding."

"How'd he find out?"

He smiled ingeniously. "Word gets around rather quickly in high school. Although there's another development— Veronka's on the warpath." Markus's features hardened. "As I'd suspected, she's initiated a bounty. She's offered some sort of reward to the demon that captures you."

Jordan gawked. "That sounds awesome," she said, her voice dripping with sarcasm. "Don't tell my mom or I'll be in protective custody forever."

Markus seemed to grow cold, and, if she didn't know better, almost—fearful? "I think your mom should be made aware—"

"Absolutely not."

Then Ezekiel emerged from the ether and said without preamble, "Jordan, get your mother, now."

Seeing the angel's mournful expression, Jordan knew something was wrong. She started to leave then turned back. "I didn't tell her what happened when we went sledding." Jordan templed her hands. "Please don't say anything. She's just starting to get a life. Please," she said and entreated Markus with pleading eyes.

Markus tipped his head in agreement, though he looked unhappy. While at the same time Ezekiel looked disturbed and shook his head.

Moments later, Seeley rushed into the room with Jordan trailing behind her. "What's wrong?"

Ezekiel said, "We have a major crisis."

Markus half-turned, masking his troubled eyes. He spoke with an edge to his voice. "We're in a quandary. It's inexplicable. Lines have been crossed."

Weak-kneed, Seeley lowered onto the bed. By the tone of Markus's voice, the news would be horrendous. Jordan stood sturdily, her hand firm on Seeley's shoulder. Then in a sight to behold, the angelic beings unfolded feathery wings. A fiery kaleidoscope of lustrous, crystalline colors danced about the room enveloping the women protectively. Markus's glimmering eyes locked onto Jordan's.

"The Powers have discovered a violation," Ezekiel stated. He paused briefly, looking at Markus before continuing. "You know that tiny voice in the back of a person's mind? It has the potential to influence someone toward the dark side. Since the beginning of time, evil has oozed into the world, corrupting human souls, but now someone or something is creating abnormal aberrations. We're presently at a crossroads."

Jordan was riveted, though not quite comprehending.

"Demons are impregnating humans," Markus explained, visibly grieving, "who give birth to half-breeds."

Seeley's head moved slowly from side to side. "No—" she breathed catatonically. "No, this can't be happening." It was an imminent vision that had been plaguing her. In her heart, Seeley knew these creatures were a reality.

"What can we do?" Jordan said. "How can we fight this?"

"Ridding the world of this kind of atrocity will be nearly impossible," Zeke admitted, but he declined to go into specifics.

Jordan and Markus faced each other wordlessly. The blast of her cell phone jolted them.

"Omigosh," she said. "I forgot, I'm supposed to be at Ronan's tonight."

Seeley rose. "You cannot go to that...that girl's house."

"But, Mom, I think Ronan's seeking help—my help. I feel it."

"Markus, Zeke, reason with her. Ronan cannot be trusted. Not now, when everything's turning upside down."

"Your mother's right, Jordan," Ezekiel concurred.

"I'll go with Jordan," Markus offered.

Jordan smiled at Markus, all her anger evaporating like a whiff of smoke.

"That wouldn't be wise." Ezekiel glared at the younger angel. "Ronan knows what you are, which could be dangerous. With The Order's resources, it's more than likely that they've trained Ronan well. Her ability could far exceed our expectations."

"God would want me to help Ronan, wouldn't He?" Jordan protested, with her hands on her hips. "I don't like Ronan. She nearly killed me, but what really pisses me off are these soulless manipulators! They have the gall to do whatever they want, take whomever they want, and kill—" Swallowing a sob, Jordan brushed at a loose tear. "Dad would know what to do!"

She ran from the room and banged the bathroom door behind her.

"I think all this news has made Jordan a bit anxious." Seeley turned to Zeke. "I'm going to take her to Sacred Heart Church with Father James tonight. Stay close—and wish me luck with my speech."

ↄ◈ↄ

"Since I'm running late, Father James is meeting us at the church." Seeley shot her daughter a darting glance while turning right. "I know you're upset, Jordan. But I think we should talk to him first, explain more about Ronan, and get his advice." The car fishtailed on the slippery pavement.

Jordan huffed. She had her arms crossed and knew there was a less than pleasant expression on her face. "Ever since I've been old enough to understand about Dad and the book he wrote, and then read his journal, all I ever wanted to do was help rid the world of evil beings. I know this is going to sound bad, really bad, but I *want* to kill demons.

"Every time I close my eyes, I can picture Dad hanging on that cross. I see and feel his blood dripping on me and hear the way you screamed. It haunts me. Maybe Asa's curse is still working, because in my dreams, I hear you screaming all the time." She hesitated and pinned a piece of hair behind her ear. "Mom, I don't know if I want to do this anymore." It felt like a wad of cotton was bunched in her throat. "I—I want to be like a normal teenager—go on dates and not have to think about demons jumping out at me. I don't want to agonize about those things hurting someone I'm with."

Seeley didn't know what to say at first. What could she possibly tell her daughter to make her feel better about an impossible life situation? Then a belief popped into her head. "Jordan, God would never make you do anything against your will. You're free to be whomever you desire."

"B–but–but I thought I was a warrior," stammered Jordan. "I can do unusual…stuff."

"True, and I don't rightly know why it was foreseen before your birth, but—" Seeley's forehead creased in thought. "We're all called to be warriors, more or less, by fighting those evil thoughts, helping people, being a good person, and showing kindness and respect to others."

"So could I walk away from all this, this demon stuff and just be a good person?"

"I don't know. I really don't know. I'd be lying if I said anything different."

"Well, Mom, you're not helping me one bit."

Seeley already felt panicky about the speech she had to make, and now Jordan was being an absolute pill. She wanted to scream. Instead, she sighed. "Father James will be here tonight. Talk to him about this, or maybe even Markus. There's the church. I'm late—he's probably thinking I chickened out."

The attendance was disappointing, scarcely fifty people. Slumped low in the last pew in the church, Jordan listened to her mother's lecture.

"It's time to take our world away from the devil," Seeley began and paused to catch a ragged breath. "The evil one has claimed our land and roams freely, devouring morality and purity. He deceives our young people into seeking vain, prideful glory as the only way to achieve success, squashing anyone and everyone in their way. Revenge is taught as the norm in today's society. We face an epidemic of materialism and commercialism."

An insatiable fire rose in Seeley. She heard her voice ringing out, speaking words she had not written. The audience clung to every syllable, slanting forward, nodding reflexively, refreshed by the words. "One person can make a difference," she continued. "And, bit by bit, little by little, moral decency *can* and *will* prevail."

Father James eased into the pew next to Jordan, his eyes on Seeley. "She's good. When I introduced her, I thought she was going to lose it. But I can tell she's touching a nerve. People are listening."

"Yeah, but there aren't many people here," Jordan whispered dolefully.

"These people will leave here tonight and, hopefully, talk to other people. Goodness spreads like wildfire. Besides, we have many churches to visit. We'll be at Saints Peter and Paul next week and more people will carry the torch."

"Why don't you tell people about demons attacking humans?" She cast him an indignant look. "That'd change things real quick."

Swallowing a breath, Father James shifted to face the young lady who had lived her life in a strange world. "Altercations between demons and humans have occurred for centuries. Most people are aware of evil."

"No, Father," she said. "Not mind control or deception. I mean literally killing humans."

He grimaced. "Jordan, I'd be afraid of people going off the deep end. That could cause panic, suicides, and depression—people would be scared to leave their homes. Civilization would come to a standstill. No, we cannot let Satan rule by fear."

Jordan fiddled with her fingers. "Father, would you be disappointed if I decided not to fight? Demons, I mean."

"Oh, I sense you're at a crossroads."

"Don't say crossroads—Markus and Ezekiel just told us about the half-breeds."

"Ah-h, now I understand." Father James's stolid face brightened into a smile. "Jordan, I have it on good authority that God's in control. It doesn't appear that way, but have faith. The greater the faith, the more is expected of you. Belief will give you the confidence to persevere in your trials. We will all have our crosses to bear, one way or another." He then observed Seeley beckoning to him. The priest patted Jordan's hand and rose, but before walking away he said, "Don't be afraid, He is with you."

At the end of Seeley's speech, people milled about, asking her questions and buying Jack's book, which Seeley had entitled, appropriately, *Beware*. The proceeds would go toward another printing, due out in February.

Shouldering their coats, Seeley thanked Jordan for her support and asked how she'd sounded.

"You did great," Jordan told her. "Your voice carried clearly. I heard you from the last pew."

Glad for the nearby streetlamp flowing into the parking lot, Seeley unlocked the doors and huddled behind the steering wheel, adjusting the seat belt. "Whoa, it's so cold." She waved to Father James as he strode from the church. "He's a good man and a holy priest. I saw you talking with him." The engine thrummed to life and she cranked up the heat." Did he help?"

"A little. Do you think I could try being normal—take a break from the doom and gloom?"

"I don't think it works that way." Hitching her shoulders up to her neck along with the lapels of her coat, Seeley shivered. "You can't say you want the demons to leave you alone for a month and then, next month, say, okay I'm back. You'd have to leave the battle completely and even then, with your past…" Seeley negotiated a turn, her heart aching for her daughter. "I can't be positive what would happen."

"I feel like I have a tracking device with a bull's-eye attached to my back, Mom. Sometimes it freaks me out."

In frustration, Seeley slammed the steering wheel. "I know, I know." She was on the verge of tears. "And I'm so, *so* sorry. I don't know what I'd do if anything…if anything ever—"

Jordan cut her off. "Mom, I'm okay, really. Never mind—forget what I said."

Seeley snuffled, wiping her nose on the back of her glove. How could she forget the danger Jordan faced daily?

CHAPTER 19

The Arrogant Have Risen.

Whistling a tune, Seeley shrugged on the lavender jersey dress and wedged her feet into matching purple suede heels. Absorbed with Declan and their growing rapport, she glowed like a teenager. She swept a brush through her hair, did a make-up inspection, then trekked downstairs into the kitchen where her parents were eating dinner.

"Phew, you look like Jordan," Henry complimented and winked. "This Declan guy seems like an okay fella."

"He is, Dad." Her stomach grumbled and she snatched a carrot to fill the hole.

"We should have him over for a family dinner," her mom said thoughtfully. "What do you think, Seeley?"

"It may be a bit soon," she said. "I don't want to scare him off."

"Are you embarrassed of us?" Henry protested in a gruff tone. "Think we'd frighten the poor guy away?"

"I didn't mean it that way," she said. "I meant he'd think I was getting serious. You know what I mean, right?"

Then Em took the initiative to ask, "Well—are you serious?"

Seeley drew in a breath, with her parents waiting anxiously for her answer. "He's...he's just right."

Enhancing her face, Em's giddy smile made her look years younger.

"By the way, Dad, Declan isn't a poor guy, and you'd never scare him off."

Amusement played on their faces when the doorbell rang.

"Here he is now. Remember, Jordan's at the diner with Thrill and should be home by eleven." Seeley slipped into her coat and swung open the door, then said over her shoulder, "Don't wait up for me."

His expression skeptical, Declan looked at her feet. "You're wearing *those* shoes?"

Seeley peered at the pretty heels. "Yes, why?"

"Did you happen to look outside?" he said. "Snow, snow, and more snow."

"Don't you like them?" She turned a shapely leg, showing off the purple heels.

Declan's appreciative smile answered that question. "They're lovely. Come on, let's go."

He clasped her elbow, and they made it to the car without any mishaps. Observing his surly brow and pinched lips, Seeley hoped a mood change was in order. Declan drove toward the city, then detoured to the north. She'd assumed they had reservations downtown. She looked curiously at Declan, whose face remained like stone.

"There's been a change in plans," Declan said sternly. He looked positively livid with his jaw clenched.

"Is there something wrong?" Seeley inquired. "You seem more than uptight."

His normally light eyes, darkened with his mood, flit to her and then back to the road. "That bastard's put me in quite a predicament," he said. "Upper management's breathing down my neck, and now I have to kiss his ass."

"What are you talking about?" Seeley said, thoroughly confounded.

"Asa Trebane," Declan seethed between his scissored teeth. "His lawyer contacted *The Courier* and said he'll sue for libel, with the goal of taking over the paper or shutting us

down. He implied the newspaper was a waste of natural resources."

Furious with Asa's latest outrage, Seeley exhaled. "He
signed the consent forms for publication. I did everything by
the book, Dec."

"Yes, well, that's not how he sees it. He claims you twisted his words and maligned his upstanding good character. 'His
benevolent disposition wrongly misrepresented by Seeley
Chase,' I believe was the exact quote."

Now it was Seeley's turn to fume. "He said that? That
contemptible, foul—"

"Okay, okay, don't get me going. We have to smooth this
over."

"What'd you mean?" Seeley didn't like the sound of it.
"How do we do that?"

"Asa's invited us both to his country house tonight for an
elegant dinner party. We are to proclaim our good host as an
exceedingly charming man of sound and upright character."
Declan's phrase tasted sour on his tongue.

"Declan, I can't go there. This is like…blackmail." She
automatically clutched her purse then realized she had forgotten the holy water.

"You have to go with me, or we'll both be out of a job by
tomorrow." He gave her a resolute glance. "His lawyer insisted."

"Oh, Dec." She covered her eyes with her hand in dismay.
"You don't understand. That man…I despise him. He's evil."

Swerving sharply to the curb, Declan slammed the car into park, endeavoring to quash his bottled-up fury. "Seeley,
these financial geniuses think they rule the world, but they're
just rich sons-of-bitches. I wouldn't give a rat's ass if it didn't
mean our jobs."

He looked at Seeley. Her tear-filled eyes knocked the
wind from his sails. Declan wiped a lone tear from her cheek,
his anger fading. "Seeley, I'm sorry. Can you do this—for us?"

Seeley wanted to tell him so much, but why hurt Declan?
And what would he think of her? A lunatic who has visions
and banishes demons?

She wanted to confide in him, spill her guts about Jack, the demons, Ezekiel, Markus and, most importantly, Asa. Would her outlandish ravings sound genuine, or would Declan drop *the loony* like a greased pig? She decided not to risk it and nodded to Declan, conceding to Asa's demand. She squelched an untimely gush of tears with a loud hiccough.

As they journeyed to Asa's, Seeley wondered how many demons he employed. She felt sure that, somewhere on the premises, he had a place to perform satanic rituals. The memory of Jack crucified tunneled to the forefront and the smell of blood. Seeley then remembered why she had avoided any romantic attachments. Now she'd broken her own rules and brought Declan into Asa's world of black magic. Her hands knotted in her lap. The decision was made—this would be their last date.

Entering the stately mansion, the pit of her stomach turned to rot. A concentration of ungodliness and impurity plagued her senses. Feeling overwhelming dread, she looked at Declan. He had a scowl fixed on his face, anticipating an unpleasant task ahead. Seeley understood his dilemma. He was not the type of a man to compromise his integrity.

A warning erupted within Seeley and she recognized Zeke's voice. '*This house is dedicated to Lucifer with consensual human sacrifice and immeasurable transgressions. I will not be able to abide for long. I'd advise you to leave.*'

She couldn't turn back now, she thought. Her sense of dread was obviously not contagious as laughter sounded from the neighboring rooms. In the foyer, Seeley gawked at an ornate painting of 'The Temptation of Jesus,' depicting Jesus succumbing to the Devil and soaring off a building. Unconventional bronze symbols decorated the walls and antique side tables held vases spilling with abundant bouquets of every imaginable flower.

An aloof man in a butler's garb led Declan and Seeley to an elaborate study. Vintage Brazilian cherry panels encased the high-rise walls and grandiose sconces set a burnish gleam to the wood. One shelved wall held a ceiling to floor library of leather-bound books. A fieldstone fireplace came into view where a blaze simmered on the hearth. To Seeley's relief, she recognized a few dignitaries in the room. Then she spied Asa.

Even the sound of his voice made her hostile. She watched his smooth performance, designed to fool the most intelligent guest. As if Asa felt Seeley's eyes touch him, he turned and held her gaze.

"Ah, here they are." Asa raised a champagne glass to toast their entrance. "To Editor-in-Chief and his intrepid reporter, may you live well and prosper."

As if on cue, a waiter proffered a serving tray full of fluted glasses. Seeley, only too happy to oblige, drank nervously, hoping to stifle her anxiety.

Asa sauntered over to the couple and stretched out his hand to Declan.

Declan sneered at Asa's hand like he wanted to break each finger. He was surprised at Asa's hard, cold grip and squeezed for good measure.

"Let's get a picture for the paper, shall we?" Asa's tone was crisp. He signaled a young man with a camera. "Over here, Jimmy Olsen."

A young man in a rented tux pushed through the people. His freckled cheeks were scarlet. "Hello, Mr. Donavan. Thank you for the assignment. You know I'm really Thomas Polanski, but Mr. Trebane likes to call me Jimmy Olsen. Um, I think you get the joke?"

"Hey, Thomas." Declan's expression softened considerably. He patted the young man on the shoulder. "Thanks for helping out on such short notice."

Asa edged between Seeley and Declan, modifying his tone from genial host to tyrant. "Everyone look pleased because we're such good friends."

Thomas adjusted the lens and snapped the shot.

Seeley brushed Asa's hand from her shoulder. "What the hell are you trying to prove, Asa?" Her voice was low and taut.

"We'll talk later." With that perfunctory answer, Asa strolled over to an assembly of notable men and women, dripping in their finery.

Inspecting those present for red-ringed eyes, Seeley spotted at least seven, plus the notorious Veronka in a risqué evening gown that left little to the imagination. Veronka taunted her with a condescending grin. Squaring her shoulders, Seeley ignored the grin with dignity. She would never provide Veronka the satisfaction of seeing her squirm.

Declan clinked their glasses together. "My apologies, Seeley, for spoiling the evening."

Seeley stepped closer to Declan, whispering behind her glass, "Let's sneak out as soon as possible."

Declan sipped his champagne, his soured expression changing drastically with a sanguine shake of his head.

They conversed with the industrious mayor, Peter Grifton, and several well-known swindlers representing themselves as lawyers and financial experts, as well as Mr. Virgil Detroit, who owned three-fourths of *The Courier Express*.

Virgil wrung Declan's hand. "You made the right decision. Trebane will let the whole thing blow over, I'm sure." Then, spying Seeley, he smiled. "So, this is the infamous Seeley Chase?"

"Infamous, no." Seeley shook his hand. "But yes, I'm Seeley Chase."

"Play your cards right with Asa and someday you'll have a Pulitzer." Virgil eyed Seeley from head to toe. "He's the right man to boost your climb."

A foul gurgle emanated in Declan's throat and his scowl returned. Irritated, he took Seeley's hand. "Excuse us, Virgil, Trebane's motioning to us."

A bell tolled to announce dinner. Guests strode along the marbled hallway to a chandeliered dining area, where chairs with red jacquard cushions lined an elongated Elizabethan table. Crystal goblets, fine bone china, and an exquisite roped garland of white and red roses, accented with boxwood greenery graced the table.

Asa appeared behind Seeley and Declan. "My dear Seeley, you have a place of honor on my right side, and Mr. Donavan will be seated...elsewhere." Asa, his hand on Seeley's waist, guided her away before she had a chance to protest.

Glimpsing back, she saw two men in tuxes step in front of Declan as he moved to follow her.

When the third course, lobster bisque, had been served, Asa gave Seeley a sidelong glance. "You've hardly touched a thing, Seeley. I've hired the best gourmet chefs from New York City to provide you with the finest of culinary delights."

"Oh, Asa, you shouldn't have," mocked Seeley, glaring scornfully.

"Tut, tut, be a good girl and eat your soup." Asa bit his bottom lip. "You'll need your strength."

Earlier, Seeley had located Declan at the far end of the table with Veronka on his left. She looked for him now, hoping to capture his awareness. Veronka's taloned fingertips flirtatiously stroked Declan's chin, then her right hand furtively slipped beneath the table. Seeley watched with an irresistible impulse to soar over the table, unsettling the grand array. In an unexpected twist to her neck, Veronka's insolent eyes locked on Seeley, blood red lips whispered in Declan's ear. Declan's face swerved to Veronka, transparently enthralled by the beguiling woman.

When the main course of beef Wellington was removed, Seeley knew the travesty of a meal was that much closer to a conclusion. Her blood pressure must be off the charts, with Asa needling her leg and artfully caressing her arm, and then hearing Veronka's unpleasant giggling, had her hair standing on end.

Asa caught her watching them. "Don't let that upset you. Veronka likes to play with her food."

Seeley cast her infuriated eyes in Asa's direction and bristled. "Why, exactly, did you want me here?"

As waiters served a decadent dessert of tiramisu garnished with chocolate spires, Asa's fingers clamped on Seeley's wrist. "Come with me."

Wanting to scream, Seeley looked imploringly at Declan, but he was trapped in Veronka's net of desire. She stumbled as Asa pulled her through a small side door.

かの

Meanwhile, Jordan bit into her bacon, lettuce, and tomato sandwich at the Elma Diner. "Umm, I was starving."

Thrill's chin gestured toward the door. "Cayden and Paisley just walked in. Should I have them join us?"

Jordan slung her arm over the back of her chair and waved the girls over. "Sure, why not?"

They brought the cold with them. Stripping off their gloves and hats, they plopped down on the chrome chairs. "It's freezing outside," Paisley declared. "I need hot chocolate." She gestured wildly for the waitress.

"Jordan we missed you at Ronan's the other night," Cayden said. "You'd promised you'd be there."

Feeling somewhat culpable, Jordan had phoned Ronan to inform her of the change in plans. Ronan had been peeved with Jordan's lame excuse, questioning whether she was actually going to church at that hour. In the end, Ronan had said she hoped they could get together soon because she'd been so lonely and needed Jordan's help. She'd wondered what kind of help Ronan needed.

"Sorry, Cayden, but my mom wouldn't let me go." Jordan wasn't lying. Judging by their slack faces, Cayden and Paisley had kept Ronan company for the evening. "So what'd you do? Did she bring out the Ouija Board or something?"

Paisley and Cayden exchanged glances, neither one in a hurry to explain.

"Like Mark said, Ronan needs to quit that junk," Thrill interjected. "Next time you girls just tell her to eff off."

Cayden snickered.

"Sometimes it's not that easy," Paisley said with spite, glaring at Thrill. "I've seen Ronan move things without touching them. I thought it was really cool."

Paisley peeked at Cayden, gnawing on a hangnail, then she looked around the restaurant and lowered her voice. "But last night—Ronan's temper totally unleashed. First a magazine flew off the table, then a plate shimmied and smashed to the floor." She swallowed hard. "And then an ash tray clunked Cayden in the head. *That* was kind of funny," she said, strangling a half-chuckle. Cayden massaged the bruise on her head as Paisley continued. "The girl's got an awesome ability that scares the shit out of me."

With distressed eyes Cayden concurred, still rubbing her head.

"What a freak show," Thrill blurted. "How's it possible?"

Paisley shrugged listlessly. "She's definitely got some kind of power. I dunno, but I'm not messing with her. If she says run, I run. If she says walk, I walk."

Jordan fidgeted, wondering if Thrill would think her a freak if he knew about *her* telekinesis. "Ronan looked so…so needy that I actually felt sorry for her at school." Feeling ill at ease, she snatched a napkin to blot the pooling moisture on her hands. "Why was she so angry?"

Cayden tilted her head to the side, narrowing her eyes as if she were thinking, then looked to Paisley. "Paisley, do you remember? It was after Jordan called, because she'd been wondering where Jordan was—"

"Mark called," Paisley interrupted, her voice matter-of-fact. "She ran upstairs to talk to him. It was after his call, and don't ask me what they talked about, I don't know."

Browsing over Jordan's shoulder, Paisley's undertone was more than a little ironic. "Speak of the devil, look who's walking in."

Their heads turned to the door. Ronan, with Markus in the rear, marched determinedly over to them. Markus grabbed two chairs from an empty table and they sat down. Ronan's intense eyes focused on Jordan, the angry flush on her cheeks was killing the relaxed mood.

"Jordan," Ronan whispered conspiratorially. "Your mom's at Asa Trebane's."

Dubious, Jordan looked at Markus, whose eyes confirmed it. She looked to Ronan. "My mom's on a date with Mr. Donavan. I think she said they were going to the city." Digging in her purse, Jordan drew out her cell phone and dialed her mom. It went directly to voicemail.

"Who's this Trebane guy," Thrill asked, completely confused. "And why should it matter if your mom's at his house?"

Jordan stalled, sending Markus a concerned glance. Rocking back in his chair, he was masked with a profound expression.

"Asa Trebane is like the scourge of the earth," she said.

The rising of his eyebrows widened Thrill's eyes. "Wow, I guess you don't like the man."

"I wouldn't even call him a man—more like a beast." she said coldly. She shoved her plate away and balled her hands into tight fists.

Ronan leapt to her feet. "We're wasting time. Let's go to my house."

Thrill checked his cell. "It's after ten. Jordan has to be home by eleven, and we have midterms tomorrow."

"Go ahead, Thrill." Markus nodded reassuringly at the befuddled Thrill. "I'll take care of Jordan."

Slipping on his coat, not quite sure what was happening, Thrill checked with Jordan. "Are you okay with this?"

Nodding faintly, Jordan walked Thrill to the door. "Thanks for dinner, Thrill. Don't worry, Mark will get me home."

"But why do you have to go to Ronan's?"

"Ronan hasn't been herself lately—you know, her games. She's asking for our help and maybe that's a good sign."

Thrill glanced at the table then met Jordan's eyes. "Are you positive you and Mark are just friends?"

"Yes." She hoped her eyes were reassuring.

"I get a feeling there's more to the two of you than you're telling me." Thrill ran his fingers up her arm then back down to her hand, curling them around her pinky and gazing into her eyes for some sign. "Be careful at Ronan's." Brushing her lips with his, Thrill left.

It was Jordan's turn to be confounded when Markus tossed her her coat and edged her out the door with the girls lagging behind. Jordan kept her voice low. "What's going on with Ronan? She's involved with Veronka, and I don't trust her."

"She called me with information, which Ezekiel confirmed," he said. "Asa's been plotting and, without a doubt,

Ronan has her own agenda. We have to be on our guard, but she's offering to help and, right now, we need her."

"Is Ezekiel with my mom?"

"I'll explain later."

Markus and Jordan halted at the car. Ronan, Paisley, and Cayden came crunching up to them. Wisps of steam clouded their heads as they breathed. "Cayden and I are going home," Paisley said. "We don't know what you guys are planning, but leave us out."

"Fine," Ronan said abrasively. "I don't need your help anyway, Paisley." Ronan got into the front seat and slammed the door.

Jordan met Cayden's eyes with complete understanding and grinned miserably. "Don't worry. Go home, I'll call..." She left the sentence unfinished.

Hooking elbows, Paisley and Cayden scuttled back to Paisley's car. Jordan didn't want to be near Ronan, either, but Markus seemed to be determined to cooperate with her. Jordan took a seat in the back.

Inside the car, Ronan declared, "Jordan, I'm the only one who can help you get your mom out of Asa's place."

"Why, and how? I don't understand—what's going on?"

His eyes glued to the road, Markus said, "Ezekiel told me—"

"Mark," Jordan yelped. "Ronan's here."

Ronan turned in the front seat, looking sour. "I know Markus is half-angel! The lake incident proved it."

"You tried to kill me," charged Jordan. "I can't believe I'm even in the same car as you, and now you're saying you want to help my mother. It doesn't make sense, and I don't trust you."

Markus kept silent, listening to the exchange.

Ronan sneered. "Jordan, I knew he'd save you," she said with an ironic snigger. "I was testing the water, so to speak."

"It's not funny, Ronan, and I know you're a member of the Order. What's your part in all this?"

"I haven't been officially inducted," Ronan drawled. "But Asa has instructed me...spiritually."

Leaning forward, Jordan tapped Markus's shoulder. "I'll do whatever you say."

A pert cackle escaped Ronan's lips.

His cheekbone twitched as he clenched his jaw. "Ezekiel said dark spells bar any heavenly power from entering Trebane's house," he said through barred teeth. "The Order sacrificed souls and consecrated the dwelling to Lucifer. Ezekiel tried everything, but he couldn't stay there—at least not long enough to help Seeley."

Jordan was appalled "He's killing people in his house?".

"Worse. Certain members of The Black Order sacrifice their souls wholeheartedly to attain a higher position beside Lucifer." Then his words were like sandpaper. "Not all members die willingly, though. The Order's known for sacrificing an innocent every year to prove their loyalty."

Jordan felt nauseous. "And, Ronan, you want to be a part of this…this sick horror?"

Staring out the side window, Ronan ignored her. Jordan heard the hum of the heater, but she felt little warmth, chilled on the inside, reflecting on Markus's disclosure. He made a left-hand turn into Beckman's shoveled driveway. Ronan leapt out and barged through the side door with Jordan and Markus on her heels.

"Is your dad home?" Jordan called after her.

"Are you kidding? He's in Atlanta for the week."

As soon as Jordan crossed the threshold into the kitchen, it felt like a million tiny insects squiggled beneath her skin, shooting tremors everywhere. Hugging her elbows, she fought her instinct to run out the door. She looked at Markus's grim features. He'd once described feeling burning pain in the presence of devouring evil. "I don't like this," she uttered from the side of her mouth. "It could be a trick."

Markus stood his ground, looking like a marble statue.

Ronan sprinted to the second floor then thudded down the stairs with an armload of equipment: the pentagram drawing, a dagger, a bowl, and herbs. She dumped the paraphernalia on the table and left the room.

Feeling a little green, Jordan regretted having the strawberry milkshake at the diner. "What are we doing?" she accosted Markus. "How can we be a part of this and...and her spells?"

His face twisted. "We need her to lessen, or remove the bonds sealing Asa's house."

Ronan returned, lugging a book of incantations, and began assembling her altar. Jordan bubbled with fear and anger as Ronan concentrated on her murmurings. When the first hint of blistering torment touched Markus, he grasped Jordan's shoulder. "We'll leave now."

"Wait," Ronan cried. "I'll need a drop of blood—from each of you!"

"Is that necessary?" Markus said crossly.

"Yes—if you want my help."

Markus stepped forward and, flipping the dagger, sliced his palm allowing his human blood to drip into the bowl. Jordan offered her hand to Markus, who pricked her finger, splashing a single drop into the bowl. Markus then brought Jordan's finger to his mouth and washed the blood with his tongue. When he released her hand, the cut was healed.

CHAPTER 20

They Have Set an Ambush for My Life.

Asa steered Seeley along a dim hallway and opened a tiny door, revealing a room furnished with an exquisite Persian carpet, a davenport, and two end tables stationed with Tiffany lamps. Asa licked Seeley's palm before she had a chance to snatch it away. Aversion etched her mind as she scoured off her hand on her dress. She turned, confirming that the room had no windows. There was a door on the opposite wall.

Aware of Asa's sharp eyes on her, Seeley recoiled. "What do you want?"

"You." His mouth collected to the side in an indecent leer. "I've wanted you from the first day Jack brought you to us. So young, so striking, and so naively uncontaminated."

Seeley took another step back. "You have a house full of people. I'll scream bloody murder."

Pretending not to hear, Asa came within a foot of Seeley, his lustful eyes raking her body. "Your eyes have changed. The innocence has fled, and now you have yearning eyes." His voice was thick. "Seeley, you're an intriguing contradiction—inviting to look at, deadly to touch. So pliable, yet unbreakable. I could break your spirit, don't you think?"

Asa made what little she'd eaten roil in her stomach. "You make me sick," she growled like a panther, spinning from the sight of him.

"Seeley…Oh, Seeley," he said with desire. "We could move mountains. As one, we'd rule the world." Extending pointy fingers, Asa weaved his hand in her auburn hair and yanked her around to face him. She flinched, jerking her knee toward his groin, but he held her too close to get any leverage. "Ah, this is better. Feeling your wriggling body against mine makes me want you all the more."

"Declan will be searching for me."

Taking delight in taunting Seeley, Asa savored his words. "Declan is in Veronka's capable arms. And, if you don't do as I say…well then, poor Declan. He'll inadvertently imbibe too much whiskey laced with a soothing drug, spend the night with a most efficient and treacherous demon, and then never wake up."

He had figured Seeley would not compromise Declan.

Seeley thought of Declan. She knew he was strong, but could he subdue Veronka? She couldn't take the chance. "What do you want me to do?"

"You will make quite a scene for all my guests to see," he said. "You will be infuriated with your lover, who has been flirting with the vivacious Veronka. You might go so far as to slap his face in order to free him from my house." Asa drew forward, his cheek rubbing Seeley's. "He will go," he related with hunger. "You, Seeley, will stay behind." He released her abruptly, yet reluctantly.

Combing trembling fingers through her tangled hair, Seeley fought a fierce impulse to kill Asa.

"I know what you're thinking, Seeley." Asa lips curled, sure of his conquest. "You wouldn't make it to the foyer. Let's not fight, you and I. I'm much, much more powerful than I appear. I could squash you without lifting a finger."

"Fine," said Seeley. "Let's get this over with." She strode toward the door then waited for Asa, who had triumph written all over his face.

People consumed after dinner drinks, mingling and talking as Asa shepherded Seeley along. When he spotted Veronka in a poorly lit bay window, working hard at manhandling the esteemed Mr. Donavan, Asa smiled with satisfaction. He nodded to Seeley.

Threading between guests, Seeley strived to convert her fear to anger, for Declan's sake. Standing with knuckles on hips, she took a vehement stance in front of the fevered couple.

Declan's slurred words, sagging eyelids, and lethargic movements made it clear he'd been drugged. Veronka hadn't lingered for Asa's endorsement.

Seeley played her part well. "What the hell's going on here?" She sounded like a scorned woman. "Declan, I leave you alone for a minute and you hook-up with this...this demon?"

Seeley scowled. Veronka was unmistakably dissatisfied as Seeley pushed forward, hefting Declan to his feet. Teetering somewhat, Declan looked from Seeley to Veronka and back to Seeley, his face stamped with palpable disgrace. Before he could speak, Seeley punched him in the chest, yelling, "I never want to see you again. I just want you to leave. Leave—now!" Tears spilled from her eyes, tracing her nose and chin.

"Seeley, I don't know—Se–e–eley—" Declan slurred in his attempt to apologize. "Let's—leave." After his immense effort to complete a thought, Declan groped for Seeley's shoulder, trying to keep his balance. His bleary, penitent eyes lost focus when two men anchored him under each armpit and dragged him away.

Wet eyes blurred Seeley's vision as onlookers clucked their tongues in dismay at Declan's behavior.

Asa sauntered up behind Seeley, issuing orders. "Put Mr. Donavan in a taxi and send the gentleman home. I'm sorry, Seeley. I'll have my chauffeur take you home later."

Declan, too drugged to resist, slumped in the arms of two men. The scene pleased Asa. A puppet master pulling the strings, he turned to his guests to broadcast, "Just a minor inconvenience. Everyone have another glass of champagne." Then, clasping Seeley's elbow, he guided her up the huge marble staircase to the second floor. "My dear, Seeley," Asa crooned. "That was an Oscar-worthy performance. I'm quite impressed."

Ashamed of her tears, Seeley wiped away the telltale signs with her free hand. "Now what, Asa?"

"I'll make one last appearance downstairs to bid my guests farewell, and then I'll return happily to you." His eyes sparked. "No monkey business, Seeley. Wait for me."

Two men guarded an open doorway. Loosening his grip, Asa thrust Seeley into the bedroom. She swiveled swiftly, glowering.

"My men will keep you company while I'm gone," he said. With a clipped nod at the two henchmen, Asa left.

Seeley shuddered—red-ringed eyes marked the men as demons, though their navy blue suits would make them appear like guests. She stepped backward until she felt the wall behind her, her eyes never leaving the demons. They traipsed in and closed the door.

✮✮✮

Gratefully inhaling the fresh, cold air, Markus and Jordan sped to the car. Once more Jordan dialed her mom's cell with no response. "Do you truly believe Ronan can break the protective enchantments on Asa's house?"

Markus grimaced. "It hurts me to the core to use her in this way." His voice tensed. "Today, a desperate time calls for desperate measures. And the most devious creatures we've encountered have proclaimed Ronan's abilities."

Buckling her seat belt, Jordan glanced up at Markus. "You've spoken to devious creatures?"

"Ronan's released many of them," Markus answered quietly. "There's a vicious war being waged, and I've been in the thick of it for years."

"I didn't realize. I guess I always assumed that you hang around watching me every minute," she said, taking a gander at his chiseled features. "Then when you're not here, I get mad. At least now I know why you're not at my beck and call every second of the day or night." A splat on the car distracted her, then pattering rain pecked the windshield. "I haven't seen rain in two months. It must be getting warmer out." She shifted back to Markus. "Of course you know where Asa lives?"

"Yes," he said. "But I'm taking you home."

"What?" Jordan hollered. "No! No, I'm going with you!"

Markus set his mouth in a determined line and continued driving.

"Markus, I'm going with you," Jordan repeated. She clutched the dashboard and faced her angel with a dogged look. "If you drop me at home, I'll just get into my mom's car and drive to Asa's on my own—without you."

He beat his fist on the steering wheel, his eyes glinting fiercely. "Why must you always be so difficult? You are my first priority. Ezekiel needs me, and I don't want you in the way."

"I can help," she appealed fervently. "I know I can."

Unequivocally displeased, Markus blurted out, "Ezekiel and I believe it's a trap to lure you to Asa's house. He took your mother hostage, knowing you'd come after her." He mopped a hand over his forehead.

"Why me?"

"It's complicated." He sighed. "Asa thought of your father like a son. Then Jack betrayed him and, believe it or not, broke the tiny speck of good left in his warped heart. Because of Jack's betrayal, Asa is obsessed with consecrating you to Lucifer to atone for the loss of Jack's soul."

Absorbing this, Jordan nodded. "Knowing Asa, there's more to his plan."

Markus grunted, impressed. "You're reading people quite well. You've seen through him. Yes, there's more." Rather than explain, he repeated, "You need to go home. We cannot give him what he wants."

But Jordan would not be dissuaded. Negotiating a U-turn, Markus sped to the highway.

∾✸∾

The bald demon's vulgar praise annoyed Seeley. His red eyes followed her body like a cat on a rat. He began to drool.

Little by little, he moved nearer to her. Apathetic in her training, Seeley's reflexes lacked their usual speed. She focused on a ceramic vase. It schlepped from side to side, then an enigmatic pulse energized her and the vase crashed into the demon's shoulder. He stopped, temporarily dazed.

Chortling, the other creature stood guard by the door, watching his partner pursue the lady. "Get a grip, mate. This is no ordinary prisoner. You'd better hurry before he comes back."

"You could help me pin her down," the bald demon muttered.

"Not on your short-lived demon life. If he catches you, you're a goner."

He stooped low on his haunches. Just before he sprang, Seeley jumped, rolling over the bed, and landing easily on her feet.

Laughter barked from the guard. "She's a tricky minx, that one."

"Chester, grab her on that side," snarled the bald demon.

Seeley concentrated on the large armoire. Its size challenged her mental strength, but she tipped it sideways, blocking Chester's advance. The endeavor taxed her at first. Her sight hazed for a second, just long enough for the demon to trounce over the bed. Her eyes cleared by the time his distorted face was within a foot. He tackled her. Seeley's head smacked against the wall. The demon hauled Seeley, unconscious, across the mattress, pinning her with his body.

A desperate need to breathe woke Seeley; she ineffectually thrashed underneath the beast. With his chest weighing her down, he'd secured her wrists above her head with one hand. And his other hand fondled Seeley's hips, tearing at her dress. His slobbering orifice bit harshly into her shoulder and nipped the column of her throat. Writhing she kicked, lacking success. She soon realized her actions were only stimulating him.

"Oy, Gavin! Gavin, I hear someone coming," Chester warned belatedly.

Asa took in the sight before him. Chester retreated, slipping out the door. "Gavin's a bad boy," Asa mocked savagely.

Lifting his head, the demon leapt off the bed and shifted restlessly from side to side. "She was acting up. I was just trying to—"

A disheveled Seeley panted. Asa, his eyes fiery, raised his hand and denounced the demon. "Back to the pit, where you will grind and gnash for all eternity!"

Gavin went rigid, then gyrated feverishly. He gave a hideous squeal as his body exploded.

Climbing off the mattress, Seeley rearranged her mussed clothing as Asa delicately closed the bedroom door. He gestured to the broken pottery and fallen armoire, smiling approvingly. "Is this your handiwork, Seeley?" He stared at the agitated woman, her lips swollen and hair in disarray.

Seeley glared hatefully at her captor.

Offering his hand, palm up, Asa mumbled something incoherently. Like a lariat, the words circled the room until they dropped over Seeley, completely irresistible. "Come. Come to me. We will be one. You will be mine."

The overpowering spell tugged on her like an invisible cable but, with all her might, Seeley fought the compulsion. Her foot stepped forward as if it had a mind of its own, submissive to his inveigled charms. Absolutely receptive to Asa's every suggestion, Seeley's body deceived her, tingling in eagerness to close the gap, craving this man's touch.

Asa's fingertips caressed her shoulders and up the side of her neck. Drawing Seeley near, his lips brushed the column of her neck, she purred like a tamed kitten. His arms wound around her back, molding her against his chest. Asa groaned. The craving sound put a chink in the spell, and distracted Seeley, fraying the cable just enough for her to resist. Turning inward, Seeley prayed for strength to disrupt the magic charm.

"No!" Asa screamed. "God has no dominion here!"

Coming swiftly to her senses, she shoved hard. "Let me go, Asa. Let me go."

Losing his footing, Asa nearly tumbled to the floor.

Mad as hell, he seized Seeley's upper arm, his aquiline nose flaring. His fingers cut into her flesh. "We should unwind while we wait for your daughter."

Seeley stared at him, incredulous. "Why would Jordan come here?"

"Seeley, you should've accepted my offer." He thrust her away, she landed on the bed. "Your guardians know of your capture. Heavenly beings cannot survive long here. Their power is nullified. Jordan will come and, once inside my domain, she will finally be sacrificed to Lucifer."

Reeling from this admission, Seeley knew that Ezekiel and Markus would not be fooled. Zeke could manage Asa, alone. And then she recalled Zeke's words: *I'd advise you to leave.* They would never bring Jordan to the devil—would they?

"At least you saved Declan's life," Asa cooed, tracing Seeley's chin. "And Veronka was very interested in the man. It was a shame to let him go."

As if on command, Veronka barged through the door, her expression belligerent. She callously slapped Seeley on the side of the head. "Ahh, I feel somewhat better now."

"Now, be nice, girls," Asa said, welcoming Veronka's abuse.

Seeley unexpectedly vaulted, tackling Veronka to the plush carpet. Adrenaline roared through her veins as Seeley bashed the seductress in the teeth. Wrestling and rolling while Asa laughed like a jackal. Demon men hefted a panting Seeley off Veronka. They held her arms behind her back. With her mouth angled crookedly, Veronka took advantage of Seeley's restraint and whacked her in the diaphragm. The men let Seeley fall to the floor.

"Well," said Asa. "That demonstration of nastiness is over. We'd best get ready for our visitors." Kneeling beside Seeley, who was gasping for oxygen, he brushed back the curls that shielded her face, bent, and planted a numbing kiss on her temple. Wet lips trailed across her cheekbone, then he bit her bottom lip. "Be a good girl and wait for me."

He hummed as he walked smartly from the room.

CHAPTER 21

What Can Mere Mortals Do to Me as I Bathe
My Feet in the Blood of the Wicked?

Markus decelerated near a three story colonial manor, fortified with a concrete barrier. The area was desolate, with no other residence in sight.

"Are we here?" questioned Jordan.

"Yes."

"What are we waiting for?"

"Ezekiel." Reaching into his pocket, Markus pulled out a small bottle. "Here" He placed the holy water in her hand.

They waited. Markus turned on the wipers to clear the windshield periodically. Tings sounded on the car's roof as the rain evolved into hail pellets.

Fraught with anxiety, not knowing what lurked beyond those walls, Jordan spurred her courage. Her mom needed her. *And*, she thought, *we might just rid the world of the man who murdered my Dad*. That seemed like bitter compensation as darkness overcame them. Her teeth chattered as a numbing frost adhered to her bones.

Worried by Jordan's presence and the need to protect her while rescuing Seeley, Markus muttered under his breath. Then he saw her trembling. "Are you all right? No, of course you're not." His jaw tightened. "I should've taken you home. I'm an idiot."

Jordan was about to object when Ezekiel materialized in the back seat. In human form, he looked like the Grim Reaper in a black trench coat with his ebony hair branching out on his wide shoulders. He glowered under his heavy brow. "Markus, it was a bad idea to bring her here," he spoke coldly, lacking discretion. "I don't care what Ronan said."

"I know, but she would've followed. Then who knows what would've happened? At least this way we can keep an eye on her."

"What did Ronan say?" Jordan turned from Ezekiel to Markus. "You're keeping secrets again."

Disregarding Jordan, Ezekiel sighed. "I'm not convinced that we'll be able to free Seeley without additional power. It's just possible that Jordan will be an asset, in some destined way. On the other hand, her presence could prove detrimental."

"Hey, guys—" *Detrimental my foot*, Jordan thought. "I'm right here and I plan to help. And one of you should have told Father James, we could use reinforcements."

Ezekiel's dark eyes started a new wave of shivers for Jordan. "I did. He's with us, in spirit."

"Let's go," ordered Markus.

Ezekiel scowled. "You said Ronan's working on the barrier, I couldn't get in earlier."

"Yes, it should be possible by now," said Markus. "But it may be advantageous to remain human."

"I disagree. We should breakthrough the main barrier angelically, then transform to our human state. Lucifer's enmeshed a web over the mansion." Ezekiel's tone was precise. "Once inside, I don't know if we'll be able to escape unless Ronan has reduced the enchantments. We will last longer in human form."

Jordan's head swung back and forth between them. "Aren't you stronger as angels?"

Ezekiel looked baleful. "The evil inside may eliminate our strength rather swiftly."

Markus felt Jordan's piercing glare. He held his head in his hands, well acquainted with the sting they were about to endure.

"But as humans you might die, right?" Jordan asked.

Neither one spoke.

"I know," she began. "Markus told me how sin grinds angels raw, though angelic power could get us in and out awfully quick, right?"

"We cannot foresee the future," Ezekiel said, his features drawn. "Asa more than likely waits for us with a few unearthly tricks. Although, he won't expect Ronan, his new protégé, to knock down his defenses."

Jordan peered at Markus. "I can't very well turn to spirit and materialize on the other side."

"You're staying here," Markus insisted sternly, giving one last order.

"No way."

"Trebane's setting a trap for you," said Ezekiel. "Your mother's the bait."

"You don't know that for sure," she argued. "Besides, as soon as you leave, I'll be out this door in a snap."

"Markus, keep her close," Ezekiel groused, surrendering. "I'll fly in, you follow." And he faded from sight.

"Let's go." They exited the car. Jordan popped up her hood against the pelting ice and followed Markus.

Markus lobbed Jordan over the brick barrier then effortlessly alighted on the snowy ground next to her. Ducking from tree trunk to tree trunk, he examined the towering residence. He spotted a two-story ornamental trellis, hoisted Jordan up, then scaled rapidly past her.

He grasped a window ledge and flew a few feet to the balcony. He leaned back to lift up Jordan, who clung to the trellis. He jarred a locked window then sent her sprawling inside before gracefully leaping in himself. Immediately, Markus and Jordan felt the force field as stinging prickles shot through their skin.

℘℘℘

Manifesting next to Seeley, Ezekiel's face contorted, feeling the sting as well. Ronan's incantations helped, but the depravity remained.

Seeley gasped, rushing into his arms. "Zeke, I thought you'd never come."

Zeke held her off, examining her bruised face. "Let's go." Cupping the doorknob, he simply tore the door from its hinges. The splintering alerted the household.

Seeley shadowed Ezekiel in the diffused light. They peered over the banister, then she said in a hushed voice, "It's a trap for Jordan." Seeley confirmed Ezekiel's suspicion. "Asa's fixated on Jordan coming here. He intends to perform the consecration."

Ezekiel furtively descended the stairs. "This is too easy," he whispered. Halfway down, he heard a thump from the second floor. "Markus and Jordan are here."

"No—she can't be here." She turned, ready to bolt toward her daughter. "We have to warn them."

Ezekiel grabbed Seeley's wrist, halting her from sprinting up the staircase. "The house is a menagerie. We'd be overtaken by the time we find them."

Suddenly, a searing pain stabbed Ezekiel. The spell struck his chest, blasting him off his feet. His body crashed against the wall, shaking the house to its foundation. He crumpled and tumbled limply down the stairwell like a sack of potatoes. With no idea where the spell had come from, Seeley pelted down the stairs after the fallen angel.

Landing in a clump, Ezekiel collected his strength. An infestation of plundering demons stormed toward him on all sides. Reaching upward, Zeke splayed his fingers as if he were waiting for a specific accoutrement. A glimmering sickle used for harvesting appeared above him. Zeke seized it and swung. He carved his way through the cursed creatures, feinting and striking on all sides. He heard a gunshot. With a flick of his wrist, he sent forth lightning. The bullets melted in midair.

Executing a knee-jerking jolt to a demon's kneecap, Seeley felt and heard the crunch of bone. The thing stumbled to the floor.

A mangy, maniacal creature scurried up Ezekiel's back. Teeth, sharpened like shards of glass, chomped the side of his neck, gnashing out a hunk of flesh, which the creature lustfully consumed. Bloodstained shards glistened as the creature opened its mouth to bite again. Ezekiel reached back, striking it in the head with the sickle's handle, but the creature stuck like superglue.

Focusing her mind, Seeley hurled a range of objects at it. One by one, the copper decorations flew off the wall and clobbered the wild-eyed creature, sending it spooling off Zeke. She mentally gripped more sculptures, impelling them to crush demon skulls. From the depths of gloom, a pernicious entity surfaced, its evil aura spreading over Seeley, blocking her telekinesis. A snarling female with half a face advanced, knocking Seeley's legs from under her. The demon pounced, tenaciously throttling her. In retaliation, Seeley's elbow connected to the demons red eye. Swiftly gaining ground, Seeley sank her heel into the creature's neck.

Then Seeley heard a scream.

"Mom!"

Whipping her head toward the sound, she spied Jordan and Markus on the second floor landing, besieged by a bedlam of soulless demons. Moving fluidly, Markus heaved two screeching carcasses over the banister. They landed headfirst with an ugly thunk. Like a bomb, grainy chunks of brain spewed over the white marble.

Aware of mind-splitting bellowing, she covered her ears to thwart Asa's psychic influence. She looked for the elusive devil, determined to eliminate him.

Out of nowhere, a rain of scorching flames surrounded Ezekiel. He collapsed. Nearby demons caught in the hex combusted in the Hellfire. Ezekiel was trapped. As Seeley watched in horror, Veronka, dressed in patent black leather from head to booted toe, ambushed her.

"Get behind me!" Markus shouted to Jordan. A cadaverous beast lunged for the girl. Markus ripped its pea head from its neck. The possessed carcass, groped like a headless chicken, percolating gore everywhere until Markus booted it down the staircase. He shielded Jordan from a torrent of descending creatures. Never one to go down without a fight, Jordan skillfully kicked and dodged, repelling a few gnarly characters on her own.

No demon could outmatch Markus's power. He parried to the right and to the left without any weaponry but his mighty hands. As he exchanged blows with the never-ending tide of enemies, Jordan sensed his pain and weariness through their inner bond.

Like her mother, Jordan used her mind, tossing demons over the banister. Sneaking silently, a predator with draggled hair reeking of excrement banded fingers around Jordan's neck. Feeling around for the bottle of holy water, Jordan fumbled open the lid and sprinkled her assailant. Juddering frenziedly, the predator smoldered and screamed soundlessly. Eyeballs rolled in his sockets. He combusted like a match head, adding more tang to the putrefied air.

Jordan leaned over the banister, pouring the rest of the holy water on malevolent creatures below.

"Jordan, smother that fire and release Ezekiel," Markus hollered.

At that precise moment, Jordan saw Veronka attack her mom, and, unable to concentrate, she faltered. Her hesitation was their downfall, she was snatched from behind. A butcher knife hugged her chest with the tip pricking her chin.

Jordan stood motionless. She felt breath on her neck as Asa backed her toward the wall. Inevitably, Markus forged ahead, matching him.

"I have no qualms about sticking this blade through her throat and consecrating Jordan here," Asa growled. "I'd prefer a stupendous ceremony, but what must be, will be." Raising his hand, he released a blast of magic that propelled Markus over the banister.

Jordan shrieked and, at the same time, felt the blade cut into her chin. A spark flared. Markus transformed and landed lightly on his feet in front of them.

"You won't last long in that state," Asa heckled.

Markus stood his ground, flinty eyes struck Asa and the knife, calculating, waiting.

Jordan was aware of Markus's waning strength and fought unsuccessfully to wiggle free. She was amazed by his rock-hard grip.

Asa met her resistance with a flick of the knife to her throat. He noted Markus's brusque inhalation as blood squirted from the gash.

Reckoning the angel would protect the girl at all costs, Asa carelessly released Jordan, whispering a hex.

She sailed up and over the banister. Within a millisecond, Markus lunged after her, snagging her wrist. Jordan dangled precariously.

Seeley's panicked cries were added to the upheaval when she saw Jordan hanging in the air. Markus yanked Jordan upward and, sensing Asa's presence, flung her protectively on his far side. Jordan landed on all fours crawling like an insect. She could only watch the ghastly scene.

By diverting the angel, Asa had created an opportune moment. After rescuing Jordan, Markus began to morph, garnering strength. Vulnerable amidst angelic and human form, Asa summarily and expertly speared him. The lethal razor-edged knife severed Markus from top to bottom; Asa relinquished the blade in his gut.

Jordan's bone-chilling scream announced the tragedy. She felt as if she had been gutted along with her angel and watched in horror as Markus gripped the hilt with trembling fingers. Baring his teeth in excruciating pain, he withdrew the blade. It slipped from his fingers, clunking to the wooden floor.

Asa shrank back, his face drained of color, fearing the angel's inexorable strength. Markus lashed out with a bloodied hand, catching the man's chest and toppling him over the banister. Markus staggered and fell to his knees, gaping at the wound. The laceration gushed copiously like a streaming gully.

The mansion quaked. An emergence of warrior angels descended. With devastating efficiency, each exterminated a demon and then escaped the wickedness. Like guerrilla warfare, more came and, one by one, fought the beasts. Seeing their power, Veronka released Seeley and fled.

Freed, Seeley used her mind to part the fire. Zeke flew to her side. He snagged her hand, and they ran toward Jordan's screams. Bounding up the stairwell, ignoring the shrieks of the beaten legions, Seeley and Ezekiel raced for Jordan.

Markus was on his knees, his back to them. Blood pooled on the floor. Then he slumped forward. Jordan crawled toward him, whimpering, "Markus, Markus, Markus…"

Ezekiel knelt and gently rolled him over. He grimaced at the mortal wound.

Seeley gasped.

Jordan bent over Markus. His fathomless eyes gazed into hers. The corner of his lip twitched, attempting a smile, as his lids fluttered.

"Don't leave me, Markus. Don't leave me." Her scalding tears washed his face. "Markus, you can't die—you can't."

Ezekiel clasped the hand of his fallen friend, his face pale.

The berserk ruckus had stopped, leaving the mansion eerily noiseless. Blinking watery eyes, Jordan and Seeley beheld an unbelievable sight. The shower of blinding effulgence was overwhelming as lucent angels surrounded them. A heavenly song, beautiful beyond description, graced their ears.

Markus's countenance altered. His body became dazzling white. The angels appeared to be ministering to him. He merged with their sheer incandescence and vanished, along with the celestial beings.

"No—No!" Jordan cried. "Markus."

Seeley clung to her weeping daughter.

Ezekiel swayed to his feet. "We must leave quickly." His voice was shaken. "Now, before they regroup."

He grappled with the two lamenting woman. Practically carrying them, he barreled down the stairwell and out the front door.

CHAPTER 22

I Will Grieve and Complain.

Suffering from total despair, Jordan had buried herself in bed. Her muffled weeping was heard by Seeley, again. Seeley inspected her cell phone to check the time. Besides it being after three in the morning, she'd found another waiting voicemail. Without even listening, she erased the apology from Declan who, wholly confused, explained that the night at Asa's was one big blur. Seeley felt it best to end the relationship completely. She needed to let Declan go, or else he would again be used as a pawn in her surreal life.

She'd taken a short leave of absence from work to weigh her options. Lacking the courage to speak to him in person, Seeley feared that, faced with Declan's wonderful qualities, she'd be in his arms in less than a second. *Give it time*, she thought. *Either he'll get fed up and stop calling, or I'll get brave and come up with some lame excuse about why he isn't right for me.*

Currently, she shuffled to her daughter's room and gathered Jordan into her embrace. Seeley wordlessly rocked Jordan, hoping to dispel the memories that caused her tears. Seeley settled next to her and, as the evening progressed, Jordan jerked intermittently in her restless slumber.

In the early hours of the morning, a variable light sparkled in the shadows. Jordan bolted upright. With numb fingers, she rubbed her eyes, intent on the developing figure. "Markus?"

When the angel Ezekiel formed, Jordan flopped back onto the mattress.

"Did they find Asa's body yet?" Seeley whispered.

"He's alive, Seeley," Ezekiel said dispassionately. "Beaten and downtrodden, but alive."

"How could he survive that fall? I saw Markus fling him over the rail."

"Yes, but we didn't see him hit the ground. No doubt Asa's sorcery saved him."

"I want him dead—dead," Jordan's tone was toxic. "He shouldn't be allowed to live." In every respect she felt eviscerated. Markus had been a part of her.

Ezekiel neared by one step then halted. His gaze skirted past Seeley to Jordan, who feigned sleep. "Soon Jordan will feel better and return to school," he said. "I don't want her to be alarmed, so I came to tell you both—Rafe has been assigned to her."

A shimmering spirit stood beside Zeke. A stranger with brown eyes and coppery hair. The angel looked oddly familiar. Then he changed, becoming Markus.

"Markus?" Seeley cried. "Zeke, is this Markus?"

Jordan leapt from the bed. "Markus!" She flew into his arms.

"No, this is Rafe," Ezekiel remarked, clearing his throat. "That's why I'm warning you both. He'll look like Markus until the end of the school year, and then 'Mark' will move on."

Jordan felt the prickly burn behind her eyes as she inspected the angel. He impersonated Markus so well, except for the remarkable shade of his violet blue eyes. She turned away. "I don't need another angel. I don't want anyone else." Her cold expression raked Ezekiel. "Do you understand?"

"I watched over your father," Rafe said sorrowfully. "And after—" He paused. "It was hoped that I would be acceptable to you."

Seeley recognized the brawny angel. "Yes, I know you. The day Jack died—" Staring at him, she remembered only too well how tenderly Rafe had carried Jack in his arms. "Thank you, Rafe."

He nodded humbly.

Inconsolable, Jordan lashed out. "Why are you thanking him? Dad died. I only want Markus."

Ezekiel heaved a dejected sigh and peered at Seeley. "I'll be near. Go to Father James. He'll help."

ᘒᘖᘒ

After enduring a week of self-pity, Jordan showered and went downstairs to the kitchen. Her grandparents and mother were eating breakfast. Henry labored up from his chair and grasped his granddaughter in a rousing bear hug. Depositing a plate on the table, Em pecked Jordan's cheek.

"My, this girl is skinny, momma." Henry looked at Seeley with twinkly eyes and tickled Jordan beneath the ribcage. "We need to put some meat on these bones."

Seeley giggled along with her daughter, happy that Jordan actually produced a smile. Em fussed like a mother hen, pouring orange juice and supplying Jordan with hot fluffy pancakes. She chatted about the weather, anticipating spring and wondering when her bulbs would flower. Henry harrumphed, foreseeing lots of hard work ahead. He rolled his eyes at Jordan. She grinned.

Seeley sensed her daughter's contained energy, like a rubber band ready to snap. She had a brilliant notion to pursue in their training and scheduled a workout at Jacob's studio.

ᘒᘖᘒ

All youthful vitality, Jordan danced on the mats in a relentless frenzy. Springing and bounding, she did front and back flips and somersaults. She weaved from side to side and then walloped the punching bag, glad to feel the grating ache.

She twirled and leapt, booting the bag until it wobbled like a drunken bum, pumping hostility into the innocent bag of straw. Rivulets of perspiration coursed her hairline, past temple and cheeks, dripping off her chin. Wiping a damp brow with her wrists, she then battered the bag with rabbit punches, using every last ounce of energy.

Then Seeley and Jordan sparred with four partners, executing various martial art techniques. Rolling, tumbling, and squaring off for over an hour, they danced faultlessly over mats. The grueling sport left Seeley breathless. "I'm done, caput."

After the workout they tramped to a nearby café. Jordan's recently dampened spirits recovered in the sunshine of a warm day. Almost lively, she sidestepped the heaps of thawing snow which generated puddles on the sidewalks. Then coming upon a pool of water, she hopped, thumping both feet into a sloppy puddle. Cold water splashed far and wide. Seeley flung back her head, laughing—her daughter was back.

ოჳოჳ

Jordan waited until her grandparents had gone to bed. It was after ten-thirty, and her mom lay on the couch, watching television. During a commercial, Jordan cleared her throat tentatively. "I'm going to school tomorrow. There'll be tons of work and I need to catch up, and I'll feel better if I'm busy."

Propped on her elbow, Seeley agreed. "That's a good idea."

Jordan shifted her feet. "And after school I'd like to see Ronan," she said and waited for her mother's objections.

Seeley sat up, pressing her brow. "Jordan, do think that's an intelligent decision?"

"Mom, she helped us. If it weren't for her, we'd never have gotten inside the mansion." Jordan saw her mom disguise mixed emotions.

"Don't you think Ronan had her own scheme? It's even possible Asa asked Ronan to help so he could trap you."

Jordan sat hunched on the edge of the couch, her elbows on her knees, hands supporting her chin. "That doesn't make sense."

Seeley's mouth puckered and a crease deepened between her eyebrows. For the past week, she'd rethought the catastrophe of that night. Over and over, she wondered what could've been accomplished differently, lacking any logical answer.

"I need to speak with her, please Mom—about—what happened, what she thinks."

Seeley realized that Jordan needed answers and closure. She foresaw only heartache. Peering into her daughter's grief-stricken eyes, Seeley caved. But she recommended Jordan be on the lookout for anything out of the ordinary.

CHAPTER 23

Healing.

The scrumptious aroma of bacon and eggs wafted to Jordan's room. With a healthy appetite, she hurried to the kitchen. Earlier she'd dug her cell phone out of the bottom bureau drawer and been amazed at the number of voicemails. Thrill must have called twice a day, and then Paisley, Cayden, and even Ronan called. Her grandparents and mom joined her at the table to lend support on her first day back to school. Jordan ate absently while listening to a couple of voicemails, then began to press delete, delete, delete.

Em sat across the table, sipping her customary tea. "A lot of your friends called the house phone, too. They were very worried."

Seeley noticed Jordan deleting. "I did the same with Declan's messages. But you'll see them today."

Jordan glanced at her mom, who tried to keep a stiff upper lip for her sake, but Jordan knew she was hurting. Her mom had finally been happy—until Hell came calling.

"What'd you tell school?" she asked,

"A death in the family."

Nodding, Jordan lost her appetite.

"Would you like a ride to school today?" her mom offered.

"No, thanks, I'd like to walk. It gives me time to think. Luckily, it's Friday. I can have my first day back and then the weekend to recoup." Jordan wrestled with her oversized book bag and looked back at her mom. With a thin smile stretching her mouth, she labored out into spring's moist chill.

Rounding the corner from the back door to the front of the house, Jordan half expected to see Markus leaning on the mailbox. Unevenly inhaling the crisp fragrance of springtime, Jordan began the short hike to school.

Her whole world had turned upside down and yet, as she jostled through the corridors at school, she realized that nothing had changed, only her. Markus was gone. How could things ever be the same?

Quickly dismissing her train of thought, Jordan headed into Mr. Basinski's math class. There she was—Ronan. Flipping her black mane over her shoulder, she waved Jordan over. "Move, Debbie, that's Jordan's desk."

None too happy, the blonde collected her book and stomped to an adjacent desk.

"Thanks," Jordan said kindly.

The girl looked peeved. After situating herself in the chair, Jordan looked at Ronan, who seemed mildly more composed than the last time they'd met. A secret exchange passed between the girls.

Mr. Basinski's eyes widened at sight of Jordan. He tweaked his wire-rimmed glasses up his nose. Deftly, from his pocket protector, he slid out a ballpoint to mark his attendance roster.

"Can we meet later at Taste?" Jordan asked Ronan after class.

"Sure, should I ask Paisley and Cayden?"

"Maybe just the two of us...for now, if you don't mind?" Jordan didn't know what she was going to say, but she needed to hear Ronan's view. Fundamentally, they had succeeded in saving her mom from Asa, and Markus and Ezekiel rescued them both. That night was forever engraved in her mind. Markus's death left her empty, with nothing but questions.

Hurrying along the hallway, Jordan spied Thrill conversing with some adoring chick. The girl said something to make him laugh, and Jordan gazed at the rightness of his features.

Then he noticed Jordan and his face turned serious. He walked toward her, leaving behind a sputtering female.

"Jordan." He said her name with sincerity. "I missed you. How you feeling?"

Squelching the sure-fire blush, Jordan caught a whiff of his delightful scent. "I'm good." She could tell he wanted to ask about the death in her family, but wasn't sure if he should.

"Can we get together tonight, maybe go to a movie?"

Jordan dredged up a smile. "That'd be great."

Thrill's cheeks dimpled. "I'll pick you up around seven."

Conscious that he was watching her, Jordan ambled awkwardly away, then looking down, she noticed a threadbare hole in her jeans. Wiggling her finger through the threads, she tugged. *There. Now I'm in style*, she mused.

Rummaging in her locker, Jordan recoiled when she heard Markus's voice. "First day back. How's it going?"

Her head swerved side to side, making sure no one was in listening range. "Rafe, I don't want you hanging around me— understand?"

He smiled sadly—Markus's smile. Jordan sulked.

"That'll be hard, seeing as I'm supposed to be watching over you."

She gave him a hard look. "If you must," she responded acidly. "Then do it at a distance so I don't have to see you."

His mouth set in a tight line, Rafe strode away. Jordan yanked up her heavier-than-bricks book bag and trudged home.

Dumping the book bag inside the back door, she snagged her mom's keys and drove to Taste. Customers and some of her classmates were assembled inside the bistro engrossed in animated discourse. Jordan ordered a caramel macchiato. With the hot brew in hand, she wedged between two full tables to a vacant booth.

After ten minutes of deliberating about what she would say, Jordan saw Ronan enter, looking pretty in her soft pink fleece. Not stopping to order coffee, she headed purposefully to Jordan's table, flung off her fleece, and parked herself almost on top of Jordan's elbow.

"So tell me all about what happened. Did my incantations work? Well, I know they did, but how well?" she blathered. "And there's a rumor that Asa gutted someone with a butcher knife, is that true? Did you see it? I haven't heard the details, although I got the gist from Mark."

Jordan started at Mark's name. Predicting Jordan's discomfort, Ronan just assumed her angel was a sore subject, and she wanted to rub in the salt. "I know you call him Markus, but *I* like Mark."

Jordan then realized that Ronan's connections had not revealed Markus's death. It seemed odd that she was oblivious to Asa's triumph. Why had she not been told?

Finally, instead of answering all her questions, Jordan asked Ronan a few of her own. "When did you speak with Markus?"

"The very next day, we kind of hooked-up."

Jordan cringed at her choice of words and she said, more than with a smidgen of iciness, "It took a while for your spells to work, but we were able to break into Asa's. The darkness remained, though." She sipped her coffee. Her hand trembled slightly as she peered at Ronan over the brim.

"What did you expect? Asa's house isn't his own. It belongs to a higher realm." She looked exasperated. "You should be patting me on the back and singing my praises since my spells allowed you to save your mother. You have no idea how much it drained me." She stroked her brow, as if easing her invented strain. "I'm still trying to get my strength back."

"Speaking of my mom," said Jordan. "How did you know? I mean, you called Mark and then met us at the diner. You knew before anyone."

"That's not true. Mark knew. He called me first."

Jordan was speechless. She deduced that Ronan called Markus, not the other way around. But Markus and Ezekiel had insisted they needed Ronan to get into Asa's. If the plan to rescue her mother had been in motion before they'd called Ronan, why would Markus come and get her at the diner?

"If Markus called you about my mom, then why'd you both come to the diner? They could've handled it without me even knowing."

Needing to feel superior, Ronan bragged, "Veronka let the cat out of the bag, discussing the fancy-schmancy festivities a few days beforehand. Veronka's discreetly acknowledged tidbits helped me use my powers to the fullest." Ronan tossed her silky hair over her shoulder. "She went on and on, she really hates the two of you. Unfortunately, you were part of the package. They needed your presence to fulfill—" Seeing Jordan's narrowing eyes and growing coldness, Ronan's voice abated. "What'd I say?"

"You and Veronka—you planned—" Livid, Jordan's first impulse was to smack Ronan in her pretty, witchy face. Conflicted, she controlled her combative fingers. Jordan then recollected Ezekiel's words before the slaughter. *'Markus, it was a bad idea bringing her here. I don't care what Ronan said.'*

Suddenly it was like solving a misleading math equation, and now it all made perfect sense. So Markus had known of Ronan's ruse and wanted to take her home to safety. Because of her stubbornness, she'd refused to stay put, and fell for Ronan's ploy. Jordan's pigheadedness was the source of Markus's demise.

Inhaling deeply, Ronan then breezed out a lungful of air. "Like I told Mark, Trebane's enchantments totally banished any heavenly beings. Once you entered the house, he'd planned to fortify the spells so no one could get in or get out. That's where I came in. I diluted the configuration long enough to let heavenly forces penetrate the shield. And then I was lucky enough to keep it diluted so you could get out. And from what I heard from Mark, Asa was overpowered by Principalities. Surely, Asa didn't count on that."

Yeah, after one of our own had fallen. Jordan shuddered, harboring a surplus of tears. "You still didn't specifically answer my question. You said I was part of the package."

"Like I said." Ronan appeared distracted, randomly checking the bistro. "Your presence was needed…to…to make it work."

Jordan cleared her throat. "Well, what about Trebane and Veronka? Aren't you afraid of them seeking revenge? You betrayed The Order."

Almond-shaped eyes glared. Ronan twisted her words like a knife. "Like your father?"

Ronan would never comprehend, thought Jordan, the pride she felt at her father's betrayal. "Not exactly like my father." Frustrated at Ronan's sidestepping, Jordan knew truthful answers were not forthcoming, at least not from Ronan.

Ronan completely changed the matter at hand, and rubbed her palms together like hatching a brilliant coup. "Mark and I work well together, don't you think?"

"Is that why you helped us?" Jordan said with disdain. "You have a crush on Mark, so you let life and deaths hang in the balance?"

"Oh Jordan, don't get bent out of shape." An odd shadow crept over her face. "I'd thought we could be like the dynamic duo fighting crime, or something."

Wanting to scream "*Mark's dead, the angel's dead*!" Jordan restrained herself. "Good idea. Take it up with Mark."

ᏇᏋᏇ

Climbing into a pair of newly washed jeans, Jordan checked the time. Thrill would be there shortly. She ransacked her bureau for her violet cotton knit sweater with the ruffled scoop neck. Then she dashed across the hall to her mom's room and held out her arms. "Well, how do I look?"

Seeley was in the process of stuffing clean laundry in drawers. "I like that sweater. The color looks good on you. Have fun tonight." She rotated to the task at hand then looked back at Jordan. "Hey, you haven't mentioned what Ronan had to say."

Crunching her face, Jordan sighed. "Can I tell you later? Thrill will be here any minute and I still have to fix my hair."

"Sure, go." A trace of a smile touched Seeley's mouth watching her grown daughter flutter back to her room. And pleased Jordan's depression had finally leaked away.

Hunting for a purse, Jordan noticed the sparkling dots that meant Rafe was coming. "Didn't I make myself clear?" She tried not to look at him. "Stay away from me. Watch from a distance if you have to."

Rafe ignored her rudeness. "What did you say to Ronan? She wants us to get together and talk about combining our abilities or something like that."

Jordan rolled her eyes. "Oh that," she said smugly. "Ronan wants you and her to be the next dynamic duo."

Rafe looked bewildered.

"Like Batman and Robin, or Bonnie and Clyde—who knows?" Fishing under the bed, she found the blue purse, blew off some dust, then checked to make sure of its contents.

"You've got holy water?"

"Would you please leave me alone?"

"I can't. I'm sorry. Not until—" Rafe winced. He'd said too much.

"Not until what?" Jordan analyzed the angel's expression closely, focusing on Rafe's eyes, which least reminded her of Markus.

His face hardened. Tilting his head, Rafe faded from sight.

⊱♡⊰

Thrill gave Jordan a speculative glance. "What movie would you like to see?"

"I dunno." Jordan shrugged. "Comedies and suspense are good, whatever. It doesn't matter."

"Elma's showing a kid flick, so I'd figure we'd go up the road and hit the cinemas at the mall. We'll check it out once we get there." Thrill kept his eyes on the congested roadway. It seemed that the entire village of Elma was out driving.

Peeking from under her lashes, Jordan scrutinized the easygoing Thrill. His customary spiky hair had grown. It curled naturally. A sprightly loop dangled over his eye. As if feeling her eyes on him, he pushed back the bothersome tendril. Sucking in her lips, Jordan remembered Markus's shaggy mane. The impersonator's hair was always in place, so unlike the real Markus.

"You're smiling. Something good, I hope."

Caught in the act of goggling, Jordan picked at nonexistent fuzz on her sweater. "I see you're letting your hair grow."

"It's so frigging curly, I can't stand it. That's why I usually keep it short." Thrill cast her an amazing smile. Jordan admired his suggestive dimple and his even, white teeth. "I heard about the death in your family." He felt better breaking the ice. "I'm sorry for your loss."

Saddened by the reminder, she whispered, "Thanks." Jordan then gazed at the early crescent moon, obscured by full-bellied clouds that glowed golden in the setting sun. For some lame reason, it reminded her of Markus.

In agreement, they'd lined up like cattle to see a new blockbuster adventure. They shared a tub of popcorn and thoroughly enjoyed the movie, even though Thrill said it was pure cheese with some swashbuckling added for spice. Afterward, with the stores shuttered in the mall, they'd ventured back to Elma's diner. Greeting friends, Thrill and Jordan made their way to a recently freed table. Warming her hands on the mug of hot chocolate, Jordan asked, "Anything interesting happen while I was gone?"

"We had a bomb threat at school on Monday. Did you see it on the news?

"Nope, I wasn't keeping track of the local news."

"The school had to vacate and wait outside for the SWAT team. A few of us took off in our cars, but my parents would've freaked if I got detention again, so I swung back. Of course, it was a hoax, but it got us out of school for a few hours."

Thrill had removed his jacket and Jordan observed how nicely his Redskins football shirt fit his chest. With spring training well underway, he looked healthy and fit. She made a mental note—must workout.

Jordan grinned, sipping the warm chocolate. Another curl dipped appealingly over Thrill's forehead, poking his eye.

"At first I thought you'd come down with Ronan's flu." His full lips blew off the steam on his mug. "She was out of school a couple of days. And then I found out that Paisley and Cayden have been hanging with her again. No hocus pocus or playing with the Ouija board 'cause Ronan's been so sick, they said." His fingers scraped the curl off his forehead. "Whatever happened that night we ate at the diner?" he asked, his tone reserved. "Did you go to Ronan's? It must've worked if she's not screwing around anymore."

Like a paradox, impeding Ronan was far from the truth. Markus had enlisted Ronan's expertise to cast spells. Jordan couldn't take credit for her stopping. Remembering the carnage of that night, Jordan could only guess what Ronan's part had been. "Yes, we went to Ronan's. Not much luck, though."

Thrill nodded. "Did you and Mark have a fight or something?" Lifting the mug to his mouth, amber eyes fastened on Jordan. "Not that I mind, and not that it's any of my business, but you seem to get all hot and bothered whenever he comes around, like you're ready to scratch his eyes out." Thrill couldn't help seeing her eyes misting and the hot pink spreading across her face.

Thrill's body tightened as he leaned toward her. "Did Mark try something? He—he didn't hurt you?"

"No, no, nothing like that. Mark's...okay. It's me. I haven't been myself lately—since...the death."

He relaxed. "Oh, sorry, I was just worried."

Thrill and Jordan strolled along Main Street toward the Chevelle. Jiggling the car keys, he said, "I love my car, though it'd be nice to have automatic locks and windows." He opened the passenger door for Jordan then went around to the driver's seat.

"What year is your car, Thrill?"

He sat straight and proud. "A 1968 Chevelle Malibu. Don't you love it?"

"Awesome. It's in great shape."

"It was my dad's car. He had it on blocks in the barn for as long as I can remember. It was a wreck. Every now and then he'd rev it up, take it for a spin around the yard, and then drive it back on the blocks. About five years ago, my dad asked if I wanted his old junker. I was only twelve and thought it'd be cool to have my own car, even though it was a piece of crap. My dad and I'd been working on it ever since. Under the hood, it's in pristine shape—now. I'm saving up for a paint job."

"I'd like to find a part-time job so I can get a car."

"I work a couple days a week, and on weekends."

"Really? I didn't know you had a job. What do you do?"

"McKenna's Collision off Grover Road. It's my dad's place." His grin was complacent. "It's not my life's goal to be a mechanic, but it helps pay expenses."

Moonlight filtered through the windshield as Thrill parked in the driveway. Jordan thanked him for the movie and was ready to open the door when he draped his arm over her shoulders, drawing her near. With his fingers under her chin, he kissed her lips, softly at first—tasting.

Bashfully, Jordan parted her lips under his pressure. Totally captivated, she wound an arm over his shoulder, surrendering to the kiss.

CHAPTER 24

He Will Certainly Scatter their Bones.

March roared in, denying spring's ambiance, as winter dumped one last snowfall. Henry revved up the snow blower and plowed the driveway. After an hour of backbreaking toil, he stomped into the kitchen, caked in snow, his sullen brow cracked in crystallized ice. His craggy face was scarlet from the cold. He stripped off his sopping gear, hanging it on a hook over the heating ducts to dry. "Em, I don't think winter's ever gonna end."

"You know the old saying, Henry. March comes in like a lion and goes out like a lamb. This is Buffalo—tomorrow it could be seventy degrees."

Seeley padded into the kitchen. "Thanks for plowing the driveway, Dad. I need to get to Saint Peter and Paul's by seven. I hope the weather doesn't keep too many people from attending."

"The snow petered out hours ago," he said, clawing his fingers through what was left of his hair. "The roads should be fine by now."

Polishing the sink, Em swiveled to Seeley. "You're speaking about Jack's book again?"

"Yup, wish me luck."

"Let us know the next time you're speaking," Henry said. "We'd like to come."

Stunned, Seeley grinned happily. "Sure. By the way, Jordan's hunkered down in her room with tons of homework. Perhaps someone could pop in on her later?"

"We know how to take care of her, Seeley." Henry turned grumpy. "You'd better get going—the roads might be a bit dicey."

Toting her high heels, Seeley trudged out into the snow, wearing boots, coat, and gloves. "I can't wait for summer," she mumbled to herself.

⁊ϣ⁊ϣ

To Seeley's amazement, the church was three-quarters filled with people of differing ages. After Father James's preamble, Seeley embarked on an impassioned speech. Her eyes strayed from pew to pew, until one person in particular caused her tongue to stick to the roof of her mouth. Losing her train of thought, she stammered until she regained control and then looked away.

Finally, Father James closed the lecture. "Seeley, thank you for sharing with us tonight."

An enthusiastic round of applause brought color to her cheeks. Routinely, Father James milled through the crowd, answering questions and selling Jack's book.

Seeley bent to collect her coat, but a large hand lifted it first.

Declan smiled, softening his hard edges. "May I be of service?"

Flustered, Seeley let him assist and channeled her arms into the sleeves.

"Coffee?" His hopeful powder-blue eyes firmly fixed on hers.

Normally so forceful, he was now reduced to begging her to accompany him for a cup of coffee. Seeley couldn't resist. She followed Declan in her car to a nearby restaurant. She had known that, eventually, she'd have to confront him. She'd been rehearsing for weeks, and now, the words flitted right out of her mind. Fidgety, afraid to look him in the eye, she aimlessly looked everywhere else. She then focused on her chapped, dry hands, waiting for the waitress to bring their coffee.

Declan covered her knotted hands with his own. "Seeley, I need to say it, again and again. I'm sorry. Every day I rehash the events of that night, and every day I reach the same lousy conclusion. I don't know what happened." He released her hands for a minute when the waitress brought coffee and asked if they needed menus. They both agreed coffee was enough.

Neglecting the brew, Declan grieved. "Honestly, Seeley, I was angry when Trebane stole you away. Then that bitch hung onto me for dear life. I drank just to have something to do besides listening to her—" Declan hesitated and wiped his large hands over his face.

"Listening to her saying what, Declan?"

Declan's cheeks blotched pink. "Cripes, she has the mouth of a truck driver. Man, I'd never been in the presence of such a lecherous woman."

"Did she make you hot?"

"More like—" His mouth puckered, just short of saying too much. Declan drank some coffee. "One minute you were at the end of the table and then the next you'd disappeared. I got up to look for you with her on my tail. She'd slapped a drink in my hand, and I tipped it back in one gulp. I handed the glass back to her, hoping she would go away. Basically, that's the last thing I remember—until you threw a punch. I woke up in bed, by myself." Remorseful, Declan frowned.

Seeley felt sorry for the befuddled man. He certainly wasn't at fault. "I should've warned you," she confessed. "Asa's people don't play by our rules."

Declan's wounded eyes pierced her through. She'd missed him terribly these last few weeks. And her leave-of-absence from *The Courier* was over. She had to make a decision.

"Seeley, don't be mad, but I did some research on my own. I know about Jack." He paused as Seeley stiffened. "And the accusations pertaining to a sect called The Black Order, and your apparitions. And now, to hear you speak tonight—you were amazing."

Seeley paled. "How—how did you find out?"

"I have my sources." He shrugged. "Then I went right to Father James. The priest holds you in high esteem. Though, he discreetly declined to divulge your...talents, he corroborated my investigation with logic, not sensationalism or misinformed gossip. You've had a rough life for such a young woman."

She didn't have a response.

Placing his fingers under her chin he raised her face and studied her sad cobalt eyes. "Seeley, would you come back to me? Please?"

Her eyelids fluttered shut. Seeley wanted him desperately. "D–Declan, I—I can't." Opening her eyes, she discerned his grooved brow. "I can't take the chance."

"Can't take a chance—on me?"

"If you've learned about my past, then you know my life is...complicated. What if you got hurt because of me, or my daughter?"

He considered her words for a brief second. "I don't know the all the details, but I do know that I want to be part of your life, come hell or high water."

Seeley drew in a worried breath. "That's exactly what I'm afraid of."

 барас

Light leaked underneath Jordan's door. Seeley tapped softly. Jordan mumbled for her to come in. Clothed in flannel pajamas, her hair in a ponytail, she was slouched over a stack of papers.

"That looks uncomfortable," Seeley said. "You know it's close to midnight."

"I know, Mom. I need to finish this report on the holocaust." Jordan kneaded her aching neck. "How'd the speech go?"

"Good." She tugged playfully on Jordan's ponytail. "Guess who showed up?"

Jordan stared at her mom with frightened eyes.

"No, not him." Seeley shook her head. "Not Asa."

"Phew." Jordan breathed a sigh of relief. "You had me going. Who showed up? Someone good, I hope."

Her mouth spread with a winning smile, Seeley expounded on the satisfying evening, the crowd in the church, and the appearance of Declan Donavan, and his desire to stick with her.

Jordan looked at her mom sideways. "You like this guy?"

"Yes, I do."

"Then I'm happy for you. When's he coming to dinner so I can get to know him?"

Chuckling, Seeley admitted that the time was right. Then noting the familiar sparks, she stepped aside to make room for the emergence of Zeke and Rafe. Both angels came into focus smiling.

"It must be good news," Seeley said.

Ezekiel crossed muscular arms over his strapping chest, looking like the epitome of a warrior. His voice as hard as nails, he said, "Even though Asa's alive, his troops are destabilized. Yes, good news for a change."

Taking in Rafe's natural appearance, his broad build, brown eyes, and brown hair, Jordan snapped, "I'd rather you looked like that instead of like Markus."

Ezekiel groaned. "You know he has to wait out the school year, and then he'll be gone."

Jordan tossed her legs over the edge of the bed. "Why can't he just say he's moving out of town or going back home to his parents, or something?"

Rafe propped his fists on his hips. "I need to be here so stop complaining." He gave no further explanation.

"Jordan, stop giving Rafe such a hard time," Ezekiel ordered. "You're being difficult. He's here to do a job, and your cooperation would be appreciated." His eyes turned compassionate. "I understand how badly you miss Markus, but in time…give it time."

Sliding off the mattress, Jordan edged closer to Ezekiel. "You must see him—in heaven?" Her eyes were pleading for clarification. "I don't understand. Markus wasn't fully human. His transformation had just begun when Asa—" Reliving the bloody scene, again, she felt like death clutched her heart.

Ezekiel squeezed her shoulders. "Jordan, He has a divine plan."

Jordan shucked off his hand. "He was still part angel. He needs to come back. Angel's don't die."

Somewhere a clock struck the midnight hour. Rafe sat in the chair with an irate thud. Seeley sat curled up on the bed, watching as Jordan paced in front of Ezekiel waiting impatiently for his explanation.

"Angels are pure spirit," Ezekiel began. "Destroying an angel is difficult. However, it can be done, as Asa figured out. Converted to human form, we're physically susceptible—"

"If you die when you're human, you can still come back as angels, right?" Jordan interrupted.

"For your edification, no, as I said, angels are spirit. Humans do not evolve into angels, like so many people believe."

Thumping despondently next to her mother, she laid her head on Seeley's shoulder. Seeley stroked her daughter's cheek before Jordan shoved away. It was getting harder and harder to placate Jordan.

The angels had begun to wane when Seeley said, "Wait! Does Asa know—is he aware of Ronan's involvement?"

Jordan's head perked at her mom's question.

"It's vague," Rafe said. "Logic says, yes. Ronan's conjuring should've been detected by someone as competent as Asa, unless Ronan conspired with Veronka for some unknown purpose. We wait, listen, and watch to see what plays out."

"I hate this," Jordan complained. "Can't angels be like…like spies and find out what's happening with Asa and the demons?"

"Remember, Jordan," said Rafe. "Angels cannot abide the impious darkness. In that way, we're stronger in human form. But in any form, angels cannot and should not interfere with our Father's plan."

Jordan opened her mouth, but Ezekiel raised his hand. "It's impossible to answer your questions satisfactorily. We're being summoned. We must depart." They nodded their heads, then their blaze grew faint.

Seeley broke the silence. "I wanted to ask Zeke why it's so important for Rafe to play the part of Markus. Why does he need to be here?"

CHAPTER 25

All Is Calm—Too Calm.

March blew by in the wind. Bare tree limbs bore plump buds and yellowed grass branched green and lush. Crocuses, daffodils, tulips, and hyacinths spread rapidly in Em's flowerbeds. Jordan spotted the first robin of the season and welcomed its tuneful warbling. Peaceful days blessed the Chase women. Father James counseled them not to become complacent—the devil is always hard at work.

Back to the grind, Seeley wrote articles for *The Courier Express,* with her boss, Declan, consuming her days and most evenings. Then she prepared for the much-anticipated family dinner. The menu included roasted chicken and dumplings, golden new potatoes slathered with butter and chives, glazed carrots, and homemade caramel apple pie. They received Declan at the table, and all thoroughly delighted in Seeley's savory dishes.

With his gift of charm, Declan ribbed Jordan in an amusing manner and her eyes glittered in admiration for his quick wit. Declan had the family eating from the palm of his hand and a smile plastered Seeley's face for days.

Jordan benefited from the monotony at Elma High. Rumors about Mark or rather, Rafe and Ronan were everywhere. Rumors that the two of them shared more than just their lunches infuriated Jordan, as Rafe continued to spend an inordinate amount of time with the witch. Every night, Jordan tried summoning Rafe for some kind of justification, but without success.

Spotting Paisley and Cayden, Jordan headed toward their table. The lunchroom was, as usual, boisterous and humming with fresh gossip. Jordan lodged her tray next to Paisley's. "Hey, guys, anything interesting going on this weekend?"

Clearly irritated, Paisley said, "What's it to you?"

"Paisley, is something wrong?" Jordan, asked, stunned by her angry reply.

"You know you'll be hanging with Thrill. "

"I thought you liked Thrill?"

"Yeah," she said. "But not for you." Paisley slurped her milk, avoiding eye contact with Jordan.

Cayden peered around Paisley, adding her unwanted two cents. "You and Ronan have the two hottest guys in school."

"Ronan and Mark aren't going out."

"I guess you're not in the loop," Paisley said. "Because it sure looks that way."

"Last time we talked, Ronan said they're just friends," countered Jordan.

Cayden nibbled on her homemade lunch of grapes and crackers. "A lot can happen in a week."

Gobbling a hot dog and fries, Jordan felt a flicker of annoyance—and nerve-racking tension. She knew the rumors were bogus, but she still wondered why Rafe was keeping her in the dark. Something was brewing. Entirely lost in her thinking, she didn't notice Paisley's stare.

Paisley, a poor judge of dining etiquette, said snippily, "Jordan, you're chewing like a cow."

Her derogatory remarked slowed Jordan down. "I'm thinking 'bout Ronan and Ra...Mark. Have you girls gone over to Ronan's lately?"

"Nah," said Cayden, "I'm too scared to set foot in that house."

Paisley shifted in her chair. "I was there last night. She has mega bottled up frustrations. She's wacked for Mark and can't seem to get anywhere. It's seriously pissing her off."

"There, I told you," Jordan said confidently. "They're friends."

Paisley threw her a mutinous look. "Yeah." She rotated completely, surveying the cafeteria. Her tone altered to a hushed whisper. "But Ronan's looking for more than friendship, and Beth Schaffer's getting in the way."

"What's wrong, Paisley, afraid Ronan can hear you?" Noting Paisley's apprehension, Cayden was sharp.

"Zip it, Cayden. She scares you, too." Paisley's face paled. "She had the Ouija board on the table last night. We played a little. I thought I was going to puke."

"Like me?" Cayden said.

"Yeah, but I was able to hold it down…until I got home." Paisley pushed her plate to the side. "I'm not hungry." She blotted her mouth on a napkin. "Ronan got a call when I was there. I heard her say a weird name like *Verona*. Then she walked away, so I don't know what they were talking about."

Jordan's scalp bristled. And the charade continues…

৵৯৵৯

Jordan walked home, mindlessly dodging dirty puddles. Her sneakers, hardly a month old, were already a filthy mess. She heard footsteps behind her. Markus's voice called, "Hey, wait up."

Jordan slowed down, seething. Rafe caught up to her, stepping in a puddle and splattering the bottom of her jeans.

"You've been calling me," he said. "That's either a good sign or a bad one."

She glared at him. "You're leaving me in the dark, Rafe. What's going on with Ronan and Veronka?"

"If I thought you should know, I would've told you," he said. "Seriously, Jordan, I don't know how humans manage. I have to deal with Beth tugging on one arm and Ronan on the other, all the while trying to keep you out of trouble."

"You're keeping me out of trouble? How's that?"

"Obviously, you've deduced my method."

Jordan's lips pinched. "By not confiding in me."

Rafe's brow relaxed. "Markus said you're competent and can handle whatever—"

"Markus said? You've spoken with Markus?"

Rafe took a deep breath. "If you thought Ronan's taken a break from her mysticism, you're wrong. Each day she steps it up a notch. With Asa and Veronka cultivating her habits, Ronan's capacity to unleash Hell soars, and Lucifer himself obliges. They're pleased to find such a gifted young woman to influence."

Jordan realized that Rafe had evaded her question, but she let it go for now. "What can I do?"

"It's perplexing," he said. "As Mark, I've befriended her, and Ronan's confessed a few tawdry facts of her unwholesome childhood. I can see why she hates her life and her father. Lucifer tempts those who feel mistreated, and Ronan's comforted by magic. The power is enthralling to her. The black arts offer ways to modify events and lure people to do her bidding, and Ronan's hooked."

"So you believe it's too late to help her?"

"That's not what I said. The danger of losing her soul doesn't impress Ronan at present. Like most teenagers, she sees death as a distant enemy. The teenage attitude of 'just do it' is engraved on her heart, without any thought of culpability. Asa Trebane's promise of reward adds greatly to Ronan's unfortunate parentage. She's discovered a seedy kind of love."

Rafe and Jordan strolled down the sidewalk, oblivious to their surroundings.

"I've been keeping close tabs on Ronan, hoping she'll leak some information about the Order's next move. She's vain about her mystical prowess and recently bragged of Asa's aspiration to blend their powers. He has only proposed blending of powers with one other person…" Rafe stopped, conscious he'd said too much.

"My mother."

Rafe's slip of the tongue did not surprise her. She knew how Asa stalked her mom.

Rafe was stressed. "Everything at the moment seems calm—too calm."

With her house just across the street, Jordan peered up at Rafe. "Ronan knows you're an angel—well, a human angel. Why is she so keen on wanting more from you? Um...do you know what I mean?" Jordan tilted her head, wondering. "You'd think she'd despise your presence, since you're a divine spirit."

Rafe grinned sheepishly, his skin stretched tightly over high cheekbones. "Ronan's intent on Markus changing masters."

"Really?" Jordan balked. "Does she truly believe you'd be loyal to Lucifer?"

"Wiser angels have fallen."

"So she wants you or, I mean, Markus to crossover to the dark side?" Rafe nodded. "What if I tell her Markus is dead, would she leave you alone?"

"Perhaps," he divulged. "She truly fancies Markus, although any angel's power, no matter which angel, would help appease her. Lately, setting foot in her house causes me brutal grief, even in my human form. I've gone as far as to attempt sprinkling holy water, but I heard it sizzle before it even touched the floor. That only means one thing—Hell's consuming fire has found another home."

ℰↂℰↂ

Jordan received Ronan's grief-stricken call after dinner. "Jordan, I can't...I can't stand it anymore. I'm hurting. I've never felt this way before. I feel like my heart is going to explode or something. Markus doesn't love me and I love him so much, but—but he keeps pushing me away," she cried. "Can't you tell Markus how much I need him, how much I love him? He's the only person who can save me. Only Markus can help me, you know that, Jordan."

Like a pot of water on the stove, Jordan came to a slow simmer as she listened to Ronan bellyaching. Infuriated with Ronan's method to drag Markus into her hell, Jordan made a decision. "Remember when you asked me who Asa gutted with a butcher knife?"

Jordan waited till she heard Ronan say, "Yes?"

"Why hasn't Asa told you?"

"Asa confides in ways you haven't even begun to imagine," Ronan declared, sounding exceptionally offended. "What are you getting at?"

"Ronan, I know you're in league with The Order and I know what you're trying to do to Markus. It won't work...because Asa killed Markus."

Jordan heard an intake of breath. "That's not true. I'd know...I'd know...why wasn't—" After a weighty pause, she asked, "Then...who's Markus?"

"A facsimile, an imposter. His name is Rafe."

Jordan believed that this was news to her. Something wasn't quite kosher. Why hadn't Ronan been informed? She then construed the deceitful Asa more than likely exploited Markus as an incentive—if—Ronan compromised her power.

"Jordan," a weeping Ronan wailed. "Can–can–you come–come over?"

Jordan was reluctant, but the clamor of Ronan's sniveling bothered her. "I guess so," she mumbled into the cell phone. "I'll be there soon."

Instantaneously, Rafe appeared in Jordan's room, looking silly in cargo shorts and a Hawaiian shirt. "What are you doing? You can't go there!"

Glad he had abandoned the Markus façade, Jordan held in a laugh. "Were you on vacation or something?"

He looked baffled. "What are you talking about?"

"Your clothes, oh, never mind." She grinned when Rafe smoothed the shirt. However her grin was quickly replaced with severity. "I told Ronan about Markus and you. She now knows Asa's been hiding important information. Perhaps I could convince her to douse the fires, or whatever she's invoking of late."

"That's unlikely." He glared at Jordan with his brown eyes, so unlike Markus'. "She's gone too far."

"I need to try, or she'll be lost forever." She yearned to believe that Ronan could be saved.

Rafe exhaled a snort. "Like I explained earlier, her residence holds my power at bay."

"Ronan undoubtedly hasn't had time to concoct a plan." Jordan raked her fingers through her hair, thinking. "She's reeling with the information of Markus's death right now. Possibly I'll catch her off-guard." She sat on the side of the bed cuffing on her high tops, while Rafe marched back and forth.

"Why don't you call Thrill to go with you?" Rafe suggested. "They've been friends a while, his persuasion might be more helpful than you think."

The last thing Jordan wanted was to involve an unsuspecting Thrill in the whole fiasco. "I–I don't think so. There's some things I'd rather not reveal and to drag him into this mess, no, that's a bad idea."

Rafe's body tensed, then a tremor shook his broad frame. "Something doesn't feel right…"

Jordan studied the peaked angel. "What'd you mean?"

His spirit was elsewhere as Rafe speculated for a split second. "Don't go to Ronan's—" His voice was unyielding and indistinct brown eyes issued a second warning. "I'm urgently being summoned. Do not leave—understand?"

At a complete loss regarding his exigencies, Jordan blinked and he was gone. The racket of her grandparent's favorite sitcom floated up the stairs as she paced anxiously from room to room. Her mom had left with Declan well over two hours ago. Her new knowledge blazed a hole in her tongue. She thought of ringing her mom, and then decided against it. Why spoil her night?

Alternatively, Jordan decided to practice the ability to probe beyond her human psyche to manufacture a sword. Since sparring with Markus months ago, she'd been secretly attempting to perform the impossible feat. Diligently and with immense effort, Jordan sought inner control. Lifting her hand, she felt her mind transcending. Feeling the powerful pull and the typical heat passing her fingers, she strived for concentration as the evasive magical sword appeared. The image took shape and hardened. Just as she was about to grab hold, a flash of lightning drew her eye from the intended object. Jordan groaned. Apparently, it was a sign—she wasn't ready yet.

While the hours crept at a snail's pace, Jordan wondered where Rafe had gone. She was ready to burst. She reflected on the possibility of him venturing to Ronan's without her, that's when the rash decision was made.

She galloped down the staircase. "Em, Henry, I'm going to Ronan's for a while. I'm borrowing mom's car," she said in a crisp voice. "I won't be long."

"Okay, honey." Em sounded upbeat and giggled at the television. "See you later."

As soon as Jordan shoved the key into the ignition she experienced an eerie foreboding.

CHAPTER 26

The Earth Quaked, the Heavens Shook,
I Took Refuge in the Shelter of Your Wings!

Ronan's side door was slightly ajar. Jordan knocked. When there was no reply, she banged louder. "Ronan?"

Her hands felt sticky. There was some sort of goo on her knuckles. *Did Ronan recently paint the door?* Pressing the door all the way open, she then wiped her sticky hands on her jeans. She stepped into the dimly lit kitchen. Normally drafty and cold, the air was muggy. An obnoxious stink filled the room. With her arm shielding her nose, Jordan tried not to breathe.

Advancing farther into the kitchen, she saw that the wallpaper was riddled with strange markings. Shuffling cautiously toward the living room, the strange markings followed. And it appeared as if the splattered crimson paint had been mixed with ash.

"Ronan?" she called again.

A floorboard creaked under her feet. She froze.

A motionless man stood with his back to her, looking out the square picture window. An immaculate white tailored suit and matching white shoes contrasted with his lubricated hair, which was black as tar. The man drew the curtains shut and leisurely turned around.

At first, Jordan thought he might be Ronan's absentee father, though every bone in her body told her otherwise. She
stared at the strikingly handsome man. He reminded her of a
legendary movie star. His uneven smile was unconventionally
appealing as he gracefully walked forward.

Heavy footfalls made Jordan glance fleetingly away from
the man, to the staircase. For some reason, she wasn't surprised to see Ronan *and* Asa. They stopped midway between
Jordan and the strange man in white. Ronan, her face drained
of color, almost looked afraid to move.

Jordan broke the creepy hush. "Ronan, what's going on?"

Coming to her senses and widening her eyes, Ronan
waved her hand at the mysterious, handsome man. "Meet...my
father."

Startled by her introduction, Jordan looked past Asa's
caustic grin to Ronan and back to the man in white.

Hypnotic obsidian eyes centered on Jordan, the elegant
man smiled wider. "I finally meet the elusive Jordan Chase."

"Mr. Beckman?"

He laughed.

Ronan's head jerked to the side, squinting at Jordan hatefully. "Mr. Beckman?" Her voice rang acid with contempt.
"I'm free of that incestuous smutty scum. The prick gave his
life to Lucifer."

Jordan's throat tightened, her eyes sliding from Ronan to
the man. "Ronan d–did–did you k–kill your father?" She waited on pins and needles, hoping the answer would be a decisive
no.

Disfiguring her pretty face, Ronan glowered, stirring
closer. "Martin Beckman was finally worth something—my
ascension to a privileged realm. Martin was never truly my
father." Her head turned to the man by the window. "Here is
my father."

The man in white extended his arms to her, his words
sickly sweet. "My daughter." Ronan scuttled into his open
arms. "My daughter, side by side with Asa, we will lead *my*
world."

"Look around you!" His brooding voice was electric. "Martin's blood offers me sanctuary. His blood consecrates this abode and—his daughter to me." He spread his arms proudly.

Feeling utter defilement, Jordan gaped at the walls as they wept blood. Barely able to speak through her constricting throat, she croaked, "Who are you?"

Jordan's question went unheeded as the man smoothed Ronan's long locks, his tone a soothing coo. "Markiel, or should I say Markus, has been like a burrowing blade in my back since—forever. Markus." The name sounded offensive on his tongue. "When he became human, I grasped the chance to rid the netherworld of that particular enemy." Then, as if he were pacifying the girl, his voice turned rueful. "I'm sorry, but we had to dispose of him. Asa's plan worked to perfection thanks to your expertise, Ronan."

A pouting Ronan crossed back to Asa.

"Ronan, you plotted against Markus? While all the time we thought—we thought you were helping." Her hackles were rising.

Footsteps clattered on the kitchen tile. Jordan twirled, half-expecting a barrage of demons. She was half-right. Veronka swept in with a belligerent expression.

Jordan glared into Veronka's soulless midnight pupils ringed in red. "The eyes are the mirror to the soul," she said mockingly. "And yours are empty, Veronka."

Veronka flung her head back, emitting a rude cackle. "If only I had a soul to offer Lucifer, it would be the blackest." In a fast motion, Veronka circled fingers around Jordan's neck and shoved her to the floor.

"You're not so strong without that angel."

Jordan yanked her legs up between Veronka's ankles and sent her sprawling backward. On her feet, Jordan crouched, ready to fight.

"Stop—"

She wheeled to face a scathing glare. The man's façade of sultry composure collapsed.

"Young lady, I don't generally make appearances. You should be honored to meet me." He wove a deadly cocoon with his silky voice. "Who do you think I am?"

She snubbed the question. She'd be more than happy to send any demon back to Hell.

His arms rose in exaltation. "I am the way, I am the life," he extolled. "I am the way to master this life, to gain wealth beyond your wildest dreams, and to live a life of carnal fulfillment."

Terrifyingly, the man's body began to blur and suddenly coalesced into a voluptuous woman who, with an eerie smirk, stroked herself obscenely. Swiftly the woman roiled into a mass of skeleton bones, then a vortex of flesh and eyes, and next developed into a coiled, scaly serpent. The serpent grew enormous, its fangs threateningly close to Jordan. A forked tongue hissed, licking her face.

Undulating, it molted its snakeskin like a banana peel, revealing a child, gazing around in wide-eyed innocence. The child's innocent eyes changed to a blazing red. His skin was ripped asunder from within as a behemoth, horned beast crawled out. Burgeoning wings, not resplendent like her angels, but greasy black, like feathers dipped in motor oil. A thing of humped sinew and immortal energy, naked and blood red, it breathed fire.

"Is this how you see me in your nightmares?" Maniacal laughter rose from the Hellfire that ensconced the room. The creature pivoted its trunk-like neck, its barbed horns fracturing the ceiling, raining plaster.

Jordan's heart hammered in her chest. Any hope for escape had fled.

Tremors rocked the beast and the white-suited man stood there once more. "I am...I am..." He gestured his hand for Jordan to answer, as if they were playing a guessing game.

"Lucifer—" breathed Jordan, knees knocking in her high-tops.

He touched a finger to his nose in confirmation.

"Jack Chase promised me his first born. Your mother—" His tone seethed with loathing. "—Seeley stole Jack's soul from me. I want what's owed. The time has come when the warrior will be one—with me!"

A pain ripped through Jordan's shoulder joints as her arms were wrenched behind her. His expression vindictive, Asa sauntered toward Jordan.

"Ronan, Ronan! Don't let this happen!"

Jordan's mind latched onto the nearest lamp and whipped it at Asa's head. With a nod from Lucifer, it crashed to the floor.

He belched a chuckle.

"To tell the *God's awful truth*," Asa said snidely. "Ronan thought she was helping. She was, in a way—my way." Asa turned a snide eye on Ronan. "The angels could not break through the enchantments—without help." Ronan looked ill. "Your blood was the key to enter. The house should've been sealed from others. Our spells were to weaken the angel and take you, body and spirit. It was Ronan's inexcusable love for that angel that destabilized the spells enough for heaven's army to penetrate."

"You promised me Mark if I gave you Jordan," Ronan cried.

"My good fortune of killing Markus was destiny, a gift for my lord," Asa went on, his tone belittling. "Ronan is an exceedingly skilled child, who must be ruled with an iron fist as she…matures." He made obeisance to Lucifer. "Forgive me. I live to do your will."

Lucifer looked thoroughly pleased with the drama and leered ruthlessly.

Jordan shook like a windblown leaf as Asa slid a hand into his jacket and withdrew a shiny dagger. "I used the one person I knew who would weaken Markus—you. And my remuneration shall be great when the warrior's spirit becomes one with my lord." Merely a foot from Jordan, Asa announced, "My dear, you've made me exceptionally jubilant. I honor Lucifer, in person, with your consecration."

"I will not be consecrated!" Jordan bawled. "I will never fight for Lucifer, I rebuke Satan. I rebuke you!" No longer afraid, she glared at them.

Lucifer's implacable eyes enflamed, his pride rattled by a measly child. "Your spirit is rightly mine."

Jordan awaited the plunging blade. Memories of her mom and dad, her grandparents, and Markus raced through her mind. She refused to cry, refused to plead for mercy from the devil, refused the consecration altogether. Closing her eyelids, she waited for the pain.

The room rattled—her eyes popped open. The last time she'd felt such a quake, Markus had died.

Pure illumination flooded over them, Jordan stared in awe at the splendorous shimmering. Veronka screamed and fled, freeing Jordan's arms. Asa scampered across the floor and hid behind Lucifer.

"Markiel!" roared the devil, growing in stature until he towered over the room.

"That's not Mark—" Ronan's voice was unraveling like a fine thread "—it's Rafe!"

Jordan stood her ground. With a sound like pealing thunder, gleaning wings enclosed her like a protective shield. In Markus's strong voice, Rafe said, "Go back to Hell where you belong."

Morphing into the behemoth horned beast, Lucifer breathed fire. "Asa, you've failed me!"

His face like parchment, Asa changed from dictatorial hit man to cowering worm at those words. "He was human when I stabbed him!"

Confounded, Jordan followed Ronan's tearful gaze to the looming angel. She squinted against the dazzling brightness. In a face like sculptured granite, velvety sapphire eyes beamed into hers. Woozy, she spoke his name in wonder. "Markus?"

A smile played at the corners of his mouth. Jordan couldn't believe her eyes and then, totally energized, she felt like fighting the devil.

"We have *also* been biding our time, awaiting your arrival, Lucifer." Markus's voice boomed like rolling thunder. "Your minions are scattered, and the supposed leaders of your army have been defeated. Your pride would not let a mere mortal, a girl, stand in your way. We knew you'd attend to her yourself."

Lucifer recoiled. "This girl is no mere mortal. Your *Father* has seen to that! But be forewarned—I will be the sure victor in this land."

"You are not God!" Markus chastised. "Your iniquity bleeds into mankind, and I take pleasure destroying your breed."

Lucifer's horned skull twisted sideways. "My breed..." He snorted fire with a gutsy noise and aimed his horns at the angel. "Markiel, my brother, you cannot win this fight. You cannot abide in my realm. Your power ebbs as we speak. And once you become human, I myself will smite you."

From Jordan's vantage point, she'd detected purplish tendons stemming out of Markus's neck. Veins pulsed in his temple as he clenched his jaw in agony. Yet the muscles in his arms flexed expectantly while his spirit continued to exude superlative power.

"I am new and improved, thanks to my Father," Markus said confidently.

"*Father!*" spat Lucifer. "I am the Father—the father of this world. Humans beg for me in their pitiful lives."

Movement came from the side. Jordan caught Ronan sprinting up the stairwell. Asa had retreated, sneaking out the front door. Veronka was either dead or gone. That left her, Markus, and the fire-breathing Lucifer. Jordan thought about chasing Ronan, knowing full well that she'd perform spectacular incantations to bind Markus. As if he could read her thoughts, he spoke in an undertone, "Go home, now."

Jordan foolishly left his protective wings and ran to the stairs.

"No—" Markus yelled after her.

Heat seared her back. She cringed. Dodging behind the handrail, she glanced behind her. Markus's muscles convulsively tightened as he shielded her with his body, deflecting Lucifer's deadly violence. In a tidal wave of fury, the devil targeted Markus. Their clash resonated like an atomic bomb.

The house rocked, raining down splintering wood and shattering glass.

Jordan fumbled for the railing with her arms. She staggered a few steps then scrambled up to the second floor.

Adrenaline pumping, her heart beating a thousand times a minute, Jordan hated to waste time hunting for Ronan. She wanted to face her and be done with it.

In the narrow hallway, Jordan suffocated a shriek as inky creatures dive-bombed her head. Bracing herself, she swatted her way through nebulous entities and ducked into the nearest room.

She had found Ronan.

Standing before her makeshift altar, Ronan slit her palm with a knife and dripped blood into a crucible. Quickly and confidently, she added herbs to the magic brew. In a guttural voice, she began her incantation.

The one flickering candle sputtered, a bluish-orange flame shot upward spinning into a golden chain.

"Ronan, stop!"

Jordan barged forward, overturning the paraphernalia. The lit candle toppled onto the bed. The sheets ignited with a *whoosh*. Jordan launched herself at Ronan, sealing her in a headlock. She thought how easy it would be to snap the girl's neck. Instead, she slammed Ronan's head against the floor. Ronan was unconscious.

Jordan clutched her limp arm and hauled the girl over her shoulder. She inhaled a lungful of smoky air, gagging, and searched for an opening. Ronan woke up with a vengeance, kicking and throwing air punches. One blow caught Jordan behind the ear. Coughing wildly, she dropped her load, and Ronan darted into a cloud of smoldering grayness.

Hunkering down on her hands and knees, Jordan crawled, trying to find the door. She mopped her stinging eyes, and peered through the sheeting gray residue at Ronan's bed. The flames were confined. Jordan discerned the dense smoke issued from downstairs. Screaming Markus's name, she groped along the floor. Her lungs began to ache, every breath seemed like a chokehold to her throat. Completely sightless, she fumbled in the opaque fog until a pair of arms circled her waist from above. Jordan literally flew away from the destruction.

Gagging and spitting, Jordan woke to Ezekiel's voice. "Jordan…"

Blinking and scrubbing her smarting eyes, Jordan realized she was propped against the trunk of a tree. She looked around. They appeared to be in the woods. She coughed up gooey dregs, spit, and felt a little better. "Where are we?"

Ezekiel, in his customary black, looked irritated and incredulous. "You blacked out, and I brought you to Emery Forest. I need to go back. Markus was right about Lucifer, though, I know it's a trap. It's always a trap."

"Wait, I want to help. I can't lose Markus a second time."

His voice detonated like a bomb. "Go home!" Squawking birds took flight. "That's the best way you can help. Please, for a change, listen. Do as I say."

Shaking her head, uncertain over the whole debacle, Jordan groaned. "My mom's car is at Ronan's."

"Don't even attempt to go near her house. Seeley will understand." Pointing south, he waved his hand. "Go straight. You'll be walking for about a mile. Rafe will be here soon to make sure you stay on your route."

"You don't trust me?"

Peering at Jordan sorrowfully, Ezekiel exhaled. "When it comes to someone you love, not in the least."

Jordan's words rushed out in one breath. "Something's terribly wrong—Markus isn't planning on coming back, is he?" Grappling against the tree trunk, Jordan fought her way to a standing position.

A stellar wingspan expanded, and a restless Ezekiel grieved. "There's little time…" The angel took flight, shooting past the tree limbs.

CHAPTER 27

Your Breath Gives Me New Life.

Shadows played hide and seek with Jordan, as moaning branches bowed to the blood moon. Voyaging in the woods amid foreign night noises, Jordan twitched at the sound of a hooting owl. *You are not scared,* she disparaged. *You are supposed to be a warrior, act like one!* Straightening her shoulders, she picked up the pace and travelled into the unwieldy woodland.

Her spirit was with Markus and Ezekiel, and she wondered where the heck Ronan had run off to. The embodiment of Lucifer was astronomical *and* petrifying. Those eyes will forever be ingrained in her brain. Inconceivably, the Beast had personally involved himself in the conflict.

Up ahead a human figure lurked in the shadows. Frozen in time, she waited—the man came into view. She gasped. She hadn't realized she was holding her breath. "Rafe."

"Ezekiel said you'd be expecting me. I didn't mean to scare you.

"I have the heebie-geebies. Meandering through the woods at night isn't the smartest move. Let's head to the road." Jordan started in the opposite direction, back to the street.

Rafe seized her arm, stopping her. "I'm here now and the road will take you twice as long to get home. Besides, they'll be hunting for you on the streets."

"Great. Demons are hunting me down like a piece of meat." Jordan rolled her eyes. "Will they ever give up?"

Rafe nudged her gently forward, looking skyward as if anticipating an answer from above. "Lucifer rarely intervenes. His legions get plenty of immoral results without their deity's help."

Her heart weary, Jordan scuffed pine needles and sticks with her sneakers. "Rafe, you were my father's guardian angel. Why couldn't you help him?"

Rafe stopped, his expression haunted. "Jack was entrenched in a bleak world at a young age. I spoke to his heart, but he buried my words deep within, and I watched and waited. Asa's influence changed Jack to such a degree that I had to flee from his side entirely.

"Then on the day you were born, Seeley nearly died. And Jack prayed for the first time, creating a miraculous chink in his blackened heart—a space for light to cultivate. Grace fractured the evil, making it possible for me to return." Rafe's palatable smile was unmistakable. "Jack fought a brave battle, never involving you or your mother. His perfidy incensed Asa, who'd promised Lucifer a warrior's spirit—"

Jordan nodded. "I think I know the rest of the story." Weighing Rafe's words during a temporary interval, she started to get weepy. "Will Markus come back to me? Why does my heart ache so much for him?"

"My Father bestows a guardian to every soul, a strong, lasting bond, where two spirits become one."

Wishing for the angel to elaborate, she was ready to drill him for information when she realized he'd commenced into a slow trot. Intuitively, Jordan sensed Rafe's trepidation. "I guess we're in a hurry."

"Yes."

The heels of Rafe's shoes troweled the dirt, stopping suddenly. A visible shudder pitched him backward, with both hands gripping his head. "They need me. I don't know if I should leave you alone." Troubled eyes pierced Jordan.

She didn't see what was holding him up. "Go. Go now—help Markus."

"Go straight home," Rafe ordered in a low growl. With a whoosh of spreading wings that looked like flaming icicles, Rafe pushed off with his feet. A distinct whir swelled the air as he dematerialized.

Alone again, Jordan noticed every spooky creak. She made a beeline for home, jogging and swerving among trees, bushes, and fallen trunks.

She braked, sloping frontward, resting with hands stacked on her knees. Swallowing deep breaths, Jordan rubbed the stitch in her side. Grime and sweat pearled her neck, arms and back as she unwound a noose of hair from her throat and plucked at her clinging shirt. Rucking her shirttail with her hands, Jordan scrubbed her clammy face. Then she smelled smoke.

Something splintered and Jordan's head swiveled to the right. Someone was there. He looked like Jordan's algebra teacher, short and squatty with grubby brown hair, wire-rimmed glasses, a bulbous snout, and a white button-down shirt, complete with a pen protector.

Jordan squinted. *It was* her teacher, Mr. Basinski.

When the man spotted Jordan, he ran faster than she expected, given his rotund bulk. She sidestepped just in the nick of time. She could see the sweat streaming down Mr. Basinski's pudgy face. He charged a second time. Hawking a phlegm ball, Jordan spat in his red-ringed demon eye. She jerked her knee up, colliding with the man's groin. Grunting, she punted her sneaker into the teacher's chin, knocking him unconscious.

Leaves rustled and two more demons attacked with hacking blades. Ducking behind a trunk, Jordan grumbled anxiously, "Markus! Markus!"

A demon popped around the tree trunk, clamping his fingers on Jordan's arm. He frothed at the mouth and chortled as he claimed his prize. She distracted the demon with a fist to his unprotected throat. He slumped, choking. Jordan took off, skirting some brambles, trying to lose his buddy.

Her throat raw, she panted, "Where the heck are you? I need you, NOW!"

Jordan spotted a rock. Would she be able to throw it with all the distractions? She concentrated, focusing her mind. The rock shook. She firmed her mental grip then chucked it at her aggressor. *Yes*!

He dodged, yet the rock's notched edge grazed his forehead, splicing open a gaping gash.

All her senses heightened, Jordan heard the *phlit* of a flying object just in time to bob to the left as the tip of the blade stabbed the tree.

She took off again, the demon in hot pursuit. Their ragged breathing mingled with ghostly night noises as they ran, trampling twigs and breaking off branches. Suddenly the demon lurched forward and his burly arms snagged her legs. She tripped and sprawled in a pile of brushwood. With the wind knocked from her lungs, Jordan couldn't breathe. *Wait just a second*, she thought, but the demon leapt on her. His blade scraped perilously near to her throat. She gulped for air.

"Thought you'd get away, missy?" His breath reeked. He gawked at her, the whites of his demon eyes unmistakably ringed with red. The tip of the knife bit her neck as he pressed harder, breaking skin.

Jordan stayed perfectly still, waiting for her chance to kill the beast. She felt warm blood stream down and soak into her shirt.

"Wait!" a battered Mr. Basinski shouted. "Trebane's waiting in the clearing. You don't want to get him mad."

The demented demon perched on Jordan's chest. "I jus' wanna little taste."

Jordan squeezed her eyelids shut. As his sweaty face drew closer, his noxious stench filled her nostrils. She gagged.

The demon's weight shifted off her chest when Mr. Basinski forcibly kicked him with the heel of his penny loafer. She drew a deep breath then heard the noxious demon swear at Mr. Basinski. He shoved the demon again. Jordan barely had time to think. Frantic, she struggled to get to her feet, only to be accosted by her teacher and a third fiend standing nearby. They wrestled with her thrashing legs and arms.

From of the corner of her eye, Jordan saw a wink of moonlight on silver but was unable to budge from their fiendish hold. The ousted demon reared back and stabbed Jordan's right arm. Again the knife flashed, searing her upper chest. A fist clipped Jordan in the temple and all went black.

Roused by burning pain and the sounds of a crackling bonfire, Jordan suppressed a groan. Before she opened her eyes, she prayed. "I need help."

Chanting droned in the background. Jordan opened her eyes a slit, confirming what she felt. Rope twined from her shoulders, across her chest and under her arms, tying her firmly to the rough wood. She knew she was trapped.

Flames sputtered in response as cowled figures threw bespelled ingredients in the pit. Spellbound worshippers rocked in rhythm to the chanting. Jordan wondered if she might recognize anyone beneath the hoods. Ronan! *Is she hidden under one of those cloaks, conjuring her black magic*? Jordan knew how effective Ronan's curses could be.

Off to one side, she observed her three demon attackers standing guard, the only ones in street clothes.

"Come on, Trebane," Mr. Basinski croaked. "Let's get on with it."

Jordan saw the nefarious gray-haired man, stooped low, clutching a wooden staff. Apparently, Asa sprained an ankle on his swift jaunt through the forest. Jordan hoped it hurt like a hellhound gnawing on his bones.

His black robe swished as he moved surprisingly fast. Standing before Jordan, he stared down at her. His creased skin drooped in folds, and his eyes reflected his black heart.

"Hello, Jordan. So we meet again—and for the last time. Now I have the advantage." His voice grated like metal on glass. "I believe it's past time for your consecration." Asa's jowls quivered, sprinkling spittle on Jordan's face. "However, I'd consider sparing you for a while *if* you conform to The Order."

"Never, you piece of slime!"

"My, my, my, what language. Such an impertinent child." His voice was an acerbic coo. "I see your mother's lack in teaching you manners." His pointy chin angled right, black eyes glued to Jordan's face. "You look a lot like her—what a waste. Speaking of your mother—how is the luscious Seeley?"

Jordan felt hatred oozing out of her pores. "Damn you to Hell!"

"I have no doubt. But all in good time, Jordan, all in good time."

Asa turned away. Approaching the hooded men and women who paraded around the pit, he halted them with a peremptory hand. Not a sound stirred in the forest. "Disciples of Lucifer, we sacrifice a most worthy offering to our lord. You come here to witness the long overdue consecration of the Warrior."

Jordan craned her neck to see heads bowing and hands clasped in expectation. Then the smelly demon grunted, dropping to his knees and tugging on her legs. Jordan, never one to give up, kicked toward the man's face, just barely catching his jaw before he secured both ankles. He lassoed them tightly to the timber and then began to run his filthy hand up under her jeans. Jordan fought the urge to puke. Mr. Basinski walked over to check the bindings, interrupting the demon's pleasure. Jordan couldn't believe she was actually glad to see him. They both vanished somewhere behind her shoulders.

Her circulation cut off, Jordan's extremities went numb. She pinched her eyelids shut, holding back threatening tears. Ezekiel's words went through her head again and again: *It's always a trap.* Right now, the angels battled Lucifer and his cohorts. Jordan wondered if all would be lost.

Asa spoke again, his voice amplified. "Tonight, the prophecy will be fulfilled! Preeminent Lucifer, in this vigil, we seek world dominance. May you reign on earth, achieving our victory of wealth and supremacy. We submit ourselves to your authority by this sacrificial consecration." He then kicked it up a notch. "Lucifer! Bind the Warrior's spirit. Create a powerful demon to win souls for your gain!"

With numb hands and no sensation below her knees, Jordan mumbled, hoping for a miracle. "Markus…Markus…"

Asa spun, sneering. "Markus? Did you call Markus? The Great One detains your Markus as we speak." He bent low, piercing Jordan with his malicious gaze. "I'm afraid you and your father will have a lot to talk about, both dying in the same manner. How long has it been, Jordan? I'd estimate five or six years now."

Horrorstruck, Jordan realized Asa planned to crucify her. Two demon men yanked her arms out, knelt on her extended wrists, and waited impatiently for the signal. The cadence of hellish chanting built, its rhythm hypnotic.

The ultimate predator, Asa raised his arm in deathly quiet.

She was scared out of her mind, however, she wouldn't give Asa the gratification of seeing her break down. Setting her jaw, she felt that every bone in her body was stretched to the limit, quaking. She never imagined the consecration would actually take place. It was a distance threat, never a reality. Her mom's face haunted her. Poor Mom!

This was another one of those realistic nightmares—no, a nightmare that was about to come true. She relived ghastly memories of her father's mangled body dying—only this time, she was going to die.

Asa's hellish words spoke volumes. He nodded, dropping his arm. Jordan felt a pinch in each palm then heard the clang of metal on metal.

She screamed loud and long, the spine-tingling cry echoing through the forest. Excruciating agony exploded her brain into a million pieces. On the brink of unconsciousness, she wished for nothingness. Her senses reeled and her body rose as demons heaved the wooden trunk upright. It thumped into a prepared hole, jarring her aching body forward.

In sheer anguish, she shrieked again. Above their heads, Jordan hung on the cross between heaven and earth. She was going to die—just like her father.

"God..." Jordan breathed.

"He isn't here, Jordan. He can't, or won't help you," Asa mocked. "You poor child, you are abandoned. The good shepherd has given his flock free will, and the sheep have scattered.

Jordan, you are the little lamb led to the slaughter. How poetic! Your mission is fulfilled."

Asa hobbled near, clinging to the cane with both hands, his smug face intent. "You've hunted and fought so hard all these years for Christ. Now you shall die like your Christ."

Jordan had heard those words before. Asa said them as her father died. She gathered courage. "That's—where— you're wrong. Christ—is alive." She gasped. "He's here—"

Jordan welcomed the hallucinations that came next. She saw her father, vital and alive, looming over everyone. He stared at Asa with a rakish grin. Gradually, his eyes came to rest on her—not with pity, not with sorrow, but with pure love! He dipped his head in affirmation, and then his mouth quirked. The quirk spread to a brilliant smile, the smile she'd missed these past seven years.

Then he was gone. Jordan accepted the sign from heaven—her father would be taking her home.

Her blood stained the ground, draining away her warmth, her pain, her life. Even in her weakened state, Jordan reacted to an indescribable flash of light. She cried out, beseeching, "Markus…"

Violent and swift, a wrathful angel destroyed demon after demon, as robed humans fled. Only Asa remained, driven past the brink of insanity by his defeat. "You can't kill me, and I will never give up. Do you hear me, *Markus*?"

Transforming, the human Markus strode rapidly toward Asa, his expression merciless, his daunting eyes darkening bitterly. "I'm human," he snarled. "Now, I will kill you."

Asa's eyes went wide in fright. He scurried backward, his wooden crutch in tow. "Your Father won't allow it! You'll be cast away! Think of the torment, think of God's rebuke."

Asa's words resounded to Jordan. She sucked air, wheezing. "No, Markus!" Her lungs inflated, trying to take the next breath. "He's not worth it—let him go."

Markus whipped about. His marble features crumbled at the sight of Jordan on the cross. "Jordan."

She looked into Markus's face, overflowing with love for the angel who had guarded her from her birth till now, her death. Motion snagged her eye. Asa's crutch had fallen to the ground and with two hands, he gripped—a gun! He took aim.

Jordan willed Markus to turn. Her chest heaved, producing a withered gasp, "Markus, behind you—"

The gun fired. Already turning, Markus's body jerked, yet he continued toward his adversary.

In his desperate need to flee, Asa tripped, stumbling headlong into the bonfire. Flailing his arms, he screeched, a repulsive blast that swelled the night.

Asa wobbled upright. His expression was bizarrely jubilant. "Master! My lord!" he squealed. "The consecration is complete!" Murky creatures slunk from his mouth, like rats fleeing a sinking ship. Flames laced Asa's legs then, steadily, the blaze devoured him.

Jordan knew she was dying. She didn't want Asa's grisly inferno to be the last thing she'd see. Her eyes blurred then refocused. Beautiful Markus looked at her. Perfect. She wasn't in pain anymore, just tired—very tired. Her eyelids lowered.

CHAPTER 28

Abuse Has Broken My Heart and I Am Weak.

Scarcely conscious, Jordan whimpered. Pain claimed every inch of her body. Disoriented, she felt restored in Markus's arms. Sheathed in his healing embrace, she stirred. Over and over, Asa's repugnant screams tore through her brain and she wept.

Supporting Jordan on his lap, Markus soothed the battered young woman. Grieving, he tenderly lifted Jordan's tangled hair from her face, looking past the bruises and lacerations, locking his gaze on her suffering eyes.

"Will it ever end?"

"I don't know—maybe not in your lifetime."

"Then let me die."

Despondent, Markus managed a dismal attempt at a smile. "You have a lot of fight left in you, Jordan. I feel it. And Asa Trebane is dead."

Jordan quivered from head to toe. Her body felt cold, her lips trembled. "No more debt to be paid—no consecration?"

"Lucifer has been thwarted—for a while. Evil never rests, but for now, it's over."

Vulnerable, Jordan moaned. "There'll be another Asa—more hideous and powerful." She grimaced, trying not to move. A searing pain branched out of her hands at the slightest twitch.

Markus's gilded hair glistened like vast lightning bugs on a summer night. Then Jordan registered the blood covering his T-shirt. She managed a faint grin. Only her angel would look dazzling after being shot. Her head slumped to one side to stare at the flames licking Asa's bones. Without taking her eyes away from the light, she said tonelessly, "We're quite a bloody pair…"

More fluidly than any human could move, Markus rose, supporting Jordan against his blood-soaked torso. He ferried his precious cargo out of the forest as Jordan lost consciousness.

෬෧෬෧

Three days in the hospital, a blood transfusion, and alternative treatments had not remedied Jordan. She seemed broken in body and spirit. Henry and Em helped during the recuperation, and Seeley was coddling. Endeavoring to mask her concern, Seeley conversed optimistically about Declan, work, the weather, anything to cheer Jordan up.

At one point, Jordan mentioned her friends, asking what the excuse was this time, and if they'd found Ronan yet.

Entirely ignoring the question about Ronan, Seeley repeated the story she'd constructed about a hoodlum's attack.

"A hoodlum?" Jordan chuckled, devoid of humor. "Wow, why not a thug, or a gangster?"

Seeley gave her daughter the universal, motherly don't-mess-with-me look, glad to hear Jordan laugh, even though it wasn't sincere.

A week later, headlines reported the unexplained disappearance of billionaire, Asa Trebane. Foul play was suspected, although, police had yet to find a body.

Squeamish dreams of Asa's fiery death obsessed Jordan. The one person—or angel—she urgently needed to see had left her to wallow in misery. Seeley breezed into Jordan's room, spreading the curtains, and grating open the window, letting in streaks of sunshine, that chased the drabness, and lukewarm air to sift the stale room.

Jordan sat upright. The mild exertion chronicled the pain in her expression. Her mom fluffed the pillow and tucked it neatly behind her back. She slipped Jordan her antibiotics and a glass of water. "Father James is here again."

Seeley watched her daughter's attempt to grip the small pill with shaky fingers.

A throbbing ache shot up Jordan's arm from the wounds in her hands. Straightening a finger or moving her arms was nearly unbearable. "Mom, he's going to want the whole story, and I'm trying to put it far from my mind."

Smiling gently at her daughter, Seeley handed her a brush. "He can help you. Come on now, I know you're raring to go."

Her mom pulled back the covers. Jordan felt like an eighty-year-old woman. She gimped off the mattress and stretched her rigid muscles that cried for a workout. She realized it was time to get back in the game.

"I'm going to take a shower and get dressed first—I feel grungy." Dismissing her mom's help, Jordan waved her off and grumbled like her grandfather. "Go talk to Father James. I'll be down in fifteen."

Toweling the condensation off the mirror, Jordan inspected the stitches on her arm and just below her shoulder. She exhaled then inspected her hands. The puncture holes would leave telltale, jagged scars, a lasting souvenir. She put ointment on each open wound then wrapped them with gauze.

The weather had gotten warm enough that she decided to unbury a pair of shorts and a tank top. Glancing at her reflection in the mirror, she stopped, astounded. Her cheekbones looked sharp, above sunken cheeks, and her clothes hung on her whittled frame. *Ugh—not only did she feel old, now she looked old.*

Her grandparents and mom made themselves scarce while Jordan sat with the priest. Alone with Father James, Jordan described the night—what had happened at Ronan's house, Markus's timely arrival, the angel's fierce battle with the devil, her own excruciating crucifixion, and then Asa's blistering death. Reliving it was exhausting.

Listening without interruption, Father James pondered the ramifications of her story.

"You do believe me, don't you?"

"Absolutely." Father James could hardly find words for Jordan's sacrifice.

"It's hopeless." Tucking both sides of her hair behind her ears, she looked at the priest. "That's how I feel right now. It's too hard—the fight, I mean."

He gently touched her gaunt face. Then he shared his euphoric apparition of the previous month. His account brought a hint of color to the girl's cheeks. "Hopelessness is never an issue, understand?"

"Father, I'm worn out—done in. Markus has left me."

The priest patted her hand. "We all need healing. Surely Markus acquires his energy from proximity with his Father."

A light flickered in her heart. *Yes.* Markus was healing. A rush of energy and relief swept away her doldrums.

℮ℌ℮ℌ

Declan joined them for dinner. His uplifting presence, humorous anecdotes, and demonstrations of how to disarm a 'hoodlum,' had them laughing until they cried. As she scraped the last spoonful of pistachio pudding from her bowl, Jordan felt a hand on her shoulder. Declan asked if he could speak to her, alone. Slightly worried, she glanced over her shoulder toward her mom then obediently followed Declan onto the front porch.

He paced around the wooden deck, his hand massaging the back of his neck like someone anxiously awaiting an execution. Jordan fiddled with a stray hangnail and shuffled her feet. Finally, she leaned on the porch rail and breathed in the succulent perfume of Em's honeysuckle tree, patiently waiting for Declan to speak.

"I'm not a man to juggle words," he said, plainly nervous, "so I'd like to get straight to the point." He clapped his large hands together, his expression serious. "Would you object to me—I mean—I love your mother. I know this is rather sudden—" He swatted at a buzzing bee.

Jordan watched the man falling apart before her eyes.

Expelling a winded breath, he managed to say, "I'd like to ask Seeley to marry me. And I'd like your permission."

Momentarily speechless, Jordan recovered. "You want my permission? Shouldn't you be asking Henry?"

"Henry's next," he said. "You are the most important person in Seeley's life. Without your approval, there will be no proposal."

Jordan inspected the crumbling man before her swabbing his face and let him off the hook. "Declan, I think you're a good guy. If my mom says yes, then I say yes."

Declan grasped her shoulders and kissed the top of her head. "Not a word, okay? Our secret until the time is right?"

His grasp sent pain coursing through her arms, she hid the twinge. "What should I tell them about why you wanted to talk to me? You know she'll ask."

Tapping his fingers on the porch rail, Declan thought for a minute. "How 'bout saying I wanted to know if you remembered anything else about your attacker, for the police, anything you might've forgotten?"

Apparently, her mom hadn't shared all the sordid details. "Yeah, sure. That's…a good cover."

"Seriously, Jordan." His eyes showed empathy. "If you do remember anything—any small detail—will you tell me?"

Nodding, Jordan agreed—*if* that occasion arose. Hiding her enthusiasm from her mom's curiosity, she headed for the stairs. "I'm going up to get a jump on all those homework assignments." She knew her mom's eyes trailed her up the steps.

Within the hour, Henry knuckled lightly on Jordan's bedroom door. "Jordan, there's a young man downstairs to see you."

Sitting on her bed, surrounded by textbooks and papers, and itching at the healing wound on her arm, Jordan wondered if Thrill had finally come for a visit. Her mom hadn't permitted visitors in the hospital or during her first few days home.

And with her cell phone lost somewhere in the woods, Jordan felt completely isolated from her friends.

Running a brush through her hair and applying blush to her pale cheeks, Jordan traipsed downstairs. She saw her grandparents and Declan lounging in the living room. Her mom stood at the front door with a smug grin. "Outside."

Jordan lumbered past her mom onto the porch. An arresting figure rose from the glider, and tears involuntarily made an appearance. Feeling no pain, Jordan took two bounding strides and leapt into Markus's embracing arms.

"I thought you'd left me again," she cried.

Markus set her gently on the ground. "Let's go for a ride." He led her to his car and helped her into the passenger seat. "Buckle up." When he noticed she was having a hard time with her sore hands, Markus leaned over and helped with the buckle. She inhaled deeply, taking comfort in his fresh clean scent.

They drove in silence. Although, Jordan had a slew of questions harboring to the surface, and didn't know where to begin. Inspecting the flawless angel she thought was lost from her forever. Invading shades of pink colored his prominent cheekbones and his hair was as unmanageable as ever. A smile tugged at her mouth as he scratched the inimical golden scruff beneath his chin. His navy and white cotton shirt stretched over his solid biceps, and Jordan couldn't help wondering if human angels bore scars.

Markus banked left onto a dirt road. Jordan knew they were headed to Hidden Lake. In summertime, a canopy of abundant foliage sheltered the road, filtering the sun's rays. Birds sang in hidden nests. Wild patches of happy-faced white daisies, Queen Anne's lace, and purple heather randomly embellished the hidden hollow. They dawdled toward the rusty bridge.

Tentative at first, Markus hesitated. "Jordan, I'm sorry I wasn't there for you when you needed me most." He relaxed, a grin lighting his face. "You gave Rafe a hard time."

"Well, Markus—first of all, I needed *you*. I got used to Rafe, after a while, but he wasn't you." She looked into his face. His eyes were hooded "Am I allowed to ask questions?"

Markus seemed preoccupied, staring ahead. When he didn't reply, Jordan shrugged. "I know now I should have listened to you and gone home—that night, at Asa's, I was in the way. Asa used me to get to you. Otherwise, everything would've worked out differently."

"We'll never know for sure." As they strolled toward the lake, his open palm browsed the feathery heather. "Ronan insisted on your presence at Asa's. She'd refused to work her magic unless you went with us. That's why I came to the diner and brought you to her house. I gambled so we could use Ronan's witchcraft." Markus's brow furrowed, as if he was somewhat ashamed at his own conniving. "I never intended to bring you to Asa's. Perhaps...perhaps it was meant to be. Something worse might've happened."

"Worse than seeing you butchered from head to toe?" Jordan retorted, her voice brittle.

He cringed. "Asa knew exactly what he was doing. He caught me while I was human. Luckily, I'd been in the process of transforming—half angel, half human," he said. "Death stood still—and then my Father took me to himself." Squatting, Markus plucked a wildflower and handed it to Jordan.

"So you didn't actually die?"

"Not exactly," he said. "I was kind of...in limbo...between life and death you might say."

They trekked over the bridge's sturdy wooden planks then stopped, side by side, leaning their backs on the metal rail. Both Jordan and Markus reflected on the enigma. Examining the sun-speckled water, Jordan remembered that, only months before, the lake had nearly claimed her life.

She turned to face him. A shadow flickered then was masked instantly. "Rafe kept me in the dark," she said in an offhanded tone. "I was pissed."

"That was the plan. Sometimes you lead...and you need to follow." Markus wheeled around, both hands gripping the rail, little bumps protruding from his knuckles. "We had to wait for the opportune time. Lucifer was on the prowl. His demon forces were weak. They needed to harvest souls. Lucifer was…pissed, as you would say."

"So before you appeared at Ronan's, Lucifer really thought you were dead?" Jordan watched varying emotions play over his face. A muscle twitched in his jaw as if he were thinking about something Jordan could only guess at.

"Yes."

She slumped to the ground cross-legged, elbows on her knees, and felt her palms smart as she rested her chin on them. She couldn't escape her own memories, yet, she wondered what Markus must've been subjected to. He slid down beside her.

"Ronan killed her father." She dropped her hands to her lap. "Her own father."

"Actually, Veronka performed the deed. Asa used Martin Beckman's blood to desecrate the house for Lucifer to inhabit."

Jordan shut her eyes, imagining the horrendous murder. "What's going to happen to Ronan? Has she been detained for her father's murder? My mom hasn't spoken a word about her."

"May I?" He extended his hands to Jordan and she laid her wounded ones in his. Affectionately, and slowly, he turned her palms over. Markus gently stroked each wound with his fingertip then sheltered them in his sinewy hands. Jordan felt a radiating sensation, like streaming hot liquid, run the length of her arm and shoulder. He then carefully removed the gauze.

The jagged wounds were healed, along with the throbbing ache.

"Suffering is an exemplary ointment for a wounded world. But I think you've done your fair share for now." His compassionate expression comforted her. "You'll always carry the mark, though."

Jordan followed his gaze. She flipped her hands over and perceived a whitish welt on each hand. She studied the marks intently. "They look like a tiny cross." She glanced back at him, slightly aggrieved, though thankful. "After all this time, you could've healed me?" She continued to contract her fingers then touched the wounds on her arm and shoulder without flinching.

"I did heal you, from your...death...on the cross." His composure was shattered as his eyes filled with liquid. "Afterwards, I was weakened." He looked down, hiding his weakness, and, with furled fists, pressed his eyelids.

Staggered by the information, Jordan stared at him.

"One way or another," he said, with his equanimity restored, "Lucifer was bound and determined to set the scales straight."

Jordan was still pondering his words. '*Your death on the cross...*' "I—died?"

Markus's eyes darkened to the blackest purple, the color heightened by his fury. "You were consecrated *before* you were born. Lucifer's arrogance in asserting a claim to your spirit makes me furious. The devil was restrained—licking his wounds—at the exact moment that he could have enslaved your spirit. And then my Father forgave me my defiance."

She didn't quite understand—if anything, Markus was saving her life. "How did you defy Him, Markus?"

"My heart cried out for revenge." Overwrought he briefly covered his face, which had flushed in his fury. Then agitated, he combed back fallen tendrils from his forehead. "Full of hatred, I wanted to kill Trebane. The thought of killing him brought me...pleasure." He hesitated. "I wanted to rip him to shreds—if not for you–telling me he wasn't worth it..."

Markus's flashing eyes struck Jordan. He cupped her face in his hands. "And then I was too late to save you. I agonized as your spirit surrendered. Afterwards, my Father answered my plea with the breath of life."

Shaken by Markus's testimony, Jordan responded in a meek whisper. "Thank you, Markus." Then she added, "He must want me here...for some unexplainable reason. Does my mom know about this?"

"Ezekiel."

Easily picking up a pebble in her healed hand, Jordan rose and threw it into the lake below. She watched the ripples lap to the shore.

"All actions have consequences that ripple outward," he predicted.

She faced him. He wore his standard poker face again. "Everyone's ignoring my questioning about Ronan."

"Her house burnt to the ground. Ronan's body was not recovered." He shot Jordan a poignant glance when she gasped. "The remains of Mr. Beckman have been retrieved. Authorities believe Ronan died in the fire along with her father."

Reeling from the bombshell, Jordan didn't know how to react. Though Ronan was obviously messed up, Jordan couldn't bear the thought of her being burned alive. She felt the cool tears course her cheeks, and Markus gently took her to his chest.

"Is she…dead?"

"Whether she's dead or alive, Ronan's not in Heaven."

"I never wanted her to…to die. Oh my gosh, Markus."

CHAPTER 29

I'll Miss You This Way.

On Jordan's first day back at school, Paisley and Cayden had accusingly tackled her, asking if she knew anything about Ronan's death. Not wanting to get into it, Jordan simply shook her head, disclaiming any connection. Life unexpectedly became somewhat ordinary. Thrill insisted on driving Jordan to and from school. Markus continued his schooling with Beth tagging after him and she glared at Jordan needlessly. Elma High mourned the loss of their classmate, Ronan Beckman. Faculty and students assembled in the auditorium for a memorial service, with psychologists nearby. The principal spoke of the tragic death of a student.

"Ronan called me—that night," said Paisley, who was picking at her food during lunch period. "I know you were supposed to go to her house. You're lying, Jordan."

Seething inside, Jordan wasn't in the mood for Paisley. "So what do you think you know?"

Paisley's face crumbled while holding back a sob. "Ronan's dead. It's—it's not possible. She was powerful—and young." She dabbed her nose with a napkin. "I talked to her around six o'clock, and she said her father was leaving, moving out—and then she said that Mark was going to move in with her soon. Ronan was so happy to be free from her revolting father. Her voice was a little quirky, and I'd thought she'd been drinking."

Paisley moved closer, her platinum hair tickling Jordan's cheeks. "Ronan hung up, and within minutes she called again. She sounded hysterical. She said something crazy—that Mark was dead!" Paisley pulled back to look into Jordan's eyes for some kind of a reaction. "She totally freaked me out, because I'd just seen Mark at school. And then I'm positive that Ronan said you were coming to her house to talk about it."

The bell rang, but Paisley clasped Jordan's wrist, holding her in place. "I *know* you were there!" Her voice was accusatory. "I was worried and drove by Ronan's house. I saw your car. I parked across the street." Paisley turned Jordan's wrist over, revealing the pale scar on her hand.

Jordan snatched her hand away. "Now is not the time." Rattled, she fled from Paisley's snooping.

ဇာဇာ

Deliriously ecstatic, Seeley prepared for her upcoming marriage to Declan Donavan. Since the paper had a policy against spouses working together, Declan insisted that Seeley pursue her dream of writing a novel. He even offered to add some of his sarcastic nuances.

One day, Jordan asked, "Mom, are we going to keep living with Em and Henry?"

In the middle of drying dishes, Seeley checked on her parents, who sat in the front room glued to the world news. "Declan has a great apartment in the city," she said. "We're thinking of moving there for a while then hunting for a house in the fall, maybe somewhere close to your grandparents. They're getting up in age and I don't want to be too far away. I haven't told them yet, but surely they must realize we'll be leaving."

Jordan finished scrubbing the last pot and glanced at her mom. "What about my school, would I have to transfer?"

"Maybe we'd go back to homeschooling for the last year. I won't be working, so it'd be ideal."

"Mom, I actually like school. At first I was leery, but now I have friends." She didn't want to be sheltered any longer. "I don't feel so much like a freak. If I go back to homeschooling, I'll be alone again, and I don't want that."

Seeley hung up the dishtowel. "What are you saying, Jordan, what do *you* want?"

"I want you to be happy," she said. "And I want to be with you, but maybe you and Declan need some time…alone…for a while." She leaned on the counter. "I could stay with Em and Henry for my senior year, then come and live with you in the city, or if you find a house nearby."

Seeley's heart took a nosedive. Elated to become Mrs. Donavan, now she felt she'd be losing her daughter.

Sensing her mom's distress, Jordan slung her arm over Seeley's shoulder. "Mom, don't worry," she said playfully. "You'll only be forty minutes away. And, knowing you and Declan, you'll be here all the time."

Sniffing back the tears, Seeley threw her arms around Jordan.

സ്ക

At a private ceremony at Saint Mary's of the Holy Angels Church, the Reverend Father James Waite presiding and with Deacon Samuel Schaffer assisting, Seeley Frances Chase and Declan Gregory Donavan were married.

Jordan was the maid of honor and Declan's friend, Virgil Detroit, was the best man. Henry walked Seeley down the aisle, unsuccessfully curbing his brimming eyes. A beaming smile lit Em's face. Mr. Detroit's wife and the entire Schaffer family, including Markus, filled a pew. And Jordan had been given permission to bring Thrill, whose infectious dimples brought color to her cheeks.

The intimate reception featured exquisite beef tenderloin, chicken cordon bleu, flavorful garlic mashed potatoes, and a medley of vegetables. As a replacement for the traditional wedding cake, guests celebrated with scrumptious flaming bananas foster. Champagne toasts rang out, and a live band set the tone with buoyancy.

Jordan wore a strapless, multihued blue and silver dress and looked beautiful, flushed with happiness. She glided around the floor with Declan, Henry, and Deacon Samuel, but especially with Thrill. She couldn't keep her eyes off her joyful mother, whose lilting laughter filled the room. It made Jordan happy to see her mom so blissfully content. *It's about time,* she thought.

Much later, Thrill and Jordan swayed together to the music. As Thrill bent near her ear, a voice interrupted.

"Mind if I cut in?"

Startled by Mark's gall, Thrill backed away. Markus instantly took his place.

"That was rather rude," Jordan said.

"I was biding my time."

"Yeah, with Beth clinging to every inch of your body. It's sickening, don't you think?"

He smiled broadly. "Angels aren't usually privy to those...feelings. I must admit, there is a certain thrill." He chuckled and pressed Jordan to his chest.

"I wonder what's going to happen now?" she mused.

"Life goes on." He hesitated. "Jordan, I'll be leaving soon."

She lifted her head and stared into his rich violet-blue eyes.

"My human self will cease to exist, but I'll be guarding you—always."

Basking in his warm arms, Jordan tucked her head under his chin, setting her cheek on his chest. She could feel his heartbeat. "I'll miss you—I mean, this way."

Markus saw Thrill watching them very attentively. He stopped dancing, untangled Jordan, and headed in another direction.

ఎఎఎ

Home from the honeymoon, Seeley barreled into her parents' house. She dropped her bags on the floor as she clutched

Jordan then hugged her parents. Full of smiles, Declan slogged behind with extra baggage.

"Two and a half weeks seemed like an eternity," said Jordan, watching her joyful mother. "Mom, you look great." Then she turned to Declan. "You look good too, Dec."

A crooked grin spread over his face. "Gee, thanks, Jor."

"We came straight from the airport," Seeley gushed. "I couldn't wait to see everyone, and Declan and I are going to spend the night here." Then she peeked at her parents. "If that's all right with you, Mom and Dad?"

"Of course, of course." Em's approval showered the room. "We want to hear all about the Hawaiian honeymoon." She linked her arm into Seeley's, and they headed into the living room. Seeley described their five star, beachfront hotel, the quantity of food, and how it would take weeks to lose the extra pounds she'd gained.

Declan and Jordan heaped the luggage in a pile next to the front door. Declan wiped his forehead. "I'm pooped."

Henry snickered, smacking Declan on the back. "My Seeley's too much of a woman to handle, eh, kid?"

Declan shook his head, his eyes laughing. "Seeley's stamina is outstanding. She's got more get up and go than I'll ever have."

"Yeah, and mine got up and left."

Jordan watched the men lumber to the kitchen and uncap two beers. Henry's attitude improved drastically with another man in the house. She bounded into the parlor to listen to her mom gush about every little honeymoon detail.

↺↻↺

Opening the window to temperate summer breezes, Jordan leaned her elbows on the sill and gazed at the gibbous moon. Inhaling moist night air, expanding her lungs to capacity, Jordan held the breath then released it bit by bit.

Oddly discomfited to have a man sleeping with her mom in the adjacent room, Jordan pulled on a pair of sweats and retreated to the bathroom for a shower. She heard her mom giggling and speedily turned the faucet on full blast. She normally didn't lock the door, but today she bolted the lock then double-checked.

After her shower, Jordan dried her hair then carefully pried the door open and tiptoed across the hall silently, only to bump into a naked man's chest.

"Thought you'd never get outta there, Jordan," Declan said, grinning affably.

"Sorry, Declan." She scrambled to her room, attempting not to look at his muscled pecs.

Tunneling beneath her pillow to block out all sounds, she was startled to feel a tender caress on her shoulder. She flung off the pillow to see her mom hovering above her.

"You and I haven't had a minute to ourselves, something we're both not used to," said Seeley.

Rucking the sheets, Jordan sat cross-legged in front of her mom. "Things are going to change. They're already different."

"Yes, I know, but you're always first, Jordan."

"Don't say that, Mom. I'm all grown—well, almost. Life's been crazy, and you and I both deserve some happiness. Take it and run."

Seeley peered lovingly at her daughter. "When'd you get so philosophical?"

Jordan snuggled into her mother's open arms, thinking that, at thirty-six, her mom was more attractive than ever.

Seeley combed Jordan's hair away from her forehead and cleared her throat. "Father James phoned me in Hawaii. He was upset. A friend of his needs our help. Evidently, there's a sect kidnapping children and he thinks it's an offshoot of the Order. People like us are meeting in a small village outside of Charlottesville. I think it's called Sherando. I leave in two days."

Jordan's eyes bulged as she shook her head. "No, Mom. No. I thought…" Her voice faded.

Seeley ringed a stray lock behind Jordan's ear. "You thought because I got married, I'd forget about my…calling?"

Jordan nodded, crestfallen. "Something like that."

"By now the Order's chosen its new leader, just as adept, corrupt, and lethal as Asa. One day I'll call it quits, but for now…well, I had another vision while I was gone. I saw two children cowering in a dark corner. The street sign read Larkson and I remember the style of house." Her insides grew cold at the memory. "The rest was bad—really bad."

Changing the subject, she nudged Jordan to lighten the mood. "What about you, Jordan, anything happening in your brain?"

"Not much. The nightmares are far and few between, but Henry grumped the other day. I guess I scared the pants off him when I screamed. It was a scary one. Other than the nightmares, nothing much is going on. I did what you wanted. I went to church and talked with Father James." Abstractedly tracing the scar on her hand, she said mildly, "I'll go with you, Mom."

"Absolutely not. Your body and mind are still in the process of healing."

Her mom's adamant decision came as a relief. Jordan knew she was physically fit, although mentally was another story. She wondered if she'd turned into a coward. Since her experience in the forest, Jordan hadn't been her confident self. Maybe her mom recognized her inability to cope.

Seeley saw the emotions wash over Jordan. "Give it time. You never know, maybe we've started on a new path." Then she added, "I've slowly been explaining everything to Declan. It'll take time for him, too. He wants to go with me and Father James on this trip. What do you think?"

Feeling guilty about her own slacking, and worried for her mom's safety, Jordan thought for a moment. "If Father James is going to meet up with his friend, then you probably should bring Declan along. How bad is it? Did Father James say?"

"No, I'm meeting with him tomorrow."

"Then make the decision tomorrow."

CHAPTER 30

If Only I Had Wings, I'd Fly Away with You.

Avoiding a clutch of heckling freshmen, Jordan reached her locker. She sorted through tattered folders and slipped the bulk into her book bag. A tap on the shoulder made her jerk.

It was Beth Schaffer. "Sorry, Jordan, I didn't mean to scare you."

"You didn't scare me, Beth. I've just been a little edgy lately—with exams coming up and all."

"Could I talk to you?" Beth looked visibly upset.

Jordan flung the book bag over her back. "Sure, what's up?"

Beth browsed the hallway then whispered, "In private—come to my car. I'll drive you home and we can talk."

Uncertain of Beth's motives, Jordan glanced around. "Sure, but let me call Thrill and let him know."

She rifled in her pocket for her new cell phone and explained to a disappointed Thrill that she'd be going home with Beth.

"Is there something wrong, Beth?" Jordan asked once she was settled in Beth's tiny hybrid. She rarely spoke to Beth, although Markus spoke highly of the Schaffer family.

Beth kept her eyes on the road, though Jordan noted how fraught she was. When she answered, her voice shook. "Mark told the whole family yesterday that he'd be leaving." She glanced at Jordan. "I'm…upset. I thought he'd stay."

Somewhat frazzled herself, Jordan nodded. She had no idea how to respond.

"I thought since you're related in some way, maybe you could convince him to stay." Beth turned her head to glimpse Jordan. "Maybe even find an apartment in town."

Jordan had to be careful. "We're not exactly related."

"Why does he have to leave anyway?" whined Beth. "I know he likes me. I asked him to call, but the guy doesn't own a cell phone. I'd like to keep in touch, but I might never see him again."

Beth's soft weeping was infectious, Jordan's eyes filled in sympathy. What could she possibly say to a brokenhearted Beth? Then she wondered if Markus possibly felt romantically inclined toward the gorgeous girl. She shook her head. *No, he's an angel—my angel.*

"Have you and Mark, uh…you know." She felt like a moron asking such personal questions. "Um, I mean…dated… or anything?" She braced herself, not certain if she wanted to know.

"I wish." Beth sounded wistful. "He's been a perfect gentleman. Kind of driving me insane. I've practically thrown myself at him."

Jordan paused to think. "Is Mark home a lot? I mean, I know he lives at your house, but is he around?"

"That's why I'm so nuts," she said. "The guy's hardly ever there. I was curious—I wondered if he's seeing someone on the sly. I've seen him with you and then—this is going to sound awful because now she'd dead—but he was with Ronan Beckman a lot. I thought for sure they'd been hooking up."

Jordan squirmed. "No," she relayed rather quickly. "Mark's not going out with anyone that I know of. And I don't think I'd be able to make him stay."

Swinging into the driveway, Beth parked the car and turned toward Jordan, her face wet with tears. "Are you lying to me, Jordan?"

Jordan stared at her, confused.

Beth's eyes locked on Jordan. "You—and—Mark?"

"I'm not lying. Besides, you know I've been seeing Thrill."

"I needed to make sure. Because you and Mark look at each other like—like you have a secret. I still remember the way you two danced at the Winter Ball. It didn't look like friendship." She lowered her voice to a murmur. "I don't get Mark at all." She paused and looked at Jordan distrustfully, as if wondering if she should continue. Then her voice changed, almost hostile. "This is just between you and me—and if you repeat this—" Her eyes narrowed. "—I'll tell everyone that it really happened to you. Understand?"

Jordan frowned. She didn't really want Beth to unload on her. But then Beth sighed. "I've been doing everything to get Mark interested, you know. I've literally thrown myself at him this last month. I wanted him so bad that I actually snuck in his room one night and waited for him in his bed, totally nude. I'd be dead if my parents had caught me."

Beth's fair complexion reddened, and Jordan didn't want to hear the rest of her story, afraid of what she was going to say.

"I fell asleep waiting. And when I woke up the next morning, I was in my own bed. He must've carried me to my room." Beth's perky nose and cute oval eyes peered at Jordan for an answer. "He must've seen—and then—nothing. Do you think he's gay?"

Jordan imagined Markus carrying Beth Schaffer's fault-less, naked body to her own bed, all without looking at her. The comical mental picture got to her and she let slip a snort.

She wondered if Markus actually had human urges. There was all his wit about Ronan wanting more than just his light, then his comment about the thrill of dancing with Beth at her mom's wedding, and then he had looked at her kind of funny after she said that she'd miss him "in this way."

"What's so funny?" Beth gawked at Jordan. "He's gay, isn't he?"

Jordan shrugged while shaking her head and keeping her face blank. "I don't know about Mark's sexual preferences.

We never talked about those kinds of things. I'm sorry I can't help much, Beth."

"Remember, this is our secret." Beth reiterated when Jordan flung open the car door. "Not a word to your cronies, Paisley or Cayden—agreed?"

"Of course, I won't say a word."

Backing out of the driveway, Beth instantly regretted telling Jordan about Mark's rebuff, fretful that her juicy bit of gossip, being naked—and rejected—in Mark's bed, would be circling the school by tomorrow. Luckily, Jordan was a little geeky and didn't have any substantial or believable friends. After mulling it over, Beth felt somewhat better.

ↂↂↂ

The next morning, Jordan plunged out the back door to discover a cloud-covered sun and drizzling mist. Shelving the book bag atop of her head in hopes of preserving her hair, she wended past the house. Jordan was a tad surprised to discover Markus waiting. Checking the street, Jordan half expected to see Thrill's car approaching. Markus drawled, as if he were in charge, "I phoned Thrill and told him I'd be taking you to school today."

"You shouldn't have done that."

"Why?"

"Well, because…" Jordan tried to clarify the situation for an inexperienced angel. "Thrill and I are…well, kind of going out. You probably upset him."

"I thought we'd walk to school one last time, for old time's sake."

Ashamed for scolding Markus, she smiled brilliantly. "I'd love to walk with you."

Popping into her mind was the conversation with Beth, and Jordan had wanted to ask him if he felt human desire. And as if he could read her thoughts, he blasted her with a fascinating smirk. Mindful of Markus's magnetism, Jordan tripped over her feet. He snagged her elbow before she landed on her face. Mortified, she straightened her shirt. No wonder Beth and half the school drooled over the angel—he was a sight to behold.

More than a bit interested, Jordan offhandedly repeated her chat with Beth. She scrutinized Markus's expression for any clues. Apart from biting his lips—Jordan guessed he was holding back laughter—he said nothing in response to her probing.

Out of the blue, he asked, "How's Seeley?"

She didn't expect her mom to enter the conversation when conferring about angels and desire. "Mom's fine," Jordan cited. "She's going to another meeting with Father James, and this time Declan's going along. Someplace called Sherando, I think."

Markus gnawed on his lower lip and stopped walking.

"Is something wrong? Ezekiel will be with them, right? I mean, you know, if there's any trouble. You'll help, too, right?" Jordan said, noting his bland expression.

He didn't reply, lowering his eyelids, but he seemed to disappear in spirit. Reopening his eyes, he gazed down at Jordan, his face disciplined, showing no emotion.

"Markus, you're scaring me," she said. "You know how much we depend on you and Ezekiel. Without our angels, we'd be dead—"

"Stop—" Markus raked fingers into his hair. "Ezekiel and I've grown close in the past seventeen years since your birth. He's helped me and I hope I've helped him. We're like a team, like you and your mother. We're there for each other."

Markus rested a lean palm on Jordan's shoulder. She stared at his hand, the hand pierced by a dagger, the hand that taught Jordan how to fight, and the hand that had slain demons, saving Jordan and her mother time and again. She thought of her glorious angel in limbo between life and death after being sliced open, and she thought of Markus battling Lucifer. She peered into Markus's dazzling eyes. Unreadable, his eyes reflected more than he would say. "I'll miss our walks, but always remember—I'm only a whisper away."

"Markus, what's wrong? I feel it."

"Life can be convoluted at times, Jordan. Believe…" His voice grew faint. Markus was gone.

Jordan wheeled around—she could still feel the weight of his hand on her shoulder.

℮⁊℮⁊

Standing at the locker, Jordan collected her books for the next three classes and turned, plowing into Beth.

"He's gone," Beth sniveled. "Mark is gone. He said his good-byes to the family last night. He said he had to leave earlier than expected."

An unanticipated tear leaked down Jordan's face.

CHAPTER 31

Consumed, this enigmatic puzzle called a dream,
Or a nightmare if you please,
Flaunts my waking consciousness.

What is it that I saw...
What more does it mean...

Dreams Do Come True.

Jordan settled comfortably on the porch deck with ankles propped on the railing and hands behind her head. Diminishing daylight had turned the mild summer sky magenta with twilight hints of a bluish-purple, a shade that reminded her of Markus's eyes. Breaking her concentration, Henry yawned his way through the screen door, "Goodnight, Jordan."

"Night, Henry, I'll be in shortly."

"Lock up, okay?"

"Yup." She waited until her grandfather's footsteps receded, then her whisper mingled with a hooting owl. "Markus, I know it's only been a few weeks, but—I—I miss you. And there's something I've been wanting to say. I regret never telling you before." Jordan waited, in hopes Markus might appear. Then, with a resigned sigh, she said, "Markus, I do—love—you..." Heatedly, her mental ability scooped up a handful of rocks that littered the road and, one by one, shot at dangly leaves for target practice, her accuracy right-on. She smiled.

Jordan dropped her legs from the rail and rose, glimpsing the secluded landscape. Raising her arm like readying to wave at a passing vehicle, she closed her eyes, contemplating.

It almost seemed too easy. Ether, hot and thick, brushed her fingers. Within seconds, a glowing sword became visible, fitting perfectly into the palm of her hand. Turning the blade, she gawked, astounded. "Markus?" At the mention of his name the sword dissolved.

Jordan stared wonderingly at her empty hand.

For a moment, she heard absolute quiet, so soundless that it truly hurt. Then the nighttime symphony returned to her ears. A twig snapped behind the house—more than likely a herd of deer was making its way through the woods. Crickets chirped, bullfrogs croaked, and there was the swoosh of a passing car. Stretching her arms, Jordan yawned and went inside.

In her room, she noticed the piled textbooks strewn across the bed. She groaned. Final exams were next week. Haphazardly bundling the materials, she stuffed them into her book bag and got ready for bed.

Summer's fragrance drifted into the room on a breeze. She inhaled deeply as she looked at the billowing chintz curtains.

"Markus?"

No response.

Jordan punched the pillow a few times before flopping into bed. She fidgeted. Not finding her comfort zone she sat up, tucking her knees under her chin. "Markus…where are you? You said you'd come if I called."

She waited. Not even a faint flicker. She plopped onto the feathery pillow and stared at skittering patterns on the ceiling. Her lids fluttered as she fought sleep.

Surrounded by strange noises, in a misty unfamiliar place, Jordan stepped lightly into the hazy hallway. She came to a standstill, studying a framed photograph. Tight grins touched the mouths of Declan, her mom, Jordan, and a swaddled infant nestled in the crook of Seeley's arm. Jordan had a hard time remembering the picture and—*what's with the baby*? Her head twisted on the pillow. *Oh yes, I'm dreaming*. A pleasant gurgly sound filled her ears and, curious, she decided to see what happened next. She sank deeper into the dream.

She padded softly to an archway. Seeley sat contently in a chair, rocking as a baby suckled at her breast. Jordan stepped forward, smirking at the greedy slurping noises. Seeley raised her striking face to Jordan, a motherly smile gracing her pretty lips. She drew back the fluffy blanket from the infant, revealing downy auburn hair.

Jordan knew she was grinning foolishly, marveling at the diminutive fingers and the tiny heart-shaped lips. She bent in for a closer look. The infant opened its wide eyes and gazed at her. Jordan gasped. The baby's eyes, in wildly varying hues of blue and black, had unmistakably defined, red-ringed pupils.

Jordan jolted awake as the vision evaporated. Wheezing and panting, she wrenched herself upright, her pulse racing. All was calm in the house, excluding her pounding heart. She searched the dim bedroom for some sign of Markus. Disappointed, she took a deep breath, pulled herself together, and thought, *Just a dream. It was just a dream...just a dream...*

About the Author

Cathrina Constantine resides in Upstate New York with her husband, five children, two Labradors, and two cats. After a long hiatus while raising her family, Constantine finally picked up her pen and paper and began to hone her craft of writing. When not with her family, baking, crafting, reading, or stationed at the computer writing, you will find her walking in the backwoods with her dogs, daydreaming. She is extremely happy to have her debut novel published by Black Opal Books.